FLORIDA WOMAN

A Novel

DEB ROGERS

HANOVER
SQUARE
PRESS

HANOVER
SQUARE
PRESS™

Recycling programs
for this product may
not exist in your area.

ISBN-13: 978-1-335-42689-5

Florida Woman

Hanover Square Press
22 Adelaide St. West, 41st Floor
Toronto, Ontario M5H 4E3, Canada
HanoverSqPress.com
BookClubbish.com

Printed in U.S.A.

for my family

1

It would have been so easy to snatch the key chain from Sari's neck, break the lock on the macaques' enclosure, and follow the monkeys as they run wild into the palmetto woods.

I wasn't supposed to have thoughts like that while touring the refuge on my first day. I was supposed to be respectfully delighted: a large troop of rescued monkeys, a devoted nonprofit staff, a remote haven of virgin wilderness on the edge of the Ocala National Forest.

I was expected to feel grateful to Sari and the others for allowing me to "dedicate myself to a summer of service and personal transformation," as Cole Calhoun, my house arrest officer, had put it. Any decent person would be offering baskets of shiny apples and spinning bushels of straw into gold in return for a live-in community service placement from which to pay her societal debts and to earn a second chance.

At the very least, I should be smiling.

But we had walked miles in circles along the narrow paths through humid, subtropical forest scrub for Sari to show me boundaries and landmarks I wouldn't remember, and I was already limping from the ankle monitor. It made me feel like an injured deer, tagged and released so I could be hunted later. I was parched, the July sun extracting the last dots of my life force, making every single being around me seem stronger, more willful and more attractive than me: the three staff members, the monkeys, the thick blue-tailed skink lounging in the ancient cast-iron bathtub in the shower house that we had visited on the tour, the gnarled oak roots impossibly clinging to the rocks at the lake's edge.

Although less than two hours inland from my hometown on the Atlantic shore, Atlas was an entire dark world away. The refuge's land—Sari's land—was verdant and rank instead of sun-washed and salt-dried, dark moss green instead of cerulean and pale sand. Atlas held court on a primitive stretch of land that had been avoided by indigenous farmers and settlers alike, shunned by thieves and developers, skipped over by Flagler and Disney. Relentlessly, tenaciously wild.

It was the best I could do.

They had given me a tour of the Atlas cabins, which were ramshackle A-frames that had clearly been built by amateurs, the surrounding flora reaching inside to repossess the soft wood construction. Sand, dirt, and pine needles from the paths swirled on plywood floors. Kudzu vines clawed toward the rooflines and snaked inside hand-stapled window screens, pinkie-sized green anoles and big-eared deer mice following right behind. The shared shower house was a fiberglass shed, and the other main buildings were hand-built geodesic domes—the larger of which tilted to the west, an ice cream scoop that was one summer second away from sliding off the cone.

The macaques had the best setup, a total environment built for their protection and for our easy viewing. Since it was feeding time, we congregated around the chain-link fence like a zoo-going family after church while the macaques ate their buckets of oysters. Cole and I watched the monkeys. The three women of Atlas watched us.

"You are so very beautiful, Jamie!" Sari said. She gathered my hair—several degrees darker and duller than her own cascading, honey-blond waves—and piled it on top of my head to assess me, or to help me cool off. "We have been waiting so patiently, and wow, here you are right in front of us. We're so happy you are here! You made the right choice in coming to us!"

Her forward contact threw me, but I willed myself to not recoil. She was too close, and I was probably a grubby, sweaty mess after slogging through the tour. Plus, Sari didn't know me. We had spoken on the phone twice. But I had been watching her throughout our brief tour to learn what I could about her, noting her beatific smile, the frictionless drape of her sundress against her thin, golden legs as they hiked the unkempt paths, the scent of juniper and grapefruit left in her wake. I decided she was simply being friendly in the way of women who breeze through every day as though they are just arriving at a music festival.

"What do you think of our little paradise?" asked Tierra. She was statuesque and olive-skinned, and like Sari, seemed unfazed by the violent heat. I estimated the ages of Sari and Dagmar, Atlas's vet and animal care expert, to be in their midthirties—a handful of years older than me, at barely twenty-eight. But Tierra's age was hard to pinpoint, with her mellow voice, lean muscles, and exquisitely shaved head.

"It's wild." I knew I should say something more, but that was the best I could muster, so my brain made me say it again. "So wild."

At least Dagmar was drenched like me, her short blond hair spiked with sweat. She described the assets of the monkeys' enclosure: it was a massive structure that housed a tire swing, a small swimming pool, and an intricate climbing apparatus over a rock-strewn clearing where the macaques loped around on all fours like tawny bears or wild coyotes. Long tails flagged behind them like whips, only to be tucked safely under their bodies moments later when they squatted to confer with each other in pairs or groups.

I would have thought the animals would squabble competitively over the food, but they worked in admirable harmony. They circled the piles of oysters and selected one or two at a time. Then they sorted through a crate of rocks for the sharpest ones to crack the shells, and ran off to their spots using their underarms and mouths as backup pockets for their treasures. There, they crouched and got to work with their tools: slamming with determination, angling the shells as needed. They coaxed with their old-man teeth. They slurped with probing tongues.

"Watch how they each have their own style," Dagmar said. "They learn from each other. See Ghost, going with the two-handed drop smash, as opposed to Curious Georgia O'Keeffe, the right-handed, rapid-fire jackhammer. Henri throws his whole body into it with an overhead lift. Bee doesn't even use a stone. See how she knocks two oysters against each other, and then she eats whichever opens first."

"Efficient!" Cole Calhoun was rapt. The embroidered emblem on his company uniform broadcast *Sunshine Monitoring* directly at my eye level. I was never going to get him to go home.

"They all have their ways, and they fine-tune them by studying others. You watch," Dagmar said.

"We love their amazing hands, don't we?" Sari said. "We learn so much by watching them. You're going to adore the macaques, Jamie. Did you have to say goodbye to any animals before moving here? I hate that we have to ask guests not to bring pets, but it simply wouldn't work out."

"No pets," I said. "I've never actually had one."

Dagmar looked concerned. "Why not?"

"I don't know," I said, turning my gaze to the macaques. "Never really been a pet person. I mean, I took care of the lobster tank at one of my waitressing jobs. And once when I was a kid, I even found a dog in a parking lot. My mom wouldn't let me keep it, because we were sort of broke at the time, and I've never been able to afford one myself, either. But I'm sure I'll do fine with the monkeys."

The women stared at me. Tierra smiled empathically.

"Animal care is very, very expensive," Dagmar said at last.

"That it is," Sari said. "Don't worry. It's going to be wonderful. When rescues arrive here, their spirits have been stripped away and left raw. You can see agitation just below the skin, a feverish terror in their eyes, exposing dueling impulses—the desire for food versus a primal distrust of the cage. They are scared of us at first, and of everything we offer." She paused to pluck a stray hair from Tierra's shirt, either her own or maybe a monkey's. "We serve them with patience, love, constancy. Cleanliness, routine. Gentle care, delicious food," she said, motioning to the oysters. "It works. And you know what, Jamie? Atlas will do the same for you."

I wanted to say something to reassure Sari that I understood the preciousness of this volunteer opportunity, that I would avail myself of every lesson her monkeys had to offer, but all I could manage was more nodding. Her gentle words sanded the edge from my scorched and exhausted mood. Her ease was a marvel. I, on the other hand, seemed to be the only one still sweating unruly rivulets. It would have helped if I had dressed to make a better impression. Next to Sari's sundress, my shorts felt too short, my old Salt Life T-shirt too tacky. I worried that I fit in better with the monkeys.

Hitting jackpot after jackpot with each smashed oyster, the macaques were engrossed with their abundant meal. They celebrated some wins by chittering and shaking their shoulders.

"Phenomenal creatures!" Cole said. "Don't we all wish they could talk!"

The sauna around us cooled, and I knew instantly Cole had

said the wrong thing. Dagmar bristled. Sari smiled and looked down, while Tierra quietly turned away.

"No, no," Dagmar eventually said. "Do not patronize them with that human wish. They are not furry people. They are macaques. They are majestic beasts made of fangs and coiled muscle, and they have their own intelligence superior to ours."

"We listen to what they say in other ways," Sari said.

"You know, I didn't mean anything by that," Cole protested.

My instinct was to smile at him, to try to soften his embarrassment, but I was grateful not to be in the hot seat for once and instead stayed focused on the oyster antics.

"They might not speak, but they understand," Dagmar said. "Rhesus macaques forecast the weather and various community events, and they even have murdered humans. More than one group have stoned people to death. In India, a man who once complained about the monkeys in his town was found stoned by bricks that the monkeys had collected and then stored in the branches of trees, waiting until just the right moment when the man was gathering firewood underneath. Then they pelted him to death. Premeditated."

Cole pursed his lips and pantomimed turning a key and tossing it to the wind. I made a mental note to search and verify Dagmar's outrageous story later, only to remember they had confiscated my electronics, and felt suddenly, queasily aware of how difficult it would be to survive at Atlas without my cell phone all summer.

Later in my cabin, Cole kneeled before me, firmly clutching my foot to fuss with the anklet. I felt a pang inside at the coin-sized ring of blistering skin on the top of his head. Everyone has something they hope doesn't show. He reminded me for a moment of my brother, Jason, the kind of guy who could back a trailer into the intracoastal blindfolded, yet was too shy to look you in the eye. Cole must have felt naked without a cap on.

"This is actually one of our older, heavier units. I had to deploy it because of the rugged environmental conditions out here," he said, knocking on the rigid vinyl of the anklet as though it were a speakeasy door.

I pictured Cole returning to his office to monitor me, tracking my blipping signal on massive computer screens. The thought was repulsive, but I tried to coax myself into feeling comforted by it. The intrusive surveillance meant that Sunshine Monitoring knew where I was at all times. They would make sure I survived my new life in the woods with the monkeys.

"Okay now, I'm gonna take your picture to document that you have been initiated, we've taken your tour, and we've checked the calibrations. And please don't grin in this particular mug shot, if you don't mind. Try to look like you've been reformed."

That stung. I had smiled for my shot when I was initially fingerprinted and booked: it was a good-girl reflex, a subconscious way to make the arresting officers like me. It clearly didn't work, and worse, the smile had contributed to my infamy—the internet loves the contradiction of a happy mug shot.

I complied and pulled a straight face for Cole's photo, letting his joke wash over me without a reaction. I wanted to tell him how much he reminded me of my brother, but I bit my tongue. I had promised myself not to bring up Jason to anyone. I wanted a fresh start, and right at this moment, it didn't seem smart to advertise my distinctive family history to the man in charge of my brand-new, remote-controlled, electronic monitor.

Mostly, I wanted him to leave so that I could just sprawl on the A-frame's grungy foam mattress—my new nest—and sleep forever. Instead, Cole slowly inventoried every item in my plastic totes, making me feel defensive about normal decisions (yes, I really did need that many tampons and off-brand protein bars) and odd ones (I winced when he gave my ancient Beanie Baby Winston a cavity search).

But part of me also didn't want to be alone. During the daytime I would be working for the refuge in the domes or at the macaque enclosure, but at night I would be in this creepy cabin by myself, far down Atlas's winding paths with no other buildings in sight. Just me and the nosy lizards scaling the makeshift screen doors. Just me and a monitor tracking my every move.

"Can you listen to me through this thing?" I asked him.

"Like I said before, our job is to monitor you, and that's all you need to know."

"Is it too late to change my mind, Cole?"

We each looked around. My crappy stuff in disarray, the busted-up building that looked like it had been furnished by fairy-tale animals with ill-fated human aspirations. Even as the words left my mouth, I knew I didn't mean them. My few days in jail were the worst hours of my life, my body hollowed by fathomless dread, every surface I touched damp from sweat and other people's breath in overcrowded rooms. Each morning was an assault of regret, the hours marked only by unpalatable meals where even the smallest bites of food were too rank or stale to swallow. Three months at Atlas was a miracle.

"Oh, yeah, way too late to change anything," he said, adjusting the sunglasses hanging from the placket of his polo shirt. "That boat left the dock three hurricanes ago."

After briefly chatting with Sari on the way out, Cole finally left, and that was that. He walked out of the A-frame, leaving me alone with only my anklet and whatever else was hiding in the spongy cobwebs littering my cabin walls. As I watched the palmetto path engulf and absorb his silhouette, it was as though the forest's door closed behind him. I felt like an abandoned beagle staring after a car it will never catch.

2

Welcome, beautiful friend!

Atlas Wildlife Refuge is a hidden gem in the heart of Florida, encompassing over eighty biodiverse acres of land bordering the Ocala National Forest. Thanks to the stewardship of our founder, Sari Sutherland, as well as the generosity of our community of volunteers, Atlas is home to a healthy troop of forty-two macaques who are cared for in peaceful, expansive enclosures. We intend to increase our capacity to serve five times this number by the end of the next three calendar years. We open our arms to welcome you to our vital work. Join the Atlas tribe!

Our promise to you, our dear new members, is the same promise we make to new macaques. As a species, baby monkeys stay close to their mamas, riding on their backs, nursing, learning. That early maternal bond is very important to their later development, but for our macaques it has almost always been broken in their journeys before Atlas. Once they arrive, we repair their spirits and bodies with constancy and attend to their every need. Healing and wholeness naturally follow.

We make that same promise to you, our precious members. We love you. We need each other, and we will take care of you just as you are taking care of us. Embrace the spiritual connection our macaques offer through our brand-new livestream, and visit Atlas's encampment in this pristine, ancient forest in Central Florida.

We are a supportive circle, but remember: circles are closed for safety and wholeness. You are either with us or against us. There is no other way.

COMMENT FROM SARI

Dagmar and Tierra, this shared document is just to get us started on our journey of writing our manifesto for the updated website, which needs to be ready when we turn on the livestream. I really want everyone's feedback and authorship. This needs to be a team project that fully captures everything we have discussed. Everything we believe. Don't forget to click on Track Changes!

You'll see how hard it is when you get started. We have to say enough to get potential members interested in supporting Atlas, and we want to be true to our beliefs, but we obviously can't say too much on a public website. I don't want to sound like we are just a roadside zoo, but I also don't want to attract trouble from unevolved people with small minds.

So, let's brainstorm together and do our best to create a website that will make all of our community dreams come true. The time is now, especially since Jamie is here. –xoxoS.

3

Instead of collapsing into a depression nap, I wandered back to the monkey enclosure, mostly because I wasn't sure where else to go. The rustic and quirky buildings that ran through Atlas were intimidating, but the monkeys, grooming and crawling about in their habitat, felt approachable. On my tour I had noticed that the area between the macaque enclosure, the main building, and the garden was the hotspot: some people sat on benches and watched the monkeys while others worked nearby, raking paths, weeding, or cleaning galvanized steel bins. I hoped if I just showed up that someone would give me a job, because I'd rather feel useful than lost.

I wondered if I would need to borrow a machete from the staff to widen the path to my cabin. Undergrowth closed in on several of the bends, and I had to pay close attention to stay the course. Now that I had walked through the property, I understood that taming this massive wedge of land into a safe environment for anything more than snakes and mosquitoes would require constant vigilance.

Somewhere along my path, I realized I had taken the wrong turn and dead-ended at a sagging, abandoned yurt, its southernmost corner caved in by a pine tree. I quickly backtracked and vowed to mark my trail from then on. During my walk-through with Cole, the paths had revealed as many abandoned projects as completed ones—a gutted school bus, an empty aviary, a rotting treehouse—each one now reclaimed by the forest to serve as the perfect nest for any manner of animal. I wondered what made the original residents give up and get out.

I don't know why I was so thrown by the wildness. I knew before I came here that Atlas was located far from town on the edge of a natural forest, which made perfect sense for the animals. Perhaps I had jumped to conclusions, or maybe I had arrived with unrealistic expectations after I had stalked the Atlas website. The photos had done such a great job of downplaying the grimy, isolated, snake-trap vibe and replacing it with a quirky boho shimmer.

Their whole website had been outdated, but it was in a charming way, describing an idyllic garden setting that had once housed a midwifery school and other communal living groups. I envisioned an eco-resort or glamping site for trust fund climate activists. Even if I weren't in dire straits, what I saw seemed a little like heaven. I had never been a member of an advocacy group focused on bettering the world by fighting climate change or funding wells for impoverished villagers— volunteering seemed like a privilege for those with money and university degrees. But maybe Atlas was offering me a chance to give an admirable lifestyle a try.

The best photo, the one that had been my lodestar during the last anxious months of selling my furniture and truck, was a sweeping panorama that must have been caught by drone. Atlas looked like a pristine village nestled in a clearing near a diamond-shaped lake that was surrounded by virgin sand pine scruff. Maybe all environments are best when viewed from above. Gritty city streets look like children's playsets. Stultifying suburbs were enticing mazes dotted with refreshing aquamarine pools. From above, even after the Fall, Eden probably looked like a verdant paradise. Only at ground level did the devil become evident.

The website had made Atlas look like an artistically designed tribute to sustainable living: the two solar-powered geodesic domes were surrounded by gardens and pathways that promised ecologically respectful housing and communally shared facilities. Anchored by a spring-fed lake and deep within a private natural forest, Atlas seemed to be the perfect tropical home for the monkeys and their devoted caretakers.

Instead, on move-in day, I saw dirt and rust animated by humidity. I saw overwhelm. No photo could have prepared me for the swarming mosquitos, or the way the thorny greenbrier vines and cabbage palm seedlings would rustle and rattle ahead of my footsteps as unseen creatures fled their cover.

Still, the potential was there, so I buoyed myself. I was fully capable of roughing it. I was no princess. My mother buckled under the weight of supporting me and Jason when we were growing up, and temporary caregivers and foster homes offered the bare minimum, and so I learned to expect little and make do. And above all else, wasn't I a Floridian? Though inland scrub was vastly different from the Atlantic coast, I could still tolerate the heat, pestilence, and decay of the subtropics. Plus I wasn't at Atlas to relax or retreat. I would just use the hardship in housing as fuel to keep me motivated and out of bed. If I gained a good recommendation letter to help me land a job at the end of the summer, at the very least, my time here would be a success.

Finally, I arrived at the enclosure. A few workers were in the area pruning azalea bushes, but no one seemed to need help, so I sat down at one of the benches nearby. Three monkeys ran to the edge of the cage to scrutinize me. The air smelled strongly of ammonia, urine, and musk, but the macaques looked clean and healthy. I wondered if anyone bathed them or if swimming in the pool sufficed.

"Hey there," I said. "It's your new friend Jamie. Guess who got lost already? Please do not let me get attacked by the cryptid living in that yurt in the woods." A sandy-haired monkey lifted his arms in the air in response, bobbing his head and squeezing his eyes closed. His two friends clasped their bodies together in a solid hug, burying their furry faces into each other.

I suppose the enclosure was the first thing that didn't disappoint me about Atlas. The animal habitat was expansive. The monkeys were boisterous and their faces expressive, all fat-eyed and pouty. I looked up to see a cluster of gossiping laundresses perched on a hanging beam. Below them was a gang of tiny-faced naughty tots racing through the village center, and grumpy old men with scraggly beards, leaning in the shade and bitching about sports. I couldn't look away from their goofy human ears. Their inky eyes and troll doll faces. Despite the intense odor, anyone would immediately fall in love.

The oysters were gone, and a new course of watermelon had appeared in its place. The macaques were having a grand time sharing a few slices between them. They adeptly pried off hunks with their hands, and one little guy was shoving his whole face into a melon before coming up for air with red pulp flying off his fur.

"That's Charlie. He's my favorite. There's always that one kid."

I turned to see a wiry man sidling up to me. He held long-handled pruning shears with a thick blade that looked like a parrot's beak.

"I'm Boris," he said. "Lead volunteer today."

"Hi, there," I said, relieved. "I'm Jamie, I'm new, not sure what I should be doing yet. Do you need—"

Before I could finish introducing myself, the macaques started shrieking.

I turned and scanned the enclosure, expecting to find some of them fighting, but instead saw the monkeys banging on the chain link. Ten yards down the cage, a squatting woman was being pulled up against the fence by a macaque with a gorgeous gray mane and powder blue eyelids. The monkey held her necklace in its grip while others screeched and alerted each other overhead and below him on the ground. The woman, slack against the cage, didn't even seem to be resisting the monkey's hold on her.

"Willow, get away from the monkeys!" Dagmar yelled from the far side of the enclosure. A few of us rushed to gather around Willow, including Tierra and Sari. Suddenly the chain of Willow's necklace popped and she tumbled back. The monkey ran with its prize up a ladder to the tire swing.

Tierra helped Willow stand and then checked the woman's neck and hands, finding only a red abrasion where the necklace had been pulled taut. Sari watched, arms folded in front of her.

"Don't be mad, Sari, he just came out of nowhere, he just jumped in front of me and reached through the fence," Willow said, her hand on her chest and laboring to catch her breath. "He didn't mean any harm."

I backed away to a bench nearby to give them space, but Boris and three other volunteers closed in on them. Sari slowly surveyed the monkeys in the enclosure and then focused again on Willow. "It looks like Cornelius didn't hurt you, not even a scratch, am I correct?"

"Right, I'm fine. Nothing happened. I'm so sorry for the commotion," Willow said. "Do you think maybe this means Cornelius was bonding with me?"

Sari shook her head. "Willow, you were too close. You have just endangered the whole troop with a choking hazard. Dagmar will now have to go in and find it. Was it just the chain?"

Willow winced. "And a gold charm of a hawk. But it's real gold, it's not a toxin."

"It was pretty big, though. Plus the chain might be in multiple pieces," Boris offered.

Tierra took Willow's arm. "Come with me. I'll put some salve on your neck."

"It's time for the volunteers to go home today, anyway," Sari said. I watched her walk to the other end of the enclosure toward Dagmar. For a moment, I wondered if I should follow her. I wasn't a volunteer; I wasn't going home. I hesitated, then just decided to stay on the bench, and a moment later they all had disappeared.

"Y'all pulled off quite the heist," I whispered to the group of five or six macaques that remained near me. I had arrived at Atlas already a little afraid of the macaques, as I had to sign a waiver that stated I would never touch them. Dagmar's stoning story was new to me, but apparently some of the Atlas monkeys were known to be aggressive after entering adolescence. Also, some of them were carriers of the serious herpes B virus that only affected humans. The staff had said the macaques were asymptomatic, but a bite or scratch could transmit a lethal lode, so the rule was *hands off.* Not a problem for me. They were cute, but I had no desire to hold them, especially after Willow's experience.

A few more monkeys gathered. They extended their leathery fingers in my direction through the chain link.

"You're barking up the wrong tree, buddies. I'm broke, sold everything to come live with you. I don't own anything worth pawning, anymore, and certainly no gold."

Nearby, a fifty-something woman in a crisp blouse turned to look blankly at me. Her ability to look fresh in white linen on a ninety-degree day at a rural animal shelter absolutely astonished me.

"You must be new." She eyed me up and down. There was no welcome in her voice. "You startled me. Because most people come here to meditate. Most of us don't talk to the macaques."

"Hi, I'm Jamie," I said. I followed her gaze to my ankle. Two little buttons on the black box glowed with an amber light, like vampire puncture wounds. "I am new, and I'm sorry if I'm doing something wrong. I was just trying to calm down, I guess. I want to get to know these little guys."

"Consider silent meditation," she said. "You can't observe if you aren't silent." She nodded promptly and then walked toward the parking lot.

Once she was out of earshot, I said to the monkeys, "She must have seen me in the news. I'm lucky you don't have the internet, or you guys would probably hate me, too."

I sighed. My stunt at Tiki Hut—my humiliating, ridiculous crime—left me blackballed in St. Augustine, not to mention penniless and vehicle-less—because at the very end I was forced to sell my truck to pay the last of the legal fees, placement fees, and ongoing house arrest fees that would allow me to live at Atlas. Every time I turned around, I owed somebody another $300. The application fee to get into the Atlas community service diversion program. An ankle monitor installation deposit to Sunshine Monitoring. Monthly maintenance charges and court fees. After all of my legal problems were behind me, the thought of a fresh start in a new city at the end of the summer kept me going—until I remembered that my infamy probably had spread to people outside of St. Augustine, too.

"You guys have it made. Watermelon, a tire swing, and an entire heist crew. And so many humans working for you. I'm in, sign me up." I eyed one beautiful monkey that was a little smaller than the others. Her cheeks were so pink they looked like blush had been applied by a senior citizen in the low light of the bingo hall bathroom. "Can we be friends? I really need a friend."

The monkey wiggled her fingers, a virtuoso playing the scales. At the distant sounds of gravel from the parking lot, I looked around to see that most of the workers had evaporated. Quitting time, right at the peak of the afternoon heat. I imagined myself being able to leave Atlas like that. I could stop at my favorite convenience store for a beer and then head down the winding state route to Crescent Beach or Matanzas and throw myself into the ebb of the cleansing, forgiving Atlantic.

It didn't matter if I wanted to leave or not. I was compelled by the State of Florida and the anklet on my body to stay. Arriving at Atlas signaled the end of one long, dark tunnel, but maybe the beginning of yet another. I didn't know if I could take one more hit. I wished I could lie flat on the bench in front of the monkeys and dream my way through the next three months. It seemed impossible that I could summon the energy needed to even make it through the rest of the day.

The enclosure clanged as doors opened. The monkeys loped to the back of the cage where Dagmar alone was able to meet their needs with more food and more water. I forced myself to stand up, and then I used my foot to smooth over the sand and mulch that had been disrupted where Willow fell backward when her necklace broke. I didn't see any remnants of gold.

4

Our primates come from four different pathways. One is by rescue from the exotic pet trade, a treacherous and exploitative industry that discards more animals than it sells. Private ownership is neither good for primates nor for owners; so many monkeys need refuge after being relinquished, abused or removed from homes.

The second way we receive monkeys is from the laboratories, which subject macaques to untold tortures.

The third is from roadside zoos, which are more prevalent and less regulated than you would think, and they are notorious for dumping their animals when they become old, infirm or even depressed. They want monkeys who smile for photographs, but who wouldn't be sad in those conditions? Forced to live in a zoo, gawked at for entertainment, enslaved for the amusement of lesser beings. We believe monkeys should be worshipped, not ridiculed! After all, they are bound to outlast us all.

Finally, we rescue wild monkeys that have been injured or rejected by their own troops. We would like to create more slots for the rehabilitation of wild monkeys, as Florida is home to over a thousand feral macaques, many of which carry viruses that make humans want to hunt or trap them, and our eighty-acre campus is environmentally the perfect refuge for them.

That's where you come in. Join our family at Atlas! We are stronger together!

COMMENT FROM SARI

Dear ones, this is a shared project. Start writing and editing! —xoxoS.

TRACK CHANGES FROM TIERRA

Dear Sari & Dagmar. This is great, Sari! But I hear you completely. You are not alone with this big and beautiful project. I am ready to help in every way. I simply don't have any suggestions on what you have written so far. It's lovely and is bound to be useful. I was chatting with Dagmar and she said she is a little confused because we are not ready to start the livestream much less invite people to stay here, but that she trusts you to prep the website redesign. You are doing great, Sari. Keep it up! Just make sure to add what you said during the last ritual about rebirth. You said it all so beautifully. Maybe leave out the part about dying? But otherwise, say that! With love and respect, Tierra.

5

The dome was cool and dark. Only Tierra was there, working in the kitchen in a flax apron. As soon as she saw me, she brightened and beckoned me in. She washed flour from her hands and prepared a tall mason jar of cold tea, another of cold water, and a big bowl of fat green grapes.

"You sit down right at that table and cool off. I'm trying to finish this bread for our supper. Willow's drama interrupted my process, so I can't promise how the bread will turn out. On hot days like this you have to monitor the dough at every stage—it can blow up in the heat, or the yeast can get choked out. It's volatile."

"It looks great," I offered. "I've never made bread before."

"Never? Not even tortillas? Not even biscuits?" she asked, theatrically shaking flour onto the chipped Formica countertop. Her incredulity was tender and bemused.

"Well, okay, biscuits. And I worked at a catering company that said they baked their own bread, but they really just pulled frozen blobs out of a box and stuck them in the oven, so I don't think that counts."

"They skipped the most beautiful part!"

I sat back and watched her shape the loaf while she narrated her process. "The yeast needs to be warm to grow," she said, "but when the humidity is too heavy, it's difficult to knead without adding too much flour into the sticky dough." She pinched four handfuls of dough as white and soft as a baby's thigh from a ceramic bowl and rolled each piece, weaving them into challah braids in a captivating, glutinous dance.

"I wanted to have fresh bread to welcome you," she said. "You've been through a lot today. I really hope it turns out."

I offered to help, but she refused, so I leaned back in my chair and marveled at the dome's ceiling, an intricately constructed puzzle of triangles. Some of the panels were fiberglass, while others were wood or corrugated steel. Globs of sealant had been applied and reapplied to most of the joints, and other junctures were marred with water spots. The triangles on the sides were screened-in. It was remarkably cooler in the dome than outside, perhaps from the many fans, or because heat rose to the top of the arcs.

A smaller dome was attached via a covered porch. That building, I knew, was Sari's home and also housed Atlas's business office. On my tour, Sari had said Atlas's land had belonged to her family for decades and had been through a few evolutions before becoming the Atlas Wildlife Refuge.

"Tierra, I've never been in a building like this. Do you know how old it is?" I asked.

"All of the buildings were here when I arrived for the midwifery school. Well, except for the monkey structures—I was here when those were installed three years ago. But Sari built the domes herself, years before that when she moved out of her parents' house." Tierra smashed chopped herbs into butter.

I could see the main area was devoted to the service of food preparation and dining. It felt welcoming, furnished with reclaimed fixtures: a chipped iron sink that Tierra said came from a goat dairy farm, a large walk-in refrigerator, old wooden church pews and mismatched chairs, and three long crate wood tables. Beyond the dining tables, a few old couches and bookshelves formed a makeshift living room.

Tierra stayed busy in a constant loop in and out of the refrigerator, back and forth to her spice rack and pantry shelves. She moved with grace and her food smelled amazing, but she seemed too inefficient to have had formal kitchen training. It would just be the four of us most nights, she told me, because all of the other community members left after lunch.

"I've grown to like it this way, one cozy little table," she said. "But it will be fun for Atlas to grow again. Sari wants more people to live here eventually, to build up the community, get more guests on the land who aren't working jobs in town. There's so much we can do. You'll see, Jamie."

"Great! Please give me jobs, Tierra. I am here to work, and I'm a fast learner. Just point me in the right direction."

"Tomorrow. Today I'm taking care of you." Tierra pulled the baking sheet from the oven. Her bread looked flawless.

Eventually Sari came to the dome to join us for dinner. She wore a fresh sundress and smelled like citrus and clove. Maybe frequent wardrobe changing was a survival skill here. My clothes were now dry from sitting near the fan, but they were still crunchy from the day's sweat, and I'm sure I smelled terrible. She greeted me as though she hadn't seen me in years, cupping her hand on my cheek.

"Tierra, Dagmar says she's running a wee bit late because of the jewelry situation," Sari said. "She's still in Monkey Island." Sari turned to me to explain. "That's the metal building near the enclosure. Dagmar's probably not going to let you in there for a while, but don't be offended. It's just her vet tech center."

"It's her happy place," Tierra said. "No worries, I was thrown off schedule, too."

Tierra removed the spotless apron and then her T-shirt, revealing a gauzy sundress that barely skimmed her sculpted, sunburnished shoulders. She had prepared a table that looked like a jewel box—white beans with microgreens, homemade radish pickles, fresh bread, braised eggplant, honey-roasted squash, beeswax candles burning in little mustard jars. And here I was, very obviously more of a convenience-store-honey-bun-for-breakfast kind of person.

"Beautiful, beautiful, you made my eggplant, you made my day," Sari said. She stretched and twisted as she talked, as though she were warming up for a yoga class. "Jamie, you are going to die for this, it's so good."

"I know, thank you. I mean, look at it," I said, stumbling over my words. "It smells amazing—I'm so grateful to be here."

"Jamie helped with supper," Tierra said.

I looked at Sari and shook my head. "I really didn't. But I do want to!"

"It's all good, little Jamie," Sari said. Her gentle smile put me at ease.

While Tierra was sorting through a notebook of CDs to find one to feed to an old boom box, Dagmar came through the screen door at last, letting it bounce in its wood frame. She took off her white rubber chore boots and left them on a mat by the door.

"Bread, bread, bread," she chanted. Cheeks pink from the heat, she washed her hands, bowed to me, and gave Sari and Tierra each a long hug.

"Yes, let's eat," Tierra said. "Dagmar is so excited because Mondays and Thursdays are my usual bread days, but I added an extra baking day today in honor of your arrival."

"Wow, I don't know how to thank you enough for all of your kindnesses." I meant it, too. Aside from my lawyer, it had been a long time since anyone had been so nice to me. I worried my bumbling words of gratitude sounded forced as soon as they were out of my mouth. These gracious women were a trio of key deer, and I was a clumsy buzzard.

"We love dinner, Jamie. This is our sacred time. Eat! We cultivate all manner of things in the kitchen and garden to sustain us, the volunteers, and the monkeys," Sari said.

"Nut milk yogurt from an ancient starter—our monkeys love it. And look at our sprouts! Have you ever had a sprout garden?" Tierra asked. She beamed and pointed to a row of fat pickle jars near her spice rack that were topped with makeshift mesh lids.

"Never. We served entrées with alfalfa sprouts at one of my last jobs, but it never occurred to me to wonder how they were grown." My mind flashed to Duke's kitchen at the Tiki Hut. "We just had them delivered in boxes like everything else."

"I thought you worked at a bar," Sari said.

"The Tiki Hut was a bar, but also they served food. Grouper sandwiches, burgers, nachos, that kind of thing. But I've worked lots of jobs," I said, trying to steer the conversation away. "Recently I've been motel cleaning. I also assist a wedding videographer. I did pressure washing for a little while before that, scooter rentals, catering. No monkeys, but I have lots of other experience."

"What do you really love?" Sari asked. "What do you really, really love?"

"Do you mean, for work?" I looked to Sari for guidance, but she merely smiled. "I had a nice job at a surf shop for a while. People were really easygoing there. And I like editing wedding videos. I got to help a videographer put together different video packages."

"Do you surf?" Dagmar asked.

"No, not anymore…just on bodyboards, you know?"

"What do you like about the weddings?" Sari asked.

Their questions made me flush. "It's more the editing, because you can take hours of video footage, and then boil it down to the best five minutes where everyone looks happy."

"I love that," Tierra said. "Sounds like magic."

"Jamie, we are so happy you are here," Dagmar said. "You truly will benefit from meeting the macaques."

"Me too." I sighed in relief. "I feel like I already have."

Tierra put the last portion of eggplant on Sari's plate, and she passed the bread basket to me. Her food was deceptively simple, each bite holding a layered bloom of flavors. "You can garden with me tomorrow morning if you want. It's the best place to be, I mean, as well as hanging out with the macaques."

"That's fine," Dagmar said. "I have a lot of volunteer help right now, and those men are coming to work on the new enclosure soon."

"That's exciting. For more macaques?" I asked.

"Of course, what else?"

"We're expanding!" Sari reached across the table to take my hand in hers. "We have such a good life here, Jamie. It's beautiful, you can see that. I predict that everything is progressing exactly how it is meant to, and that we'll find good work for you to do, and you're going to be truly happy here."

"I think you're right," I said, nursing a drop of confidence, and hoping I had finally passed their impromptu interview.

"By the way everyone, Willow will not be coming back," Sari said, standing up. "I handled it. Let me know if you see her again on the premises."

Dagmar and Tierra nodded impassively, as though they expected as much. I wanted to press more about what happened, if only to avoid the same fate. I wondered, too, if any monkeys had been harmed from Willow's necklace. But no one said anything else, and I didn't think it was my place to ask.

Sari changed the music to Brittany Howard singing about Georgia. The women commiserated over an ongoing issue with spots on their rows of lettuce while Dagmar sliced mangos with the competence of a surgeon. It made me wonder how a Danish veterinarian who looked like an Olympic ski champion had found her way to a monkey refuge in Central Florida. She fit in though, the three of them rich in the currencies of beauty and charm, with Sari and Tierra more closely resembling the surfer girls I grew up with, or the women I served at the bar who drank tequila by night and fed themselves on hot sand and the assault of waves by day.

They refused my attempts to help clear the table.

"Relax, Jamie. I bet you are tired," Sari said. "You had to do so much in order to move here."

"Moving is so hard," Tierra said. "I hope I never have to move again."

"Actually, I couldn't afford to keep my rental or my truck, so I've just been selling stuff on Craigslist," I said. "It's good to be free of it all. I feel like I've been through a cleanse."

"It's so important not to waste. We don't need many belongings to live." Dagmar was eating her melon rapidly but with precision, utensils in both hands and her fork curved down.

"It's true, I really don't miss anything. And when I start over, I can be extra careful about what I buy or what I accumulate."

What I didn't say is that it was also terrifying to own so little, or that those last days in my house grew eerie as items went missing one at a time, as though the building itself was eating them. I felt like an untethered balloon. After this summer, I would need to start from scratch, which is daunting when you're broke. It had taken me years to acquire basic items like a table, a bed, a couch, and a television, usually settling for whatever was cheap or free. But I also didn't say that it somehow felt just for me to lose everything. Like I deserved to have my life burnt down to the ground. "It's funny, last year seems like it happened a million years ago," I said.

Dagmar cleaned the last of the dishes. "Tierra, we should send her home with some tea." She turned to address me. "There's potable water in your cabin. Please drink plenty. We're afraid you may have become slightly dehydrated today."

"Of course," Tierra said, "and we will pack you a sandwich in case you get hungry tonight. Do you like peanut butter? Or I could whip up some hummus? In case you want a snack."

"I'm full from this spectacular dinner, but sure, anything is fine," I said. "Y'all are too good. I don't know how to thank you for welcoming me so graciously."

"You know," Sari suddenly extended her hands upward, "we need to commemorate this moment and show Jamie how to give thanks!"

Dagmar said, "Sari, I think we're waiting. Let Jamie settle in first! Plus it's getting late. She should be home before dark."

"We have plenty of daylight. And we are not waiting when there is so much abundance that needs celebration. We need to give thanks for Jamie! She just said she wants to give thanks for us."

"Sari," Tierra said, already fixing my to-go bag. "I think Dagmar has a point. Jamie must be very tired."

Sari ignored them. She took my hands in hers. "Jamie, sweet thing. You are a blessing to us. I am going to show you what we do on nights like this, when we have so much to be happy for."

She ducked behind the counter and grabbed a large stainless-steel bowl. She strutted into the refrigerator. Dagmar and Tierra kept their eyes on me. I assumed that Sari was going to come present some sort of dessert, so I was preparing for birthday-cake-and-singing kind of awkwardness. But instead, she arrived with a bowl of what appeared to be raw meat, the flesh dark and puckered.

"Is that...chicken?" I asked, trying not to stare at the way Sari cradled the large bowl so close to her clean clothes. I didn't want to food shame them, but I had been certain Atlas was 100 percent vegetarian only.

No one answered.

"Come," Sari commanded. I followed Tierra to join Sari in a small circle right outside the dome door as she placed the bowl of flabby meat at our feet. Mosquitoes flocked to my ankles and knees while we waited for Dagmar to hop into her boots and catch up with us. When she did, we all joined hands.

"We don't do this every night," Sari said, "but today we have much to be grateful for. It is at these times that we give back to our precious land with a small sacrifice. Jamie, just as we fed you, and just as we fed the macaques today, we will now offer this food to our land and to our lake in gratitude for all of our blessings."

Sari took a deep breath. Dagmar closed her eyes, and Tierra gave me a reassuring nod.

Sari spoke in an odd whisper that almost sounded like a song. "These animals lived a useful life, and now will have a useful death in service to others. We offer this sacrifice in gratitude for all that is given to us. Blessed be."

"Blessed be," Dagmar and Tierra said. And then the women hugged each other, and each of them hugged me.

"The alligators will be very happy to receive this," Sari said. "See how it's done, Jamie? It's easy to show gratitude, and it's very important. Well done!"

I stared at them, petrified about what would come next. Dusk was a terrible time to go down to a Florida pond bearing meat, and feeding alligators was a pastime for drunk teenagers. I could always hang behind them if we all were going to walk down to the lake together, but I didn't know what I would say if Sari told me to go down on my own. I wouldn't even know which path to take.

Fortunately I didn't have to decide, because Sari dismissed us.

"Good night, dear ones," she said, picking up her bowl. "I will deliver this to the lake with your love. And I will see you in the morning, Jamie! Remember, we don't wander at night because we don't want to disturb the monkeys or each other."

"We roost up like birds after dinner and stay put," Tierra said. "But you'll get used to it all. The best thing to do is make sure you get tired during the day, and that way the night isn't as long."

I slapped a big mosquito that had landed on my arm. The thought of alligators snapping at meat in Sari's hands had left me twitchy, and the mosquitoes were making it worse. "Yeah, no, I'm looking forward to the quiet. It's been really chaotic for me lately, and I plan to get good and tired working for you guys. I'll get used to it, I will."

"You know, one thing I learned about living in Atlas is that time can feel different out here. Days are liquid, and it's perfectly normal to feel like the nights are really long. It's so dark and so very quiet, but that's a good thing, ultimately," Tierra said. She elegantly moved her hands when she spoke, as though gently reminding the air to make room for her words.

"You are like a new monkey, Jamie," Dagmar said. "It is normal to feel very weird now. Soon it will feel like home." Her accent was faint, but I heard a charming lilt in her vowels when she said *monkey* and *Jamie*.

"Okay, I really have to leave now, because after the lake I have to go to my mother." Sari turned to me to explain. "She's very ill."

"Oh, oh! I'm so sorry," I said.

"Don't be sorry," Sari said brightly. Bugs were landing on the chicken blood that was pooling in the bottom of the bowl. "We've been on a long journey with her. It's all a very natural process."

I wasn't sure what I was supposed to say to that, so I just stood there. Dagmar and Tierra were unfazed. Quiet smiles and nods rose like paper lanterns. Earlier I had wanted dinner to never end. I was dreading walking down that skinny path to sleep in the ratty A-frame shack. But this ominous silence, while Sari held a bowl of meat shreds like they were apples for pie, made me want to dash to my little cabin as soon as possible.

We exchanged more embraces, Tierra's dress smelling like rising yeast, Dagmar's touch warm and solid, as though we were
long lost friends. It occurred to me that I didn't know where
their homes were. I wondered if they stayed up late in Sari's
dome together, listening to music and telling stories about the
monkeys or their worries or whatever they hope to do next.

Once we parted ways, I followed mental breadcrumbs and
sheer instinct to find my way to the cabin. I passed Dagmar's
Monkey Island. Then the monkey enclosure and benches. I
stopped for a second to say good-night to the macaques, who
were already clustered in one of the covered shelters within
their habitat.

"Don't worry, it's just me, your new friend Jamie, tucking
you in. Good night, moon, good night, stars, good night, little
monkey paws."

Then I hustled along. I didn't know which would be worse:
to get in trouble for breaking curfew with the monkeys or to
get lost in the dark.

I doubted myself at points. Knobby roots tripped me now
and then, and I accidentally veered off once and hit a stand of
saw palmetto clumps. And then all of a sudden, there it was, my
cabin growing out of the ground like just another cypress knee.
I knew that inside, a damp quilt covered the bed and a layer of
pollen and mildew coated everything else, and things I couldn't
even imagine lived under and near my space. It was not a house
that could keep bugs out—or anything else, I feared. A wolf
could blow a kiss and it would all tumble down.

A full moon had escorted me home, but otherwise I could
see no other lights. I wondered if any of the women would even
hear me if I screamed.

6

You are a valued member of Atlas wherever you live on this precious, imperiled globe. Plan a visit! You are welcome! We are stronger together! Imagine the joy of observing the macaques in person. Picture yourself sitting on a Bonding Bench immersed in the natural beauty of a subtropical forest as you meditate up close and personal with our troop.

You are also a valued member of the Atlas community when you are in your own home. Donate now so that we can fund additional macaque enclosures and an orchard of VIP eco-cabins on our campus. We want to host you!

Of course, your work contributions are how you will become the most intimately involved in Atlas's mission. You might find yourself clearing paths, chopping fruit and vegetables for the monkeys, or helping us construct more cabins and enclosures as we grow. Every single member of our community will attest that working together on behalf of the macaques is deeply meaningful, and we can't wait to share this joy with you. Your well-being is our passion.

We are ready to reach out to infinitely more people with the wisdom gifted to us at Atlas. We have learned that every animal relaxes when they realize they are surrounded by good energy and caregivers who will listen to them. Don't you want to join us? Don't you want to grow with us?

Please donate to our building fund and blessings will follow.

COMMENT FROM SARI

Hello? We need everyone to pitch in on this. Rewriting the website is one of the hardest tasks we have on our plate right now, so please weigh in and start writing. Dagmar, I know you are busy, but this means you, too. If you say it's great, just keep doing it yourself, Sari, I will lose my ever-loving mind. –xoxoS.

7

I knew early on that I would be spending long nights alone in my cabin. My attorney, Kayla, had instructed me about the restrictions when she initially sold me on the placement, and Cole had also ordered me to stay in my cabin at night to keep my monitor happy. And, like Sari explained at dinner, if the refuge wasn't quiet at night, the macaques would be alert and anxious. Giving the macaques a restful sleep in the forest was a huge promise Atlas made to them, Sari said, and it went a long way toward their emotional rehabilitation.

I would have preferred staying in the dome listening to music with the Atlas women to help stave off the darkness of my first night. I had held at least two jobs at any one given time for as long as I could remember, so most of my waking hours had always been consumed with work, running around to solve one crisis or the other, getting my electricity turned back on or paying tickets for driving with expired tags. I bar-backed one spring break while feverish with walking pneumonia; I couldn't remember the last time I had an evening off with nothing to do.

When I packed the few bags I'd brought, I tried to think like
a tourist, or a sunbird anticipating leisure: I brought an arm-
ful of books, a notebook to plan my next moves, and a fat pad
of crossword and word search puzzles for when I didn't want
to think about anything. Maybe one night if I grew desperate
enough, they would appeal to me.

My poor little cabin was much more remote than I had envisioned. I suppose I had pictured something more like a summer camp where all the dormitories were clustered together. I
could see that the women of Atlas had done the best they could
to make it feel homey—braided rugs, small candles, and a vase
with flowers centered on a small café table—but there wasn't
much to be done about its general disrepair or the unsettling
quiet. I knew I couldn't have an emotional support pet here, but
I was beginning to understand their appeal.

The only thing to do, then, was to get to know the place.
The lights ran on solar power stored in a wall-mounted battery
bank that looked like an advanced science fair project. A com-
posting toilet had been installed in my cabin that was basically
just a complicated litter box, and the bucket of coconut coir that
was supposed to handle the odor seemed atrociously inadequate.
Eventually, I would need to figure out laundry and bathing in
the communal shower house.

Tierra had reminded me that cooking was discouraged when
she gave me my sandwich, but there was an electric kettle and
tea bags on a handmade shelf. I remembered, then, how Tierra
had so thoughtfully given me a take-home jar of her sun tea.
I took a sip. I had never tasted anything as refreshing: citrusy,
mildly spicy, and thick from a honey emulsion. I took another
sip, and then another. I couldn't stop.

I pulled a ceramic plate from the shelf and put it on the dresser.
Earlier in the day I had pocketed a smooth stone from the path,
and I centered it on the plate.

"One day, Cole. That's what one day looks like. Before you

know it that plate will be full, and then what?" I said to the room, or to my monitor, in case Cole could hear me through it. Part of me hoped that he was listening. Maybe Cole could be my emotional support dog.

They left me two T-shirts made of fair-trade organic bamboo, one featuring a macaque and the other that said *Atlas: We Are the Fountain of Youth.* Maybe the swag would help me look like I fit in. I've always loved uniforms: A fresh stack of T-shirts or a colored apron at a new job always told me who the boss wanted me to be. No guesswork, no mistakes, no standing out. In a uniform, I could count on looking the part, and these Atlas shirts were going to make it easier to weave myself into to the spirit of the place without calling attention to myself.

When I picked up the T-shirt with the monkey, an index card shook free and fluttered to the floor. Handwritten in a looping script that was accented with vines and flowers, it looked just like the instructional cards propped by the solar power switch and toilet. This one said:

> *Soon enough you will come to love this simplicity like we do. After living at Atlas, returning to the city will feel indulgent and wasteful, gallons of water pounding through a house just to handle a half cup of your body's emissions, lawn mowers sputtering out of every garage once a week, a massive refrigerator gulping electricity just to chill leftovers in Styrofoam for a few days until they are tossed into a landfill? We will never be able to see that as luxurious again.*

The other T-shirt held another card:

> *The universe has a way of reclaiming excess. Understand the power in that. We all hold a capacity to better our environment each and every day through eliminating waste.*

At first, I thought the cards were general notes the Atlas women might slide into all of their merch, but then when I went to check the sheets on my bed for bugs, I found one on the quilt.

Some people need to relinquish things in order to see they never needed them anyway. If you are sad right now about your truck or the things you lost, just know we have everything needed right here for you. Nothing has been lost.

I paused at the specific mention of a "truck." That was targeted at me. I studied the handwriting. Something about the swirling vines and big capital letters made me think they were written by Sari. I sniffed the cards. They smelled faintly of a campfire and molasses, though maybe that was from the candle on my bedside table.

And then, as I arranged the pillows, I found one more:

It doesn't take the macaques long to realize that Atlas is the best thing ever to happen to them. They know we are ready to receive their brilliance. Before you know it, you'll be ready, too.

8

I was still wide-awake late into the night, unable to find that final tumble into sleep. I was exhausted, but everything about my new situation crashed in on me whenever I closed my eyes: the isolated cabin, the lack of phone (I craved it like a missing hand), my raw ankle that was now the property of the government—or worse, the property of a corporation that leased me for profit.

Massive insects bristled against the windows and clawed feet clamored on the roof. At least I think they were on the roof. I hoped they were on the outside, along with all of the snakes, spiders, and wind demons I imagined.

Both the dreadful quiet within my cabin and the variety of forest noises outside it were terrifying, and not to mention those index card notes. These women were so different from me. I was never going to fit in here. Every mistake I had made seemed to slam into the forefront of my mind. Every loss. Every fear about supporting myself when my stint at Atlas ends. I had decimated each facet of my life, lost every friend, turned my town against me after turning myself into a laughingstock. A Florida Woman headline. I didn't even have a car to sleep in. I was going to end up in a motel where you pay by the month but have to move rooms on a weekly basis because they don't want customers to earn tenants' rights. I heard the creaking pine trees overhead and thought about the one that had crashed into the yurt. I had never felt more forsaken or alone.

I got up and paced around my cabin, because when I was lying down, I felt like my heart would climb out of my throat. I needed to get a grip. Think more positively. That's what my brother used to tell me to do when I spiraled into worry or fear as a child. Jason would make a silly face or a goofy noise, and say, *Don't be sad, Jamie. You've got to bright side yourself!* He was right, but resilience was easier for him. He was older. He was always the confident one who could glide atop any wave and become fast friends with everyone.

I finally drifted off, but it was a nightmare-fueled jag. I careened in and out of disturbing visions as though I was trying to sleep off a liter of well gin, my brain melting and my mouth dry. I dreamed of monkeys howling and strangling me with my own shirt, earthquakes crashing trees on top of cages, monkeys screeching and pounding on the metal fencing of their enclosure with oyster shells. The dreams were so unsettling and so vivid that even when I jolted myself awake I could still hear the reverberations deep in my brain, the agitation carrying forward into an ache just beyond my jaw and a chill under my skin.

Morning came. I don't know how much I had actually slept, but I resolved to throw myself into life at Atlas and wrote off my shaky feelings to first night jitters.

On my way to breakfast, I wandered up to the monkeys and Sari intercepted me, pulling me by the hand into the dome for breakfast. "Look at you in your Atlas T-shirt! That blue is amazing on you."

"Good morning, Jamie, so wonderful to see your new face

here," said Tierra when we entered the kitchen. "I woke up so happy about getting to know you."

"Not that you have to wear a uniform," Sari said, pouring herself the last of the coffee. "You do you. I absolutely love you in that blue, though!"

"Are you kidding? I could live in this shirt forever," I said. "It's super soft."

"You are going to have a gorgeous day, Jamie!" Tierra said, pushing more coffee through her press. "Sari, someday it would be amazing to make our own clothes. We could plant more bamboo. It grows so fast. Truly a solution plant for the planet."

"Beautiful idea," Sari said. "When we have more hands and hearts in the community."

I assumed Sari was going to give me my work schedule for the day, but she instead kissed the top of Tierra's head and swiftly left the building.

Bouncing between the dome and the monkeys during those first few days gave me a fairly good sense of Atlas life. I learned that the day-to-day labor of keeping the monkeys safe and well-fed fell to the dozens of volunteers. Dagmar served as the vet and supervisor of the grounds. Tierra helmed the garden and kitchen and managed the throng of workers.

Tierra told me the locals were the regular helpers, and then closer to the weekend, carloads of volunteers would arrive from Jacksonville, Gainesville, Daytona and even Orlando, mostly women in their twenties and thirties, but retired folks, too. Most of the locals only came for an hour or so every few days, and out-of-towners worked longer shifts but visited even less frequently. No minors were allowed—an insurance restriction, according to Sari.

Back when I thought more people would be living at Atlas, I envisioned us getting to know each other at bonfires or while swimming at the lake during our downtime, sort of like camp counselors at a sleepaway camp. But now that I understood people just came and went, I couldn't envision how building relationships would work with such sporadic scheduling. Plus I really didn't want my ankle bracelet to scare anyone off. I wore jeans that first day hoping to camouflage the monitor a little bit, but I had no idea how I looked because my cabin only had a small mirror. The bulge most likely drew attention instead of concealing my ankle, and probably wasn't worth the extra clothes in the oppressive heat, but I felt too vulnerable in shorts.

While I was at the enclosure with Dagmar that morning, I watched the macaques for a little while from the benches with a few other volunteers, who were studying their antics with solemn attention. I could understand why: the monkeys' expressive faces were fascinating, with plaintive eyes and protruding pouts that made them look like infants and old men all at once. No wonder people took them as pets.

Dagmar let me shadow her as she supplied, removed, and cleaned a series of puzzles for them to play with. I spent thirty or so minutes hiding nuts in a group of six containers that were nested like Matryoshka dolls, only to have the macaques access the treats in a matter of minutes.

Watching them reminded me of the horrible two weeks I spent as a childcare worker. The preschoolers blew through piles of activities like frogs eating bugs. I knew it wouldn't work out long-term from day one—I've always found the vulnerability of children very stressful—and then I finally had enough when one of them bit me because I wouldn't let him eat a crayon. I happily returned to waiting tables and never looked back.

Fortunately, the monkeys were cuter, and I hoped they stayed behind the chain-link fencing, because their bites came with higher stakes.

Dagmar showed me the new enclosure Atlas was building near the old one, with a few rows of benches between the two cages. Contractors were almost finished with construction. The expansion, she informed me, would allow Atlas to double its monkey population.

"This is my baby," she said as she showed me the new cage's features. She carried herself regally, as if to suggest there was no higher calling than a zookeeper, no greater service to perform than tending to animals. "I also drafted the first enclosure myself, but this one will reflect its perfections. We live, we learn, we enhance."

She had designed improvements to the freshwater system, and the drawers that were used to push food into the enclosure would be safer and easier to clean. Both enclosures featured climbing and shelter structures for the monkeys, and most importantly, a double gate system. Even if one door was accidently left open, the monkeys would be held back by the other.

"So will some of those monkeys get to move over to the new enclosure?" I asked.

"Oh, no, no, no. These macaques are now an established troop. We won't split them up! Never."

"I just thought maybe they would be spreading out, to give them more play space. An upgrade."

"They have plenty of space," Dagmar scoffed. "They have an ideal amount of space."

I quickly backpedaled. "Of course, and I'm sure they are very happy where they are."

"Yes, very content. Change comes at a cost, and that's a cost they have already paid. There is no need to change their environment." Dagmar turned away from me and tested her new feeding drawer again. "Our new enclosure is for different macaques, an entire new cohort that I will build one or two at a time, carefully introducing them to each other."

I tried to think about the things I had researched before arriving at Atlas. I wanted to sound smart to her. "Dagmar, I was wondering if any of the monkeys know American Sign Language, or any other kind of sign language. I watched some videos about talking with animals before coming here, and..."

"No. Some may know commands from their previous owners, but we don't do that."

"Okay. I just thought—"

"Jamie. Listen well. They are not our little minions. They are not here to perform tricks." Her disgust was animated, her eyes daring me to try to save the conversation.

"But don't some primates know sign language? They are smart enough."

She tilted her head and smiled, like I was a child too old to be asking about Santa. "That was debunked. Even apes don't use our language. They are learning commands from positive feedback, but commands are different from language. It is forcing them to do parlor tricks."

My cheeks were on fire. "I guess I have a lot to learn."

She turned and walked toward Monkey Island. I tagged along, trying to keep up as she continued. "You will learn. You need to study the historic records and esoteric texts to understand why they are revered. Think of macaques as experts on the environment, Jamie. They are messengers of ancient mountain gods, messengers of the rivers. God of the wind, reborn! They communicate with an ear and a vocabulary we cannot yet grasp, and what they are telling us is of dire importance to the planet. It is insulting to teach them the sign language for water. They are water. They are the wind."

"Well, I definitely don't want to insult them," I said.

"Okay, we are done, I have other work to do in Monkey Island. Bye now." She disappeared into the unassuming prefab metal building, unlocking it with a key tethered to her belt. I wasn't sure what could be inside other than storage cabinets, and perhaps exam tables for when Dagmar needed to perform veterinary services on the macaques, or maybe office space.

I noticed, as heat waves bounced off the metal siding and as sweat collected behind my knees, that Monkey Island was air-conditioned. There were no windows on the front—which made it look like an overgrown shed—but I could hear the tantalizing hum of a unit placed somewhere behind the building. The main dome wasn't even air-conditioned, and my cabin certainly wasn't. I would pay good money, if I had any, to crawl into a dark cabinet in Monkey Island to cool off for an hour, but the Atlas staff didn't seem to believe in siestas.

That afternoon, I learned that Tierra was much less stressful to help than Dagmar. She spent the day gardening, canning and cooking, and I slid easily into her projects like a kid at recess hopping into a schoolyard jump rope.

We harvested every available tomato, ripe or not, into two large baskets—mostly Romas, but at least four other varietals as well. The tomatoes were hot in our hands, their skin blasting back the heat of the sun. "This might be the end of tomatoes this year," Tierra said. "It's already too hot. They're cooking on the vine. Some luck and magic might bring them back, but I doubt it. It's lucky you are here to help me, though."

"Well, I'm glad you are putting me to work. I've always wanted to learn how to do all of this back-to-the-land stuff anyway."

"The thing about canning is you must do it at the peak of season—in this case, the hottest days of summer—and so we need to boil vats of water to sterilize jars on a ninety-degree day. I love it, though. You'll love it, too. As they cool off, their lids will pop like happy little children, and then the food is all ready to be stored for our beloved family."

"I'm going to be honest, I've never really cooked for anyone, so not sure how much help I'll be. It would take me years to eat this much salsa. I pick up tacos on the way home from work and get a few extra hot sauce packets, and I'm good to go."

Tierra's eyes and nose crinkled as she laughed. "I can't believe you haven't ever cooked a meal for a friend, or a sweet-heart. Or something to bring to a party. Never? My family was always cooking. I'm half Puerto Rican, half Italian, so maybe that's part of it. But everyone has to feed someone."

"Maybe that's where I've gone wrong. I've only ever had two relationships, and neither amounted to anything long-term. But maybe they would have if I had learned how to cook."

"Maybe they should have cooked for you," she said. Tierra seasoned her sauce, but I could feel her listening, still and open. It made me want to continue talking.

"I don't know. I had a girlfriend one year, and then she took off for a surfing competition in Indian River Shores and never came back. Then about two years later, a friend from work and I flirted on and off for a long time, and it felt like something was building," I said, watching the big bubbles breaking the surface of the boiling pot. "But then it sort of fell apart. And I haven't met anyone since. Pathetic, I know."

"Not pathetic. Who knows? Some of us here at Atlas are a bit like nuns, fulfilled entirely by our work. Or maybe you're just not in that cycle of life."

"It's so weird, I shoot all of these weddings for girls my age or even younger, and they have these happy families and rows of friends—all the pieces of their life fit together and are cheering them on. It always looks like they have it all figured out already."

She nodded. "I always thought I'd have a baby by now, and I don't, but I don't mind. I have forty-two macaques." She extracted a batch of clean jars from the boiling water using a large pair of tongs. "And I'm close to having a dozen jars of salsa, plus more for dinner. I've just met a new friend. You never know what the universe will provide, but you know it will be perfect."

"You mean Cole, right? He's my new best friend too," I said, and was delighted to hear her laugh.

"I mean you! But you know, I'm going to make you sit down and drink some water, Jamie, because you look like you're suffering. I shouldn't have worked you so hard in this heat. Are you feeling okay?" She poured me a full glass of sun tea from the five-gallon jar on the counter.

"I'm just tired. I'm fine, and I'm used to working in the heat," I said, although that wasn't entirely true. Even at beach bars or working as a motel maid, I could take air-conditioned breaks and then go home to an air-conditioned house. It felt so much hotter here. Atlas was far from the tempering breezes of the Atlantic Ocean and the inland air was stultifying, thick and heavy like the scraped insides of succulent leaves or melted cane sugar. "And I didn't sleep much last night. I had these horrible nightmares about the monkeys and I don't even know what else, and I couldn't wake up and get free of it."

"Poor thing. I hate when that happens. Once I was upset with Dagmar all day because we had argued in my dream." She sat down with me, allowing her salsa time to cool. "You know what, you are still settling in. You've got years of toxic life that must melt off of you. That's why I don't want you to work hard right now. Just rest, Jamie. The work will be here."

"Yeah, maybe you're right." I thought about Cole and my raw, sore ankle. I needed to soak and bandage it.

"When we get new macaques, it takes them months to feel at home. I think it's like soul jet lag, where their spirits haven't caught up with their little bodies just yet. Change is hard. But once you get those toxins out, and you look around and see how loved and safe you are, you'll be golden."

I thought a shower might be a good idea. I wanted to change my clothes and appear refreshed at dinner like Sari had the night before, her golden hair free of the day's sweat and grime. Down at the shared shower house with my clothes and toiletries in one arm, I reached to pull back the door and let myself in, and felt a sudden, fiery pinch on my hand.

I recoiled, my eyes welled up, the pain sharp and hot as it

traveled from my right hand up to my temples and back again. Spooked, I scanned the door and the door handle, but didn't see any insects or possible culprits, so I rushed back toward the dome. The pain was intense, tight as a knife wound, and immediately my hand began to swell in the crook between my thumb and first finger.

"Hey, speak of the devil," Sari said when I entered the kitchen. She was sitting at a table with Tierra and a gaunt, older woman who was wrapped in a towel, her head lost in a floral bathing cap. "Come over here and meet my mother. Mama, this is Jamie. Jamie, this is my mother, Flora Sutherland."

"Hello, ma'am," I said, feeling instantly awkward for barging in on them. "Very pleased to meet you."

"Just call me Flora. I'm very glad to meet you too, Jamie." She had a gentle smile, but her face was drawn and tired.

"Did you have trouble finding the shower house?" Tierra asked.

"Oh, I found it, but then something bit my hand at the door. I didn't see snakes or anything, but you don't think it could have been a pygmy rattler, do you?"

Tierra frowned. Sari said, "Doubt it."

Flora inspected the bite. "Not a worry, just a wasp or a bee," she said, nodding reassuringly, the petals on her bathing cap fluttering in ascent. "It will be fine in no time."

"I'll get you some ice," Tierra said.

"That's a very good sign, the bees," Sari said. "Very good omen indeed. I really should get some hives going again."

"I've been bit by many a bee living here," added Flora. "Your daddy, too."

"My father kept bees for a while," Sari explained. "He and Mama ran lots of different farm businesses. I'll show you where we used to grow ferns and flowers later."

"We delivered our altar flowers to churches as far away as

Tallahassee, every week," Flora proudly proclaimed. "Cut and arranged them on Friday, delivered on Saturday."

"The best was the palm leaves for Palm Sunday," Sari reminisced. "We shipped them everywhere in those huge boxes. And we wove crosses from the palms, too."

"The preachers loved Daddy, didn't they?" She patted Sari's hand. "He could have been a preacher himself, but he was a farmer in his bones, isn't that right?"

"You could have been a preacher too, Mama, just as much as Daddy. And he would be real proud to see all that you've done for Atlas."

Flora looked down at her hands in reverence. "I'll see him soon enough. I know he's always looking out for you, Sarahbelle."

"Well, thank you for helping me, all of you," I said, pulling away from their private moment. "I am so sorry I busted in on you, but truly, thank you for allowing me to stay on your beautiful property, Miss Flora."

"You are very welcome. I've heard a lot about you, and I know many people are happy you're here," she said, patting Sari's hand. "But you know, don't leave, it's really time for me to go home, not you. Why don't you settle in on the sofa—I picked that out myself in Deland way back when I was carrying Sari..."

I woke up hot and disoriented on an old denim couch, having accidentally fallen asleep right there in the small living room area of the dome. I sat up and slowly tried to remember where I was. Tierra was singing quietly along to Fleetwood Mac; onions, peppers, and garlic sizzled in a pan.

I heard the screen door open, and Dagmar and Tierra began speaking with an urgency that kept me at a distance.

"Sari is very upset about her sister," Tierra said. "Anna Beth called and said that she's coming to get Flora."

"No, we don't need that right now. No! When?" Dagmar asked.

I tried to listen to their conversation without looking like I was listening, which was incredibly hard to do without having a phone to look at. I coped by pretending to read a copy of *The Moosewood Cookbook* from the dome's bookshelf beside me.

"Soon. That's why she has flipped out. Anna Beth wants to take Flora to her house. She wants her to get treatment and has already booked appointments for her in Missouri."

"Outrageous." I could sense a protective rage bubbling in Dagmar. "This is about the will. Sari needs to tell Anna Beth to mind her own business. Flora can make her own choices and to do things her own way."

"Sari did tell her that, Dagmar. That's why Anna Beth is coming down."

Dagmar and Tierra stared at each other for a long time. The air bristled. I wasn't sure if they were mad at each other in addition to being mad about Anna Beth. I certainly didn't want to have their ire directed at me. I stayed busy reading about gentle lentil soup on the couch.

"I'm telling you so you can process this information without adding to Sari's upset feelings. Fume and catastrophize for a bit if you need, but then we all need to strategize."

"Anna Beth already has the life she wants. The house, the husband. Why can't she leave Sari and Flora alone? She pops up like a ground hog. Destructive, aggressive, territorial, even cannibalistic. She hates Atlas and wants to ruin everything."

Tierra placated. "Sari will get it under control. We will be fine. We always are."

I wasn't entirely surprised to hear all this. No family controls large estates without some inheritance squabbles, and Atlas was a substantial piece of land. Surely it was big enough to divide fairly, but it also sounded like their conflicts went beyond that.

The gossip was intriguing, and I could breathe a little easier knowing I wasn't the only person at Atlas with baggage. But I felt terrible that Flora had to confront family drama while she was in such a tender condition. And Sari had so much on her plate. I couldn't imagine the stress of expanding Atlas and managing a family crisis all at the same time, yet they still dropped everything and tended to me, each of them in their own ways.

I needed to somehow let Sari know I was on call to help her. I would start with supper. I got up and walked to the kitchen area to see if I could assist Tierra or help prepare our tomatillo salsa. Maybe the women would talk more about Anna Beth and include me in their problem-solving. I could offer to help care for Flora, but her house was off-campus and not in my anklet's approved range. Perhaps we could have Cole change that.

Before I could reach the sink, though, Sari entered the kitchen. She looked energized, fresh from a swim with goggles still hanging around her neck, and greeted me with a bow. She smelled like coconut and sweet basil.

"Jamie, we're about to teach you something life-changing." Sari nodded at Tierra and Dagmar, both of whom looked away. "Because today is a vitally important day, and I want to include you in what we as a community need to do. You want to be included, right?"

"Of course," I said.

"Sari," Dagmar started. "Jamie has worked so hard all day. We all have. Let's sit down and eat."

"But Jamie says she wants to be included." She smiled at me. "That's what I thought, Jamie. You want to be a part of Atlas. I can feel it. We appreciate your hard work, and the love behind it. I thought about sending you home with your supper instead of inviting you, but then I realized, no, we need you, and I think you have earned the right to participate." Sari surveyed the kitchen. "So, let's all help Tierra pack this up."

Dagmar groaned and protested. Tierra asked, "Sari, are you sure?"

"It's necessary. Only tea for us tonight. We need to make a

sacrifice," she whispered to me through a sly smile. She was bristling with energy. "For Atlas."

"Do you mean like last night?" I asked, wondering if she fed her alligators every day. I had peeked in the refrigerator earlier and hadn't noticed any bowls of meat. I wondered what it would be like to watch her feed them. If she dangled the food on a stick for small alligators in the water, or if she left it in a pile for a large one to claim—but I didn't want to know badly enough to stand by her side.

"No, a true sacrifice. Last night was about giving thanks through the sacrifice of animal flesh. Tonight, we sacrifice our own comfort. We need to show the monkeys that we will fight for Atlas. Fight for their future!"

Tierra resolutely found a box and layered our dinner preparations in it. Dagmar relented and started assisting. Beans and rice, a pile of fresh tortillas, a big bowl of salsa. They scraped it all in the container.

When everything was ready, Sari snatched the box and trotted outside and down toward the monkeys, trailing us behind her. I tried to get Tierra's attention but she was focused, head high, walking straight ahead with a stainless-steel bowl full of salad in her arms.

Down at the enclosure, Sari motioned for us to sit on a Bonding Bench. She addressed us, some of the monkeys assembling behind her.

"We have been useful today, but tonight we will make this sacrifice to remind us that greater sacrifices inevitably will come, and we must always be ready to give and then give more. We offer this humble food to the monkeys of Atlas, and tonight we dedicate our fast to them. Blessed be the monkeys of Atlas."

"Blessed be the monkeys of Atlas," Tierra and Dagmar said in unison.

Dagmar carried the box around the cage to the feeding drawer and pushed the entire lot in. I looked over at Tierra. I was baffled at the tremendous waste of food, and more so the rude dismissal of Tierra's time, but she appeared to be stoic and resigned. We watched the monkeys investigate their twilight bounty and feast on the contents, my stomach twisting more and more aggressively with each of their squeals and grunts. They tore at the cardboard with bared front teeth, and a few lucky ones ran their hands through the mess of food. The box was not very large—it was only dinner for four—so the mass of monkeys pushed and plucked at each other to get in on the goods. One macaque broke away with several of the tortillas and deftly climbed up a beam to protect her booty. Silhouetted against the low light of the closing day, she clamped down with her bared teeth and savagely shredded her way through each one without sharing.

I was amazed that neither Dagmar nor Tierra continued to protest. I wondered what they hoped to accomplish through all this. Maybe it felt like wishing luck upon themselves, like blowing on a pair of dice or tossing salt over one's shoulder. It had been a long time since someone had snatched a meal away from me, but I supposed it was better than not having been invited at all. I briefly pictured myself back in the dome, eating tortillas alone while the others gathered outside, and the image made my stomach constrict even more.

Later, back in the kitchen, the three of them chatted casually as if nothing had happened. Dagmar and I washed dishes, which was the worst part of the night. Few things are more torturous than washing dishes when you're hungry, something I was all too familiar with from my long nights waitressing, but Dagmar sang an old folk song and the pile of work slowly dissolved. Sari swanned through the dome tidying up, and Tierra prepared mason jars of her sun tea for us to take home, two jars each. If they needed good luck, I wished for them to have it. Sari was under unthinkable stress, and no one was at their best when worry rattled behind their ribs.

Tierra whispered to me as she pushed the jars into my hands. "Just sip throughout the evening. We'll eat at breakfast."

When I passed the monkeys on my way home, one of them was dancing with the salad bowl as his partner, step one, two, step one, two. All I could think about was doing the same with one or two of the precious protein bars from my stash.

9

I panicked on the path on my way home, getting lost again, and felt myself spiraling from hunger and sensory overload. Stands of scrub pines and coontie palms looked odd to me in a couple places, and some plants on the path seemed bent or broken. The sky had grown dark and nothing looked the same. It made me think about large animals trudging down my path, though it was likely from something smaller, like a raccoon or a coatimundi. I needed to head home earlier in the evening. I needed to be more attentive on the paths in the daytime. Look for scat. Look for teeth markings.

It took me at least twenty minutes to find my way back. At last in my cabin, I tossed another stone on the counting plate and took a sip of tea. It didn't make up for a lost dinner, but I did love Tierra's concoction, full of orange blossom honey and some dark spices that reminded me of clove cigarettes, and I knew I would rally after a few snacks. I pulled out my tote to grab a protein bar and some nuts, grateful for my own forethought, but the canvas collapsed into my hands, empty.

All of my food was gone.

Fury exploded, setting my hand on fire again. How dare they, I thought, itching from the inside out with righteous insult. I quickly searched my room in case I had unpacked my stash, but the stockpile of snacks was nowhere to be found.

Then, on the heels of reactive ire, I was just simply confused. Perhaps I had broken a rule, one of the lacy, subtle policies that community members just knew without leaders making them explicit. Cooking was discouraged in the cabins, except for tea—I knew that. I guess it was possible I'd offended community sensibilities with my off-brand protein bars, tainting Atlas with GMOs and nonorganics and noncompostable wrappers. Either way, I didn't like it that someone went through my belongings.

I hadn't been able to shower earlier, but I certainly wasn't leaving my cabin again that night. I did the best I could to wash and bandage my ankle anyway. Water trickled out of my hand-pumped sink, and I was grateful for every drop. My skin was torn up from the rigid plastic of the monitor, and the whole apparatus was filthy from the dirt pathways. The little lights glowed, so I guessed the tracking mechanism was working seamlessly.

"Are you there, Cole? It's me, Jamie. I hate to be a Goldilocks, but listen, this thing is too tight. Or too loose. Too something. When you check on me, is there a setting that would work better? Otherwise I'm good. As you know. Thank you."

A thick palmetto bug flew down from the rafters, its wings scratching through the still air like course sandpaper. I had officially somehow arrived at a new stage in my ever-declining life, awkward even when talking to myself. I was struggling without a computer or a phone. I couldn't count how many times during the day I wanted to research something. Tomatillo vs. tomato. How to become a vet. Monkey gods. Honey bees in Florida.

If I had a phone, I could have looked up photos of Sari's sister, Anna Beth from Missouri. Few things were more satisfying than finding relevant Facebook pages to match an overheard story and figuring out the players later on. I didn't want to gossip in a malicious way or anything. I just wanted to be able to slide into their conversations and support them without having to bother with questions or making the wrong assumptions.

It sounded as though Anna Beth didn't like the medical care Flora was accessing here. I wondered what that entailed, and why exactly did she hate Atlas? Did she just hate the monkeys? It was likely more than that. I fell asleep thinking about the macaques' inquisitive eyes, the way they bit and skinned oranges with such focused glee. Who could hate that?

Later, I woke with my head spinning, as though gravity no longer served me, and my thoughts roamed untethered. It was just after midnight. I was sweating and covered with mosquitoes, my screen door snapping open and shut against its frame. I could hear the high-pitched squalling of monkeys in the distance— or almost hear them. I wasn't quite sure what it was the more I tried to isolate the sound. It may have been more of a vibration, like in my dream, and then I thought I must be dreaming still. But that couldn't be. I was awake, my ankle screaming in its own pain, and then I wondered if the disturbance was from the earth itself, the start of a sinkhole, maybe. Or oncoming hurricane winds?

I thought about going outside to check, but I was too exhausted to move. I drifted back asleep and watched waves of colors riding the sounds—and then the colors were the iridescent wings of moths, and also Tierra's long eyelashes opening and closing, and an undulating honey bee hive the size of my bed—leaving me unsure the next morning if I had really been awake at all that night.

10

Dagmar met me at the door to the dome, told me to open my mouth, and fed me a slice of almond butter-covered banana bread.

"Isn't this heavenly." She nodded. Like a toddler, I nodded back. "Tierra was up early this morning. Come join the party!"

Breakfast was a feast of fresh tortillas, scrambled tofu and mushrooms, beans, rice, sliced red peppers, and a jar of our fragrant salsa. We ate like triumphant tigers, laughing with mouths full of food, allowing our appreciation out in sighs and smacks. Midmeal Dagmar jumped up, ran to the other side of the table and hugged Tierra from behind, and then Sari joined them. I quickly, shyly leaned against Tierra while walking dishes to the sink, wishing I could press my head against her warm shoulder a moment longer. It felt amazing to be with them all, the food magnificent because of our hunger, the four of us ready to make the most of a new day.

No one mentioned Flora, or Anna Beth for that matter. Sari and Dagmar hurried off when they heard the turn of gravel that meant the volunteers, or perhaps the construction crew, were arriving. I stayed to prep lunch with Tierra. We had our work cut out for us, with massive piles of onions, garlic, and potatoes to dice.

"Jamie, please stop if you get tired. Sit and keep me company," she said.

"I'm good, thank you. I'm just a little off. Lots of sounds in the night, you know? Insects, the wind, the monkeys. I'm also having those kinds of dreams again that are so vivid that they almost seem real." I washed the baking sheets for the potatoes, thinking about what bugs might have crawled on these exposed shelves at night. "I don't know where your cabin is, but do you think the monkeys might be howling at night?"

"No, no way. They weren't howling at all. Plus, even if they were, you could not have heard them crying from the A-frame. Do you mean you came up here to the enclosures last night? Or to the dome?" Tierra stirred onions in a large sauté pan. From behind I saw tiny beads of sweat clinging to the nape of her neck.

"No, I definitely did not leave my cabin. I don't want to sound like a baby, but trust me, I am not going on the paths in the middle of the night."

"Good. But, no, absolutely nothing happened last night. No disturbances. It might have been feral hogs in the distance, something like that, and you assumed it was the monkeys because you have the monkeys on your mind." Her voice was all cool breezes and easy shrugs, but my eyes widened at the thought of being chased by a razorback.

"I forgot about hogs. They are freaky. Do you have those in this part of the forest?"

"You're not used to the woods. Sounds can echo and play tricks on you. What's that thing called where a small handful of toads know how to sound like millions of toads to protect their turf? Dagmar would know what it's called. Or maybe you're hearing alligators," she continued. Gold and hammered silver bracelets and braided cords adorned each of her tan arms, moving in a way that captivated me. If I tried to replicate the look, I would be a sweaty mess. The jade and quartz beads tinkled now and then as she cooked, like faraway chimes. "I've heard them bellowing before from here, but that's usually during mating season, which should be done by now. And not all the way at our cabins."

"Okay, so about those alligators. It kind of freaked me out that Sari feeds them. Is that a frequent thing?"

"It's a spring-fed lake; of course we have a few alligators. Sari likes to feed them, you saw that. She knows this land so intimately it will blow your mind, and I can't imagine her getting hurt here, not at all. But they stay in the water. I've never once seen them anywhere else."

"Yeah, I don't think it was the alligators I heard last night."

"Maybe it was bats. I think they sort of scream if there are a lot of them. Dagmar could check your roof. I mean, I don't think we have panthers up around here, but it's a possibility. That would be awesome, actually. Though maybe not, not for the monkeys."

Tierra must have seen it all register on my face and quickly backpedaled. She picked up my hand and unclenched it from my knife.

"It's just a lot to get used to. Hold still. I'm going to do an energy transfer. It will give you strength." She flattened my hands between hers, pressing firmly while she closed her eyes. I closed my eyes, too, unsure of the proper etiquette in such an impromptu experience. She held me there, silently, as my hands melted into hers, and then she dropped them abruptly and went back to tend the range.

I opened one eye and when I saw she was done with me, I tentatively returned to my knife and cutting board. "I'm sure you're right. This is all new to me."

"Oh, it was to me, too. I grew up in Tampa, in the suburbs

sort of. There were no snakes or bugs hiding in shower houses. My mother hates them. She believes flying palmetto roaches are signs of the devil. She thinks I've lost my mind to want to live out here—she won't even visit—but she had to let me go my own way. I respect her for that, because she had always expected me to stay with her in the city, and lead a better version of her own life. So living naturally out here didn't come easy to me at first, but I've learned a lot from Flora and the others who have come and gone from this land."

"Flora's amazing. I was happy to meet her. I can't imagine having a mother like that." I flashed to her and Sari together in the kitchen. "I don't actually even have a mom anymore. Not functionally, anyway. My dad left when I was a kid, then my mom took off with a new boyfriend when I was in middle school, and I haven't seen her since. She used to call on my birthday or whatever, but then that eventually stopped, too."

She made an empathetic cluck and pouted.

"It's okay," I continued. "She knew her limitations. My brother and I stayed with a friend of hers for a while, but my brother was older and kind of wild, so he messed that up, and I ended up in foster care for a few years. Somehow I'm still kicking, I guess. But I definitely didn't have anyone like Flora taking care of me."

"Oh, Flora is the kind of mother I would want to be, for sure. Strong, in every way." Tierra pushed a large cast-iron pan full of potatoes in the oven, but we had many more batches to roast before our workers arrived.

At the end of the day, I found I still had daylight to spare, so I stopped to chat with the monkeys. Seven or eight gathered near me, with two of the bigger guys scaling up and down the fence, and others arriving on the ground one after the other. I walked along the cage, and they slowly moved down the row with me.

"Let me ask you this, you little freaks. No one is giving me a time sheet or a list of tasks to complete, and it occurred to me that Cole never said when he would come back to check on me. Should I be worried? Is Cole not going to verify my days or something?"

One petite flower of a monkey shook her head and pursed her mouth. The two big macaques wandered off when they were certain I didn't have any food to share.

"I know, I know. I need to get over myself, work on my stress. I like living with y'all, but I want this jewelry off of my ankle." I scanned for the gray-haired heist crew leader and didn't see him. I hoped no panthers or forest monsters were terrorizing the macaques at night. It was reassuring to remember that the same cage that kept them in would likely also keep a predator out, save for the snakes and bats.

I made it home that night for the first time with no issues. I was very proud of myself. I plunked my calendar rock on the saucer, flopped on my bed, and stared at the connecting angles of the A-frame, occasionally rolling over to steal a sip of my sun tea. Dagmar was right. It did help to stay hydrated. Sometimes remembering my childhood left me sullen and moody, but Tierra made it easy to share. I hoped I hadn't blurted too much, but I was in a deficit from the last year, having emotionally withdrawn in the aftermath of the Tiki Hut situation. I so often tried to cauterize my past because it was too painful to talk about all of my losses and mistakes. Connecting with Tierra was an unexpected balm.

Relaxing at last, the knots in my brain started to diffuse like sugar into warm water. If the monkeys cried in my dreams, they didn't wake me, and the only sound that registered was the wind nudging my screen door open once, twice, three times, but I couldn't pull myself awake to latch it shut.

11

I hated the horrific ankle bracelet and all it represented. It was shredding my skin, and maybe it hit on trigger points of some sort, because I began to blame it for my waves of intermittent anxiety and the struggle to wake up at dawn. It was inconvenient, shameful and cumbersome, but I gave up trying to hide it because the jeans were untenable in the heat.

I even had a breakdown in the shower house after stripping down and comprehending that despite my growing cache of stones, the monitor still wasn't coming off anytime soon. It was now part of my naked body, and I would likely have scars forever from the raw abrasions. It was part of my shadow. Part of me.

I never mentioned it to the women, hoping they had stopped noticing it in the way that familiarity erases details, but I still complained about it to the monkeys. I was beginning to think of them as my buddies, so enamored was I with their close-knit ways, and how some of them would scamper toward me when I walked near their cage, cooing or jabbering at me, coaxing me to respond. Dagmar said they were merely hoping I had food for them, but I knew better. They tilted their tufted heads and made excellent eye contact, and when their hands gripped the chain link, I saw they actually had fingernails instead of claws. They listened attentively, forming grooming lines or mimicking my voice tone back to me as if they were a Greek chorus.

"I know what I did was wrong, but haven't I been punished enough, in the scheme of things?" I asked. Cornelius the jewel thief scratched his ears and huffed, unmoved by my plea, which I found deeply hypocritical of him.

"What if you guys take turns wearing it for me? Cole probably wouldn't know. We could turn it into a game!" The chubby red head ran away, bounding up one of the beams to eye me warily from above.

"What's that? Every day spent at Atlas puts me one day closer to getting it removed. Ah, you are correct, little monkey. I shall work on my patience. Thank you!"

The paths and the wooded area outside the shower house were as dark as those around my cabin. Ancient ferns and palms rose up between trees, and fast-growing kudzu vines fought with dripping Spanish moss to possess tree limbs. It was better to be outside in the sun. There were only three bright clearings in my anklet jurisdiction: the monkey habitat, the pier at the lake, and the garden. I loved the garden. It felt good to harvest lettuce with Tierra. I felt needed, too. Sari hadn't given me work yet, and Dagmar was very rigid about helpers coming near Monkey Island, so Tierra's projects became my default.

That morning, she was teaching me how to loosen root wads when replanting and how to turn the kitchen cuttings deep into the compost pile. She reached over and positioned my hands on the shovel to get maximum purchase, her long, defined arms resting on mine for a moment, putting them to shame.

"This is my favorite thing. This beauty!" Tierra exclaimed. "Compost is alchemy. Do you know how powerful it is to know nothing is wasted, ever? Compost is life!"

She marveled at the worms that haunted each shovelful. I felt nothing but disgust, but I envied her excitement. I don't know if I've ever cared about anything properly if other people could muster this much passion for compost.

I admired the easy way Tierra and Dagmar moved and managed Atlas's workload. As volunteers came and went, Tierra served as a coordinator, steering them to where the work was most needed, and Dagmar provided on-the-ground oversight.

"I'm glad Sari wants you to try all the different work areas," Tierra said. "My joy is matching volunteers with jobs that will make their time at Atlas feel the most purposeful and joyous. Some people want to be as close to the macaques as possible, so they like chopping food, cleaning enrichment toys or landscaping near the habitats. Others need a break from the toxins in the city, so they work in the garden and or on the paths. Retired people love repairing and building things, like the dock or the yards of screen that lined the domes. Everyone finds a purpose!"

At any point when someone wanted a break, they were welcome to come to the dome for sun tea or to observe the monkeys from the hand-hewn Bonding Benches.

"You should definitely spend time with the macaques. Just watch them. Some people meditate here, so we designate the area a quiet zone. Most of the people who come to Atlas are working specifically to earn that special time."

"So do people just show up here to volunteer?" I asked. I went to the hose to rinse the red bandanna Tierra had given me. When I wiped my face, rinsed it again, and replaced it on my neck, the cool water instantly lifted the heat.

"No, absolutely not. There's a process, and not everyone is right for Atlas." Tierra leaned in and lowered her voice, prompting me to lean toward her in return. "Soon you'll understand that only very special people are allowed time here. You are a major exception in that we're doing things a little out of order. Typically, Sari has people prove themselves in a few different ways."

"I really don't know how my lawyer secured me this program slot," I said.

"Yes, and we're so glad you're here. Your situation is atypical. Atlas workers are handpicked. Sometimes Sari has tour days where she tells people about the refuge, and that's when new people get to visit, and if they seem right, Sari takes them to the next stage. Education, deep understanding, etcetera. Because we're a community, you know, we're not a zoo. And then after that, we have strict work schedules, eleven to two. And then we have special events. Everyone votes on who gets to go to special events, Jamie! It's just a bit jumbled with you, but soon it will all weave together. You'll get it."

"I feel really lucky, in that case. I can't believe it all came together." I did also feel a bit like an impostor, though. I jumped at the chance to live at Atlas because it was a pathway out of trouble. I hoped I wasn't taking the place of a die-hard monkey devotee. I wanted to learn, but if they expected that I would obtain some sort of spiritual awakening, I was bound to disappoint them. It made me wonder if my lawyer, Kayla, had somehow fibbed about my background in order to swing the deal.

"I think we're the lucky ones," Tierra said. "Oh no, look at these eggs!" She flipped a lettuce leaf over to show me an opaque cluster. A small anole peeked his head out from a nearby plant to look as well. "This is what hurts my heart. If I kill these eggs, I'm affecting this butterfly's reproduction intentions. But if I don't, we lose our lettuce to hungry caterpillars."

"But you have to protect your food. That seems fair to me. The butterflies have acres and acres to choose from. I bet they'll find another spot."

"But they like the sunny clearings! One year I thought I could give them some parsley as a peace offering, but they took over the whole garden anyway. It's so sad—the planet needs butterflies, and maybe I only *want* lettuce." She ripped the egg-ridden lettuce leaf off the plant and scoured for more damage. "And now both that leaf of lettuce and the eggs are gone. Such a waste. Sorry, Mama Moth, please lay your babies elsewhere, I beg you."

As if Tierra's lamentations were heard by the mother of the eggs herself, a sharp scream cut through the air. I froze.

It was a human sound, very human, clearly the breathy wails of a woman who was crying out in fear or pain. The monkeys followed with screeches and alerts, a chilling call-and-response of danger and discord.

We bolted from the garden and saw Dagmar leading a limping worker into the dome. Tierra followed Dagmar, but I stayed outside with the other buzzing volunteers and picked up pieces of the story. Earlier a volunteer noticed that the padlock was not firmly securing the enclosure and entered without permission. She was a local woman named Jodie. The witnesses disagreed about her intentions, some saying she wanted to touch the monkeys, and others saying she was looking for Dagmar. Someone suggested that we text her husband, and then someone said, "Absolutely do not, wait for Sari." But everyone agreed: when Jodie was inside the enclosure, she picked up one monkey and was bitten by another.

"Isak bit her. No doubt," one of the volunteers reported.

Tom, a sturdy man in saggy khakis, agreed. "It was Isak. I saw the whole thing. Jodie picked up O-Ren, and then Isak bit her calf hard, and Jodie yelled but held on to O-Ren, and then Dagmar was right there." He demonstrated the bite, fully extending his jaw and then slamming it shut. I felt it vicariously, like pins and needles jabbing my legs.

"Jodie has been hinting that she was going to hold O-Ren someday. I thought it was just wishful thinking, but I should have talked to Sari."

"I can't believe she did this to Sari," said another volunteer.

Dagmar suddenly walked outside the dome and onto the

two-step-high covered landing that protected the door. We assembled and listened.

"I'm going to give Jodie a few stitches, that's all that is happening, and Sari is talking to Jodie. Everyone is confident that the bite was from Isak, who does not carry the virus."

Tom exhaled audibly, and Dagmar nodded and continued. "So now let's go home today and meditate on lessons learned. Most certainly, confidentiality in the community is essential. To be clear, do not talk about today at all to anyone. Email Sari later if you have questions. We love you and we appreciate you."

"Dagmar." Tom was anxious to get her attention—he had tried raising his hand a few times during her speech. "I want to make an extra donation today in O-Ren's honor. Can I leave that with you?"

"Yes, certainly, appropriate and auspicious. Okay, let's walk to the parking lot now." She motioned for the crowd to scoot, and slowly led them away. After weighing the risks of intruding on the Atlas women, I decided to go into the dome.

Inside, Sari was angry. She was barefoot and pacing in front of Jodie, who was crying with her head tilted back. Her leg was elevated on a chair; Tierra was cleaning it with a cloth.

"How can we trust you?" Sari said, her sharp, enunciated words like claws on fabric. "What's next, Jodie? Which other community guideline is meaningless to you?"

"I'm sorry, Sari. I can't explain it. I don't know why I did it."

"I know why you did it. Because you don't love this community. We follow protocols because we are devoted and committed. But you don't respect the macaques. You picked her up like a baby doll! Like a plaything."

"I love O-Ren."

"You did not demonstrate love today." Sari's eyes flashed, her contempt uncontained.

"What can I do? I promise I won't go to the doctor."

"What if your husband sees this bite, Jodie? What if he reports it? Then the police are here. Then the state is here. The licensing board is here. The monkeys' very lives are in jeopardy."

Jodi's face was reddening and I was worried she needed ice for her leg, but I knew better than to interrupt Sari's scorching reproach. Having listened to many restaurant owners train me about insurance, food safety, and alcohol service liability—not to mention my Tiki Hut debacle—I knew a little bit about legal exposure, and managing an animal shelter on your own land must be infinitely riskier. If a bar owner can lose everything by serving someone who commits a DUI, Sari could probably be sued and lose Atlas over this, even though Jodie made the personal choice to enter the cage. I realized on an even deeper level than before that Sari was taking a gargantuan chance on me.

"He won't see the bite, he barely looks at me. Plus, I sneak out of the house to come here. He doesn't even know that I came to work with the macaques today. Besides, I know the oath. I would never, ever say I was bitten at Atlas."

"That's the point, Jodie. How do we know you'll abide by any of the agreements when you've just broken the biggest one? You gave yourself permission, is that how it goes? You invited yourself to that honor."

"I promise I'll handle it. Please don't ban me. I'll absolutely die if you do, I swear I will. I am devoted to the monkeys of Atlas. To you. Please." Jodie was wide-eyed, seeking an absolution that even I knew wouldn't ever arrive. Tierra bit her lip. I looked down at my monitor, a constant reminder that I was in no position to judge.

Dagmar arrived back at the dome, now carrying a plastic basket. She washed her hands and then draped a chair with a sheet before beginning to stitch up the gashes on Jodi's calf. As she threaded the long, curved needle with a thick and waxy thread, my knees turned to warm swamp water and I had to sit down on the sandy floor to keep from fainting. Dagmar stitched in silence, with not one whimper from Jodie or another word from Sari.

12

We love Florida for a reason. We love our land. We dig carefully when we clear paths or space for cabins and macaque habitats because we find treasures from the earth. Shards of pottery left by Timucuan people predating European settlements. A saber-tooth tiger's incisor that is now in a museum. Bone fragments and fossils from the animals and sea life that predate native inhabitation. We find lush vegetation exploding from all that died before it.

We find life everywhere, proof of its previous glory, proof that nothing is wasted if it is given back to the land.

Atlas was built on ground that is rich with legends, and we feel them as we walk the forests or sit under the particular alignments of stars that travel over our heads.

We know that youth does not mean perpetual life. Youth means usefulness, in every carbon form we take. In fact, youth often means the reuse that is only made possible from death. The legends are true. The Fountain of Youth can ensure a cycle of unending purpose.

We know the Fountain of Youth is right here in Florida. We feel it running through Atlas. We feel it running through every being living here, and most especially in our macaques.

We are the Fountain of Youth. Join us.

COMMENT FROM SARI

Dagmar, are you even reading this? I need to know how much to say. I want people to understand that by visiting us they will be receiving special knowledge, healing and the truth about life and death. Is that coming through? It's like I have it all in my head, but I feel like when I try to write it down, it all evaporates. —xoxoS.

COMMENT FROM DAGMAR

Hello, this is Dagmar. See my notes above.

COMMENT FROM SARI

I don't see any notes above! Did you have Track Changes turned on? You have to have Track Changes turned on.

TRACK CHANGES FROM TIERRA

Dear Sari & Dagmar. I think it is very beautiful to see it all written out. You have a glorious gift, Sari. I believe in us. You are doing great. Keep it up! With love and respect, Tierra.

TRACK CHANGES FROM DAGMAR

Hello, this is Dagmar. Of course I have Track Changes turned on.

COMMENT FROM SARI

You 100 percent do not have Track Changes turned on.

13

The monkeys were low key when I stopped on my way home to tuck them in. I wondered if they knew how much the bite had derailed the day. I would have paid good money to hear their thoughts.

"Good night, little troublemakers," I whispered. The macaques looked supremely innocent, grooming each other in clusters of two or three, nimble fingers gently combing through tufts of hair and then snacking on bugs they plucked. With their close-set eyes and exaggerated frowns, they were like a Kabuki or an overperformed mime show, and it was easy to project human dialogue onto their group squabbles.

It was only when they moved as a chaotic gang, rushing to their food or clamoring for the best spot on the tire swing, that I remembered their feral potential. I quietly moved on because I didn't want Dagmar to overhear me talking to the macaques.

Back in my cabin, I put another stone on my plate and tried to wash off a layer of grime from the sunscreen and bug spray mixed with pine pollen from the path, all baked in with sweat and thick humidity. I didn't know how mosquitoes penetrated it, but they had by the scores.

I couldn't get Jodie off my mind. Her gruesome leg certainly needed a doctor, but Sari did not seem to like that idea. I bit my lip and thought about Jodie trying to defend her inexplicable drive to pick up O-Ren. When she said she didn't know why she did it, Sari didn't believe her, but I did. I still didn't know why I acted so impulsively sometimes. Like that night at the Tiki Hut. Many people asked me what drove me to do something so terrible—and they had a right to wonder—but in all truth, I didn't fully know myself.

Kayla Dixson, my attorney, especially hated that response. When Kayla sought me out and offered to represent me pro bono, it made me believe in angels. She had seen the videos and had read the newspaper articles about me, so when she helped me post bail and launch a defense, I assumed she did so because she was hungry for publicity.

"I know there's more to the story. Lay it on me, girl. You can't shock me. I'm a Florida defense attorney," she had said.

Kayla wasn't troubled that I stole money from the owner, Duke. She wasn't worried about whether or not I was a good person. She just couldn't discern a motive for such a terrible plan. Kayla was a strategic woman trying to mount a defense, and she could not see any strategy behind my actions.

"You must have known all along you wouldn't get away with it," she said.

"I don't know what to say. It just happened."

"But why all of the destruction? Were you acting out in retribution against the owner? Did Duke harm you?"

"Sort of. Duke was definitely a jerk." For years, he perpetually ripped all of us off and harassed us. But I didn't think I was harming him, at least at first. I couldn't find the words to help Kayla comprehend. "It's more like a prank that just got out of hand."

"I know it got out of hand by the end of the night, but how

did it start? I'm trying to understand your state of mind before you even took the first dollar."

She was frustrated with me, and I understood why. "Kayla, you're right. Duke was an ass. He made me do stupid things. Like cover up his affairs so he didn't get in trouble with his wife. And I had to learn how to buy and sell cybercurrency for him because he was gambling online with the bar profits. Things that weren't even close to my job as a server. He just ordered me to do them."

Kayla pursed her lips and nodded for me to continue.

"That Saturday night, Duke was supposed to be there to close, but he wasn't. Presley and I had to do it, and her boyfriend, Hank, our line cook, stayed too. We were pissed about getting stuck with all of the closing tasks again, so we had a few shots, and the idea to take the money just came to us."

"Presley and Hank deny any involvement," Kayla said.

Presley and Hank were lying. The whole thing was Hank's idea.

"I don't know what else to tell you," I told Kayla. "I thought we were doing it together to teach Duke a lesson, and then it escalated from there."

I narrated the whole story to Kayla while she took notes on a yellow legal pad, starting with the money. When Duke took over the Tiki Hut seven years ago, he celebrated by signing his name on a single dollar bill and stapling it to the wall above the bar. He encouraged patrons to join in, and before long, the posting of dollars—scrawled with names and sweet notes—became a treasured tradition. "I'm a genius," he would crow, pointing to the bills. "I don't have to tend bar and I still get tips."

So, that night, we drank and fantasized for a while, door propped open for the cool island breeze. They left to get pizza and to round up more coworkers to help us.

Presley and Hank were tight with the group of staff who partied and fished together on their off days, but they usually called

me to cover their shifts instead of inviting me along. I tried not
to add to the awkwardness when I overheard their group plans
or their private jokes, but it always made me feel invisible. With
our impromptu event, I finally felt connected with them, col-
laborating on a big comeuppance for Duke that somehow, in
our minds, was going to compel him to become a better boss. It
felt like a party, or a community project, or maybe even something more.

Presley pocketed about forty bucks for pizza and they left.
Eager to help, I got started while they were gone. I drank shots
of Patrón by myself, pulling hundreds of single dollar bills off the
Tiki Hut walls and cramming them into my backpack, server's
apron and bra, working long past the point when I should have
realized Presley and Hank weren't returning. I cranked up the
music, dancing to Little Big Town and Kelly Clarkson while
working relentlessly to remove staples and bills.

It was an odd pleasure, but I was aware of a darker compul-
sion, too, the anger and resentment freeing itself with each buck I
unstapled. Yes, anger at Duke, and also at Presley and Hank, and
everyone who didn't do what they said they would do, and also
every customer who had stapled a bill on the walls, the tourists
and snowbirds and students at a college I would never be able
to afford, blowing through town but expecting to leave their
mark with a dollar they should have tipped to their server. My
name wasn't on a dollar bill. If my brother were still in town,
or my mother or father, maybe things would have been different. Maybe we would have gone to Duke's on my birthday and
graffitied a bill using a pink highlighter for luck, but that wasn't
my life. My life was unstapling the dollars and cramming them
wherever they fit.

I suppose all of this is why I didn't notice the arrival of the
pelican. He had somehow strutted through the open door behind me when I was working on a patch above the bar, grand

and grotesque, his dinosaur accordion beak opening like a bucket to collect my haul.

According to the video, as I lifted my arms to drunkenly reach for another dollar, he too spread his massive wings—perhaps to challenge my turf—and knocked over three hurricane candles near the door. The candles ignited a thatch basket of paper napkins, the pelican fanning the flames with his own wings. I heard an unsettling clatter I had thought was the wind, and then felt the air growing heavy and stifling—smelling not exactly like smoke, more like sulfur and grease. I thought Presley and Hank had finally arrived with food, and then I turned around.

If it weren't for the bird, I might have been able to put out the fire before it spread. But the pelican was stuck within the early flames, flapping his wings in place, and his helplessness terrified me. Not thinking, I went in, scooped up the big bird like a toddler and ran out the door to free it. I had abandoned my phone, my backpack and my keys inside, but there was no use trying to reclaim them—smoke was billowing out the door by the time I got out.

So I set the pelican down in the parking lot, and it stayed with me for a few minutes. We watched the fire from outside the building, waiting for sprinklers that never turned on.

And that's what was featured on the footage that was leaked after my arrest. I had forgotten that Duke's security camera recorded everything.

Two days after the fire, the video was published by a Jacksonville news site. The bizarre theft, the pelican, the fire, the lack of context behind all of my actions—every detail fueled its popularity. Online threads debated lots of theories during the height of the video's circulation. Most people said that I was merely drunk, others thought I looked distressed, and still others blamed meth or bath salts. Some thought I was angry, exacting a #metoo revenge scenario. Some just thought I was a greedy thief.

The video was short and soundless, a plastic sand strainer through which to filter their own ideas. I saved the pelican's life; I was a destructive agent of chaos; I was Robin Hood; I was faking it; I was she-ro; I was a crook. I was either doing what every viewer wishes she could do, or I made viewers feel superior by doing something they couldn't imagine doing themselves.

I became a meme, a trending topic on Twitter, the discourse of the day. People set highlight reels of the video to songs. They were laughing at me. *Only in Florida.* But they were also right there with me, stealing the money. Taking cash out of the sky like it grew on trees.

I became a shorthand of my headlines, and people called me Florida Woman.

National viewers did, anyway. Locals saw things a little differently.

What the locals didn't like is that I didn't pay any attention to what the dollar bills said. Many of them were elaborately marked, signed with highlighters and ink pens servers kept in our aprons just for them. Tourists scrawled their hometowns or drew stick figure families on their bills. Locals wrote holiday messages and anniversary commemorations on them. Miniature obituaries. *Go Gators!* Love notes to the universe. Others had doodles—hearts and male anatomy mostly.

The locals who went to Duke's felt ownership over those dollars. They had signed their bills; they looked for them on subsequent visits. I stole their birthday dollars. Their bachelorette parties. Their portraits.

Nationally, I made "Best Gif Lists" because I was an off-kilter, working-class hero from freaky Florida, but locally, I became an embarrassment, and worse, someone who carelessly robs her neighbors.

What the video hadn't revealed was that I didn't want the money, that I left most of it behind, or what I did after I fled with the little I took. When we heard the approach of the fire trucks, the pelican took flight and I left the Tiki Hut and walked straight across the Bridge of Lions—raw and almost numb, hugged by low-slung clouds against a glorious pink dawn and the briny air of the Atlantic Ocean.

The most beautiful parts of my morning didn't make the GIFs or memes. No one else saw the sun rising like gold over the bobbing yachts in the Matanzas Bay, or the 450-year-old masonry of the Castillo de San Marco staunchly guarding the old town for another day. The statues of lions at the end of the bridge let me enter, and I paid their toll by heading straight to the Cathedral Basilica. There I lit three candles and crammed the embellished money from my pockets, apron, and bra in and around the offertory.

Though I didn't yet know the extent of my impending banishment, deep inside somewhere I knew that I was free of waiting for my family to return to the town where they had left me. As I peeled the dollar bills and put them in the cathedral box, the worn paper was almost as soft as the hands of the woman who was preparing for morning Mass as she gave me a damp paper towel, right after she called the police.

Most of the newspapers came as close to the truth as possible, given what they had to work with. FLORIDA WOMAN DESTROYS TIKI BAR IN ATTEMPTED ROBBERY, BLAMES PELICAN. Duke managed to milk the victim angle locally, and the community replaced the dollars tenfold for his new bar.

That's why, after burning my workplace and my entire life to the ground one random night a year previous, I believed Jodie when she said she didn't know why she entered the cage and picked up O-Ren. Sometimes, like Tierra said, we're confused by the soul jet lag, the brain and the body are in different time zones, one trying to catch up with the actions of the other.

Being at Atlas at the end of another long day at the end of my long first week, now lying in bed with a wet bandanna on my face, I tried to forget the ache of the past and block off the terror of what's next. I tried to root myself in my rough plank house in the wild pine forest dead center between the Gulf of Mexico and the Atlantic Ocean in the middle of the improbable peninsula of new beginnings.

And then the macaques started screaming.

Their periled shrieks invaded my dreams, and I saw the shadows of unseen predators moving slowly in the middle of the dark, sticky night. The shrill cacophony broke through the humid air in rapid, chaotic howls that electrified the hair on my arms and legs. I knew their screams were real, and I tried to wake myself to go help them, but I was too tired to find my way out of sleep and into consciousness.

14

Mornings at Atlas were rough, nights were miserable, but I almost always felt good by the afternoon after a solid day's work or a chat with the monkeys. Dinners were the best, though. The volunteers were gone and along with them, their demands on the women's attention. We became more natural, less wary, less stressed. Dagmar often needed to vent about them or, more commonly, the workmen who had been hired for various construction projects.

"They waste so much, it's offensive," she said one night over roasted vegetable pizza. "Lumber, water, time. Their own efforts! If a man doesn't have the dignity to conserve his own effort, how can you get him to conserve planetary resources?"

"Sari, we must at least tell them no chewing tobacco on the land," Tierra piped in. "They come in here to eat and..." She trailed off, too disgusted to finish.

Dagmar pointed at me with her fork. "Jamie, if Atlas teaches you one thing, I hope it is an understanding at a cellular level, a deep biological level, that waste is an affront to nature." In the low light of the dome, Dagmar's blue eyes looked like steel. "Waste is killing Earth. We have been lied to, encouraged to consume *ad nauseum*, told we should attempt to live forever, and it's an abomination to nature. Americans are the worst, in abject denial about the state of our oceans, our lands, our global resources."

Dagmar often lectured me like this. At first it worried me, but I was coming to love it. She sounded like a know-it-all father.

"It's soullessness," said Tierra. "Vacant, empty soullessness. But Dagmar, don't lump us into that. We're modeling a better way."

"Jamie, let me ask you this. Have you ever seen the monkeys waste anything? Do you see them bemoaning their natural aging process, lining up for Botox?" She ate her pizza and shook her head, looking very much like one of her macaques, and I could see she didn't want an answer.

"That's why we need to get our messages out to people," Sari said. "Jamie, Dagmar is reminding me that I need you to help me with our website. Soon. Yesterday. I know I keep saying it, but we need to do it. People need our information." She picked the mushrooms off her pizza and stacked them in a cairn. "I wish you had email. I could send you the link to the Atlantic Rescue Center so you can see how they showcase their videos."

"Ugh, speaking of soulless," Dagmar said. "The ARC is basically a zoo. They treat the monkeys like animals."

"So many missed opportunities," Tierra said. She left the table to switch our music to a Taylor Swift CD. I saw one of her braided bracelets was fraying precariously to a single strand. I wondered each time she moved her arm if it would break, freeing the three green beads it held close to her wrist.

"True, but they have so many resources because they have a great website for their videos. Zelda says their donations are mammoth," Sari said.

"Cole won't let me have email, I'm sure of that, but if he says

I can work with you on the website, I'm game anytime. As long as we use a template, there's lots we can do."

"Yes, we are going to fix everything, aren't we, Jamie?" Sari put the last square of pizza on my plate, then leaned across the table and gave Dagmar a swift kiss, managing to snuff the candle in the process. "Though I do love how you flare your nostrils when you are angry, Dagmar," she said. She walked to the refrigerator to gather chicken without saying another word.

I constantly woke up exhausted from the unsettling night-time sounds, now certain I was in fact hearing something real emanating from the Atlas campus, or from the woods itself, but unsure of what to do about it. That's how my first weeks became a blur. It would take me all morning to shake my queasy sleepiness and headaches. It didn't help that Dagmar wanted us up at dawn to beat the heat, or that every few days Sari made us bless bowls of meat for the lake before getting started on the day's projects. It also didn't help that there wasn't enough water or tea in the world to combat the heat and long days of work—it almost didn't matter if the sounds were real or from my dreamscape, because my real problem was a hunger for sleep.

The macaques didn't seem to be suffering when I saw them during the day. As we fed them a fruit snack one afternoon, Dagmar pushed the trays in, and most of the monkeys hopped and wiggled and leapt over each other, dancing in praise of their feast. They gathered in clusters and plucked at grapes and berries. They sank diamond-sharp teeth into the giving flesh of apples and bananas. Henri grabbed one of the baby watermelons, held it high overhead, and threw it to the ground while little Charlie cheered. It smashed like a paper piñata.

What perplexed me was that the women themselves said that the monkeys were easily disturbed. The entire reason we closed down Atlas early each night was to let the monkeys have peace. Dagmar, or was it Tierra, had mentioned that many slept fitfully when they arrived, trauma left over from midnight predators or poachers, or from the pain of the medical experiments. Atlas was meant to be a refuge of continuity and comfort for them.

Maybe they howled and cried despite all of that care, and the women didn't hear it. Or maybe they did, and they were simply in denial that the macaques were troubled. It would be tragic if their refuge, while perhaps the best option for an at-risk macaque, might be adding to the animals' trauma, but it would make sense. The more I thought about, the surer I felt.

Perhaps that was the real reason I was told not to explore at night. They didn't want me to see unhappy monkeys, crying for their mamas or old owners. Maybe distressed noise was a reality in animal rescue, but a hard one to cop to when you are invested in a savior myth.

The paradox of exotic pet rescue seemed daunting. Most of the Atlas monkeys had been stolen at too young an age and then lived unnaturally as pets or even as proxy human children, wearing tutus or onesies or wacky fedoras. Yet they couldn't be completely free here either. At Atlas, they lived in a cage with minimal human contact: neither beloved pet nor truly wild. But I knew it was essential the macaques were protected from escape. They wouldn't survive in the wild and could end up a danger to themselves or humans through violence or virus transmission. They needed care, which the massive habitats and loving attention at Atlas clearly provided.

Maybe it wasn't complicated at all. Maybe they scream at night because they sense a predator. Or maybe they simply don't want to be caged. I could relate to that.

There were many consequences to my Tiki Hut crime, but the worse was being booked into jail a few days later. I thought I had nothing before the fire, but the moment I was cuffed I realized what nothing really meant. A primal rebellion rose up in my core against being locked up. Maybe sometimes, it does too for the macaques.

With so much good offered to the monkeys, how could Dagmar or Tierra, much less Sari, admit to themselves that it wasn't sufficient? That all of their love couldn't possibly be enough when caretaking meant cages? I didn't want to be the one to remind them.

One bright morning, Tierra was dissolving Epsom salts in a bucket of water to let me soak my ankle and drink an extra cup of coffee while she prepped lunch.

She washed the peeling skin under the anklet for me and looked at it from several angles, allowing me to study her dark lashes, the tip of her nose, and the line where her tender scalp met the darker skin of her face. "I think it's healing, but slowly," she proclaimed. "You know, if a physical wound is not healing, that means you are holding on to old emotional resentments somewhere."

"I don't think so. I don't really have resentments."

"We all have them. Old bosses? Disappointing friends or exes?" She returned to a big bowl of chickpeas that needed to be mashed into hummus. "It could be anything. Family issues, sibling rivalry."

"No, no way. I loved my brother. I couldn't resent him."

"Didn't you say he messed up when you were younger and that's why you went to foster care? It could be anything like that. Just think about it, let the idea roll around, maybe it will bloom."

I took the bucket to the sink to scrub it clean. The anklet clung to my clammy skin. "Maybe I said something like that, but I didn't mean I resented him for it. He was just a kid himself." I heard the tightness in my voice and tried to smooth it out. "My mom's friend who took us in, Nedra, she had two kids of her own. We all slept in the living room and we loved it. That was the best time of my life, all of us together for a couple years in that little apartment. But then Jason got busted for drug dealing—he took off, actually—and social services got involved, and that's when I ended up in foster care, never to hear from him, or my mom, or my dad again. That's my life in a nutshell. Everybody leaves. But it's not his fault."

"That's true. Maybe you've let go of it. Every single cell of yours has changed since then," she said, her muscles firing as she bore down into the mound of hummus. "My own family has a lot of addiction and alcohol abuse running through it. My mom went back to my dad again and again, even though he is a toxic mess with no intentions of staying sober. It's why I don't look back often. It's my personal timeline, but it doesn't define my journey, not at all. Our paths will cross again if they are meant to, that's the truest story."

She fed me a bite of the hummus on a spoon, and I smiled. "It's perfect."

"Maybe more garlic?"

"I think it's just right," I said.

Sari was present for dinner only sporadically as of late, as she was often needed at Flora's. That evening, she arrived halfway through the meal topless, wearing only a gold necklace, her key chain, and underwear (or perhaps it was a bikini bottom. I tried not to stare). Tierra stood up and welcomed her as a hostess might, looking improbably pristine in a long white sundress, and even Dagmar looked overdressed in her typical T-shirt and khaki shorts. No one batted an eye at Sari's attire.

Sari sat directly across from me. I was happy to see her because I had prepared an especially elegant salad from freshly harvested figs, the first of the summer, and Tierra told me that Sari's father had planted the trees and that they were a special joy of hers.

She was, in fact, delighted. "This is absolutely wonderful. Nothing compares to sweet figs!"

"Ripe figs won't keep, *tra la!*" Dagmar sang.

Tierra served Sari bread and a sweet potato, but she only ate the figs, plucking the fleshy pink wedges from the arugula and walnut salad. Hard as I tried, it was impossible to ignore the lack of tan lines on her golden shoulders or the way the glow very gradually paled toward the lower curve of her breasts.

"Jamie, you've fallen in love with the monkeys by now, haven't you?" Sari asked. "I've heard you talk with them."

I blushed—I thought I had been so careful. I wondered if Cole had been listening to me via my anklet and had ratted me out. "I do love them. It's true. They've won my heart."

"They are very sacred beings. I am so grateful Dagmar brought them into our life," Sari said, beaming at her friend. Dagmar was busy devouring a sweet potato.

"Me too," said Tierra. "And they are excellent judges of character."

Sari dangled her knife over her plate, rhythmically pricking the skin of her potato. "Did you know they are very ethical? They support each other, they share, but they don't ever let themselves drag down the group. They help one another give birth and can administer CPR or save a choking monkey. But if it's time for them to go, if they get sick or old, they wander off to die properly. They don't drain and drain and drain. Like us. Like humans draining the planet."

"Of course." I popped a Roma tomato dripping with balsamic vinegar into my mouth.

"It's the waste," Dagmar said. "They don't waste fossil fuels and water. They know we do, and they are trying to tell us. Oh boy, they are trying to tell us."

"Jamie, I want you to study them this week. They are so wise. We need to tell people about them. They need to be understood. In fact—"

"Sari, do you know what?" Tierra interrupted. "Jamie taught me a great way to wash dishes with buckets that saves water. Cleaning up goes faster after lunch, too."

"It's just something some restaurants do," I said, feeling suddenly shy.

"In fact," Sari continued, "some of the macaques are revered as gods, did you know that?" She fished in the salad bowl, making sure she had not missed a fig. "Their ancestors crawled right out of the Buddha's head, and do you know what else?"

Tierra stood up to wrap her arms around Sari from behind, whispering in her ear. The air bristled. Dagmar began scarfing down a second potato, eating it like an apple out of her hands.

Tierra sat down again, smiling at me. She marveled at a forkful of arugula. "The salad is so good, Jamie. I love the balance of the sweet against the bitter, and then the balsamic is perfection!"

"Thank you," I whispered.

Tierra always seemed to know what needed to be said, or who needed a dose of kindness. She saw the small, important things, and obviously didn't want me to feel self-conscious that Sari was picking at my salad. "Sari," she said, "we set aside a bowl of today's fig harvest so you can bring some to Flora, too."

Sari mood darkened suddenly. She stabbed her knife into her food. "Sacrifice!"

Abruptly, Dagmar stood up, chewing an enormous mouthful of food before I'd even figured out what was happening. It was clear she knew a sacrifice was coming long before Sari said so, like reading the wind before a hurricane, that's why she had started eating so ferally, whereas I had hardly taken two bites.

Tierra took my plate away with a blank smile, along with all the rest of our sweet potatoes, bread, squash, and the precious bowl of fruit set aside for Flora. Sari also snatched a box of bananas that Tierra had planned to bake with the next day. We followed Sari to the enclosure.

Down at the cages, the monkeys celebrated their meal, wrapping their fists around whatever they were lucky enough to claim. Cornelius snagged a few figs and savored them, eyes closed while he chewed, while Stella washed hers in the pool. Clutching my jars of tea on my walk home, I thought about the brown, womb-shaped figs, the way they split open at the fissure to decadently reveal the miraculous, lush fruit beneath. I wanted nothing more than to return to the cage and let a monkey pop one of their figs in my mouth like a communion wafer.

Dear Sari & Dagmar. I want to do my part on behalf of the website, and I've been thinking hard about what I can do to add value that is infused with love and respect for our community and our prospective members.

Would you like me to compile some of our recipes?

We could have a section of the website called The Heart of the Atlas Kitchen or Atlas's Garden Table. I could share some of the yummy, nourishing recipes that we enjoy here. Perhaps that will encourage others to cook with garden ingredients and inspire people to say, *how beautiful, yes, I want to work and live at Atlas!*

That is my idea for today. Otherwise I think you are doing a gorgeous job telling our story. With love and respect, Tierra

COMMENT FROM SARI
Or maybe a cookbook? Or a cooking documentary?! I LOVE that idea. Start jotting things down! Not all of your recipes, of course, like our tea blend. Dagmar, please add your brainstorms too! –xoxoS.

16

I was in and out of sleep for a good part of the night, tortured by vibrations and screams. By morning I decided to risk asking one more time about it. I needed answers, and if the sounds truly were only in my head, then maybe I needed to talk to Sari about sleeping in the dome, or moving to another cabin that wasn't so isolated and eerie. I would try anything to make life at Atlas work, at least for the summer, but something had to give. As I paused at the entrance to the dome, I overheard Dagmar and Tierra in a heated conversation.

"It's just that we are not a boardinghouse, or an artists' retreat. The mission should be central and demonstrated through long-term focused action and sacrifice. That should be the sole determinant for who gets to come here. Short-term doesn't work for me."

I blanched. Was Dagmar talking about me?

"What does Sari say?" Tierra asked.

"You know I'm not going to question Sari. She knows my

opinion anyway. But we just have too much going on now. It's so complicated."

"Like you said last night, Sari knows what she's doing. It's just stress and she needs help remembering."

"I know. I know," Dagmar said.

I decided to simply walk into the dome as if I hadn't heard anything, because it would be more awkward to leave and get caught. Tierra looked up at me and winked, and then went back to talking to Dagmar, pointedly changing the subject.

"What were you saying about the new enclosure?"

"Um, it's going well, and also I wanted you to know I made a new batch of arnica and hemp salve for Zelda, because she's visiting today, and so I made extra for us. Help yourself," Dagmar said, nodding to the bench holding a plastic tote containing small jars.

"Oh, excellent! Jamie, you need some of this. It is amazing medicine for bumps or bruises. You know what? Apply it where that insulting thing rubs your ankle."

Dagmar busied herself making coffee in a French press. I felt like a complete leech for taking a jar with nothing to give her in return, but I also sort of wanted some of her witchy remedy. Dagmar worked nonstop in grisly conditions—cleaning enclosures, wrangling monkeys for procedures, clearing trails—and yet her fair skin was flawless, her hands elegant like a piano player's, and her hair like pale silk. She reminded me of a swan. Tough, strong, and pristine. I wanted whatever potions kept her looking like that.

Sari floated in. She dispensed hugs and good-morning head tussles to us all, as though she hadn't taken my dinner and given it to the macaques hours before.

Then she spied the box of salve.

"Dagmar! You heavenly goddess. You delicious angel. What did you make?"

"Arnica and hemp, and a few other niceties." Dagmar poured the coffee and started on another batch.

"Yes, gorgeous, yes. Thank you for your labors. I need this. You know what, this deserves a circle."

A circle. My stomach filled with acid at the thought of skipping breakfast.

Dagmar softened, turned off the burner, and grabbed the tote of salves. Sari left the dome without getting a bowl from the walk-in. Tierra smiled and pulled me along, and we followed Sari outside to an open space between the Bonding Benches. The sun was still low. Despite my apprehension, it felt good to be there. I had come to love dawn in the woods. The light danced through the trees and bushes, casting shadows that glowed with possibility. Stars had pierced through the early-morning sky in a close cluster for the last few days, and cloudy skies were still magical in a different way, making the day feel as sleepy and slow to wake up as I was.

In front of the enclosure, Tierra and Sari playfully started jostling me back and forth, Tierra's earrings tinkling like chimes.

"Are you thinking she's West? I thought North?" Tierra said.

"Definitely West. Look at her, she's the Queen of Cups," Sari said.

"I'm South today," Dagmar said.

"Yeah, I can see West, but also North."

"Jamie, when's your birthday?" Sari asked.

"February."

"Pisces or Aquarius?"

"Pisces."

"West," they all said in unison, and then pushed me in position. Dagmar put the bin full of jars in the middle.

We joined hands, and they proceeded to sing and chant about the four directions and the elements, all with the refrain *return, return, return, return*. They did some unison posing and pointing in response to Sari's odd commands, but without explaining to me what we were supposed to do or why. She would say *Saturn* and they would walk in a circle, stopping at the halfway point. She would say *wolf*, and they would tilt their heads back and howl.

At first I tried to keep up, a radio-delay echo to their synchronized dance. It felt nonsensical to me, like yogic sun salutations meets a playground game of Mother May I, but it was light and full of energy. By the third time we looped around in some sort of May Day procession, I had given up all but the most basic movements. I noticed the monkeys came to watch the commotion: humans on exhibit.

Then Sari said, "This land gives us everything we need, and we are so blessed. These botanicals will heal us, fruits of this earth of the ancient ocean floor, the Fountain of Youth, we love you, Atlas. Thank you for this salve. Let it soothe our sacred monkeys' hands. Let it soothe our own hands to do good deeds. May nothing ever, ever, ever go to waste. Blessed be."

"Blessed be," we answered in unison. I felt the harmony of our voices in the back of my jaw.

"Your first circle!" cooed Sari. I wasn't certain what made a circle different from gathering to bring chicken to the gators or our dinner to the monkeys, but they seemed proud and enthused.

"It feels so good to have you in our circle," Tierra said. "You are like a new color in our rainbow. We didn't know it, but we have been missing you for a long time." She turned to Dagmar. "It was more powerful with four, wasn't it?"

"One for every direction," Dagmar agreed.

Sari hugged me. "I told them we didn't need to wait to include you in our rituals. They wanted me to wait, but I was right! I told you, Tierra. The circle is so much stronger with you in it, Jamie! We are so glad you are here, little sister. Oh, and later on I want to chat. I have a minor video project I need some help with. Our website needs your magic. You are ready, right?"

"Yes. I have been dying to help you," I said. "But remember my restrictions. I am bound by those terms."

"I don't think it's a problem. We can talk about it."

We walked back to the dome to finish breakfast. I was bursting with endorphins, as though I had just come in from a long swim in the Atlantic and a sprint on the beach. Sari's prayer, despite its unfamiliar approach, had reminded me how special it was to be at Atlas. I felt moved by how easily it came to her to appreciate the natural world. I wanted to get to work on Sari's website project so that I could be of help to Atlas in a concrete way and have something to proudly share. Each of the others offered their skills so generously, and I wanted to do my part.

As we went into the dome, I decided to postpone asking the women about the nighttime noises. I was being foolish, undoubtedly hearing things. The women of Atlas wouldn't let the monkeys suffer.

I walked through the screen door first, and then a minute later I looked back outside. No one had followed me in. They all had vanished.

Assuming they went to Flora's for a bit, I drank some fresh coffee and quickly ate two bananas for breakfast. I was famished, but also feeling like a lost kid in a storybook witch's cottage.

I walked back outside, figuring I would hang out with the macaques for a while until they returned from wherever they were. But the women were right there, loading several bulky boxes into a van that was parked in front of Monkey Island. If it was Dagmar's hemp salve, it was a lot of it. After stacking the last boxes, Sari put a carrier that I was almost certain contained a small macaque into the passenger side of the front seat.

I cocked my head and walked toward them to get a better look, wondering if one of our monkeys was ill. Dagmar noticed me and closed the back van doors immediately.

The black van featured an emblem for the University of Florida. The driver, a redheaded woman with gangly arms, tapped on her own car door and drove off.

Sari finally motioned for me to join them, and I walked over.

"That was Zelda. She's a friend of Atlas and a vet, like Dagmar. A very evolved woman. You'll love her!" Sari said. It was an odd thing for her to say, as any of them could have introduced me mere moments ago. No mention was made of the sick macaque, and I could see they didn't want me to ask any follow-up questions.

"Let's grab coffee, and I need to bring in the sun tea," Tierra said. "Volunteers will be here in half an hour."

Dagmar ignored her and disappeared into Monkey Island, firmly closing the door behind her. Sari grimaced at Tierra, and Tierra nodded in response.

"You know what?" Sari said. Her tone was bright and full of energy. "Y'all go on. I think I'll stay here and help Dagmar."

17

I occupied myself that afternoon by working with Tierra. She was making candles in tall jars while also baking guava turnovers for some sort of community meeting, gliding between work-stations so quickly her gray linen apron billowed away from her body in the movement. Hours with her in the dome were hot and long, but we always had something exquisite and nourishing to show for it, and usually I had learned a new homesteading skill.

"Kind of wish I could bring my mother one of the pastries. She loves guava," Tierra said.

"Does she like to bake?"

"Not really," Tierra said. "But in Tampa, there are tons of little places selling pastelitos that she liked. What about your parents, Jamie? Do you know where they live?"

"My father? I'm not sure. My mother always thought he went back to Texas, but who knows. I know she moved to Colorado with her boyfriend. He worked in hospitality or something. They're probably still there for all I care. I always sort of wondered if Jason ran there when he skipped bail to see if she'd help him. Probably not, because that's the first place they'd look for him." I busied myself cleaning the counter. "Who knows? Bygones."

"My first girlfriend took off like your mother did. One day, she came to me and told me she fell in love with someone else and that they were moving that very night to Las Vegas. She wanted me to be happy for her new adventure. It took a long time, but eventually I was. The universe is big and wise beyond all comprehension."

She didn't sound brokenhearted, but I immediately disliked her long-gone ex all the same. "Tierra, you deserve so much better."

What I loved most, was how Tierra gave the dome a loving vibe. She stayed upbeat and busy, listening to a playlist where every other song seemed to be a Janelle Monáe or The Internet track, making time feel both slow and full, where every minute stretched and contracted into a new shape, standing still or falling back. We sipped tea and moved on to making vegetable and fruit empanadas for the freezer, Tierra feeding me bits of guava paste on the cores of apples because she knew I was always hungry.

"What kind of community meeting are you cooking all of these things for?" I asked Tierra. "Do you mean the Atlas community, or the local town?"

She gave me a tender hug and then swiftly, before I knew what she was doing, firmly grabbed my shoulders and twisted my back, my head swinging roughly. A crack resounded, leaving me stunned.

"There, I released toxins for you. You need to work on your fear of death," she said, smiling beneficently.

I took a step back. I had no idea what I was supposed to do when she or Sari said cryptic things or performed spontaneous rituals like this, other than play along and hope eventually it would resonate. I did want to understand, and to be more spiritually connected like them. *Evolved*, Sari called it. It didn't come naturally to me, but even though it was awkward and sometimes shocking, I found I didn't want them to stop. Deep inside, I loved the way they whispered and conjured, the way they believed I was capable of feeling something.

Right before supper, Tierra and I went to the garden. She said she was working on harvesting the last of the summer growth. It was becoming too hot for anything more than peppers or herbs, so Tierra didn't plan on planting new seeds, but we cut arugula and leaf lettuce from the raised bed rows until we had enough for our supper. Tierra also found some radishes and a kohlrabi, and she babied the few remaining squash, narrow pea pods, and persistent cherry tomatoes with a ridiculous amount of water.

I liked the openness of the garden. To the far north, a short fencerow and gate marked the end of Atlas—I knew that much from when Cole mapped out my territory. On the other side sat a large, mowed yard and a ranch-style house that faced a dirt road. That was Flora's home. Tierra said that Sari and her sister had grown up in the house, and that Sari's father had intended to someday expand his fern farm throughout more of the land.

"He passed, and Sari has been carrying the dreams of turning his acreage into a more successful homestead ever since, just in a different way, as Atlas."

"But the land wasn't called Atlas until recently, right?"

"She called it The Argo a while ago. I think that was the first community, and then different things through the years. I came after Argo, when it was going to be a midwifery school called Vessel. But now it's Atlas, because the macaques are our guides to a healthier planet." Tierra yanked a dead tomato plant from the ground.

The lake was a short walk from the old homestead. I wondered if Sari and Anna Beth were allowed to go down to a gator-nested lake to play when they were young. Jason and I had roamed wild. We didn't have a large piece of land like Atlas, but we did have the entire coastline to explore. Jason built the most extravagant sandcastles, teaching me how to cup a slurry of sand in my hand and then drip globs to form towers and turrets, and we spent hours exploring rock jetties and oyster beds.

The beach wasn't far from Atlas, but I felt worlds away from the seagrass and creeping wildflowers of the fragile dunes. The surrounding woods here were jungles—dense with shin-eating scrub, saw palmettos, split pines, switch cane, and hackberry, hornbeam and cabbage palm tree sapling. The dark, snaky, impenetrable land was probably partially responsible for the claustrophobic panic that unsettled me at night.

Sari never collected me for our meeting, and in fact she didn't show up for supper. I was disappointed, but I talked to the monkeys about it on my way home. I hadn't learned all of their names yet, and I tried to count them only to find it was simply impossible to tally over forty moving macaques. I knew many of them by sight, though, and fortunately none of my favorites were missing: not the cranky redhead or the pink-cheeked beauty, not gray-faced Cornelius, nor O-Ren, and not the crooked-tail bossy one that often picked the fights.

"I know, I know. I should just cut up more fruit for you and stop worrying about Sari, shouldn't I? The internet is nothing but trouble, anyway."

Two of the monkeys squabbled back and forth like siblings. "Yeah, she's probably just busy with her mother and her sister. But I wish they'd let me help, you know?"

I let their impervious frolicking console me until I couldn't manage the mosquitoes any longer. A small crescent moon was already climbing the sky as I made my way along the path. I thought I saw a distant light south of the enclosure and wondered if perhaps Dagmar had a house in that direction, or maybe Tierra.

On the last turn of the path, I could see that my screen door was ajar, which was annoying, because though it wasn't much, it did keep some bugs out. I needed to be more careful to latch it each morning, or maybe see if it needed to be repaired. I should be more like Dagmar and Tierra—more proactive, more attuned to my surroundings.

Once inside, I reached in my pocket to extract a rock for my countdown pile, and then I recalled walking out that morning: I definitely hadn't left the door open. I remembered latching it, because I had surprised an armadillo outside and double-checked the latch to be sure he couldn't wander in.

Someone else had been in my cabin. New notes were positioned around my room.

Keep working. You're almost ready.

Be not afraid of anything, not of life, not of death.

And propped up on my plate of stones: *Don't be in such a hurry to leave us. We want you here.*

18

Sari and Dagmar were squabbling about who should make the next pot of coffee when I walked into the dome.

"Let me do it," I said. "But is this container something I should be worried about?" I pointed to an open quart jar with a few inches of dark red liquid, completely out of place next to the organic honey, yogurt and granola. I was certain it was blood because I could smell the iron.

"It's sacred menstrual blood. Don't be ashamed of it," Sari said. Tierra had pulled a chair to sit behind Sari and was weaving her hair in an elaborate fishtail braid while Sari sat still and straight. To Tierra, Sari said, "She's very shame-based. It's quite oppressive."

Dagmar rose. "I can move it, no worries."

Tierra offered me coffee. "We collect it every month. Do you have a menstrual cup? I can get you one."

"Jamie, every month, women have a heavenly opportunity to experience both life and death at the same time. It's basic stuff, really." Sari sighed.

I hadn't had a period yet at Atlas, though I was starting to feel a hormonal tug on my emotions. I was already wondering how I was going to manage it on long workdays, as neither the toilet in my house nor the communal outhouse in the woods was very accommodating, which made me dread my period even more.

Everyone looked as tired as I did, and I wondered if Flora's illness was weighing on them. I wished I understood more about her situation so that I could share their burden. I wanted to ask if Flora's other daughter, Anna Beth, was already in town, or if her trip had been abandoned. If I had only arrived at Atlas earlier in the year, by now I would have gained their trust, and maybe they would have even brought me into their inner staff circle. But I still had too much to learn, and was at a loss over what I could say or do to encourage them.

I gulped my coffee and started to slink out of the kitchen, but Sari stopped me.

"Jamie, I keep running out of time to chat with you so I'm just going to cut to the chase. I need you to do a job for me. We have a camera that is almost ready-to-go in the macaque enclosure. We want a livestream of our macaques on our website, but the volunteer helping us only knew how to install it, not how to get the video to play live. How long would that take you to get it rolling? You know what I'm talking about, right?"

"I think so. I mean, I helped edit videos for a wedding photographer, and sometimes we did livestreams. Did Cole tell you that?"

Sari looked at me quizzically. "Uh, yes. No. I think Kayla did. Anyway, let's do that!"

"Add a page to your website to host a livestream?"

"Yes, whatever it takes. It's going to help people who want to support our work to see the monkeys. To be delighted by the monkeys. We need more donations, and livestreams really work to engage people."

"Well, more to the point, we want to share the monkeys with the world," Dagmar said.

"Yes, and that," Sari said.

"I can look at what you have so far and give it a try, but honestly, I'm far from an expert. I know a few basics, and then I just learn as I go. And I'm not sure I'm supposed to be on the internet right now. Have we heard from Cole at all?"

"Oh, don't worry about it. You won't get in trouble." Dagmar rolled her eyes.

"Jamie, Jamie," Sari said, using her preschool teacher voice. "Cole doesn't care what you do. He is a corporation that wants to get paid. The court just wants a successful check mark after your name. Guess what? We give you the check mark! We are the check mark!" She waved her hand in a grand flourish. "And I'll babysit you while you're on the internet, that will make it okay."

"I'll show you where the camera is later and give you the manuals, and we'll start from there," Dagmar said with brittle authority. If the setup was similar to Duke's or to the wedding livestreams I worked on, that would be a relief, because I knew how to upload files and grab the code to embed it onto her site. If not, I'd read the manuals. I was excited for a shot at real work, a true contribution to the growth of Atlas.

The day melted by. I took a few breaks to see the monkeys, but it was too hot for me to sit on a Bonding Bench. We needed a cool afternoon rain, but storm clouds gathered only to pass us by. The meditating volunteers had a stamina I couldn't muster, and the monkeys seemed almost as lethargic as I felt in the thick heat. I preferred to catch them in the early morning or on my way home at night when they were crawling on the beams or swinging on their tire.

At one point, I walked over to peek at the camera setup, but right as I arrived, a macaque ran toward the enclosure, twisted and leapt, throwing its back into the fencing. The metal resounded, monkeys howled and clamored in protest, and two volunteers yelled and jumped back.

The macaque bared his teeth in a snarling growl, his mouth revealing two sharp eyeteeth, his facial hair standing on end.

"Too close," said Natasha, a veteran volunteer from Jacksonville, to the surrounding group. "You need to stay on the benches."

Later, Dagmar let me look at the livestream setup in the enclosure, and I could see it was going to be a piece of cake to do what Sari wanted. Atlas had an upmarket network camera capturing a nice shot of the tire swing, a weatherproof box for controls, and a buried line of ethernet cable connecting it all to Monkey Island. Presumably, inside they had a modem and router powerful enough to do the job, but Dagmar wouldn't let me in Monkey Island to see it.

"You'll be able to do everything from the box or Sari's house. That's what we were told," she said.

"That's good that the software is on Sari's computer, but there must be a router in there for the Wi-Fi. I just need to check the hardware in case I have to troubleshoot when it's time to go live. Honestly, when I see things, sometimes they make more sense to me. It would really help to see it."

"You don't have to look. Just tell me what you need."

"I won't touch anything. I can take off my shoes, wash up so I'm sterile, whatever." I didn't know what I needed to do to pass the test to get into Monkey Island. I wasn't suggesting I should go alone. Even Tierra didn't have keys. But I was going to need periodic access to the equipment, and I was starting to feel bullied by her resistance.

"I assure you the setup is good." Dagmar set her jaw and pursed her lips into a tight bow. Conversation over.

Sari didn't come to the dome that evening. The three of us drank some of Tierra's iced tea and relaxed as though it were happy hour. I had been too distracted to notice the extreme temperature all day, but when we finally sat down I was light-headed and the heat shimmered around me in visible waves. It was the same experience I had at night in my cabin, when I finally stopped working and the exhaustion left me feeling hammered on a cellular level.

In their presence, I could see through the surface of things to a deep, underlying goodness. Dagmar created a cozy setting with a tablecloth, wildflowers, and candles that had been poured into various mustard jars. Tierra queued up a '60s playlist, and when Ella sang about rich daddies and good-looking mamas, I sang along because we felt almost like the beginnings of a sweet little family, these women so beautiful and Atlas rich with everything we needed. We brought bowls of food to the table: roasted blue potatoes, curried chickpeas, fragrant rice, seared asparagus, the salad from lunch braised with leeks, and a plate of shaved mushrooms. We feasted.

I watched to see if the others were setting aside food to bring to Sari, and I almost offered to walk over a plate to Sari's dome or to Flora's house. Her absence was worrisome, but it also felt a bit like a respite. When Sari was around, she drew Tierra's attention in a way that left me feeling forgotten, and there was always the looming threat of a sacrifice. Without her, we lingered and ate luxuriously.

They told stories about old friends, including some who had been banished from Sari's life for various, vaguely described infractions.

"That reminds me, Dagmar," Tierra said. "You know how Harper's been bringing her mother? We need to watch her, because she's been caught trying to slip food through the cages to Colette. At lunch I saw her put grapes in her pocket, and then Jasper came over and told me why."

"It never ends."

"He said she calls Colette her spirit animal."

"Colette's the big golden one who acts like everyone's mother, right?" I asked.

Tierra nodded. "The super groomer."

Dagmar rolled her eyes. "Colette would very happily grab Harper's mother by both ears and drag her across the enclosure."

Tierra smiled. "I talked with Harper, and I think she'll handle it, but I just wanted you to be aware."

We delighted in the food before us, as usual, discussing at length how beautifully it was prepared and the other food we hoped to soon have for dinner. Dagmar suggested taking me on an outing to the local melon U-pick farm before the season ended. I said nothing, because I was prohibited from leaving the campus, but I secretly hoped she meant they were going to help me break that rule, too.

Tierra brought out tiny plum and almond milk tarts for dessert. This surprised me—I had no idea when Tierra had whipped them up. They were decadent, and I thought maybe they had been infused with a secret stash of liquor, because with each bite a languorous tide of ease washed over me.

They noticed I was growing sleepy and let me watch as Tierra scrubbed the dishes, and then Dagmar sat next to me, her arms flung wide and resting on the pew back. I leaned toward her and let her arm support my head as we watched Tierra's final domestic dance of the day, the evening's glow silhouetting the curve where her head dropped down to meet the nape of her neck. Even though I was relaxed on the bench with Dagmar, I found myself wishing she would leave the dome so Tierra and I could be alone.

Tierra eventually finished and came to the table. I watched her lean over to blow out the last candle. When she looked up, I realized I had been waiting for her to meet my eyes, and we shared a fiery exchange, something more intense and provocative than the comfort of Dagmar's arms.

★ ★ ★

I stopped on my way home to say good-night to the monkeys and sang them a little lullaby. When they gathered, I noticed Colette was in the front of the group.

"Girl, you're in trouble. They're on to you, Colette. Don't get busted for a few grapes, it's not worth it," I told her. Colette rubbed her eyes and flapped her elbows like wings.

At home, my mind drifted to Tierra: her tapered hands selecting mangos and the sound her silver charms made when she toyed with the chain on her necklace. But I knew better than to indulge my growing attraction. I made myself think about Dagmar's pretty dinner table to distract myself, and then I decided to unpack a few of my things—it was way past time. I placed a rainbow-striped juice glass from my grandmother's house on the dresser, and next to it, a framed photo of my mother and me at the beach when I was around eight. We were walking toward the water, and then Jason yelled "butt shot," and took the photo just as we were turning around, laughing and ready to chastise him for teasing us.

I dangled two chain necklaces from a tack in the wall, one with a gold cross charm my mother gave me on my confirmation and the other with a tiny silver giraffe I bought for myself because it made me smile. I couldn't imagine wearing them at Atlas, certainly not near the macaques.

I pulled a tiny stone out of my pocket and put it on the plate. I had taken the handwritten note from the night before and put it away, because I liked seeing my daily collection. Even a drop at a time, they were adding up. What then?

My belongings looked out of place in the A-frame, but I forced myself to leave them out on display, because it helped to remember the good times. Then I crammed some of Dagmar's salve under the monitor strap and onto my ankle without looking. I didn't want to see it. I planned to take a long shower in the morning, but at that moment all I could imagine was falling face-first, arms open onto the bed, fan on full blast.

I peeled back my quilt to uncover a rainbow skink lounging on my pillow, and I sucked in my breath.

"Mister, no one invited you to this slumber party," I told him as I gently picked up the entire pillow and crept outside. He stayed put, as though he were a king who was quite accustomed to traveling atop cushions. Outside, I coaxed him onto an azalea bush, and then I heard the monkeys.

It was clear to me then: the screams were real. I felt them, vibrations that nestled as a cold creep against the nape of my neck. A wave of nausea came over me, buckling my legs, then compelling me to stand up, and then immediately making me want to lean over again. Hands on my knees, I tried to talk myself down. *It's just anxiety. It will go away. Breathe. It's all in your head.*

I could almost convince myself, were it not for the monkeys. The monkeys were real, and they were just down the path. And those very real monkeys sounded very upset, howling and banging against the metal of their enclosure. I didn't feel up to investigating—my body felt ill and lethargic, like I had just been beaten up. But I promised myself that the next day I would look into it. I would find a simple solution to the problem, to be of some actual help to Dagmar, Tierra, and Sari, and to the unhappy macaques.

Here's our promise to new members. We will take care of you. We will find a place of purpose for you so that you can contribute to Atlas. We will not waste your good intentions, your true potential, your beauty or your generous gifts.

We will not waste you.

COMMENT FROM SARI

Jamie is ready to work on the website. We have got to get this crap done. We have to get that livestream up and some donations running in. I feel like I am being taken advantage of again and again and again. Why am I the only one working on our expansion? Why am I the only one with this massive burden on my shoulders? Is this a collective? Do we truly live out our commitment to consensus and decentralized power? Am I losing my ever-loving mind? –xoxoS.

COMMENT FROM DAGMAR

Hello, this is Dagmar. I am working night and day, Sari. Too much is spinning at one time. None of us are sleeping. Why are we making this particular project so hard for ourselves while we have so much else going on, that's what I want to know. We aren't ready for visitors to stay here, anyway, so all the philosophy and manifestos don't have to be up there yet. And honestly, you can't put those on a website, anyway. You are making it hard for yourself. Just write interesting things about the macaques, put the camera footage up, and ask for donations. I say keep it simple.

COMMENT FROM SARI
Do you mean I should start over and delete all this work?!?!?!?

TRACK CHANGES FROM TIERRA
Dear Sari & Dagmar. No, no, no, don't delete anything. Maybe it's good as is, I think that's what Dagmar is saying. Just use what you've already brilliantly written, and that will be wonderful! With love and respect, Tierra.

TRACK CHANGES FROM DAGMAR
Hello, this is Dagmar. YES, delete the part where you invite people to stay here. We aren't ready for that.

COMMENT FROM SARI
By the way, Dagmar, your latest batch was too strong, but I'm grateful because no one else has my back and everything is depending on me and me alone, so at least I have this boosting me up. Small mercies.

20

I woke determined to figure out what was up with the wailing monkeys, one way or the other.

"I'm sorry it's taken me so long to understand that you are upset, sugar babies," I whispered to them the next morning. The sun was still rising, the light as red and translucent as a melting Popsicle. "It took me a while to get settled, but I'm going to make up for lost time."

Wandering the property so early in the day felt several kinds of weird. First of all, I wasn't confident I remembered all my anklet boundaries. I certainly didn't want to come close to any potential alarm zone. On top of that, I didn't know how welcome I was to wander. Sure, Sari had said to make myself at home, her voice an open jar of honey. The women were unfailingly, abundantly generous with their food and resources. But still, the social boundaries were clear. I knew not to show up at any staff member's cabin, for instance, an unwritten rule that was easy to decode when they said *we keep early nights* or *when we want company, we come to the dome*. Sari's house was right there by the dome, but I hadn't been inside it yet, and I didn't even know where Dagmar and Tierra stayed. I sensed they each had their own homes, but I wasn't sure.

More importantly, Dagmar was clear that I should not enter Monkey Island at all, ever. She had overtly blocked me from even catching a glance inside. For all I knew, I could accidentally stumble upon another outbuilding that she also wanted me to stay away from. I really did not want Dagmar to hate me.

Nevertheless, it was time for me to fight anxiety with information. The first thing I wanted to do was visit the lake. I needed to find out how close it was relative to the monkey enclosure to see if gator activity could possibly be scaring them. I didn't know how I would fix that problem if that was what it was, but at least I would be aware.

The path to the lake was wide and had been kept in good condition. A volunteer must have recently cut back the palmettos and vines, and the forest was less dense than the heavy growth around my A-frame and the shower house. The grade was rough at a few places and would have benefited from some stairs, so a few exposed root wads tried to trip me where the downward tug of erosion had been particularly steep, but overall, it was an easy walk. At one point, a second path opened to the right, and I wondered if it tracked to the far side of Sari's dome, or maybe all the way to Flora's house.

I finally arrived at the spring-fed lake. It didn't feel particularly swampy to me aside from one darker corner of downed tree and overgrowth. Any body of water in Florida could attract alligators, but they particularly loved dark coves and murky habitats that allowed them to lurk. This lake was clear. The water was a pristine mirror to the sky, free of the pond moss and duckweed that made some other lakes unappealing for swimming. I imagined that the sixty-degree water would feel magical, like ice in summer and warm as a bath in winter.

I shed my shoes and slowly walked toward the edge of the

bank, feeling slightly illicit. It was going to be so restorative to soak my sore ankle. I must have been too nervous during Cole's walk-through to appreciate the knobby cypress that lined the bank, or to see how the water's reflection of Spanish moss from the leaning live oak tree looked like a floating lace doily.

Why didn't the women come down here to escape the heat? I remembered Flora's bathing cap, and realized maybe they did but hadn't invited me yet.

I couldn't help but think that if I lived at Atlas, if Sari offered me a staff position after my community service, my lifestyle would be almost as good as owning a house here, and I would be able to spend time swimming and kayaking on the lake with community members or other new friends. As long as I could make weekly trips to the ocean—maybe on Sunday mornings, stopping for bottles of soda and bags of boiled peanuts from my old guy on the corner of US 1—I could imagine that I might be happy with Atlas as my new home base, all of my restrictions behind me and my worries about where to live resolved.

Just as I was envisioning myself floating carefree on Triangle Lake on a rainbow-colored raft some balmy day in late August, I looked up to see three water moccasins racing like assassins toward me, heads above the water, tongues flicking in horrific white-lined, fanged mouths, their bodies forcing the charge with barely a ripple.

Adrenaline raced through me. I didn't wait to see where they were headed. I scooped up my shoes and ran from the bank and a few yards up the path before turning back to assess.

The snakes were gone, but right behind them, an adolescent gator lumbered her way up out of the water, one sinister step at a time. I froze, suddenly nauseous. Even though I knew she wasn't big enough to be much of a danger to me, I wanted to carefully evade her without disturbing any others.

She stopped on the clean, sandy bank, either sunning herself or staring me down. She may have been defending her lake, or perhaps she thought I was Sari, here with chicken for breakfast. Either way, I didn't want to stay and find out, so I continued up the path, and thankfully she didn't follow.

On the way back, I decided to poke my head down the off-shoot path I had seen earlier. The opening was narrow, so I tied the red bandanna from my wrist to a thin slash pine to help me find my way back to the lake path, and I ventured into the woods.

The ground was heavy with pine needles and the tree cover was much sparser, letting the broiling sun inside to dry the forest floor. When I was a few hundred yards down the trail, I could see some sort of white, wooden structure that I imagined to be a child's play set. Maybe Sari and her sister played down by the lake many years ago, a young Flora watching them bob in inner tubes all morning and climb on monkey bars—idyllic summer days in a private paradise. I hoped by seeing it up close I could envision what it might have been like for Sari to grow up here.

But as I drew closer to the clearing, I saw the structure wasn't a jungle gym or a slide.

It was a large pergola, constructed from long, twisted branches and bamboo poles that had been lashed together and white-washed, big enough to host a wedding or summer party. Beneath the archway stood an egg-shaped rock the size of a barstool. An assemblage of objects surrounded the rock: hurricane candles; shells and crystals; painted bottles; handmade tiles inlaid with broken dishes and mosaic glass; dozens of porcelain and clay statues of women, monkeys and a mermaid sitting on a rock. More items that would otherwise be viewed as trash, like small liquor bottles, an empty can of Diet Coke, a blue Danish butter cookie tin, one orange flip-flop, and a plastic University of Florida Gators stadium cup.

Beyond the eclectic assemblage, a black kettle grill was dropping chips of rust onto the dirt behind the rock, looking fragile and defiantly out of place. Then I realized what was especially eerie about the display. Florida destroys everything quickly through corrosion, mold and dank rot, especially deep in the woods. But these items by the rock weren't particularly wet or weathered, and they bore only the faintest dusting of green pollen.

The area was clearly cared for, or at the very least the candles and offerings were relatively new. I returned to the kettle. The ash had been swept out.

I tried to picture Sari or the others standing here having the oddest picnic imaginable. Or concerts, I thought. Maybe they held concerts and barbecues near the lake.

Surveying the area, I saw another rock, maybe ten yards away. It was much smaller and flat—not big enough to even use as a chair. I went to investigate and saw there were other flat stones just like it positioned in a ring around the pergola, each of them painted with elaborate rows of symbols. Some of the marks looked like backward numbers, some like geometric shapes, and then I recognized regular letters mixed in with the complex marks. The letters spelled names, one on each stone. My ears burned, my breath shortened. I read them out loud, quickly moving from stone to stone, as though hearing the names would awaken ghosts who could help me understand Atlas.

Marcos, then next to that, *Eva*.

Audrey, Xavier, Jenny.

William, Dylan, Sarah Ann.

Emma, Khalil, Terry.

I walked in circles around the wheel, studying each painted rock. I forced myself to fight back the rising bile. There must be a simple explanation. Maybe the names represented Atlas volunteers, a guest book of sorts. Maybe the pergola is where they honored generous donors with some version of Sari's circles.

With trepidation, I forced myself to step outside the circle and turn the stones over, hoping they would provide a useful clue, a *VIP Sponsor* label or something similar. Instead, I saw *Bryant, Ian, Katrina, Noah*—additional names.

The flowers, the candles—the entire display felt like a roadside memorial at a treacherous state road curve. I didn't want to think it, but my gut told me that I was standing on small graves, maybe for monkeys. But the names all seemed like they would belong to people. A vision of unspeakable problems at Atlas's failed midwife school loomed large, but I scrubbed it away.

I thought about the notes left in my room. I remembered Sari talking about women being in touch with life and death on a monthly basis. I shuddered. I studied the names. I went back to the altar collection, but none of it told a story that I could unravel. I picked up the butter cookie tin, first removing a white porcelain flamingo from on top of it. The tin uncomfortably rattled from within. *Be pennies*, I prayed. *Be buttons.* I pried open the lid and my stomach dropped.

Inside rested a clutch of bones. They weren't curved or distinctive like a T-bone, either. Only straight bones, lined up neatly so a hand could easily grab them like a bouquet.

I needed to get away from here before I got sick. I replaced the tin and raced out toward the main path, turned at the cypress tree and then bolted up the hill. Soon, the reassuring tire wheels from the parking lot told me I was almost there. I stopped to catch my breath, and as I tucked my hair behind my ear, I realized that I didn't have my bandanna, and couldn't remember seeing it on the slash pines where I had tied it as a trail marker on my way back.

I must have missed it, but I had no intentions of going back.

21

I went straight to the dome but was still the last to arrive for breakfast. Sari was there, with one arm wrapped around Tierra as they swayed to Cat Stevens, and her other hand gripping a lopsided coffee mug that looked like it had been formed by hand instead of thrown on a wheel. Dagmar's eyes were closed, but she greeted me anyway. "Good morning, beautiful Jamie."

I fixed a cup of coffee and joined Dagmar at the table, and then Sari came behind me and began playing with my hair. I recoiled from her touch, then felt instantly ashamed. I shook my head as though I were just waking up.

Sari put her hands on the back of my neck. "What's up? You're very warm. Are you having a low biorhythm day? We need to get you straight because we have work to do."

"I'm fine," I said, but something stuck in my throat and set my nerves on edge. I was not fine. Words kept bubbling out of me. "I don't think I'm sleeping right, maybe it's the heat, I wake up feeling half out of it, you know? Last night there was a rainbow skink in my bed, on my pillow actually, it could also be the nightmares…" I stopped myself before I babbled more. "It's just transitional anxiety, I think."

"You haven't eaten anything yet. We saved you some melon and coconut. We're about to have granola," she said. "I'd like you to eat. Of course, you are feeling stressed, and that's when the mind plays games with us. It's sneaky like that, gets us when we are down."

"Did you know our macaques often have nightmares when they are newly arrived?" Dagmar said. "But then they settle in. It will be okay. We're your troop. We'll make it so."

"Don't worry. We are your troop now," Sari echoed. I felt slightly embarrassed for provoking all of this attention, but it made me remember it was okay to ask for help. I wondered if it might also be okay to ask more questions.

Tierra emerged from the refrigerator with nut milk in a large canning jar. Dagmar handed out bowls for granola.

"That's right," Tierra said. "It will be okay. Which would you prefer with your granola? Cashew milk or yogurt?"

"Cashew milk, yummy," Sari said. "Not that I don't love your yogurt, Tierra. Blessed be the bacteria and the garden and the teas you create." Sari squinted at Tierra as though she were a glowing goddess too bright to gaze upon.

I panicked for a moment, thinking Sari's theatrics meant she was about to compel a sacrifice of our breakfast.

"Either is fine," I whispered.

Dagmar smiled disarmingly. "No. We won't accept that answer. Maybe it's true that you like both and don't mind either, but today, let yourself have a preference. Think for a second. Ask yourself which you prefer today."

I felt my cheeks start to burn, and I tried to will the heat away. I think they wanted me to say milk, because it was fresh, whereas we had yogurt pretty frequently. The question was a test I wanted to pass, but it also felt like a game that I was already predestined to lose. But Sari might sacrifice it to the macaques regardless of what I said. I waited one more beat and said, "Cashew milk."

"Lovely choice! Me too," Dagmar said. "Now, didn't that feel wonderful?"

Sari smiled. I exhaled, even though all of a sudden neither were very appealing.

I wanted to be happy with my new, easy life. In the light of day, warmed by fresh coffee in a warm mug, all three of them working intently on bowls of grain, I didn't know why I went out of my way to make everything harder for myself. Why I let my imagination run away with me about the pergola and the noises at night. I needed to stay focused on work, on giving back, on earning their confidence and kindnesses.

Tierra started a burner, the gas catching a start with a gasp.

Still smiling, Sari turned to me. "Dear one, I am so excited to spend time with you today. Please tell me you have time and energy."

I nodded, my mouth full of granola, and quickly swallowed. "Of course not, I mean, of course, whatever. I'm here for you whenever."

"Good, good. Let's finish our breakfast, and then I'll show you our dinky website. Or, Tierra, can we help you before we move to the office?" Sari asked.

"No, no. Black beans are already in the pot. They'll cook themselves."

Tierra moved on to rinse her sprouts. She maintained three large pickle jars of mung beans in various stages of sprouting. Several times a day she rinsed them with cold water, draining off the excess through the mesh mouths of the jars. I was learning that four days were needed for each growth cycle, that's all it took, and then we had mounds of fresh sprouts for salads or cooking. I could imagine having a sprout garden of my own someday. The seeds asked for so little, and yet were bursting with life force.

Sari must have been thinking the same thing. "I like watching you tend to our sprout garden," she said.

"I was just thinking it reminds me of getting Sea Monkey kits from the dollar store when I was a kid. We sprinkle an envelope full of tiny specks in water and then they'd hatch into brine shrimp, like magic!"

"Sea Monkey kits?" Dagmar asked Tierra. "We didn't have that in Denmark."

Sari admired the jars of Tierra's sprouts and then began kneading her neck, Tierra leaning back deep into Sari's hands. I could feel the ache from across the room, or maybe the ache was mine. Energy flowed between them like the tide on sunbaked sand. It was a language they used fluently, reaching out to hold hands or lingering in embraces, filled with grace and tenderness. I spent hours with Tierra but could never imagine myself wordlessly reaching out to massage her neck. I had never had that kind of physical familiarity with any other friends, either. I couldn't even remember my own mother brushing my hair.

It looked like we were moving toward work, but then Sari had to fix a mug of tea, and I could see that she was bound to get distracted again, or to change her mind, or to simply say *later.* It felt possible we could get just stuck inside this moment, like a beetle in amber, forever having breakfast in the dome.

The Atlas office was located in Sari's house, which was the campus's second, smaller dome. A covered gazebo of sorts (fiberglass panels bolted to beams) had been put up to join the two, presumably so that she could easily walk from the dome to her house in the rain.

As I followed Sari inside, I saw her reach up to touch one of three prayer wheels mounted on a shelf that also contained plants, seashells, and a Venus of Willendorf statue that had been painted bright teal.

I wasn't expecting much of a setup. My A-frame, the shower

house, and the main dome were austere, with worn furnishings and junkyard appliances that were maintained with duct tape and baling wire.

Walking from the main dome into Sari's house was a revelation. It was markedly cooler and darker than the other buildings. Had I not known better, I would have guessed we were underground. The abundance pulled me in like quicksand. Tapestries, batik sheets, and vintage quilts covered a mosquito-netted bed and a large living room full of furniture. Plants, animal skulls, and jars that cupped rainbows of overflowing candles filled every corner.

I paused in front of an easel holding a portrait in progress, featuring a queen on an elaborate giltwood throne with monkeys at her feet. The monkeys were joyously posed as though they might be jumping or dancing; the ruler was stern, with icy eyes that promised dominance.

"I still have a lot of work to do on that one," Sari said. "Forgive my mess!"

She tugged me away and led me down two steps into a sunken room. I stopped short. A massive black-and-silver fur rug was splayed across the entrance to the office area, the posed head of a wolf still attached.

I was shocked. I would have thought that as devoted animal lovers, the people of Atlas wouldn't have permitted taxidermy at their refuge. The lush rug was splayed, with all four legs reaching out, and its head was facing squarely forward, ears back, black lips taut in a teeth-baring snarl. I cognitively knew that the cutting green eyes were glass and that the tongue was formed plastic, but the effect was as close to real as anyone could want, as though the beast was temporarily trapped on sticky tar paper but would momentarily rise to avenge the insult, and it was still intimidating enough to raise the hair on the back of my neck.

"I hope fur doesn't offend you," Sari continued. "She was my loyal friend. Now she is my coworker. She guards the office."

"Cool," I said, and stepped carefully over the wolf's head. I was very afraid of saying the wrong thing.

The office itself left me speechless too, filled with Sari's high-end computing and video tech. I saw a desktop and two laptops running, a docked tablet, plus several cameras and drones on a shelf—not to mention a small, sputtering air conditioner that spilled out in all directions—wastefully, I couldn't help but think.

Sari explained that she had invested in equipment that would allow high-quality video and audio recording, editing and uploading because she had plans for live camera feeds and other documentary projects.

"If you get too cold, let me know and I'll bring you a blanket," she said. "The AC runs to keep the humidity from damaging everything. I keep losing laptops to mildew!"

"I really expected, you know, just a laptop. Sari, I need to confess to you that I might not be as skilled as you hoped I would be," I said. "I'm used to updating templates, or easy video software, that sort of thing."

"You can do it, little sister. I know you can. What you don't already know, you can learn."

"I just worked for a wedding videographer, my friend Charlotte, not a documentary filmmaker. Sometimes we did a live feed for destination weddings or relatives who were stuck at home, and I also edited footage into short clips for them to share on social media. Basic stuff. I can update your website, probably, but I've never used something like a drone camera." I pointed to three drones still in their cellophane-wrapped boxes.

"I don't think you understand what a big deal livecams are. Do you know how many people love livecams? Animals of all kinds. People have livecams of their bird feeders, their backyard bird feeders, Jamie! And millions of viewers dial in to watch the simplest things, like a cardinal prancing and squawking because she was given new sunflower seeds. The Atlantic Rescue Center gets obscene amounts of donations just because of their cage cams, and we're almost all set up in our macaque enclo-sure. I don't think you know how special your video skills are."

"Yeah, but I've never been to school for this stuff. Not for anything. I just learn on the job, and that has limitations."

"Not as many as you think! Your bosses knew that too; they just didn't want to pay you fairly." She sounded so confident. "Plus you went viral. Your videos were seen by literally every-one!"

I flushed. "Oh, but Sari, I didn't do that. That was done to me. Two different things."

"Not really, not if you think about it." She smiled. So she had seen my Tiki Hut videos, and believed in me anyway. I had nothing left to hide.

"Listen, let's get started. I will do as much as I can and then some. I just don't want to oversell myself." I sucked in my breath. "I don't want you to be disappointed."

"Of course. I know. No expectations at all," Sari said. "I know that you have aptitude and interest though, so what I'm saying is please feel free to experiment, read some manuals, watch some tutorials, learn however you like to learn."

"Okay, cool, yeah, this is quite the setup. Wow, Sari."

I felt nervous, not only about the capacity of the machines around me, but also the sheer expense of it all. Thousands of dollars' worth of equipment, sitting in a weird, leaky dome in the middle of the woods. Part of me also felt proud that Sari was trusting me with the collection. That was the most faith anyone had placed in me in a very long time.

What Sari wanted was attainable. I could build the pages she asked for, especially since I could crib quite a bit from her nem-esis's website. I knew how to upload to YouTube and then grab the code needed to embed the videos on her site and other so-cial media platforms. I already had tons of ideas about promot-ing the content to animal lovers.

"Animal lovers are merely the beginning," she said. "I need

you to understand something important, Jamie. Yes, there are bird rescues who do the work because they love birds. There are big cat rescues because people love cats. So what? Love is superficial. Atlas is something much deeper—a spiritual community."

"Right." I nodded, still not comprehending.

"We are devoted to the macaques. We learn from them. We worship them. We are building a community around them. The macaques aren't animals, is what I'm saying." She raised her arms heavenward.

"You need to find people who want a spiritual community."

"Exactly! Atlas wants more supporters because we know that our macaques teach us to embrace life and also to embrace death. And we have to hurry, we have to grow immediately. We need to share their ancient wisdom!"

She held my gaze, seeking something I wasn't sure I knew how to offer. All the same, I very much wanted to please her. "I have to say, I don't yet understand how that relates to watching videos of our monkeys," I said reluctantly. "Unless we are featuring them like mascots, like Smokey Bear?"

"No, that's my point. Trust me, it is all related, and we just need to get started. Your job is to get the livestream of the macaque enclosure up. It shows them playing and interacting with each other on the tire swing. It's a perfect bubble of community. We need to start by reaching people who love animals, who love the planet, and who know that our society is broken."

She played with the cover of a nearby book entitled *Planning for When the Last Leaf Falls*, opening the cover and letting it fall shut. Other volumes weighed down the desk. *The Uninhabitable Green. Rising Tides, Fragile Coasts.* "We need them to understand that there are too many people and too much waste destroying the planet. That we have to fix that problem, whatever it takes, or prepare to face death. And that the purer beings in our midst, the macaques, can guide us. Atlas can guide us."

"So basically, you need to reach people who care?"

"Yes!" She gave my arm a firm pinch.

I could see that Sari knew what she wanted. She saw her potential audience as limitless, and as she talked, her plans felt expansive and golden to me, too. I started to envision helping her with tremendous projects to share the macaques with the world. Social media interactions, virtual tours, livestreams. Connections to universities and schools for educational programs, or to nursing homes, prisons and other places where people are isolated and could benefit from the macaque community. So many possibilities ignited.

"We've been in here forever," she suddenly said, standing to signal her desire to wrap up our meeting.

"Let me get out of your way," I said, also scrambling to stand up, "but this has been super great, because now I can think about what you want me to do, and when we have time to work on it, I'll be ready to go."

"Oh, I can't wait to spend more time with you, brilliant Jamie! You are so smart! Why are you just now here at Atlas? You've been wasted working at bars, sister. Wasted at weddings for what, middle-class, straight, unevolved dummies?"

"Yeah, pretty much."

"You are an absolute balm! Now, go ahead back to Tierra. I need to spend time with Flora right now. She's only going to be here a very short time."

"I'm sorry for what you are going through, Sari, I'm so sorry. That is so hard," I said, trying to slowly tiptoe out of the office without touching the wolf. "If I can help you with that, let me know, too."

"Oh, don't be sorry. We are surrounded by community!" Sari looked intently at me, her eyes tinted more purple than blue in the low light of her dome. She hugged me goodbye, whispering, "You are too, dearest. All is well, don't worry about one little thing."

Then she physically pivoted me by the shoulders and quickly shooed me out of the house like I was an unwelcome fox.

Standing in the courtyard between the two domes, I realized how hot my cheeks suddenly felt. The big dome exuded heat in visible shimmers. I could smell bread baking and I was hungrier than I remembered being in a long time.

22

We are happiest when we renounce the wastefulness of outside life.

We are happiest when we take care of our simians and each other. Service every day is key. It starts with being consistent and reliable with their morning meal. First thing, with the dawn, they are shown here that they are loved, that they are safe, that they are in a good environment. Then we care for the land surrounding them. Their home is guarded by live oak trees that are dripping with ancient moss and by blooming plants like spiral ginger and sanchezia that vibrate with healing frequencies. You'll benefit from this environment too!

We carefully prepare meals and tend to their grounds throughout the day. Through our actions, we show them that we are worthy of their message, and that we will heed it. Service is the best way to give of yourself. We must be ready to sacrifice everything when it is our time, so practice now.

COMMENT FROM SARI

Jamie is amazing! She knows exactly what to do on all of this website stuff. This is a game changer! We have to get everything written and then after that she is going to fly with it! We are going to reach millions of people! We are going to change their lives and ours! I know we have a lot going on but I truly believe this is our priority, because once we get money streaming in from the internet, one, we'll have the funds we need to pay Zelda and to fight Anna Beth, and two, we will be able to give up everything else!!! Part of me is thinking we just put it all on Jamie. I bet she could write this stuff overnight. Wolfie disagrees with me, but what do you think?!? This is so amazing. It's like with the pregnant mamas when we were Vessel midwives, Tierra. I feel like a midwife to the rebirth of Atlas, and she's screaming and crying and furiously full of life! Push, push, push! Make sure Track Changes is on. −xoxoS.

TRACK CHANGES FROM DAGMAR

Hello, this is Dagmar. Absolutely not. I agree with Wolfie. Jamie is not at all ready. I'm very happy she will be useful to you with the camera and the website but be cautious. She is still a very shaky monkey. And she is still attached to your court system. And with Flora right now? Please wait. Also, delete the sentence where you mention sacrifices. Otherwise, it's fine.

TRACK CHANGES FROM TIERRA

Dear Sari & Dagmar. With all due respect, the court system is not "ours." Please, Dagmar. But I do hear what you are trying to say about Jamie's readiness. And I am very pleased that you are so positive, Sari. Those positive vibrations are manifesting our abundance in ways we don't even know. I feel deep healing happening, and I do believe we have Flora to thank for that, as well as the labors and wisdom from all of you. I believe in us. You are doing great with the website, Sari. Keep it up! With love and respect, Tierra.

23

I sat on a Bonding Bench and watched the macaques through new eyes, imagining them on the livestream being seen in homes across the country. Their delicate grooming rituals could calm an anxious viewer in Seattle, or their persistence when solving a puzzle could delight a discouraged spectator in Arkansas.

"You're going to be a rock star," I told Darla. Next to her, Freddie decided to use that as a prompt to begin taking a dump. "No one wants to see that, dude," I told him.

Kayla had called me a rock star to bolster my spirits before I went before the judge. "You're more famous than he is. Don't let him scare you. Remember, you saved a pelican from fire! You gave money to charity! Define the narrative, forget the rest. That's the secret to PR," she said.

I smiled, remembering her charm. Kayla was the real star. First, she secured delay after delay, hoping to pursue a harassment complaint against Duke as a way to explain my state of mind when I committed the crime, or at the very least secure an electronic monitoring punishment. Even when every avenue

dead-ended and it looked as though going back to jail was un-
avoidable, she persisted.

I liked visiting Kayla's office. My friends were ghosting me,
or I was ghosting them, and my daily life was grueling. The
only job I could land was cleaning rooms at a budget hotel two
highway stops south of St. Augustine, since no other restaurants would hire me after Tiki Hut. My appointments in Jacksonville kept me going. They reminded me that even though I
had snuffed out my entire life in my small hometown, a bigger
world existed. Kayla always gave me hope, too. When everyone
thought I was a joke, she called to offer me a lifeline.

I also looked forward to seeing her assistant, Cheyanne, an
obsessive Disney cult devotee, one of those Minnie-polka-
dotted-bow girls who made a pilgrimage to Orlando at least
once a month. Kayla never sat down, her office was a wreck,
and I had given myself the chore of tending to her perpetually
parched ferns and spider plants: giving them love and water,
pinching leggy growths off the golden pothos so it could conserve energy until rebounding.

"I don't know why people keep giving me plants," Kayla said.
"It's like I don't notice they're turning yellow, and then poof,
it's too late."

"They're coming back to life," I said. "Look at how this one's
greening up."

Resuscitating the plants had given me something to look forward to. When I couldn't summon optimism for my own legal
drama, at least I could hope for the promising curl of new leaves.
I even began using the health of the plants as a fortune-telling
device, convincing myself if the plants were better, it's a good
sign for me, too. I would panic if they died. I would give up if
she had thrown them out.

After Kayla took an Easter holiday (and after a miserable spring
season spent cleaning up the fried chicken bones and sandy bed-

sheets of tourists), I expected to return to very sorry-looking plants and very bad news about my case.

We had given up suing Duke, and I had given up on the idea of securing house arrest. I had researched it and knew I neither had a family member to live with nor the ability to prove the high-level financial stability the court required. I was tired of wasting Kayla's time, and I was tired of limbo. I was ready to serve a few months in county and put it all behind me.

Heading to that last meeting, I awkwardly punched the elevator button with my elbow because I was balancing a bottle of plant food and three iced coffees I couldn't afford. In my truck I had drawn a Hidden Mickey on Cheyanne's cup.

But the plants looked surprisingly healthy. Kayla, too, was well beyond healthy. Once a peacock had tried to mate with its own reflection on the door of my car, and that's the energy Kayla had as she bounced back and forth from the shiny mahogany glow of her desk to her own reflection in the plate-glass office window.

Kayla was tough to compliment because she already celebrated herself so freely, but this time she deserved it. She secured me a place to live and perform valuable community service, and she found an electronic monitoring company willing to oversee my activity, packaging a solid deal. Atlas Wildlife Refuge would give me everything I needed to avoid jail time, and everyone was signing off on it.

I was rescued, maybe for the first time in my life, and the rarity of the relief let me possess the glow of optimism for a small moment. I was in no position to turn it down, and I remember thinking it even sounded adventurous. Kayla didn't say much, just that Atlas was a rehabilitation center for monkeys, and that she sometimes represented them pro bono.

"You're a lawyer for monkeys?" I couldn't help but picture little chimps dragging briefcases in front of a baboon judge to plead for their freedom.

"No, I've represented the place. The nonprofit. The founder,

Sari. Amazing woman, a visionary type. You are going to fall in deep, deep love with her. Everyone does."

She went on and on about how the deal is a win for everyone, enjoying her own voice, peacocking some more.

"Jamie?" she said, snapping her fingers at me. "Hello? Stick with me. Be happy. This is the best thing that could happen to you. Do you see how brilliant and lucky this is?"

"Of course! It's almost too good, you know. I just don't want to wish for it if it's not going to happen." That was me, always trying to stave off disappointment. "Of course, I'm down if it means no jail. If this is real, you are a goddess, Kayla. And, I mean, who doesn't love monkeys?"

"Who doesn't love monkeys?" she echoed, but with a cheerier tone. "It is real. It is happening if you agree. Why wouldn't you? Your food, everything's covered. It's house arrest, but you can be outside! You're going to get so healthy, too, because they are vegetarians! Or vegans. You know, very spiritual and healing minded. And you love plants. You'll fit right in. You're going to love it and you don't even know. Compared to living in jail? No contest. Thank God for me!"

"I'm so relieved and deeply grateful, seriously. Thank you, Kayla."

"I'm jealous, actually. I wish I had a Kayla for myself, putting together a three-month deal perfectly timed for a beautiful summer in the woods. Well, okay, that part is not great. It's going to be hot, not gonna lie. But otherwise, so lucky. I really scored on this one!"

I stood up and gave her a hug to soak up her good energy as much as to thank her. Cheyanne cheered from her desk, and I thought she was excited for me too, but it turned out she finally found the Hidden Mickey on her cup.

It all truly did come together fast after that. I didn't even visit the Atlas campus ahead of time, because it didn't matter. I would have taken any diversion deal. When Sari gave me the website project, I knew it was working out better than I could have imagined, giving me a chance to complete a project that was meaningful—professional work that I would be proud to claim.

"Maybe Kayla was right and we're all rock stars, me included," I whispered to Colette. A big male with a long red face and unruly gray hair came to eavesdrop. "Odin, definitely, I can see your potential. You've got star quality."

24

I ignored the noise at night because Tierra, Sari, and Dagmar wanted me to. The sweltering days filled themselves with work, but it was easy because most of my other worries dissolved. No looming bills, no constant juggling between part-time schedules. I found freedom in devoting myself to one day at a time. Satisfaction came from knowing my monitor release day was creeping closer every minute. The pile of stones on my plate was testament to how quickly single drops can add up.

I spent mornings with Tierra in the garden and dome kitchen, and I spent the afternoon caring for the monkeys or the property. No matter what project I worked on, I was always thinking about how I could help Sari expand Atlas.

Hanging out with the volunteers reminded me of people-watching at the airport or at the beach. They were a peaceful lot, quietly meditating and then nodding off on the Bonding Benches. Dagmar assured me it was fine when they slacked, but seeing them out-and-out napping frustrated me. Paths needed clearing, monkey toys needed sanitizing, barrels of donated pro-

duce needed to be sorted and processed before it was overcome
with rot. Beyond that, I wanted Atlas to look camera-ready, so
that meant building repairs and grounds cleanup. We could accomplish so much more if some of them showed a little hustle.
But it wasn't my job to assign tasks.

Even so, I couldn't wait for the volunteers to leave at the end
of the day. When the gate closed after the last car, Atlas returned
to its rightful balance for the ochre hours of the afternoon and
early evening. Plus I could freely talk to the monkeys again, as
long as Dagmar was in Monkey Island or away from the area.

"If you persist in anthropomorphizing them or seeing them
as comical," Dagmar had said once, "how will you learn from
them? How will you hear what they are trying to tell you if you
keep interrupting them with reductive nonsense?"

Still, I loved talking to the monkeys every day, and sometimes I felt a reciprocal interest from them. Just like the puzzle
toys, many of them responded to me with their own curios-
ity or amusement. I enjoyed calling out to Stella in my Marlon
Brando voice when she was perched on a high beam. It was fun
imagining Meaty Joe as a cantankerous truck driver and Darla
a gossipy housewife on a reality TV show.

For the most part though, the players acted only marginally
aware of their starring roles in my skits. They were more concerned with their internal dramas and pecking orders than with
us, clustering in grooming groups to chatter, scaling the chains
suspending the tire swing, or working on various enrichment
puzzles we doled out to let them feel like they were foraging to
discover a cache of snacks.

Dagmar showed me how to watch for Curious Georgia
O'Keeffe and Bee, as they were the two who most relentlessly
sought out the puzzle toys, and then particularly delighted in
sharing their spoils with others.

Some of the monkeys were protective over their food, but
most of them seemed to share. Dagmar said some never recover

from the damage of being forcibly weaned too young, but that the goal here was to provide consistent abundance. I loved seeing them put food directly in each other's mouths, though I loved the petty squabbles, too.

While I was sanding mold and pollen off the Bonding Benches one afternoon, I kept an eye on Tierra as she was leading volunteers clearing the area around the new enclosure. They hacked at clumps of palmettos with machetes, sometimes needing to run a chain beneath a root wad to pop it out with a truck. They were finding an alarming number of pygmy rattlesnakes, dislodging them from the dark recesses where the heart of the palmetto began to fan out.

Sari came out to join the commotion, bringing her mother with her. Flora wore a caftan full of hibiscus flowers that looked like flames dancing around her pale face and thin, white arms. Sari held on to her elbow and led her through the area, slowly surveying the clumps of dirt.

Dagmar was walking toward the enclosure, so I hopped to catch up with her.

"Dagmar, does Sari know how many pygmies they're disturbing in that area?" I asked, pointing to where Flora was receiving a glass of water from Tierra. "It seems dangerous for Flora, doesn't it?"

Dagmar sniffed. "They are simply getting air, Jamie. But come here, look at the macaques. They love this." Dagmar shook a container of dental floss, waving it in front of the enclosure. Summoned, a clutch of monkeys gathered, hands outstretched, waiting for a thread. They immediately grabbed it and started running their prize through their teeth.

"The monkeys floss?" I was amazed at the juxtaposition of our tools to their world.

"Yep, they love it. They'll use bird feathers, blades of grass, whatnot. This stuff is perfect for them. It's made of coconut fiber."

Bee, a silver macaque with a sweet pink face and fluffy cheeks, twice discarded the floss Dagmar gave her. She climbed up the chain link to rest at eye level with us and reached her paw out, grabbing toward my face.

"Why doesn't she want a piece of floss?" I asked.

"Stay back. She wants a few strands of your hair."

"My hair?"

"Just a strand. She wants to floss with it. It won't be too effective, but there's no harm. She seems to like your long hair. She likes Sari's, too."

I felt honored, but then immediately cautious. Was it another test? I could rarely figure out what Dagmar allowed and what she forbade, so I was bound to err. I stood frozen.

"Well, aren't you going to give it to her? Just one hair. Pluck it at the root. Dangle it so she can take it without touching you," Dagmar said.

She was clearly offended that I was ignoring Bee, a high-level female, who was extending a request.

I fumbled, rushing to pluck one and ended up pulling three. I did as I was told, and Bee pinched them with her perfect little fingers and cackled.

I took a deep breath.

"There," said Dagmar. "Now you are friends."

Mischa, a sturdy, tan volunteer who always interrogated me about the ingredients in our lunch offerings, joined our conversation. "Dagmar, can I butt in for a second? If you wouldn't mind, please tell Sari how grateful I am. I was so excited when she invited me yesterday that I don't even know if I properly thanked her." Mischa gave Dagmar a quick hug and started to trot away, waving at us both. "See you later!"

Dagmar shrugged at me. "Just helping with Flora," she said,

and then walked off as well. Bee sat down and stared at me, unblinking, while she flossed her teeth with my hair.

"Such a beautiful girl," I told her. She pulled back her lips and opened her jaw wide to reveal two rows of jagged teeth—her long canines like shards of broken milk glass—and laughed at me before beginning to floss again.

25

We are of nature, so we are like nature. All things are not equal. Some things grow, some things die, some things never get started.

You will come to understand. Think of it like seeds.

Did you know some seeds need a little nick in order to sprout? They have a hard shell. They need to be trampled, torn. Bit or gnawed at. You can do this artificially by scratching a seed with a knife before you plant it, but it's not the same.

Nature provides the right amount of scarification. The right animal or insect in the environment comes along to scratch the seeds that are meant to grow there.

You are not wasted if you let yourself be cut open so that you can grow and bloom. Lay down and let your hard shell be trampled away. Join us at Atlas and we will help you.

COMMENT FROM SARI

I am losing it. Absolutely losing it. I am close to tapping out. Something has to give. Anna Beth is chapping my hide and will be here any minute. The new will won't hold up in court if Flora is declared incompetent, which is obviously what Anna Beth will try to make happen. If we get stuck with the old will, we'll need enough money to buy out Anna Beth for the land or we are screwed. Meanwhile, Zelda wants more money or all kinds of work in trade, which we don't have time to do. And this website. We've got to get this website done. We have to pivot or one, all our dreams will crash down and never become a reality, and two, I don't know, I just lost my second point. See what I mean, I envision things in my head, and they are beautiful and whole, and then on paper, poof. Nada. Help me. –xoxoS.

TRACK CHANGES FROM DAGMAR

Hello, this is Dagmar. Calm down. Ingen ko på isen. We can only do so much at one time. Right now, we focus. We finish the second enclosure because that's paid for. More importantly, we offer Flora everything she needs during this time. We will not let Anna Beth touch her. We will secure the land for Atlas. That's enough for right now. The website can come later.

COMMENT FROM SARI

It is driving me absolutely mad that you are NOW in Track Changes, but you aren't actually tracking any CHANGES. You aren't editing a thing and I seriously don't think you are even reading what I'm writing.

Here's why the website is urgent: Jamie is here and can be working on it. We are wasting the opportunity of her. And you know what, this chaos is going to be the norm until we get more people in our circle, living and working here. And the only way to do that is to reach out with really enthusiastic education about who we are etc. Meaning, the website! The livestream! Do you see? It always comes back to the need to share all of our teachings with the world. And to share the macaques. It always comes down to the damn website!

Everything needs to be done! Otherwise, what's the point of any of it?????

Dagmar, I know you have your own agendas and reasons for things, but you need to trust me that building the community, the global community, supports everything you want to do. It's easy for you to say wait, but do you have a trust fund hidden away in Denmark we can tap in the meantime?

COMMENT FROM TIERRA

Dear Sari & Dagmar. I am very concerned that we are not honoring our commitment to consensus decision-making and conflict-free communication. Our thoughts might be better shared in person. I would also like to suggest, with my heart in my hands, that Flora is confronting a beautiful reality, but it is also hard and harrowing and different. Our bodies and minds are trying to catch up with universal truths, and it's exhausting. I know I am feeling it. I own that. I am committed to helping us all see this through, even the parts we didn't expect to feel. But about the website content? I love it! I believe you and Jamie will do a beautiful job! With love and respect, Tierra.

26

Days went by and Cole still hadn't checked up on my progress, and no one at Atlas was keeping time sheets, of that much I was sure. I started to keep a notebook of all of the homesteading skills I was learning from Tierra in case I was asked by a judge to account for my time. I wanted a repository for myself, anyway. I didn't know how these women, who were only a few years older than myself, knew so much about surviving and thriving in the wilderness. They fed themselves and made healing teas, soaps, and ointments with locally harvested herbs. They used laborers or tradespeople for big projects but were always making or repairing things: the buildings, ad hoc baskets from kudzu vines, candles, garden supports. Most importantly, they had a mission. They took care of the monkeys, and they took care of each other.

I didn't know how to float the idea by the women that I would be interested in staying at Atlas past my required date. I was only now able to contribute meaningfully enough to give back in exchange for all they were offering me this summer, and we hadn't yet been able to push publish on Sari's livestream project. Even if I couldn't stay here, success might help me get a sustainable job when I left, too.

Dawn poured in fast that morning, joining the bright light of the moon remaining from the previous night's sky. Sitting by the monkeys, I watched clouds fade from pink to canary to white until the unrestrained heat on my sunburnt neck told me it was going to be another long day.

"Bee, you look hungover. I feel hungover. Atlas food is too healthy, isn't it? We need some sausage gravy, biscuits, and Diet Coke, on mornings like this," I said. Colette and the other mamas toddled over, squatting on their tails and haunches in a semicircle. "We need Waffle House sliced and smothered potatoes. Oh dang, M&M'S. I bet at least one of you misses M&M'S."

Then I thought about Tierra, her strong arms punching down glutinous bread dough. "I'm just kidding. We don't need garbage groceries. But I do need to talk to Sari to get your camera rolling. Put in a good word for me, will ya? Everyone is just so busy with the new cage."

Bubbles chirped a consolatory song, wrapping both of her arms around Colette and pulling her into a full-body hug.

In the dome, the humans looked beat. Tierra, who was outrageously elegant most of the time, like a moonlit doe, was puffy and bloodshot. Dagmar was lithe and fit and yet today moved like a rusted wrench. That morning Sari had fallen back to sleep in her kitchen chair, the strap of her vintage slip riding off her left shoulder. Instead of letting me sit for breakfast, Tierra quickly sent me back outside to start the day's work with a jar of overnight oatmeal and a cup of coffee.

"Jamie, I would be lost without you. Literally lost. You are my angel right now," she said, guiding me down the dome porch steps.

"Sure thing, but I didn't know we were starting so early today."

"I didn't know the contractors or volunteers would be here so early either. Dagmar has gone a little rogue on her enclosure project. These plumbers are incredibly difficult men. Please make sure none of them get anywhere near the macaques. Do you know Farrah? She'll help you. The men, be careful, they can be slick."

"Oh, they better not be. I'm on it." Tierra crinkled her nose and smiled, which is exactly what I hoped would be her response. I clutched the jar of oatmeal to my chest like I was greeting a precious infant. I was starving because Sari had given our dinner (tiny fork-crimped ravioli stuffed with eggplant pesto) in a sacrifice the night before, and I couldn't wait to dig in.

Farrah was a wispy-haired blonde with a slight frame, but she had a way with the workers and could manage the odd stray visitor with a flummoxed "hey, dude," and that was that. The macaques prompted some men to regress by grunting and scratching under their arms like apes. Chastised by the babysitter, they would sheepishly turn around and head back to work.

I spent an easy morning in communion with the monkeys, and while keeping an eye out for wandering plumbers, I also kept watch for Sari. Most of the macaques seemed wary of the activity and were more vocal than normal. Farrah knew all of their names, and when I asked for tips, she tried to teach me to recognize the differences in coloring, gait, and facial features.

"My favorite is Stella, that one with the rag doll, being a good mommy all the time. I like it when she bosses the other monkeys around." A pained look crossed Farrah's face. "I wonder how many babies they made her have?"

"You mean the breeders?"

"It's so terrible. Atlas is essential for the rescued mamas." She twisted the corner of her *Fountain of Youth* shirt and tied it into a knot at her hip. "Even so, we think we are saving them, but it's really the macaques who are saving us. Wouldn't you do anything for them?"

"I love them, I do. Stella is one of my favorites, too. And that little gray one. He never gets his share of food, but Bee makes sure he gets the leftovers."

"Oh, that's Ghost. He's a senior citizen. Isn't he gorgeous? He comes to me in my dreams sometimes."

Farrah was right about the breeders. It was incomprehensible that people would abuse these creatures with their hairless faces and soulful eyes. Ghost ran his hands across the fencing near us, fingers strumming the wire like a guitar.

After Farrah left, Mischa arrived to take her spot on the bench, wearing the Daytona uniform of a black concert T-shirt and impossibly small shorts.

"Monkey see, monkey do," one man said as he passed, pantomiming a dancing chimpanzee. From the benches, Mischa hissed; he cowered.

Unlike Farrah, Mischa didn't want to chat about monkeys, even when I asked her to describe her favorite ones. Instead, she wanted to grill me about my emotions and spiritual development. Did I feel the presence of gods and goddesses when I sat with the macaques? Did I have a good relationship with my own spirit guides? Was my evolution rapidly advancing because I lived at Atlas? How long had I known Sari?

Mischa also had a lot of thoughts about what I should be thinking about, including about the power of the sun.

"Of course, Sari knows best for the macaques, but I'm surprised by how often they choose to sit in the shade. The sun is so important to me. Without it, we would literally die. When it is gone one day, we will." She swooned and closed her eyes. "I did almost die once, in the hospital and rehab center, because I couldn't get them to give me daily sunlight in enough quantity to heal. I had to escape so that I could take in the sun. And then I got better!"

"Wow. I'm definitely getting plenty of sun, thankfully."

I thought about my few days in jail, how the guards only let us in the yard for ten minutes each day. Even if this girl was over-the-top, she was right. I was lucky to be at Atlas.

"We need Vitamin D. You can survive on Vitamin D energy alone, actually. Nothing but the sun. Prana, baby. Look into it. So I don't understand why the monkeys are in the shade all the time."

"I bet even in the shade, they get indirect sunlight. And in the summer, shade is so important. They probably get dehydrated and sun damaged, like us."

"I'll have to think about that. Indirect sun. Indirect." She screwed her features into a squint, as though that was the first she had heard of the concept. "You know, it's a myth that the sun is dangerous. If you are getting burnt by the sun, it's because you don't have a good relationship with the sun. Think about it. Which animals get sunburnt?"

I had no idea what she wanted me to say. "I think you're blaming the victim there. We have skin; most animals have fur. Or feathers." I looked around for Tierra or Dagmar, trying to figure out how to get out of the conversation. "You know what? Maybe food is their delicious way to capture the sun. The monkeys love watermelon, which is basically sun and water, so I think they are okay."

"I say, cut out the middleman! But I'll think about your very valid points. I'll sit with it. Hey, can you do me a favor?" Mischa took my hand, her grip wizened and compact.

"I will if I can. What's up?"

"Do they let you give out Dagmar's medicine bags? Mine was short last month, and I absolutely don't want the bad energy of complaining, but I just thought if you could quietly replace it, it was worth asking."

"Uh, no, I don't have anything to do with that."

"Cool, cool. Well, forget I said anything." She dropped my

hand fast, sending it swinging, and squinted at me again. "I'm gonna sit with your ideas."

Mischa meant that literally, because she left to sit farther down the bench to meditate. I was on my own to guard the macaques, so I decided to pace along the fence line in patrol, giving Mischa's bench a wide berth. I found myself suddenly exhausted from trying to follow the interaction. Did she mean salve and other herbal remedies when she asked for Dagmar's medicine? My pacing caught the attention of Cornelius and Henri, who starting walking with me along the fence.

"Prana, baby," I whispered to them.

Mischa had made it hard to do my second, self-assigned job of keeping an eye on the Monkey Island door. I was fairly certain only Tierra and Dagmar had gone in and out, with no hint of Sari. Dagmar stayed particularly close to the door, probably to make sure the men stayed away.

When everyone left for the day, I headed for the dome feeling relieved in a proprietary way, like when all of the customers finally left Duke's after last call and the place felt like mine. Atlas was becoming my home and anyone else was an interloper— sometimes necessary, but intrusions all the same. The real day began after they left.

I hoped we were planning a big supper because I hadn't been able to score lunch for myself. Tierra wasn't in the dome, so I went searching for her. She wasn't in the garden either, but as I walked past the greenhouse, I saw a volunteer, a woman in a white sundress adding scraps to the compost pile.

From a distance, that's what it looked like she was doing, but when I drew closer to offer help, I saw that she actually was taking things *out* of the food waste pile. The woman was very thin, with twig-like arms and legs. She held half of a soggy eggplant in one hand, and in the other, the stem from a red pepper, which she was gnawing like a dog with a rawhide bone.

"Ma'am, is that I good idea? I mean, I think we're done for the day here and it's time to go home," I said. I assumed I had stumbled upon yet another freaky volunteer who needed to be shuffled off the property, but up close, I was taken aback to see that the woman was Sari's mother. She was wearing a night-gown, her hair was matted, and as she peered up, her eyes were glassy and feverish.

"Miss Flora? Oh, Miss Flora!"

She didn't answer. I stammered and tried to make eye contact, but her attention was darting around the garden. "Ma'am, are you okay?"

She smiled warmly, pointing the pepper at me as though it were her finger. "Well, you caught me. Hello there, Jamie." She took a small bite of the raw eggplant, deftly avoiding a rotting lettuce leaf clinging to the skin. "I'm just having a little snack."

Flora bent down to root through the compost some more, pushing past liquified tomato skins and coffee ground muck. "Look at all of this waste!" she exclaimed. "Sari would be so mad if she saw all this waste."

"Let's go find Sari, Miss Flora."

"Oh, Sari? She's been running all over hell's half acre and back." She dropped the vegetables and looked at me. "Jamie, I want you to promise me that you will take up for Sari. Help her and be loyal to her."

"I am, of course I am."

"I know you will. You're a strong girl. All of you are such good girls," she said. "It's the only thing that gives me hope."

"Flora!" Tierra appeared, sprinting across the garden. "There you are."

Without meeting my eyes, Tierra maneuvered herself between me and Flora, and she began to steer the tiny, barefoot woman home. "Let's go get you situated. You know you aren't supposed to be out and about like this."

"Let me help, Tierra. I can help you with her."

"No, we're fine, aren't we?" Tierra ushered Flora across the threshold into her own backyard. She did not look back again.

Returning to the dome, I felt lost once again, unsure if I should start preparing supper for the group. I wished they would let me help care for Flora, or at least share the details with me so I didn't feel so out of the loop. I thought about the previous night, how Tierra and Sari left the table three times to whisper to each other in the walk-in refrigerator. I wouldn't know how to be of assistance until they decided to clue me in. And other community members were helping Flora. Why not me?

As soon as I entered the dome, Dagmar exclaimed, "There she is!" She was refilling her water bottle, looking grimy where dirt and sweat had settled on her neck and in the crooks of her arms. Her socks were soaking wet from being trapped inside her chore boots. "Jamie, do you know how to sew?"

"Do you mean giving people stitches, like you did for Jodie? No, and I still have nightmares about that."

Dagmar shook her head. "Sewing fabric. Here, I'll show you what I mean."

She extracted a colorful quilted purse from a plastic storage container and motioned for me to sit with her at the table.

I looked at the purse as she arranged various tools. "Dagmar, I didn't take you for the crafty type. What is this?"

She showed me how to remove a few stitches from the bottom of the lining in each bag and then sew them back up after packing them. "Can you do this type of work?" she asked.

"Yeah, I can fix a hole, for sure. But what exactly are we putting inside the purses?"

"Jamie, I wouldn't ask this of you if I weren't stuck, but here's the situation. And it's going to sound odd, but it's not really. It's a chance to help people. And also, Atlas, of course." She extracted a second plastic tote box from within the larger one and popped it open. With one hand she pulled out small, sealed plastic bags containing brown chunks that looked like dried mushrooms. "Pangolin," she said.

"Pangolin? As in, the armadillo-like thing?"

"Yes. These are pangolin scales. It's a long story, but essentially they are from pangolins that died at a sanctuary. It would be a shame to let them go to waste because pangolins are valued in many cultures to treat everything from stomach ulcers to impotence to the effects of malicious witchcraft. You get the picture. It's hard to get pangolin supplies in some places. These scales are a very good type. You can imagine."

I nodded. I pointed at a bag, not particularly wanting to touch it. "This feels a little weird, to be honest. But the pangolins died naturally, right?"

"Oh, yes. Our friend who is also a vet handles many exotic animals at refuges and in the area. Zelda, you met her. We help each other. I'm a better dentist than she is, while she's better at surgery, for example. We trade services. With these animals, Zelda gave them a clean bill of health on their death certificates, which squared everything away as far as licensing goes, no worries, but she couldn't bring herself to actually cremate them. So now they belong to her, and since we owe her a favor, we need to help."

"Okay, I guess," I said.

"All you have to do is duct tape one baggie of scales to the bottom of each purse and then sew it back up. Is this something you could do for me please, Jamie?" She looked at me so hopefully. I couldn't remember Dagmar ever needing anything from me—typically when we worked together, she reminded me that she was doing me a favor by allowing me to assist her.

"You will save my life. If not, fine, just say so. It is okay with me either way." She packed everything back into the large tote and snapped the lid. I knew absolutely that it would not be okay with Dagmar if I demurred, and in fact I might not get another chance to prove myself worthy of her trust.

"Is everything I need here? How many, and what's my deadline?" I smiled.

Dagmar clasped her hands together and bowed her head. "Thank you, Jamie! There are thirty. We need them by the morning."

"Tomorrow morning?"

"There's food in the tote for you too, and let's fill up your water bottle. Maybe put on some music? That's how I would do it, get in a rhythm."

Thirty was a lot. I didn't know if I could physically do that many by myself, but I was going to have to try. I slowly walked home with the box, wondering what Dagmar had packed for my dinner, and stopped at a Bonding Bench to say an early goodnight to the macaques.

"I think I got in trouble six times today, but I also got out of trouble seven," I whispered to Bubbles and Freddie. "So that's what counts."

They walked the length of the enclosure with me, Bubbles on the ground and Freddie hopping from fence to ground and climbing back up again. "What about y'all? It's apparently a free-for-all out there." Mr. Nilsson and John Doe joined us. "Psst, fellas, can I interest you in some fresh pangolin? They are buy one, get one free at the moment."

John Doe opened his mouth and unfurled a strip of cantaloupe rind. I didn't see any fruit bits left on it, but he gnawed on what remained, his hands pushing the rind into his teeth, until he stopped and stuffed it back into his cheeks again. I thought of Flora, her pale hands trembling as she held the eggplant stem, and hurried toward my trailhead.

27

Here's something we've learned from our macaque troop.

There's nothing to fear because we have each other.

We know each other because we are one. The hand knows the mouth. The mouth knows the apple. The apple knows the tree. The tree knows the seed. The seed knows the hand. The hand knows sacrifice.

We know everything, if not now, soon. Soon enough.

What are you waiting for? Join Atlas now.

COMMENT FROM SARI

Never mind, I had a long talk with Wolfie, and we are just going to take care of it all ourselves. As usual.

COMMENT FROM TIERRA

Please don't ice us out. We are entirely devoted to you and to our dreams. We all came to these understandings together. Through Dagmar's brilliance with the macaque communities. Through all that you and I went through cleaning up after the

Argo community, and then the midwives, and when the rifts broke out and all of the sad times. All of it. Who stayed, Sari? Dagmar and I stayed. And we are building Atlas and building a way to share our ideas. We know so many truths now. It's hard, that's all. Sacrifices are hard—if they weren't, you wouldn't get gold in return. And speaking of gold, it's always been hard for us without money, but we are so close to fixing that problem. When you own the Atlas land free and clear and Anna Beth is gone, we will get the loan and we will feel so much lighter, and abundance will flow our way. Don't shut down your heart simply because it's hard here, hard at the time of sacrifice and hard to build communities as radical and new as ours.

It's like you just wrote. There's nothing to fear because we have each other. That is so true. We know each other. I'm coming over to hug you and talk to you face-to-face.

28

My rock plate was overflowing. I needed to count out the stones one of these days, but I was too tired most nights to take on that chore, along with all that it would force me to think about.

I truly didn't mind my pangolin sewing project, but I wished I didn't have to do it alone. It would have been so much better if I could have spread out in the dome, with music or conversation going, at least with Tierra. It still grated on me that she had rebuffed me in the garden with Flora. I craved her attention, but Sari and Flora always came first. As good as the days were—Tierra standing beside me, her strong arms bumping mine as she taught me how to use a wheel to cut pasta, the whisper of the Ouija board pointer under Sari's fingertips as she sought an auspicious moment to launch projects—I knew in my heart I was not included in what mattered most to them, and was starting to think I never would be.

The knottiest vine of my loneliness was that I had no one to help me interpret the day, no one to process my problems with, no one to explain to me what I was doing wrong with Tierra,

Sari, and Dagmar. In my worst moments, I thought I must be a leech and a loser in their eyes, shamefully doing penance, and that was that.

"Cole, you are no use to me, not one bit."

I couldn't bear to look at my ankle. I shoved some salve on it and half-heartedly tried to wash up. I had been foolish not to go to the shower house earlier, and now it was too late.

I was so tired I fell asleep twice. I wondered who had loved and fed this pangolin at a sanctuary or zoo, and if they had grieved its loss, and what the scales were for. For all I knew, I was holding a miracle cure to all of my mosquito bites and muscle pains right in my hands, oblivious to the bounty. What was more impressive was the item I found under the pangolin scales: beneath the baggies shone an elegantly curved claw, the same mottled brown color as the pangolin scales. It was from a big cat, a tiger or a lion, I guessed. I ran its tip along my forearm, leaving a thin white scratch where a stronger stroke would have slashed through my flesh to lay me open.

At around nine o'clock, the noises start again, low at first. A distant howl that could have been any animal. A vibration that might have been wind rattling the A-frame's rooftop. The sounds felt diffuse and far away, making it easy enough to convince myself that the women were right. Maybe all along I had been overreacting to a jungle trick of the night wind. I ate my almond butter sandwich and went back to my sewing project.

Then the sounds escalated to an undeniable disturbance, the high pitch rattling my jaw, a palpable terror riding on top of the noise directly into my bones. The monkeys were crying and banging against their enclosure, I was sure of it. A chill cooled the sweat on my back; I suddenly felt queasy. Something was happening to the macaques.

Or maybe it was nothing. Maybe it was parties that I simply wasn't invited to attend.

But no, I didn't believe that Sari would be in the mood to host parties when I knew the women were caring for Flora during her illness. In fact, it was highly possible that Sari, Tierra, and Dagmar were all at Flora's house taking care of her at the very moment I was hearing the monkeys cry. If so, maybe that was the explanation. They were too far away to hear the distress in the enclosure.

That meant it was on me and me alone to stop the danger. I needed to take it upon myself to follow the noise and protect the monkeys from whatever was terrorizing them, instead of just waiting and wondering.

As I laced up my boots, I tried to prepare myself for the predators I might see: cougars, hogs, wild dogs. By approaching the enclosure, I would become the new bait that was outside the cage, accessible, a slow morsel, an easy target for an animal to track and then pounce, paws darting through openings in the path, jaws ready. Since the macaques were physically safe in their enclosure, I decided I wouldn't try to scare them off, but instead would retreat quietly and then give a report to Dagmar the following day—unless the situation felt dire enough to bother Sari at Flora's house.

But surely I was more likely to find a small pest than a threat. A gang of raccoons, maybe.

If it was the men from town back to harass the monkeys, then I would yell. I would chase them to the parking lot and get license tag numbers. I wouldn't let them get away with it.

Forbidden or not, I stuck the tiger claw in my pocket for protection, opened the screen door, and stepped out toward the unsettling screams.

29

The full moon was obscured by dense layers of clouds that I begged to part so I could see the path. Mosquitos swarmed my ears, but they couldn't possibly drown out the shrieks that grew stronger and more solid with each transgressive step I took. I was headed toward it, but it felt like the howling was also accelerating toward me, like the rumble of a train before it becomes a rapid cacophony of wind and furious metal.

My path felt narrower because I wasn't used to being out at night. Ivy vines, fingers of palms, and clouds of moss reached out to ensnare me. I sensed the eyes of nocturnal predators tracking me through the thorny underbrush only they could navigate. Out in the pressing ink of the night, I grew certain the noise was caused by predation. I could feel it in myself, a scream building in my chest, a distress signal of my own that would ring out to protect me.

The howling and pulsating grew loud, insistent. The more I could hear, the more the vibration sounded like purring, something guttural and deep. It was close; I was close to it. I had battled for days about whether the sounds might be coming from the lake, or the pergola, or the dome, but even halfway down my path I knew it was undeniably emanating from the cage.

A few steps farther and I stopped to listen, knowing the enclosures were just around the bend.

Most prominent was the noise of the monkeys. Now that I knew them better, I could sense they were animated and in alarm mode, screeching and bounding up and down the beams and the bars. But beneath the monkey howls was a hum, most certainly not an animal bellowing. It was music. Humans were singing.

The music delivered tremendous relief—it fell in a full river of sweat rivulets down my face and neck. The vibrating bass of music. I was ridiculous, torturing myself with what would likely turn out to be some sort of midnight Atlas choir practice.

I pressed my back against a tree to catch my breath. My head was spinning, drunk on adrenaline and night air. The bark felt alive with beetles writhing just below the surface. I shuddered and jumped away from the dead tree before I was swarmed.

A smart, secure woman would have returned to her cabin at that point, not wanting to look lonesome enough to break the rules. A good worker would go home to her pile of contraband mending. But being that close to the enclosure compelled me to move forward, at the very least to see my troubled monkeys.

And truthfully, I did want to see the Atlas party. If they weren't going to invite me, maybe I would just invite myself.

Just as I decided to press on, a woman's shriek sliced through the night. I gasped and held still, and so did the rest of the forest. All other noises stopped, including the monkeys howling, and we waited to hear what came next.

I thought she might cry out again, or that I would hear people calling out in response. Why didn't I hear everyone from the gathering also clamoring for help?

There was nothing. When a feral scream rings out like that, the real terror comes in the quiet aftermath.

I exhaled and slowly moved forward. The ground fought my steps, coming at me like quicksand and killer vines, my head reeling and finding the here and now impossible to hold steady. I thought of Stella and Curious Georgia O'Keeffe. Bee flossing her teeth with my hair. Sari caring for her amazing mother. I tried to trust those truths. I forced myself to remember what the dome looked like during the day. What it smelled like when Tierra was cooking. The inviting Eden of a garden haul on the counter, waiting for me to wash the sandy soil from crisp leaves. The joyous, blooming promise of it.

It was a good space. A safe space.

The monkeys began howling again. I quickened my pace into the darkness.

Finally reaching the end of the path, I took cover behind the trees at the trailhead, afraid of being heard. Eventually, I approached the macaque viewing area, and then I stopped cold.

The people I expected to see in the dome were right there on the Bonding Benches.

The moon broke through the cloud cover to shine on the chain link, just enough to show me its boundaries. Some flashlights beamed from outside the enclosure. I only saw the blurry shapes of monkeys within, but I could hear them running and squawking and shaking the metal of their cage.

And then the music began again from the Bonding Benches where about two dozen people sat. I tried to count, but it was hard to separate them in the shadows. They were moaning, or maybe chanting, in a loud, low tone, like a throng of animals giving birth.

As I crept forward I could see the silhouettes of a few volunteers I recognized. The chanters were watching Sari and a very large, bearded man pace in front of the enclosure. They marched in a slow, uniform tempo, each step labored and exaggerated. Above the chants, an otherworldly music was amplified from speakers or a boom box somewhere back in Monkey Island, distorted and disturbing.

I had crept to the farthest bench unnoticed and slid down to sit. I don't think I could have looked away if I had tried. I could feel the humming of the woman nearest to me as she pushed vibrations out from the bottom of her throat like a growl.

Sari and the man disappeared. Clouds again blanketed the moon, and I couldn't tell one monkey from the other as they screamed and threw their bodies down from the beams or into the fence.

And then I saw a dark-haired woman standing in the cage. She twirled around, pumped her hands in the air like a boxing champion, and gave a powerful kick. I caught sight of cutoff jean shorts, and something clicked.

The woman was Mischa, prana-loving Mischa.

The music and throaty singing boomed louder like a growing fire.

I stroked the tiger claw with my thumb, fevered with panic when I remembered Dagmar's story about the monkeys who stoned a man. I thought about the virus they carried and their potential for violence. Sari's anger at Jodie's bleeding leg, Bee's sharp canine teeth bared at me. I thought of our dinner sacrifices, the monkeys devouring our food after it was pushed into the enclosure.

But Mischa was in with the monkeys, and no one was concerned.

Had she been the woman who had screamed earlier? I spotted Tierra in the row closest to the cage, and on impulse I stood up to go to her, but then I stopped myself, spotting Farrah and a few others in the process.

The music crescendoed, along with more of the awful humming, Mischa now at the gate.

"Okay, let me out now. We did it! I'm ready," Mischa yelled

over the screeches of the circling monkeys. "Dagmar, come unlock me. Please. I'm done."

Sari was now walking alone—I didn't see the bearded man anywhere. She ignored Mischa's plaintive cries as they escalated, as did the macaques' lamentations, and I wondered how much longer the community would make her endure the chaos.

At last, minutes later, the music stopped, the door to the lockout clicked open, and Dagmar pulled Mischa out of the enclosure.

Sari bellowed, arms reaching outward. "Not one bite! The monkeys have decided! Blessed be!"

"Blessed be!" the crowd replied.

The viewers burst into applause and the music began again. Awash with confusion, I leaned forward and craned my neck until I found Tierra, her silhouette shoulder to shoulder with others on a bench. Behind me, I felt a hand take hold of my ponytail and give it two firm tugs. I slowly sat up and turned around to see Flora walking away into the crowd.

I knew I should leave. As unobtrusively as I could, I slid away from the enclosure, and as soon as I was past the cover of the trailhead, I started running. The moon was so big and low it felt like I was running toward it instead of toward my house.

Back at the cabin, I reached in my pocket and threw the tiger claw onto my pile of stones. I chugged the last of my tea and as much water as I could get out of my tap. My thoughts coursing fast like lightning, I tried to piece together what I had just experienced. Once, a beach wedding I shot had ended with a firewalk at the reception, people cheering each other on in a grand parade of brave survival. A superpowered jolt of love and community. It was exhilarating for the firewalkers and for the viewers. This new ritual felt similar, leaving me stirred up, unsettled, awake. I had a million questions and was hungry for more.

Just as quickly, though, I hit a wall: I couldn't ask any of those questions. I wasn't invited, wasn't even supposed to be there in the first place.

I had been close enough to call out to Sari and Tierra or to respond to Flora, but I ran. I retreated. I didn't want to ask them about their community, or about what the monkeys were deciding, or what exactly was upsetting them. I did want answers, but I also wanted something I couldn't have at that particular moment, something that hadn't been offered to me, which was an invitation. So I hid on the periphery. I left.

I sat at the table and stared at the mountain of purses waiting for my needle. Low howls echoing through the trees taunted me. I ached to return to the community's gathering, but more than that, I wanted them to want me enough to bring me there.

30

We love all that you contribute. We love you for you. For who you truly are.

We believe in you. We trust you.

We want the best for you. The best for you is the best for all of us.

We know that our wastefulness as humans makes us destructive to the planet, to animals, to ourselves. We keep life simple at Atlas, and we look to our monkeys to guide us. They know the way.

Living in community diminishes excess. One thing for you to consider is your lifestyle. You can conserve with more diligence. Join us as we work toward radical usefulness and a waste-free experience.

Another thing to consider is your deathstyle. We can help you with that, too.

Together we'll learn from the animals in our care.

You will do anything for us, and we will do anything for you.

COMMENT FROM SARI

Let's forget about this for a few days. Zelda has everything worked out on her end, but we now have a ton of extra work, plus the inspection, plus dealing with Anna Beth. I know we can do it. We never fail to show up and honor the work at hand. I love you and can't wait until everything hard is behind us. –xoxoS.

COMMENT FROM TIERRA

I love you all.

COMMENT FROM DAGMAR

I love you, too. Nothing will be wasted.

31

The air was steamy at first light, much too hot to linger in bed even though I only slept an hour or so after finishing my sewing. I walked the path slowly on the way to breakfast, careful not to drop Zelda's pangolin project. My feet kicked up dozens of green midges that had hatched overnight, and I was chased by a quartet of the tiniest dragonflies I had ever seen.

As I approached the macaques, the empty Bonding Benches brought back flashes of the ritual. I silently asked the macaques if they were okay with what was going on in their precious home at Atlas. They seemed the same as always, chattering in small groups, loping around the structure, happily claiming shares of the breakfast bowls that Dagmar provided.

"Need any help?" I yelled out to Dagmar. I knew she would say no. She never let me help with breakfast, only later in the day.

"I'm almost done," Dagmar called back. "See you in a minute for a good coffee."

Walking into the dome with the plastic bin of purses, I swallowed a moment of panic. What if Sari confronted me about crashing her ritual? I couldn't decide if it was better to tell the truth, or if I should feign ignorance, just as they had to me when I originally asked about the shrieks and howls invading my dreams.

Now with the workday approaching, the whole thing seemed too confusing to discuss, and I wanted to chase it out of my mind. I mostly hoped Flora hadn't told her about seeing me, and that I could forget I knew anything. It wasn't my job to worry about the macaques at night. The women of Atlas had their own private, complicated lives, and that was as it should be.

However, as Sari and Tierra began inspecting my handiwork on the purse contraband project, cooing over my impercepti-ble seams, and as we ate our breakfast in the gentle light of the dawning day, I found myself craving more of their attention and pushing away the same stupid old feelings of being left out. These women were so close, the way they casually touched each other, finished another's sentences, knew the tiniest things like who needed the honey jar next. I could never wedge into this coterie, and it hurt to watch them while wanting it so much.

Sari called out to Dagmar as soon as she entered the dome. "You won't believe Zelda's pangolin bags, Dagmar. Jamie sews like a machine!"

Dagmar scrubbed up, slowly dried each finger of her hands on a linen towel, and then carefully inspected my work. "Jamie, you are the surgeon in the house. Beyond my wildest dreams."

"You really saved us with this one, sister," Sari added.

"Not a problem," I said. I stood at the counter and fastidiously balled a watermelon, digging deep into the sugary pulp. Tierra popped them in her mouth and crushed them against her pal-ate. Sari speared hers on a fork and sucked the juice out of each piece before eating it.

"Jamie, you have so many mosquito bites, sweet baby girl, you're torn up to heaven! What are you doing, sleeping on your roof?" Sari said, looking at my legs. "Are you using the salve?"

I panicked. Was this her way of confronting me about being outside so late last night?

"Yeah, they're still going to town on me."

"Because you are so sweet. Sweet-blooded, that's who they bite," she said. She stabbed another round. "Don't itch them, slap them. Itching spreads the toxin. Okay, Dagmar, I'm going to go get the little angels. Zelda will be here soon."

"I'm sorry about these pupsters. It's always hard," Dagmar said. She reached out and walked with Sari hand in hand like schoolgirls, or an old, married couple. "Let's go get them."

Tierra fiddled with the wild beautyberries she was straining to cook into jelly. I drank my coffee, praying the caffeine would make up for lack of sleep. I studied Tierra's face, looking for signs of exhaustion, or perhaps even hoping to catch her eye, but she was distracted and content with her project.

I was pleased they were happy with my work. But if I was good enough to sew for them, why couldn't they invite me to their nighttime rituals? Or at least tell me about it? Hadn't I already shown them that I was a loyal worker, a team player? Were all of those other people in attendance somehow more worthy? I had admittedly hoped that Tierra might even be fanning a special interest in me, but obviously not, as I had been excluded by her, too.

Perhaps it was too soon to receive such an invitation—though before I knew it my time at Atlas would be up. Perhaps, then, it was my own fault for being guarded. I needed to learn to let people in. The relationships these women had with each other ran deeper than simple coupledom. If I wanted what they had, I should learn from them. Be patient, aim higher, work on becoming more open and more vulnerable.

But I didn't know how to do anything more than I was already doing, or how soon I could hope for their inclusion or reciprocation. How patient I should be.

I could feel myself shutting down in self defeat. The opposite of what was needed.

Sari whistled for Tierra and me from the clearing outside the dome.

"Come say *ciao* to the pups before they go bye-bye with Zelda," Dagmar said. "She's on her way."

Outside, Sari was waiting with a large green animal carrier. She made an exaggerated pouty face. "I don't want to take them out. They're pretty stressed already."

Tierra squealed with delight. "Jamie, look at these exquisite wolf pups! Oh, Sari, can't we let Jamie hold the little fluff balls?"

"Oh, no, that's okay," I said. I briefly pictured the wolf rising from her stuck position in Sari's dome and felt my throat constrict. "Not if they're stressed."

Tierra ran her hands over the front of each carrier and blew air kisses. "Peace and love, may our paths cross again." She took my hand and brought it to the cage. The pups weren't interested in us, remaining coiled together, eyes open. Their buff-colored fur was almost as red as a fox, and their ears and eyes were comically outsize.

"How old are they, Sari?" I asked.

"Three months." She sighed. "A little early, but so it goes."

"They'll be fine," Dagmar said. "They'll grow fat and happy. The Bortnik family loves rare wolves and will treat them like royalty."

Sari huffed. "They are royalty. I know they'll love them, but I love my pack, too."

"Jamie—" Tierra tapped my shoulder "—we better get our gardening done. We have another long day of guarding the monkeys from workmen ahead of us."

Before going to the garden, Tierra led me on a hike along a rough, unfamiliar path, her long strides challenging me to keep up. We ended in a clearing where a cast-iron bathtub had been abandoned and filled with forest debris.

"Wow. I've been taking showers," I remarked, "but all of this time I could have been taking pine needle baths."

This caught her off guard. She let out a charming, breathy laugh. "Jamie! That's a ceremonial tub. If we swept the ground around it, you'd see stones in the shape of the symbol for woman. Lots of useful herbs are still thriving up here, too."

"What kinds of ceremonies?" I asked.

"We don't use it now. It was really a Vessel thing. Before Atlas, Sari and a woman from Oregon named Eva started a community to train traditional midwives. That's when I moved here, to study midwifery. But that's ancient herstory now."

She homed in on a big plant with leaves shaped like dinosaur tongues. "Comfrey, hello, my beautiful goddess! Jamie, hold out your arms. I'm going to load you up with leaves. Comfrey is a deep taproot plant, reaching down into the age-old nutrients of the forest ground and bringing them up into these incredible leaves. Look how green they are!"

"Okay, never eaten comfrey before, but it's huge. One leaf is an entire meal."

"We aren't going to eat it. We're going to feed it to the compost! The comfrey will enrichen the compost with ancient food. Such a magnificent transfer of energy!" She was ecstatic, and it made every step of the trip worth it.

We trudged back to our garden with arms full of thick leaves, periodically stopping to shake small beetles from our arms. I tried to picture how exactly a bathtub would be used in a ritual with no source of water nearby—and ended up imagining Tierra swimming in comfrey leaves. I wanted to ask her about the pergola and couldn't figure out how to do it without appearing nosy, but the bathtub reminded me not to jump to conclusions about things I found on the property. Atlas has had many evolutions, so artifacts are likely and not necessarily scary.

★ ★ ★

By ten, I thought I might pass out from the heat. It was intense, the kind that dissolves the hard lines between objects. I drank so much tea I started to worry that my sweat smelled of it, but Tierra assured me I was fine. I took a break to wash off and was so tired I fell asleep standing up in the shower house. Thumbnail-sized frogs woke me by hopping on my feet. I got dressed and went back to work.

Sari had disappeared with the pups and the box of pangolin bags. Dagmar fought with the construction crew. She was brutal, jutting her jaw like a mean dog when dressing them down about a few angle miscalculations in the fit of the special doors. Time and materials were wasted, and she let them know exactly how much she hated that. She also let them know other things in Danish. I was dying for a translation, but I knew better than to ask.

The men were unfocused. All day long, one or another would drift off toward the macaque enclosure, even though they were asked countless times to stay away. Dagmar caught one sticking his fingers in the cage and told him she hoped he contracted herpes B from the monkeys, and if so, that he should come back to Atlas so that she could do his autopsy.

"Let me learn from your mistakes. You obviously won't," she said.

"I'm not going to get herpes, my dude. I want to pet a monkey, not mate with it. What the hell you girls getting up to out here, anyway?" He laughed, but no one joined in.

"Dagmar," I said, "I know it's been a pain, but the new enclosure looks amazing. I can really see how grand it is, and side by side all of the improvements truly shine."

"It's true," she said, sighing. "It's going to be worth it."

"They're really almost done. And soon, when Sari has time, the three of us can think through where cameras can be positioned. Or maybe you already know what you want? We only have the one in the old enclosure, but we could be very creative with your new one."

"Oh, yes, that's already part of the plan," Dagmar assured me. "From the very beginning, the new enclosure was designed for broadcasting with several cameras."

We were interrupted by a construction worker yelling, which was quickly followed by a chorus of monkey shrieks.

"One of the monkeys just reached through the cage and snatched my sunglasses!" The man was outraged, his face crimson and wide-eyed as we approached him.

"Consequences. Your actions have consequences. You were too close," Dagmar spat. "Next time they will grab your eyes. Go back to work, and I will go make sure that the monkeys don't hurt themselves with your cheap plastic glasses."

Tierra and I made fruit and fennel gazpacho and bright vegetable wraps she called Sunrise Tacos at the end of the day. It was so hot we took turns ducking into the walk-in refrigerator to cool off, and at one point she put her whole head under the sink spigot and let the cool water run over her face.

"We really shouldn't tax the refrigerator like that," she lamented. "That old thing is a terrible electricity drain as it is. But I guess we waste that much or more trying to keep Monkey Island and Sari's dome cool. Which is ridiculous, actually. A ridiculous indulgence."

"I think it's because you can't let expensive equipment like that get moisture in the works. Humidity will wreck them." I carefully dried the blades of the blender with a cotton towel. "So it's probably smart. Maybe less wasteful in the long run?"

"Expensive equipment is right," she said. "What does that say about where we are putting our efforts?"

"Oh, I know. You should see the camera equipment my old boss had. I couldn't believe the cost." I thought I was commiserating with her. I had always hated the expenses, too, because

I couldn't afford the technology. I could've made more money editing videos, maybe even leave restaurant work, if I'd had a better computer.

But Tierra rolled her eyes at me. I tried to slide out of it.

"Is Flora doing okay? Do we think Sari will make it for dinner?"

"It's hard to say, really," she said, propping open the door with a bucket.

"These tacos are going to be amazing, Tierra. I hope you all never find out what kind of tacos I ate before moving here. Though there is this place—"

"You know what, Jamie? Why don't you come back with Dagmar at dinnertime? I can finish the dishes myself."

She looked more tired than annoyed, but her obvious displeasure wounded me more than I cared to admit. I wiped my hands on the towel and set it down on the counter before leaving her.

Dagmar, Tierra, and I ate in relative silence. I was distracted by swaths of pink light that poured through the skylights, dissolving like watercolor paint on paper. I figured I was feeling the effects of too much sun. I brought half of my dinner home, along with extra tea. Dagmar also gave me another tonic for my irritated mosquito bites, so my sole evening agenda was to apply the medicine and then to lie still in bed until I fell asleep.

I desperately needed rest, but as I walked past the cages, I couldn't resist the temptation of visiting the monkeys. I wanted to check in on Bee. Did she mind Mischa entering her enclosure? Did it stress or anger her, or did it feel like play? I also wondered if she would request more hair from me. I know Dagmar didn't believe in pets or playing favorites, but I felt a special bond with Bee's adorable pink face and glimmering teeth.

A few monkeys were walking around the enclosure, crawling over others like parents turning off lights throughout the house, but most of the animals were quiet on the upper row, cuddling in small groups, and some were already clustering in the shelters. Three or four of the monkeys looked similar to Bee, and I realized again how lousy I was at discerning who was who in the lowering light of dusk. Then I keyed in on her steel-colored fur and her determined gait, and she paused on the beam and gazed back. I imagined how shielded and safe they must feel falling asleep, cloistered amid their troop of friends.

"I hope you guys have a quiet sleep," I whispered. "They don't come around and bother you every night, do they? I wouldn't know. Someday I'll find out, maybe, if I'm lucky."

Ghost and Charlie loped over, listening intently. Charlie flapped his lips along with my voice.

"Who took the man's sunglasses? You can tell me. It was Cornelius again, wasn't it, with the old snatch-and-run? I know, I'm one to talk. Believe me, I'm not judging."

Voices rose and fell, and I heard a noise in the distance. It sounded like Tierra. Part of me wanted to go to her and apologize for anything I said that had clearly offended her, but I also immediately felt the red-hot shame of being caught out too late again. I wasn't sure how much time had passed. Would she tell Sari?

I recognized the prolonged metallic screech of the property gate opening. My shame slid into panic. Was it Cole, coming to check on me? Or were the ritual attendees arriving already?

I decided to wait and watch from behind the stand of azalea bushes between the Bonding Benches and my trailhead. That way, depending on who had arrived, I could decide if I wanted to quickly run home, return to the dome—or stay and watch.

The monkeys, at least, were chill and unperturbed. I tried to mimic them.

I expected the vehicle to park in the lot, but instead the sound of tires on gravel grew closer. Dagmar and Tierra emerged from Monkey Island to greet a black van that parked right in front of the building. I saw the silhouette of the driver—slight build, a crest of red hair, stork-like legs. It was Zelda, and Sari exited the passenger side. I assumed they were back from delivering the wolves to the buyers. The monkeys stirred a bit at the ruckus, but I stayed put.

The back doors of the van opened, and the women grappled with something heavy on a blue tarp. They clearly needed a cart or a gurney, because the middle bulk of their load was sagging, but they didn't get one. They moved slowly, with halting steps and misdirection. Probably Dagmar was pulling too hard while getting mad at the others; I could imagine how trying to move something with her would go.

Whatever it was, it was bigger than a macaque. Maybe it was several macaques? Or something larger, like a chimp or a gorilla? But no, Dagmar wasn't ready with the new enclosure yet, and they had always said Atlas was exclusively interested in hosting macaques.

On the other hand, I had also just learned that Sari was apparently a wolf breeder, despite the fact that Atlas loathed monkey breeders, so all assumptions were off.

But then, when they squared at the door threshold, they tilted the tarp toward me as they fumbled to navigate the entrance. On the plastic, illuminated by the light from inside the building, I saw a large animal lying on its side. The fur's coloration was as distinctive as it was unsettling: stripes, black against honey gold and white.

A tiger, its big white belly a moon, its powerful body pinned midleap against a cloudless blue sky of plastic.

Then they disappeared inside, Tierra hoisting the last corner of the tarp into the building. The door slammed.

It couldn't be an actual tiger. Wouldn't a large cat be transported in a cage, even if it was anesthetized? I must have seen something else. A big dog, perhaps, or another animal. I tried to remember what Dagmar told me about dental work, her surgery skills, and Zelda.

I waited. The sky was pastel green as the sun set all around me, calling more mosquitos and crickets to the stage. The monkeys curled into each other in their shelters, exactly in their rightful places.

The women finally came out of Monkey Island, this time with a very large box on a cart. Again, it took all of them to hoist it into the van. They stood there talking, vexing me with their secrets, and eventually walked off toward the dome.

Back in my cabin, I couldn't hear whether Zelda's van left or not, but I figured that she might be staying for a ritual. I again thought about attending, uninvited. I chugged tea and tried to calm down, but almost immediately I felt dizzy and groundless. My stomach roiled; my throat closed in. I thought I would be sick, and then I panicked, thinking my throat wouldn't open to let the contents of my stomach out. The idea of fighting nausea made me feel alien in my own body, and I cascaded into a sort of anxiety attack that I'd never felt before. My hands looked odd, like they were transforming into paws, and then back to hands again. I started to cry, at least I thought I did—I couldn't feel tears on my face. I wanted my old life back. I wanted my old self back, screwed up as it was. I wanted to go home, and yet I didn't know where that was yet.

I fell asleep and dreamed of my bare feet sinking deep into Sari's wolf pelt, and then I felt the fur breathing under my feet, coming alive, rising up, bones and sinew whole again, and the wolf twisted her neck and sank her gleaming teeth into the anklet monitor, shearing it off and narrowly missing the meat of my leg.

32

Sari sacrificed our supper again. We gave up panfried tofu, sesame noodles, and shaved vegetables, to which she added the fruit we had precut for breakfast and a hefty bag of tart green apples.

Down at the monkey enclosure, Tierra cried silently. We had worked well together all day, which was a huge relief after the tensions of late, but I knew she had been looking forward to a peaceful meal. I reached for her hand and noticed her wrists were free of bracelets. She laced her fingers into mine. Dagmar's face was solid and inscrutable as we sat on the bench.

The macaques assembled. They knew a treat had arrived. Sari's voice was full of gravel, as though she was exhaling after holding her breath much too long.

"Tonight, we make this sacrifice to remind us of the greatest sacrifice. We must always be ready to give and then give more. There is little reason for humanity to go on. Every sign from the planet tells us so. Our only hope is service to these monkeys so that they teach us, and more importantly so they will live on and heal the planet where we have failed. We offer this humble food to the monkeys of Atlas, and tonight we dedicate our fast to them. Blessed be the monkeys of Atlas."

"Blessed be the monkeys of Atlas," we echoed.

We watched them feast. I don't think I felt anything except flat and empty inside. Nora-Nora-Nora's red head was easy to spot, and I saw that she nabbed sliced mango. Odin and Henri each claimed handfuls of noodles and crammed too much into their faces at once. River took two apples to the top of the climbing gym, quickly ate some of the flesh and then pelted the rest like rocks in our direction. The cores bounced off the fence with wet thuds. I could smell them and feel the sting their tart juice would have left on the back of my tongue.

Each of the women wandered off separately when it was over, evaporating like steam, leaving me alone on a Bonding Bench. The tiger in Monkey Island had hovered in my thoughts all day, an unspoken mystery.

Bee and Stella came near. I whispered, "I don't know what's in there, friends, do you? Dagmar and Sari keep that place completely secure. I'm sure it was dental work, right? The tiger was here for a procedure and left the same day. I wish you could tell me what's going on."

The monkeys were quiet, watching me. A flash of heat lightning cut through the sky as I left to follow my path home.

Except for the macaque enclosure, Monkey Island was the only building on Atlas that was locked. I didn't want to intrude on Dagmar's space, but I couldn't help but think it wouldn't hurt anyone if I took one small peek, just to set my mind at ease about Zelda's delivery. I had always wanted to know how to pick locks. Growing up, my brother could almost always wiggle back into one of our apartments when a landlord had changed the locks after our mom was late on rent, but I had never learned. Once again, I had failed to develop the survival skills I wanted to possess, failed to learn anything at all from Jason before he disappeared.

I was relieved to close the door to my own house, even though I knew without tea I would be miserably hungry all night. I reached into my pocket for my daily stone, gratified beyond measure to be one day closer to freedom from my anklet, but there was no place to put it.

Someone had confiscated my collection plate and the entire pile of rocks.

33

"Jamie, there you are! Sister, we need your help!"

Sari pounced as soon as I entered the dome. The vibe was frenetic, dirty dishes uncharacteristically lined the counter, and a large wire cage was randomly in the middle of the floor. Tierra wordlessly handed me a cup of coffee and rested her head on my shoulder for just a moment, leaving behind the scent of sandalwood and honey. I sensed she was tired or perhaps intentionally slow and heavy to serve as a counterweight to Sari, who was far from her usual languid morning self. She let me take one sip of coffee—nowhere near enough to catch up—and then said, "Jamie, I need to tell you some things, some very important, private things, and I really need your help. Can I count on your help?"

"Of course. No question." I flushed, trying to be cool. "What's up?"

"Well, Atlas is experiencing some growing pains right now. Some stresses. They are good stresses, the kind that come with opportunity and well, growth, you know?"

"Gotcha." Maybe I read her first question wrong. Her mood was weird. She was wringing her hands and scanning the room. I noticed Tierra slip out of the dome without saying a word. Based on past experience, I began to worry that Sari was about to fire me.

"It's like we are preparing for Atlas's true birth, Jamie! We need to boil water, we need to build a cradle, we need to reduce disruption, we need to do a lot of things."

Relief washed over me, and I felt suddenly solid again. Sari needed my help. I was more than ready to dig in.

She twisted her hair into a loose bun and secured it with a bobby pin from her pocket. She looked like an art nouveau advertisement selling me absinthe. "Unfortunately, right now we have arrows coming at us from every direction and we can't do what we need to do. It's going to be okay. It really is. Better than okay. But we need some help right now, and we think you can be that help."

"Of course. Anything. Are you talking about the website?"

"No." Sari sat back and thought for a moment. "Not exactly. Not yet. But okay, just bear with me here. We have a tiger here at Atlas. The tiger's name is Chaanda and she arrived yesterday. Chaanda belongs to a friend who needs a favor from us. Who deserves a favor from us."

"I don't understand. Is the new enclosure going to be for tigers?" I said brightly, trying to sound as though a large apex predator was the most perfectly normal problem to address, and also trying to feign surprise about its existence in the first place.

"No, no." Sari shook her head, disappointed in my question. "We would never have a tiger next to the monkeys. Of course, Chaanda is dead. Why would we have a live tiger here?"

I wanted to say *well, why would you have a dead one?*

I felt like I was back in the sheriff's interrogation room after they linked me to the Tiki Hut incident. I couldn't process the information fast enough. I had a million questions, but I didn't know how much each question would end up revealing, and Sari was speaking too inexactly. She continued so rapidly and so intensely that I feared she might be on some sort of speed.

"Chaanda died after a beautiful life. And her owner sent her off to be cremated. Our friend manages the cremations of large animals for zoos and whatnot. But sometimes that is very wasteful! Especially when a massive beast is so valuable and precious. And our friend wants the beautiful fur preserved, and we know other people will benefit from the medicine in Chaanda's bones, and Atlas owes our friend a favor. So instead of cremating Chaanda, Dagmar will preserve her, but the timing is very stressful because we have an inspection coming soon, can you believe it, probably tomorrow, and we need to finish today."

Sari paused for a moment to see my reaction. I didn't want to say anything definitive, although in truth I was agog, and also a bit miffed she kept saying *our friend* when she clearly was referring to Zelda. "When you say 'preserved,' what exactly do you mean?"

"Just the taxidermy. Saving the bones for medicine. That sort of thing. Dagmar is a pro. It's a spiritual practice of communion with an animal when done correctly, actually."

I was dubious, but decided to accept her rationale at face value for now. I said, "Of course, I'm on it. I can clean for the inspection or handle the macaques' daily needs so Dagmar can get out of the weeds. Whatever!" I hoped she read between the lines: I was happy to care for the monkeys and free up Dagmar, but that I was in no way interested in learning taxidermy.

"Check in with Dagmar. She'll guide you. I would do it myself if I could, but that's the other problem."

"What do you mean?"

"Tierra and I have to leave. Today. We're taking Flora to a hospital. And we're canceling volunteer time for a few days. Everything is just crashing in at once and that's why I have to ask you to step up. Plus, Jamie, you are ready to do more. I don't want to have secrets from you. I know it's been very confusing here lately, and I don't like that." She looked at me earnestly. "I want to be able to trust you with everything going on, and I think you are ready for that, too."

Sari finally took a breath, fluttering her eyes closed for the briefest of moments after she exhaled. I wanted to encourage her to slow down for a minute more, but I understood why she couldn't. Flora's health was rapidly deteriorating. I felt ashamed of my initial resistance about the tiger.

"Sari, of course, please count on me. The most important thing is Flora. If Flora needs to go to the hospital, then go. We'll cover everything else."

"You are a blessing. I knew you needed to be here with us. So listen now, most importantly, my sister is arriving today. Soon. She is very dramatic and also very problematic. Whatever she says or asks, just say you don't know. Which is the truth."

"Okay? Yeah, that's for sure. Got it." Flora must be in critical shape if Anna Beth was here and they were going to a hospital. Sari had delivered a huge flood of bad news, but it only made me listen closer. It meant everything to hear Sari express so much trust in me.

"Just try to stay away from her. Dagmar knows how to deal with her—she's tried to shut us down before, long story—but we don't know how it's going to go. Just, ugh, she's very toxic, so please stay away. Put up an energy shield and follow Dagmar's lead. We did a protective ritual this morning, so that should help. You weren't up yet, or we would have included you."

"Awesome, thank you." I tried to conceal my disappointment.

"And you're so very smart. If you come up with better ideas to fix all of this mess, please pipe up. Elegant solutions are most welcome." Sari clasped her hands and bowed toward me.

"I'll be sending good thoughts to Flora. And to you."

"Also, I'm sure Monkey Island needs to be scrubbed. It's all a little ridiculous. Inspections are fine, just part of the business, and we always get good marks because we take excellent care of our macaques, but they are still stressful. Tierra in particular hates them because they are so intrusive."

"Don't worry. I know all about inspections." I had done many a scramble in my waitress days to scour fryers, degrease sinks, ditch expired food. This couldn't be much different. It was my time to shine.

"Dagmar will show you what needs to be done." Sari kept talking as she breezed out the door, leaving me half-waving from the table.

Then, a moment later, she trotted back in and embraced me ferociously. She held me firmly and said directly in my ear, "You are one of us, Jamie. I know you don't know that in your heart yet, but you are. This is just how life is. Sometimes nothing is happening on the surface but when it's ready, it all tumbles out at the same time. Trust that you will have big rewards coming soon."

She let go and began walking away, leaving me stunned.

"Okay, *ciao*, Jamie, and thank you, thank you, little sister."

Sari blew kisses. The screen door slammed shut behind her.

34

I was already on my way to Dagmar when she whistled from just outside Monkey Island. The monkeys alerted, little busybodies that they were.

Dagmar's hair was secured under a white bandanna upon which rested safety glasses. She was wearing a lab coat and knee-high rubber boots.

"Jamie, I need you to stay near the gate at the picnic table just off the parking lot. You'll be able to hear an auto coming on the gravel road. There's a sign on the gate that says we are closed, so anyone should see that, turn around, and go without our intervention."

"What do you want me to do if I see someone?"

"Just watch them leave and then come tell me who it was and what you saw. And if anyone comes in anyway, don't confront them, but run to get me. I'll be here. Pound on the door."

Dagmar took a deep breath of finality and resolve, and I went to my station with one jar of tea and one jar of water.

I felt bad that there was so much physical work to be done, but at the very least I wanted to be a good guardian. I felt naturally protective of Atlas after my weeks here. I wanted to stay and dig in more. On any other day, this picnic table in the parking lot would be a charming hangout spot that I had never noticed, tucked under a majestic oak tree whose gnarled branches fanned down like tentacles to create a mossy alcove. I don't know why I had never come out to sit under the canopy of the old tree before. Sometimes I worried I walked through my days in a fog without noticing the beauty all around me.

I was just getting started at Atlas, and now it sounded as though I might be able to stay longer. But until my anklet was off and my case was resolved it felt like any minute, Cole could show up, violate me for any number of reasons, and take me to a jail, where I would no doubt moon under fluorescent lights bemoaning this lost Eden with its troop of friendly simian neighbors.

I pledged to help them get it together here. I knew I could be an organizational asset and a marketing assistant for Sari if she could just find the time to work with me. I hated seeing her so stressed and I wanted to be part of the team that moved in concert to aid her. They weren't perfect, but I agreed with Sari that Atlas had unlimited potential.

I held the sweating glass jar to my face, letting the merciful cool steady me. Dagmar appeared in the parking lot, pushing a large wheelbarrow. Growing restless, I trotted over to check in with her. Her hands and lab coat were covered with blood, and the cart was loaded with full trash bags. I would have helped, but she walked by me without saying a word and headed for the lake.

Now on top of worrying about Flora, I needed to keep an eye out to make sure Dagmar wouldn't be pulled into a death roll by an alligator lunging for tiger meat.

I went back to the picnic table and tried to wrap my head around the tiger situation. Exotics were highly regulated, and to prevent unlicensed trade, I knew an animal like Chaanda must have a paper trail documenting its life, from birth to death to the final disposition of her remains. I wanted to know who originally owned Chaanda and who brought it to Zelda to be cremated. I thought about Sari's sadness at losing her red wolf cubs, and Dagmar's sewing project, and Zelda's black van. I wondered if Dagmar thought of the tiger remains as a spiritual sacrifice to the alligators, or as protein, or simply waste in need of disposal.

Or maybe Dagmar wasn't going to the alligators at all. Maybe she was headed for the pergola.

Then I thought of the midnight monkey cage ritual. I didn't understand the spiritual reasons Sari assigned to a lot of what she did, but I could see how entering the monkey enclosure could appeal to some. Exiting unscathed would probably feel like cheating death, and that's a high that's chock full of endorphins. I wondered if, in a way, surviving it was like proof of one's faith and protection from a higher power. Feeding the alligators might be like that, too.

But what about the people in the audience? Were they waiting their turn? I wanted to know what they did when someone was bitten or otherwise attacked. Did they think of that as a sacrifice as well?

Uselessly trapped in a cycle of dark thoughts, I decided that when Dagmar returned from the lake, I would leave my post—where nothing was happening at all—and insist on cleaning. Or I would do what Tierra did on a difficult day. She would make tea, probably. And bake something. A custard pie with a honey brittle garnish. I could do that.

Just as I was thinking through the possibilities, a dark vehicle turned in off the main road, the driveway gravel churning as the car approached the gate. I panicked, picturing Dagmar down at the lake, her hand inches away from the snap of a bloodthirsty alligator.

The driver of the sedan laid on the brakes and blasted the horn several times. As instructed, I stayed put. Then a woman with ponytailed blond hair exited the car, leaving it running, and stood at the gate, tugging it open.

"Sari, I know you're somewhere on this property and I'm coming in. I want to talk to you," she yelled.

Anna Beth. I prayed for her to leave. She sounded furious. I wasn't sure if I should get Dagmar from the lake or not.

Anna Beth went back to her car and then pulled into the parking lot. Dagmar came running from the lake, without the wheelbarrow and without her lab coat. I heard the monkeys begin to howl faintly in the distance.

Dagmar joined me and we walked toward Anna Beth's car. She climbed out and pointed a manicured finger at Dagmar. She was slightly shorter and more pale than Sari, but their faces mirrored each other, and both sisters had the same gunmetal eyes framed by waves of blond hair.

"I'm going to talk with Sari. Don't even try to stop me."

"I'm not going to stop you, but Sari and Flora are not here," Dagmar said.

"I want to talk to Sari before seeing my mother, but if you won't let me in, I will ransack all of Sari's shacks on my family's property, one by one, until I find her."

"Anna Beth, be my guest, but neither of them are here. You would be wasting your time." Dagmar's voice was low and monotonous, like she was trying to talk a child off a high tree limb. "I'm telling you the absolute truth. They left this morning at about nine for the hospital, and she has not texted me an update. She was headed to Gainesville to the university hospital, because she was not happy with the smaller local ones in the county."

"Why is she not answering her phone?"

"I don't know. You know how she is. She's probably very busy either driving or looking after your mom, or probably they are waiting, and she will text us when she knows what to say. You can go to them, or you can wait in Flora's house for word from Sari."

Anna Beth eyed me warily. I nodded with solemnity.

Dagmar continued. "Anna Beth, I know this is a very challenging situation and I just want you to know, you have my deepest sympathy."

"Oh, you are full of horse crap," Anna Beth said. "You only care about protecting Sari and your monkeys. Well, let me remind you—this property is as much mine as it is Sari's, which makes it a hell of a lot more mine than yours, and the way you all have tricked an old woman into letting you take over her acreage with your diseased monkey cult is criminal. You can't lock me out of my family's estate."

"Now, please don't make drama like this again," Dagmar said firmly. Then she softened. "But Anna Beth, it's more important that you don't waste your time. Go to your mother. That's what you want. Isn't that what is more important? Now, do you know how to get to Gainesville?"

Anna Beth tilted her head back and howled. The monkeys screamed back, like a distant echo from a mountain. "Do I know how to get to Gainesville? I grew up here! But if she told you to tell me she went to Gainesville, that probably means she went to Orlando and I'll be two hours in the wrong direction."

Dagmar said nothing.

"I swear to God, if you are lying, I am coming for you two personally." She scowled and started toward her car, but then turned back around. "She better be at a hospital, or else I will have a sheriff and a warrant here ASAP, and I will toss this entire ramshackle commune and you will lose every license and permit and roof and meal you ever had."

"I promise you, your mother is not here," Dagmar said.

Anna Beth slapped a mosquito on her wrist, flicked it away, and looked at me. All I could see was Sari. I shrugged and shook my head. I wanted to defend Dagmar, or at least to echo her assurances, but I didn't want to say the wrong thing.

Anna Beth glared and pointed her finger at me. "Oh, aren't

you precious? I knew who you were the minute I saw you. Don't think I don't. Trash. Complete trash. And you are all in trouble, every one of you."

Anna Beth walked slowly to her car, but even with her back turned I could feel her rage. She drove away in a cloud of dust and pollen from the dirt road. Her words replayed in my mind and I shivered like the devil was on my back. Dagmar, on the other hand, was upbeat.

"It's good we got that out of the way." She waved as she headed back toward the lake path. "Could have been much worse!"

I spent the rest of the day taking care of the macaques. Dagmar took one more disgusting load to the lake and then holed up in Monkey Island, presumably cleaning the pelt.

The entire campus of Atlas was mine. The monkeys were all mine. I chatted with them, gave them food puzzles through the drawers in the lockout area, and scrubbed their water troughs. I sang folk songs and they gathered like preschoolers. Bee and Stella kept as close to me as they could, scrutinizing my movements and reaching their paws through the enclosure.

"Okay, Bee, here you go, only because no one is looking." I plucked a hair from my head and extended my hand toward hers. She carefully pinched it between two fingers and then did a few hops and twirled away.

Curious Georgia O'Keeffe bustled back and forth to the sliding drawer checking for new puzzles, and Charlie banged a bowl like a drum.

I missed Tierra. When I was exhausted or beat, she would know to swoop in with a cold glass of sun tea or an ice pack against the nape of my neck. I missed the electric surge I felt in her company. The way I tracked her movements and craved her touch. I planned to take similar care of her upon her return.

★ ★ ★

I knocked on the door to Monkey Island late in the afternoon and told Dagmar I was going to cook dinner. She didn't answer me, but she drifted up to the dome quite a bit later looking haggard and dazed. I gave her one of Tierra's anise blends to sip, and then she watched me melt onions, red peppers, and garlic into olive oil; add basil, capers and fat olives to the sauce; and then stir in drained pasta.

"Sublime," Dagmar mumbled, pushing more food in her mouth. She groaned, her eyes half-closed and her head lowered over her dish.

"I can help," I said. "If you have more to do tonight."

Dagmar said, "This was the biggest help in the entire world. I needed this. Thank you."

I knew my food was nothing special compared to Tierra's vegan gourmet creations. Dagmar had been ravenous from physical work. Anything would have tasted good to her. Still, I felt proud to have fed her.

Anna Beth had been so ugly to us, and it made me feel instinctually protective of Dagmar. Of Sari. Of Atlas. They tried so hard. How dare Anna Beth attack us. How dare she call me trash. Not that I wasn't used to it. I'm sure she thought of me as an untrustworthy, infamous criminal. But who was she to bring that all up here?

No wonder Sari was trying to take care of Flora without Anna Beth's intrusion.

"Dagmar, are we safe to go to sleep tonight?"

"I think so. She probably will stay at Flora's house. Sari gave a heads-up to the sheriff that we're being hassled, so that's good. The sheriff knows Flora and Sari, and they also know Anna Beth is the troublemaker Prodigal Daughter from Missouri. They won't come out here with her unless she somehow gets a judge's order or something like that."

Dagmar closed her eyes for a moment. "We've got some more

maintenance and recordkeeping to do tomorrow, but it will be easy. We'll give oysters to the macaques so we can clean the freezer, too. Keep it simple."

"Of course, whatever you want. I'll be here early."

A man's voice boomed from outside the door.

"Hello, hello? Anybody home?"

"Oh, hell no," I whispered, my heart racing. "Would an inspector come this late?"

The door swung open swiftly, but it wasn't the inspector.

Cole plowed into the dome and then loudly knocked on the kitchen counter. "Surprise check-in, Jamie. Oh, look at my most excellent timing. Dinner smells great!"

I blanched and stammered. Cole clearly knew he had disarmed me with his impromptu visit, and he strutted a bit as he joined us at the table, enjoying it. Then he saw my face and softened.

"Don't worry. I was out in this area and thought I'd kill two birds with one stone. Nothing to worry about."

"Please join us for supper. Jamie made an excellent dish," Dagmar said.

"Don't mind if I do."

I fixed Cole a big bowl of pasta. Dagmar said, "Sari is not available right now. She's actually out of town."

Cole stabbed a mound of noodles and shoved as much as he could into his mouth, biting and letting the loose ends fall while he hovered over the dish. He nodded in appreciation as he chewed. "This is fantastic, Jamie. I'm really impressed. It's hitting just right."

"It's only pasta." I scrubbed my hands and started cleaning the kitchen, suddenly aware of how filthy and sweaty I was, and how dirty the kitchen looked. I wondered if Dagmar was as worried as I was about her tiger butchery.

"We're just super busy as you can see, but I like being busy. I like taking care of the monkeys. It's good work. There's always something to be done." I prattled on, trying to sound upbeat. I figured he would want to know that I was productive and reformed, though I resented how easily I slid into the role of happy prisoner to garner his favor.

"Sounds like you are hitting all the benchmarks. Have you been off the property at all? Broken curfew? Disobeyed any rules?"

"No, of course not." I tried to avoid thinking about my late-night wanderings. I tried to avoid thinking about the ritual, the pangolin, the tiger. If any of it was on my mind, I might send out a tell. Then a new thought flooded my brain—Cole, via the anklet monitor, already knew about everything and was at Atlas to bust me.

Dagmar said, "I'm afraid we give her a very boring life here, Cole. It's not Jacksonville with the big city lights."

Cole laughed. "As if."

I channeled all my attention into a board of strawberries on the counter, dicing them to create a fruity dessert for Cole. I calmed myself. Cole wouldn't let me wield a sharp chef's knife if he was about to give me bad news. And he wouldn't have come alone to Atlas by himself if he thought anything unscrupulous was going on.

"What's it like to work for Sari?" Cole asked.

"She's amazing! What they all have built here is admirable and inspiring." I nodded to Dagmar.

"You like the monkeys and everything?" Cole dug into the yogurt parfait I gave him. From across the table, Dagmar got up and spontaneously trotted out of the building. I felt a moment of panic about handling Cole alone, but then I realized Dagmar was probably locking down her taxidermy project.

"I love them! I meditate with them, too. It's surprisingly calming, the way they hang out with together. They groom each other, and they feed each other—which I didn't expect. I thought they'd fight more or something. I've even learned all of their names, and it feels meaningful to take care of them. Honestly, it's the best job I've ever had."

He nodded, clearly more interested in the nuts, granola, and honey in his parfait. I had made a good call.

"I've learned a lot about what they've been through before coming here, and it's really heartbreaking, and amazing that Atlas exists. I so feel lucky to be here, Cole, and I promise I'm making the most of it."

"I think you sure are. Sounds like you might want to stay after your release date."

"That would be awesome!" I said it without thinking, instantly regretting the way I had opened my mouth. I shouldn't have gone on like that about the monkeys, because if he wanted to go visit them, he would be dangerously close to the tiger (or whatever remained of it) in the Monkey Island building. I also probably shouldn't have sounded so happy. I should have taken the opportunity to talk about lessons learned and about my plans to be a better citizen after Atlas. I definitely shouldn't have spoken to Cole about living here, because that's a conversation for Sari first.

"In that case, maybe I'll get a promotion for making such a perfect placement, so thank you very much for that. Sounds like we got us a win-win."

Just as I was about to agree, Dagmar bounced back into the dome. She was carrying a small white paper bag.

"Well, unless you have questions for me, let me get you to sign this screen on my tablet confirming we chatted today, and I'll leave you to your evening. Good job, Jamie."

I was shocked and relieved that he was leaving so soon. We walked out of the dome, and Dagmar said she would escort him to his car. It was a good feeling, like leaving a cinema after a first date or walking home after the first day of school.

I cleaned the dome and waited to see if Dagmar would return. Eventually she did, grabbing a banana before heading home.

"My, what a cozy little dinner," she said scornfully. "You did a good job flirting with him to keep him away from Monkey Island. Whatever it takes, I guess."

35

The next day came fast. I hurried to greet my monkeys. Work needed to be done, and we were staring down at a long day with no outside help.

I worked without resting until lunch, which I spent on a Bonding Bench watching the monkeys eat. Oysters were a prize, for them and for me. It meant everything to see them happy. Even though I was a late bloomer, I was grateful to know the pricelessness of friendship with animals. I had spent so much time feeling alone in the world, when all along I could have been offering care and companionship to a lonesome pet or wild creature in need.

I would never make that mistake again. I could see myself coming home in my new life to a kitten or taking a dog on long beach walks. Maybe a scruffy, short-legged mutt. Maybe an aging golden retriever with stringy yellow hair that I could groom.

Or I could just stay at Atlas. I was still riding high after surviving Anna Beth and Cole in one gruesome day, and I had more energy running through my veins than I had felt in weeks. All the possibilities in the world were at my feet. Dagmar seemed better rested, too, and it was a great relief to see that her testy mood from the previous day had been replaced with efficiency and stoic resolve as we took on our chores.

Oysters, I learned, were not a simple meal for the macaques. After they ate, we had the laborious task of luring all the monkeys to one side of the cage and using a movable fence to isolate them so that we could recover every shell and rock from the opposite side, and then reversing the process to clean the other. The monkeys yelled at us and shook the cage as we swept their space, making me feel like a soccer star or a gladiator in the Coliseum. It felt momentous for Dagmar to allow me to assist her with a higher-level job, but she didn't make a big deal about it, so I didn't either.

"Dagmar, I can finish up if you have something else you need to do," I said, knowing the shells and stones needed to be scrubbed and stowed away. I had no idea how much progress she had made on her tiger, or how many other jobs she wanted us to do while Sari was gone.

"No, we're making a swift go of it," she said. Without mapping it out, we had divided the area into quadrants and managed to efficiently split the workload, and we did the same with the rocks. "You know, you are a very good worker, Jamie. No one works harder. I really do appreciate you."

After the oyster activity, we went to the dome smelling like rotting seaweed, rubber gloves, and strong disinfectant. We made bread and peanut butter for ourselves. I drowned mine with honey and blueberries; Dagmar added neatly sliced bananas to hers. She laughed at my concoction.

"Don't knock it until you try it," I said. "This is how we ate them growing up. We called it a Chunky Monkey."

"I'm familiar. You know, I didn't even have peanut butter

until moving to the States. Chunky Monkey," Dagmar said. "Sometimes English is a delight."

I stirred lemon and honey into the sun tea, but it didn't taste as good as Tierra's. I cleaned the counters and rinsed Tierra's sprouts. As dusk fell, the candles on the table held on and we stayed late, Dagmar playing DJ, me reading old hippie cookbooks and textbooks from the Vessel era.

"Dagmar, this midwifery book is really intriguing. Do you think I can borrow it if I promise to bring it back?"

"You can have anything you see at Atlas, but promise me you'll read other books, too. I have many you can borrow. Birth is far from the most important concern for humans right now. Birth is the one thing we're good at. I'm also wondering if you would benefit from a painkiller. It's been a long day."

I thought for a second. The muscles in my back and shoulders were burning, which was nothing new. The prospect of a good night's sleep, however, sounded heavenly. "Yeah, that would be great."

Dagmar reached into one of her many pockets and palmed a small brown bottle. "Under your tongue," she said, and when I complied, she released three cold drops, then administered the same to herself.

"Dagmar, do you think Sari and Tierra will be back tonight? If she is going to hold another protection ritual when they return, I'd really like to be included. If possible." I didn't understand it, but I wanted desperately, in a way I had never wanted before, to uncover anything holy and intentional and communal the group designed.

"I am really happy to hear that, Jamie. I don't know when they'll be back. Anna Beth went to Shands in Gainesville and figured out that Sari wasn't there, so Anna Beth came back to town and will probably be following through on her threat to file a missing person report on Flora. We'll know more tomorrow."

"A missing person?"

Dagmar looked at me. "It's okay, don't worry. We expected this."

"If they aren't in Gainesville, where are Sari, Tierra, and Flora?"

"They are taking care of Flora, exactly as we said. Now, the monkeys need quiet so they can get to sleep, and so do we." Dagmar offered me her hand to help me stand up. "We are not going to worry about anything. It's all okay now. We couldn't have survived this week without you. You are not 'trash,' Jamie. You are glorious. We are so glad you are one of us."

As I stood up my head spun. Without Dagmar bracing me, it would have been a struggle to walk out of the dome, my legs slow to answer my brain's commands, my path erratic as a sidewinder's. The air outside the dome smelled like honeysuckle, and when I looked to the sky, I saw it was later than I thought. The stars were close overhead, and they looked like they had burst open like honeysuckle blooms, too. I turned to ask Dagmar if she also saw this beautiful, odd coincidence, but she had vanished.

When I passed the macaques, I heard Nora-Nora-Nora call out to me. *Jamie? Jamie! Jamie, are you okay? Dagmar should have walked you home. Where is she? Where did she go?*

"It's okay, Nora-Nora-Nora, I'm fine," I slurred. "I'm a million percent fine."

36

I woke with a start to find a heavy, black snake crossing the top of the quilt at the foot of my bed. Her grotesque silhouette pulled against the fabric—at least four feet of oily slither—and I involuntarily scrambled backward in my bed. She darted down the other side, and then just as quickly a dozen smaller snakes followed like ducklings, up and over and out through a crevice at the door in a cursed parade.

I sucked in a breath and reminded myself she was a safe snake, a danger only to rodents, but that knowledge couldn't undo my revulsion.

"Did you see that, Cole?" I asked my anklet, my heart still beating its way outside my throat. I was reminded of waking up from nightmares as a kid and always immediately wanting to wake Jason. I would throw my flip-flops at him from across the room so that he would silently wave or give a shaka sign to let me know everything was okay.

I shook out my clothes and shoes before putting them on and took a look around the cabin for more evidence of snakes. Everything looked suspect, a perfect nest for a mama snake or any of her left-behind children, but at least the morning was damp and slightly cooler than usual.

I stopped for a minute to chat with the monkeys. "Snakes in my bed this morning, kiddos. You ever have those just walk across your feet in there?"

I saw a few discarded oyster shells we had missed and remembered the monkeys' deft rock smashing skills. Is that what they would do to a snake, split it like an oyster?

I had researched macaques a little before arriving, but without context I hadn't retained much. I still had tons of questions, but I only wanted to bother Dagmar so much. I definitely planned to improve Sari's website with more content about the macaques' days, and the details about each one, like their oyster techniques and their friendship groups. People who couldn't volunteer would love to read that sort of detail, and certainly watch the livestreamed videos. I was determined to put Atlas's equipment to use when Sari was able to work again.

Today, I would do whatever Dagmar needed: cook, watch the parking lot for the inspector or Anna Beth, feed the animals, whatever. First, though, I needed something hearty for breakfast, because I was famished.

I opened the dome door feeling as though I owned the whole place, only to find I was the last to arrive. The table was already full of coffee mugs, bowls of fruit and bread, and pots of jam, Tierra and Dagmar chatting above a Cat Power playlist running in the background, and Sari holding Dagmar's hand palm up, like she was massaging it or assessing it for omens.

My heart leapt to see Tierra. Sari, too, of course, but it was Tierra whose eyes I sought, Tierra whose demeanor I tried to read.

"Yay, Jamie is up!" Sari exclaimed.

"Jamie!" cheered Tierra.

"*God Morgen*, Jamie," Dagmar said. She sounded as though

nothing terrible had ever happened to her, as though stress had never even crossed her shoulders.

"Get in here for some coffee, baby love," said Tierra.

"Jamie! We were just learning what a superstar you were while we were gone," Sari said. She popped up to give me a warm embrace and then led me by the waist to the table. "We can't tell you how pleased that makes us."

"Truly good, our best girl," cooed Tierra.

"Oh, good. I'm so glad. But of course, I'll do anything for y'all," I said, though I knew I had done nothing special in their absence. I wasn't particularly proud of sitting in the parking lot or making pasta, but if they were happy to see me, I would accept it.

Tierra's head was freshly shaved, and Sari was wearing a bright floral sundress. They seemed rested and undistracted. Flora must be doing better. What a massive relief. It looked like their rituals, odd as they may have been, did Flora some good, not to mention protecting her—and us—from Anna Beth's negativity. I wondered if it was like the women had been saying, that by facing her death, Flora had been adding quality to her life. Such an interesting woman, so welcoming and protective, and I admired her for handling her last years on her own terms. I had a lot to learn from her.

Sari paced and stretched. "Jamie, I have to go in just one minute to meet with my sister at Flora's house. But we want to invite you to join us tomorrow—some friends of Atlas will be there too—to the house for a little circle. We absolutely want you to come."

"We insist, actually," Dagmar said buoyantly.

"We think you'll really get a lot out of it." Tierra handed me a big glass of sun tea, even though I hadn't finished my coffee yet. "We think you'll love being with the community."

"Oh my gosh. I would love to, thank you." I was practically swooning, I was so happy, and I for once didn't even try to hide my elation. I wondered if after gathering at the house they would then go to the monkey enclosures, or if it would be a circle like the one we had held celebrating Dagmar's salves. Either way, I had been invited at long last.

"It's basically a white party," Sari said. "We're all going to only wear white. If you don't have something..."

"Oh, I don't, no way."

"...that's okay, I have dresses I can share with you. Don't worry about your shoes. We all slip them off anyway. It's going to be perfect!"

Then my heart plummeted. "Oh, but I can't. Flora's house is not in my monitor-approved zone. I can only go as far as the garden."

"Well, shoot, right, we should have remembered that thingie," Sari said. "You should be done with it by now anyway."

"Can we move it to the dome? I'm worried we need the bigger space, anyway," said Tierra.

"Much more practical," Dagmar agreed.

"Maybe, but I'm hesitating because Flora asked for the house. You know, let's just call Cole. I actually have to call him anyway," Sari said.

Tierra shrugged. "I bet he can adjust it from his office. It's probably easy. And if not, we can adapt from there."

"I don't want to be any trouble. You have enough on your plate." But I did want to be trouble, or at least I wanted the problem resolved. Their reassuring nods, Sari's upbeat tone, it all tumbled inside my throat, threatening to close it in with choked-back tears.

"You are never a trouble. If Cole can't do it, we'll move over here, but if we can, we'll meet at the house. Beautiful!" Sari sang, and we all took a deep breath with her. "I might not see you all until then, so love to you and you and you, and I will see you all tomorrow, sweet lovelies."

Sari blew me a kiss, then nodded to Dagmar to follow her out the door. Everyone floated off like balloons and it wasn't until I was at the macaque enclosure, watching them eat mounds of raw kale and piles of peanuts, that I was floored with questions, and that I remembered I didn't tell anyone my snake story at breakfast, and I realized I needed to squeeze in time to wash my bed linens. Nothing mattered, though, not the day's work or the little fears bubbling up.

Odin hauled peanuts to a corner of the enclosure near me and was privately enjoying his horde. "Guess who scored a VIP pass to the white party event of the summer? That's right, your girl Jamie," I said.

Odin freed a nut from a shell and placed it onto his back teeth to mash and grind it. He offered me another one through the bars, but then instantly pulled it back and hid it in the gray tufts of his beard.

"Psyche, I didn't want it anyway, Odin," I teased.

He crammed a handful of empty shells in his mouth, chewed a few times and then spit them forcefully at me. Bee dipped down from a high beam and knocked Odin to the ground. They wrestled, outsize-ears back, jaws jutting, until Isak distracted them by thumping Bee on the head with a bouquet of kale, which they all proceeded to eat. I didn't like seeing their aggression, but I told Bee she was a champ for sticking up for me.

37

Sari wanted us to fast all day long. Lately, too many hours without food had left me feeling cored out and flat. But on the day of the event, I felt nothing but the buoyancy of anticipation.

Not needing to cook left me with a little extra time to spend primping in the shower house for the party. I had become quite feral, letting go of nonessentials like eyebrow plucking and shaving. At Atlas, showering was an event that required planning. On workdays, it took too much time to do more than wash up, plus, wasting water was highly discouraged.

Showering also meant confronting my monitor and all the gouges and abrasions it created. I was always aware of its permanence in the shower: my shackle, my stalker, my scarlet letter.

Dressing up would be a special event, though, so I took a little extra time to remove the layers of wilderness that had conquered my body. I thought about how arresting Tierra's tawny skin and lean muscles looked in white. I wanted to look beautiful too, to fit in at Sari's white party.

Lost in thought, I jumped when a large thud reverberated

against the shower house walls. It sounded like a rock had been thrown against the building, but that couldn't be right. Maybe a large bird crashed into the wall, or someone was trying to open the door. I desperately hoped it wasn't Cole—or worse, a lost and wandering Flora again.

I called out in case it was one of the Atlas women waiting for the shower and I had taken too long. "Sorry, I'm almost dressed, just a minute."

No answer. I didn't hear any other noises. Maybe it was a tree branch or the wind. Maybe the pipes.

I collected my things, slipped on damp flip-flops, already annoyed that by the time I got to the dome to meet Tierra and Dagmar my feet would be dirty again, and opened the shower house door to the sight of a monkey seated no more than a few feet away, jaw jutting forward, four glistening canines meeting in an unnerving grate.

Bee. She was as still as a statue and holding a stainless-steel feeding bowl, as though she were a neighbor in search of sugar to borrow.

I slammed the door in her face and started screaming for Dagmar.

The macaque pushed on the door. I pushed back to brace against it, but I felt squeamish. I didn't want to hurt the monkey—her hand could slip through the door and snap from my push-back. But I remembered Dagmar saying the macaques were not furry babies, they were pure muscle with fangs, and they never smiled. What looked to us like a smile was a grimace that meant fear, or aggression.

More than one monkey might be loose. Others might be right behind this one. I assessed my options, looking for an escape route I could use if any of the monkeys scaled the building and squirreled in through the screened windows.

Just one scratch, everyone had warned.

In between bouts of calling for help, I tried to plead with the macaque.

"Please, little Bee, remember me? I'm your friend. Go back home, please. It's time to go back home."

Finally, Dagmar called back from down the path. "Don't move, don't hurt her, we're coming."

I focused on deepening my breathing. I heard footsteps grow closer, and then heard Dagmar talking to Tierra.

"I see her, at the door. Do you see her, Dagmar?" Tierra said.

"Okay, I'll go to the right."

"Is it just the one?" I asked.

"Yes, and it's Bee, who is a virus carrier, so please don't come out here yet," answered Dagmar, who then started speaking gently to the monkey in Danish.

"Okay, good, that's right, eat your banana," cooed Tierra.

Then both of them grew quiet, though I could hear their footsteps outside the building where their weight slightly shifted against the roots and vines on the path. Finally Dagmar said to Tierra, "She's dosed, so just use the blanket, not the net."

There was some rustling, and then their footsteps receded. I waited several minutes, long enough for my mind to wander to that banana and how good it would taste and what a perfect way to break a fast it would be.

I hoped the loose monkey didn't mean the ritual gathering would be canceled.

When I finally opened the shower door, I saw that Bee had left behind the stainless-steel bowl, and inside it was a porcelain figurine of a mermaid sitting on a rock.

Tierra and Dagmar were already back in the dome, as promised. Tierra wore a white linen column dress, and Dagmar wore a white T-shirt and off-white chinos. They looked tan and powerful, the clothes making them look wealthier, younger, and more relaxed than their workaday selves. Still damp and in my cutoffs, I felt more like I should skip the party and stay behind to mop the floor. They were deep in conversation and barely glanced at me when I entered, which didn't help.

"But isn't it the most likely possibility?" Tierra asked.

"I know what you mean, but I don't think Anna Beth visited Atlas, and even if she did, I think she'd be very afraid to open a monkey cage."

"Yeah, but Anna Beth wants us shut down. And she has every reason to be volatile right now. Think about it from her point of view."

"That's true. But to sneak on the property twice to let out a monkey? I don't think so. Plus how would she know where the keys were?" Dagmar pursed her lips and shook her head. "You would need to have two keys to open both doors, wait for one monkey to get out, and then lock up both doors again. It would be very hard to do all of that."

Tierra made a sweeping gesture in my direction and changed the subject. "Good news, Jamie. Cole said it's perfectly fine for you to go to Flora's house! He fixed it! So here is a dress you can wear. Just slip it on."

Tierra shook out the garment, and the light, gauzy fabric smelled alluringly like the smoke and heady perfume of Sari's incense. I felt suddenly shy. I had so far managed to avoid any nude awkwardness in the bathhouse by showering quickly when the others seemed occupied elsewhere on the campus. The idea of stripping down and standing in my underwear and ankle monitor in the dome, every infected bug bite and heat rash on full display—in front of Tierra no less—sent flames to my chest again.

I attempted to look nonchalant while slipping out of my T-shirt and shorts, but I couldn't quickly put the dress on with all of the white layered fabric, the drop shoulders, and at least four sleeves. A cool girl would think nothing of exposing her smooth body. A cool girl would have known how to wear this dress. Instead, I flailed clumsily, vulnerable as a child.

"Here, let me help. It flows like this." Tierra guided the dress over my head, the glow of the attention more overwhelming than the incense, her warm hands slowly lifting my hair over the fabric. "And then falls like this." She stepped back and smiled; the space let me take a breath.

I had no idea how I looked, but I felt like a kid in a costume, as I never wore dresses with sleeves that big. The expensive fabric draped effortlessly—it was a dress that a free-spirited traveler with an unlimited trust fund might twirl and float through a summer in. I felt like I was dancing already.

Tierra nodded in approval. "Let's brush your hair, and then we'll go help Sari get ready. Our friends will be arriving soon."

"Oh my gosh, I didn't even thank you for rescuing me this morning! Are the monkeys okay?" I said. "Is Bee okay?"

"Bee is in a K-hole, and we'll need to check on her later," Dagmar said.

"Is that how you got her, with a drugged banana?"

"Yes, she'll be fine. We don't use ketamine on them that often, so they respond well when they get it. She's in an isolation cage in Monkey Island."

Tierra pouted. "We'll check on her soon."

Dagmar said, "My theory is she must've thought Jamie knew where the oysters were. Bee loves her oysters."

38

Nothing is more important than gathering.

COMMENT FROM SARI

I just wanted to throw this idea in here to remind us to write more about circles and rituals. Though of course that's tricky. How much do we want to say online about these precious things that can only be introduced to our most trusted members??? Can you see how hard this has been for me? I wish there were another way to bring people to our beautiful community. Don't answer yet. I'm just getting us warmed up to take on this website project again. First, things first, though. We celebrate! —xoxoS

39

I wanted to sprint with my arms wide open into the threshold of Flora's yard. I felt free, even though it was only for the night and the monitor was still tight as a jaw around my ankle. Or maybe I felt the opposite of free, and was flushed with transgressive fire. My brain knew that Sari had secured permission for me to visit Flora's house, but stepping over the formerly forbidden boundary was exciting all the same.

The others felt the wave, too.

Tierra said, "We're breaking you out of your cell, Jamie. Come and be free!"

"Break on through to the other side," Dagmar sang, bouncing with swagger as she led us to the house, and then Tierra sang too, skipping and twirling around until she grew dizzy.

I couldn't remember the last party I had attended. I lagged behind, watching them, playing an air tambourine, the fabric of my sleeves catching the breeze like a sail, all of us gliding over the expanse of yard toward the fairy lights glittering in the trees. Such a luxury, a mown lawn on the edge of the forest. Such a luxury, this night.

And then near the back patio, Tierra said, "Hush, hush," and Dagmar thought she was still singing, so she breathily replied in verse.

But Tierra shook her head until Dagmar got it and stopped, and then we all heard sublime instrumental music playing in the house, a cello mournfully welcoming us.

Stepping through the sliding glass door, I soon saw that Flora's house was much larger than I had envisioned. An old midcentury brick ranch home, it rambled on in every direction, with a deep screened-in porch that ran the length of the house. A dozen people were already there setting up catering tables and moving furniture and plants to the edges of the space.

I looked for Sari and Flora but didn't see them at first glance. I was honored to be invited to this circle in Flora's home, and I wanted to thank her. Sari had been unfailingly gracious with me, learning who I was as a person past my headlines, as someone she could rely upon, all while dealing with the illness and strife of her family. Her care moved me, and I wanted to keep that thought front and center and not get lost in the raw glee of simply being dressed nice and socializing at an event.

I looked down at my monitor and it was still showing two amber lights for "on." No one told me if the anklet had been switched off for the evening, or if Cole had amended the coordinates of my boundaries. I didn't know how far I could go or what would happen if I decided to sprint out of the house and into town.

I made myself stop thinking about it. I didn't want to run away. I had no reason to run. In a few short weeks my house arrest would be finished. I didn't even know how many days I had left; it had all become a blur.

Atlas wasn't flawless, but I had never lived in a perfect place, nor worked with perfect people. It was starting to feel like a home, somewhere I could do the most engaging work of my life, with friends who truly accepted me—plus the monkeys. And maybe even more than that: Atlas promised me something glorious and life-affirming if I could only understand their philosophies. I trusted Sari to guide me there. I felt hopeful. And here I was, at a circle community gathering in the most beautiful dress I had ever worn, looking like someone worthy of a good life.

Tierra trotted off and fetched three mugs of tea for us. I was so hungry I could hardly focus, but my attention was drawn to an elaborate display in the corner where a tiered cake decorated with sugared dandelions and pansies glittered on a table surrounded by small, white gift bags and a slatted box labeled *Love Offerings*. The cello and the cake reminded me more of a wedding than the spiritual gathering I expected, and I wondered if the event might even be a birthday celebration for Flora.

Adjacent to the porch, I saw that more people were arriving. The house's dining room and open kitchen held an overwhelming kaleidoscope of food and people, indistinct voices and arms groping for embraces. The guests in all-white looked like one shimmering feather, pale angels in silk and gauze swanning about in the quiet way of the Atlas volunteers.

I tried to see if I recognized anyone, but it took focus to place them because they looked so different out of their paint-splattered shorts and Atlas T-shirts. Some details jumped out—Farrah wore elaborate gold eye makeup; Mischa looked transformed, her brown hair freshly dyed platinum—but everything quickly collapsed into a blur.

Sari moved effortlessly through the room in a backless maxi dress, setting candles aflame with a long butane lighter. She embraced us.

"Jamie, we love it that this is your first circle. Nothing could be more perfect. It's truly a circle, in and out, new and old, never-ending," Sari whispered and then passed me to Dagmar.

She left a thick cloud of orange essential oil vapor in her wake, taking Tierra with her.

We sank votive candles into small brown bags weighted with sand and positioned them along the front walkway. Lighting the bags felt like resuscitating them, the flame a heartbeat creating breath for the simple, glowing body, and with each one we added, the beats grew stronger. I could imagine continuing to line the driveway with them forever until I hit the road, bags flickering and glowing for miles until the light was a pure line connecting then and tomorrow. They would look amazing when night fell.

Done with our chore, we waited on the front porch. Zelda arrived, her red hair decadent and lipstick violent in contrast to her white linen shirt. Dagmar greeted her, the two women immediately tumbling into animated whispers while hugging each other and leaning in close. A wave of jealousy joined my hunger pangs.

Zelda elbowed me. "I wouldn't have picked this job for you, firebug," she laughed, and then to Dagmar, "Is Wolfie here?" Before Dagmar could respond, Zelda answered herself. "Oh, Tampa, I remember now. Whew, my brain shuts down when I'm fasting."

Without saying more, Zelda extended her hand to Dagmar, palm up. Dagmar extracted a slip of waxed paper from her pocket, unfolded it, and then peeled a small lump from its surface. As soon as it was placed in Zelda's hand, she popped it into her mouth.

Dagmar peeled one off for me as well, and then another for Natasha, a volunteer who had suddenly appeared behind me with her own hand extended. Since others were taking it, I decided it would be safe for me too, hoping that it would calm my ravenous hunger and anxious nerves. I expected it to be mint-flavored, but instead it tasted like pine needles floating in swimming pool water. I let it dissolve slowly on my tongue.

Dagmar and Zelda began walking to the house along with the other newly arrived partygoers. Dozens of guests seemed to have emerged from the trees, including more familiar faces, but I suddenly felt lost and overwhelmed without anyone telling me what I should do.

I followed Dagmar inside, knowing I needed to get a grip, get some food.

The living room itself was decorated with framed paintings and old scrolls of monkeys and apes, walls of books and layers of Persian rugs, and a large taxidermied alligator head. I tried to find the bathroom but dead-ended at a door that was locked with two keyed dead bolts. A bedroom, I figured, perhaps the master. As I stood in the hallway considering the locks, I felt a puff of air on my bare feet. At the slight gap between the ceramic tile floor and the door, a large black snout snarled at me. Sari's wolf. I knew it must be Sari's wolf. I put my ear to the door, and as soon as I heard my own pulse it felt like the wood dissolved under my touch, allowing me to enter a mossy den where I could pile in and sleep with the wolf pups—but then suddenly I was in the hallway with everything back to normal.

By the time I made it to the back room, most of the attendees were already gathered. There had to be at least a hundred people present. The air was humid with the competing aromas of bougainvillea, cumin, white sugar, sweat, Nag Champa, and the dank odor of wet dogs. I smelled my pits to see if I was adding to the foulness. I wondered about the order of events, praying I didn't embarrass myself with any circle faux pas or spill food on Sari's gorgeous dress later on.

Just then, the music stopped and the crowd quieted.

Sari stepped onto a small plywood stage to join the three musicians: a woman straddling a cello, a volunteer named Rose hugging a concertina, and a third woman dangling a battered guitar as though it were an exhausted toddler clinging to her neck.

I searched again for Tierra, but she was nowhere to be found.

I wondered if she was with Flora in one of the bedrooms, maybe preparing to enter. I needed her. Dagmar's pill had replaced my hunger with a disconcerting sense of disembodiment, as though I had misplaced my shell—and it felt like if I didn't find Tierra soon, I would lose her forever to the cacophony of voices and the blur of souls and dust around me.

"Dear ones, dear ones," Sari began, her voice commanding like a preacher's but also warm, like liquid butter and honey, "we are so beautiful when we're together."

The whole room seemed to inhale, yielding to the sway in her voice.

"We are here on this happy day of dedication for our dear Flora Anne Sutherland, née Morse, one of us forever, just as the monkeys decided it should be. Flora found great comfort and care in our community, and no one was more dedicated to our principles. Flora, like my father, knew this was blessed land. She protected it ten times over. She knew the time had come to pass it to me, as steward for Atlas's vision. She died happily and full of purpose, and she wanted you to gather here in her home, which she has generously gifted to the sacred macaques of Atlas, to celebrate the end of her wasteful life."

She died happily.

My gut dropped. I looked around, but no one else was reeling.

Wasteful life.

Was she actually announcing that Flora has passed away?

I couldn't have possibly heard that correctly, and yet Sari's every word was offered with precision and resonance. She held the space with her breath. Tierra and Dagmar were still missing from the group, and I was desperate to lock eyes with someone, but the entire audience was mirroring Sari's beatific smile.

"We all saw how my mother, your Flora, faced her fears head-on, she faced death with dignity, she faced the inevitable consequence of human existence, and I'm very proud of her,"

Sari continued. "We were there to ease her journey and we will be honored to follow her soon. Flora believed her most useful accomplishment was being able to gift her estate, this green and wild paradise, to Atlas—to the blessed monkeys of Atlas—so this is a celebration for all of us, just as Flora willed it to be."

Sari briefly paused, prompting a few voices to mumble *blessed be.* "We must rise to the challenge of protecting the land from division and development, and we must expand Atlas carefully and mindfully, and we must all prepare to face our deaths with as much resolve and trust as Flora, when the monkeys decide. And we shall. Blessed be."

"Blessed be," responded the crowd in resonant unison.

I scanned the room. My lips felt cold and my throat ached. I couldn't seem to swallow my own spit. The accordion player began, and then the cellist, and Sari swayed silently. With her head bowed she motioned for the attendees to begin humming the throaty vibrato I had heard the night Mischa had entered the enclosure. Sickening growls surrounded me.

I couldn't take my eyes off Sari. She wasn't crying; she didn't look sad. I hadn't known Flora very well, but I felt overcome by a dark wave of emotion pulling me under. Their song rose around me, and I could not process information fast enough to do anything but sway alongside them, while my mind flashed through images: Flora raking her fingers through compost; Sari leading Flora through snake nests; Mischa locked in the cage; Anna Beth's fiery glare.

At last Tierra appeared by my side, steadying my shoulders with a long, strong arm in a one-sided hug.

Sari sharply clapped three times, hushing the room again. The guitarist held one hand firmly against the strings to halt the music. Sari smiled broadly, opening her arms wide.

"So now we feast in honor of Flora's passage! She will be useful forever! Feast like a she-wolf provided us with a hunt to sustain you tonight, for she has. Feast like a matriarch has gifted us with fertile land to sustain us evermore, for she has. After we feast, we will gather in the cemetery to consecrate her stone. Blessed be, my dear ones, blessed be."

The white-clad mass responded in kind. After a heavy silence, the room jolted back to life with laughter, embraces, and activity. Some people drifted to claim a spot in line for food, others for a gift bag, and the crowd swallowed Tierra before I even noticed the absence of her touch.

My brain gasped and sputtered as I attempted to wrestle it all into something coherent.

I was attending a surprise funeral, except I was the only one who was surprised.

Flora died, even though none of them had said a word earlier today when we fussed about dresses and permission slips.

I didn't even know when Flora had passed, though it probably happened when she was taken to the hospital, or maybe even before I lied to Anna Beth about Flora's whereabouts.

Something primal in me, deep in my marrow, told me to run away, all the way to my old childhood home, and dive into the Atlantic Ocean where I could shed every layer of this white dress in the waves and hide in a cove, far from these people with their love of death and wilder lives.

But another impulse, green and searching like a vine's tendril, told me that I had been invited to stay, that I could choose to stay. That I could cease mourning my family, my hometown, and my pile of losses—that I could follow Sari's lead by looking ahead. I could celebrate. I could be useful.

I needed privacy to center myself, eventually finding a small bathroom behind the kitchen. The walls were painted mint green to match midcentury tilework. I ran cold water over my hands and bent down to splash my face. When I looked up in anticipation of a mirror, I instead was met with a large print of Frida Kahlo's *Self-Portrait with Monkeys*, Frida's face mirroring the size of my own, and four monkeys right there surrounding her, all of them staring back at me. I could feel them breathing near my ear, grooming my hair with practiced hands.

Tierra found me hiding alone in the kitchen. She gave me her plate.

"It's beautiful food, carefully prepared," Tierra said, savoring a spoonful of curry. "Eat, Jamie. It's sort of fun to have food we didn't prepare, and it's going to taste so good because you've been fasting."

I tried to eat the jasmine rice but my throat struggled to swallow. I coughed and needed big gulps of tea to avoid choking.

"You seem off. What's the matter?" she asked. "You didn't quite understand what was happening, did you?"

I shrugged. "Stuff is coming up about my family. I'm sorry." Tierra looked resplendent, glowing in the golden hour light, kissing each spoonful of food to taste when it hit her lips, then slowly putting the whole bite in her mouth. I took a breath. "Just, actually yes, I'm a little confused."

"It's okay, I'll explain everything later. Relax, and remember that you are beloved here. Sari, Dagmar, and I, all of us, we love you. We wouldn't have brought you here if we didn't."

Dagmar swooped through the crowd. "Eat something, Jamie!" she said, and then pulled Tierra away.

I milled about trying to find a place to stand, eventually hiding behind the cake and gift bags while the trio played haunting, old world folk music. The cake was melting in the heat, sugar grains separating from the gloss, the airy pockets in the fluffy cake filling with moisture. The tiers were headed for collapse. Impulsively, I snatched a gift bag and hid it within one of the pockets created by the layers of fabric in my dress.

Eventually I felt ready to rejoin the crowd, wondering if we might gather for a circle after all. Outside on the lawn, Sari sat on a wrought-iron chair and next to her stood Dagmar, who was holding a large macaque on a short leash atop a rock pedestal.

It looked like Colette—a golden female with tender eyes and bushy cheeks—though I wasn't certain. Colette wasn't known to be a carrier of the disease, but still, Dagmar baffled me. I didn't understand her inconsistent rules about the macaques. Even without her lectures about virus transmission, the evils of anthropomorphizing and monkeys performing emotional labor as pets, how was it not just as wrong to take a rescued animal from the enclosure and bring her out in the open, surrounded by so much chaos? Even more concerning, after people chatted with Sari, they lowered themselves in a bow and kissed the monkey's paw.

I watched Zelda take her turn. She knelt down before Sari and spoke with her, and then she picked up the macaque's hand as if she were a dapper gentleman, and kissed the top of Colette's leathery fingers.

A sudden new desire shot through my muddled thoughts: I would not be outdone by Zelda. I jumped into the line, and knelt dutifully when it was my turn. As I bowed, I saw that Colette was standing on a rock the size of a bed pillow that was inscribed with familiar symbols and letters. In the middle, it said *Flora*.

Sari leaned in and whispered, "Don't be sad. I thought you understood. We'll explain everything after we go together to the lake. We love you, Jamie."

She meant the pergola, I knew. The looming dread made the back of my knees feel unsteady. I didn't think I could do it. I sat on the ground to collect my strength, staring up at three large pine trees silhouetted against the dusk sky. A few squirrels traversed the trees, up and down the trunks, branch to branch, leaping between them and landing in the green needle clusters, and then springing down to the branches again. If they stopped moving, surely the needles wouldn't support them, and they would plummet. Instead, they were flying as they magically catapulted down to a sturdy branch on sheer momentum, out-smarting gravity itself.

Farrah joined me on the ground, leaning her head very close to mine.

"Hey, Jamie, I've been meaning to say—someone told me who you are, and then I googled you. You saved that pelican last year, didn't you?"

I looked over at Farrah. She smiled, gold makeup glittering in the creases of her eyes.

"That was me. It surely was."

I wished the pelican would reappear, its enormous, ancient wingspan opening to cover my entire body with raspy feathers, telling me what to do with my dueling wishes and fears, and then Farrah in her white dress became the bird, and then came back into focus as Farrah again. I said, "It's weird to think about the volunteers talking about me, but I know it's bound to happen."

"Don't feel weird. We think it's very cool. You saved it. No wonder you get to live here with Sari and the macaques. You're a true hero."

Tierra walked over and extended her hand to me. In my dizzy state, I let her help me slowly stand up.

"It's time to dedicate Flora's stone," she said. "Are you ready to join us, Jamie?"

I closed my eyes for a moment to steady myself, and then Far-rah and I joined the small group that was assembling to walk to the cemetery with Sari. They had invited me. Atlas was where I belonged.

40

Tom, one of the volunteers, pushed Flora's stone in the Atlas wheelbarrow until the path to the cemetery grew too narrow. Zelda picked it up and carried it for a beat, and then she passed it to Dagmar. Farrah took hold of my arm to steady herself, her grasp as insubstantial as a fern. In her other hand she held a small bust of Medusa.

Sari headed the informal procession. Dagmar lagged toward the end, cradling a box, followed by Rose with her concertina. There were only about twenty of us, the majority of guests having peeled off and gone home early, gift bags in hand. I wondered if Sari was disappointed by this, or if the evening unraveled exactly as she expected.

The day's light was almost gone, and the clear sky was the color of new denim. There wasn't much of a moon, but the stars were revealing themselves one by one, giving us plenty of light to work with. We poured into the clearing, carefully stepping over the ring of inscribed stones. The white pergola, the rows of statutes guarding it—everything looked the same as when I first discovered it, though now, in the hush of evening and in the company of others, nothing felt out of place. The centerpiece, the large egg-shaped rock, looked as though it had emerged from the forest floor to serve this very purpose.

Tierra struggled to light the candles that surrounded the altar because their wicks were too wet. She settled for the two that caught and held their flames without sputtering out. We had just enough light to see the box Dagmar had positioned on the rock, to see our shadowed faces, and to see some of the small statues and objects surrounding us in the clearing.

We watched as Tom added a few coins from his pocket to the assemblage, and Farrah added her statue. Then Dagmar picked up the blue Danish cookie tin from the ground nearby and shook it. I remembered the small bones, and choked back bile. She pried open the lid and added a few to the collection.

Slowly we drifted into an oblong ring beneath the pergola, joining hands. Sari motioned for me to take hers with my left, and Tierra grabbed my right. The white pergola wasn't quite large enough to hold us; as we gathered within, its twisting branches and bamboo frame wove around us like a twine basket trap.

I talked down my fears and tried to slow my pulse. I knew I needed to push through my discomfort to support Sari. I looked around the circle at the tender, open faces of people who showed up to care for one another. This community had accepted me without judgment, and so it fell to me to do the same for them.

"Dearest ones," Sari began. "Rose has offered to sing for us this evening. We will use her song to call into the wind from all directions of the night, announcing our presence and our intention to be of use to this sacred space."

Rose played a slow lullaby, the exhales from her concertina manifesting a gentle cloud of mournful sound around us. I closed my eyes and bowed my head, and the music wove its way into long-empty caverns and gaps with its earnestness, unearthing a nostalgia I didn't know I could claim and a longing that made my chest ache. Somewhere in the circle a woman began to cry, stifled gasps breaking free, and as if in silent concert, tears streamed down my own face. Tierra's bracelets rested again my wrist, and I was overcome by how resilient all three of them perpetually needed to be for each other, and of how hard I worked to keep my own grief at bay, and how the same was true for each and every person in the circle. None of us were alone in this moment.

When the refrain began again, I sobbed openly, unable to stop, for Sari's mother, for my own mother wherever she was, for my father, and for Jason, and my friends, and my home, and for losses I had pushed so deep, they had knotted into impossible, immovable scars. The song ended, Rose repeating the ending line *don't go, don't go* so plaintively, despite the truth revealed to us by the names on the stones: we will all go, and we will be left, again and again, and we will go.

"Dear ones, my most trusted friends," Sari began. "Before this land was known as Atlas, it nurtured mothers and midwives as Vessel, and before that, artists and dreamers called it The Argo, and before that, my parents provided stewardship under the name The Sutherland Place. And what a blessed spot it is. Centuries ago, the Timucuan leaders steered Ponce de Leon away from this Central Florida region so he would not find the Fountain of Youth. As a child, I found mammoth and tapir artifacts on this very spot. This land has always fostered the full spectrum of life and death and ensured that after death there is no longer waste, only usefulness. Now this land welcomes Flora, as it has many others before her, as it will welcome us. Commit to us and Atlas will receive you. Sacrificing her life for our betterment was noble, and we honor Flora today and for all of our days. When the monkeys decide my work is done, I will happily follow her here, as I know you will as well. Blessed be."

"Blessed be," we replied. I could sense the effects of Dagmar's pill waning, leaving me terribly thirsty and raw and frayed. I wondered what they would do if I passed out at their feet, if they'd leave me be, if someday, I would get my own stone here.

Sari opened the box of ashes and plunged both hands in, sweeping up a deep, full scoop that immediately began trickling between her fingers. She tossed it against the rock, opened her arms and draped her body on top of it, holding herself there in a long embrace.

Dagmar offered the box outward to each of us, and some of our contingent cupped small handfuls and shook them onto the various stones, but I could not, I could not stop crying and did not want to touch Flora's ashes because I was not crying for her alone. I couldn't stop thinking about the sources of those bones, who might be buried near those stones, which monkeys or tigers or bodies should also be remembered as we gathered around their names.

We heard a surge of water from the lake, trailed by two smaller splashes. Sari stood up, her white dress filthy with soot, her hands coated with ashes. Everyone around me was dirty with it, faces smudged, pristine clothes soiled. I looked down, and I didn't want anyone to see me. I was overcome with emotion, suddenly petrified they would walk to the lake to wash off, scared that I, too, would follow and would fall from the broken pier, my white dress billowing on the surface like a sail, my grief rolling me over until nothing was left. The water splashed again and I flashed to the three moccasins slicing toward me, and just then Farrah sidled next to me and slid her small hand into mine. "Who do you think might be next?" she whispered.

My nerves bristled with one message: run. I bolted up through the path to Flora's house, not missing a step, then through her yard, and didn't stop until I ended up at the garden gate, where I felt a shadow running after me. I turned, expecting Tierra, only to see a big man with a burly beard in the distance, his arm raised. I didn't know this strange volunteer or what he wanted.

I needed to be alone, and I didn't want to be out of bounds one minute longer. I crossed the threshold into Atlas, and I ran fast as I could, looking back twice to make sure he didn't follow me.

I listened to my feet thud into the dirt and my heaving breath. Told myself to stop thinking. To not let anything slow me down. I didn't even turn to look at the monkeys as I ran by, not stopping for anything until my cabin door slammed shut behind me.

I sat down at my table in that awful dress and removed the gift bag that I had crammed in its layers when I was hiding at the cake table. I tossed it under my bed. I rested my elbow on the table where my pile of daily rocks used to be and held my aching head. I wept, heaving sobs that scared me more than anything had for years, my body violently purging itself, my heart feeling every age at once. All of the pain I had accumulated was like a fire in my chest, and I feared nothing could be done with the charred ashes that would fill me, so then I cried in recognition of that until nothing was left anymore.

After some time Tierra came in, and then Sari, sweaty and bedraggled in their dirty clothes, with containers of food. They said only a few words as they washed my face with a cool cloth as though I had a fever. They gave me tea to drink and found fresh T-shirts for us to wear, lifting my dress over my head and removing their own. I could barely move. Tierra spoon-fed us all a few bites of a curry and then a few bites of cake while Sari brushed my hair and gossiped about a love triangle involving the musicians, and then we tried to sing Rose's song by memory. Eventually I must have fallen asleep because when I woke in the morning I had been tucked in, the pile of discarded white dresses the only evidence that they had been there at all.

41

I showered before breakfast, wanting to do nothing more than sneak back to my A-frame to crawl back under the covers for the day with a box of crackers and a gallon of water. I knew I should report to work, but instead I lingered with the macaques. I wondered if Bee was still recovering in Monkey Island. I scoured the enclosure looking for her, but she was nowhere. I even called out to her, peering into the darkest corner of the shelter and all sides of the tire swing, but there was no pink-faced Bee to be found. The other monkeys, at least, were not worried. Dagmar had given them hefty wedges of cantaloupe, and they looked like the Cheshire cat with the rinds against their faces. None of them were too interested in my party confessions.

"Curious Georgia, can you believe I had a breakdown like that at Flora's funeral? I'm going to be honest with you. Something like this happened to me at a wedding I once shot, where I drank a bottle of champagne by myself and wept during the father-daughter dance. After that, I was only allowed to edit videos. And this was ten times worse. A hundred times."

Charlie used two rinds like drumsticks on Darla's head. Instead of dealing directly with Charlie, Darla screeched at Nora-Nora-Nora. River offered me a half-eaten slice through the fencing.

"That's right, River. Head up, tits out, apologize and move on. Good advice."

As I walked in the dome, I immediately hung my head at the sight of the women, but they didn't give me a chance to apologize.

Tierra hugged me and pulled me to their table. "We weren't going to wake you, poor thing. We wanted you to sleep."

Sari poured coffee for me into the green earthenware mug, everyone's favorite. "We're so sorry, Jamie. We shouldn't have thrown you in like that."

"We thought it would be good if you saw how happy everyone was, but we should have explained more," Tierra said.

Dagmar jumped in. "I thought Sari and Tierra had prepared you better, Jamie. Or rather, we all thought you understood from what we had said. But we needed to be more direct."

"I'm the one who's sorry. I did not mean to make the night about myself, Sari. I'm truly humiliated and can't apologize enough," I blurted. "It's not what's in my heart, which is tremendous affection and care for you and for your loss of Flora, who I really admired."

"It's okay, it's okay," Sari said. "I left you stranded. I am so spoiled with support from Atlas, and I forgot that you are not used to having that much love around you, are you, little sister? It must have been so overwhelming to see in action. We should have prepared you."

"We typically do," Dagmar said as she sliced cantaloupe and honeydew rinds away from the lush fruit. I wondered what Dagmar meant by *typically*, and exactly how many others there had been before me. Dagmar looked at Sari. "We thought you were rolling with it. Perhaps we misread you."

"I think I..." I stammered. "I think I have a lot bottled up. It's been stressful. My court case. I need to work on that."

"No, you need to let us help you," Tierra said. "We will take care of you."

"You don't understand, but we all have been pre-grieving Flora's death for at least a year," Sari explained. She stood up and moved behind me, running her palms gently along my shoulders. "It has been a long process. A beautiful process, actually. We forgot you didn't experience that. Everything was done the way Flora wanted, almost everything, except that it took forever. But our whole community was there, all of Atlas guiding us. No one has ever helped you, have they, you poor thing, so you don't know what that feels like, and when you felt it, your old pain crashed in on you. That's all. When is the last time your burdens were lifted?"

This question made me want to start crying again. I've been helped immeasurably at times in my life. Nedra nurtured me and Jason, foster families shared their food and their homes—in the past few months alone, Kayla saved me pro bono and Atlas was wholly supporting my physical needs.

But even with that, Sari was right: most of my life I had been moving forward on sheer muscle memory, never being able to afford the time or emotional capacity to understand the past, let alone to count on anything or anybody for the future. The strain was becoming too much to bear alone. My tears made embarrassing plops on the table.

Sari comforted me, and then she began to sniffle, which prompted Tierra to tear up, and then though she tried to wipe away her tears, Sari buried her face in her hands and cried. These beautiful women had been joyous at their event, aglow like paper lanterns, but now because of me they were mired in the dark throes of my vain and futile grief. They had divined a spiritual community and practices that both comforted and elevated them, whereas I had nothing to draw upon. The last thing I should do was to bring them down with me.

"I want, with all of my heart, to have what you have. I want to learn." I looked from one face to the next, so each of them would know how much they meant to me. "I can work. I have ideas to help you with Atlas. I know it doesn't seem like it right this minute, but I will make it worth it to you, to reward you for all your patience. And I'm so, so sorry."

Dagmar smiled beneficently. Tierra kissed the crown of my head. "Don't be ashamed. We love you."

"Jamie, listen when we say we love you." Sari finished her coffee and unfurled her arms, a swallow about to soar. "I will take you at your word. Let's get to work on that website."

Sari had canceled volunteers for a while because the heat was expected to be over 100 degrees all week. That left us more time to work. Sari and I tweaked designs for her site, creating a way for the livestream to play on multiple platforms. She showed me the Atlantic Rescue Center's website, and we borrowed liberally from their photo gallery and video display pages.

"But look, you can easily tell they have no spirituality, no reverence. Look at those cartoon drawings. I don't want any of that," she groaned. "All the money in the world, and they have it, believe me, but if you don't understand the spiritual reasons for macaque devotion, you are no better than a jailer."

"We'll have no cartoons or animation," I agreed. "Don't worry, our sensibilities will show through."

"Someday I'm going to free those precious macaques from Atlantic, I swear I am." She growled. "But even if I did, Atlantic would probably just cry to their donors, make a million bucks and buy more monkeys." She tossed a large pink crystal from one hand to the other. "We should do it anyway."

When her attention capped out, Sari took a nap. Dagmar had been busy all day with walks through the grounds. I figured she was preparing for the inspection or developing a new building project and I offered to help, but Tierra told me not to bother Dagmar when she was in "hunter-gatherer mode."

I was still worried about the inspection and about Anna Beth. It concerned me that either of those two forces could be an existential threat. If anything happened to hurt Atlas, over forty little lives, including those of cranky Meaty Joe and nosy Darla, would be in jeopardy. But I didn't bring it up because I didn't want to be a force of negativity—not today and not going forward.

I let them be in charge. They knew best.

Tierra asked me to help with an emergency kitchen project. "I have a feeling the refrigerator is going to fail this week. It can't hang on through many more hundred-degree days, so I want to roast all of the tomatoes and peppers today, and then we will can salsa tomorrow."

"A fire, and then canning? Isn't it too hot for that type of labor?"

"I can't bear the idea of waking up to wasted food in a hot refrigerator!"

"Maybe we could do it at night, have a fire tonight and then can tomorrow night, when the sun goes down?" I suggested. I knew that the sun didn't make that much difference, not when the air was this heavy and immovable, but it sounded like a slightly more tenable plan.

"No, we have to do the roasting today and the canning tomorrow. In the daylight. Last night was chaotic. It's so important that we return to gently abiding by the daytime-only rules for the macaques," she said.

I bit my lip, fighting back questions. I still didn't understand why some rules about the macaques were so rigid when I had just witnessed a monkey on a leash receiving kisses and volunteers entering the macaque cage for random midnight rituals. I wanted to know how all of it jibed cohesively—these oddities

versus Dagmar's tales of violence versus a beatification of the
macaques as spiritual guides.

I also wanted to know if tonight they would be entering the
macaque enclosure again—but I decided that given my recent
breakdown, I needed to wait to be invited to that, too.

I built an oak fire in a band of bricks, and Tierra hauled out
trays of sliced gems. Soon we were trapped in a bell jar of smoke.
Heat distorted the grill, making it look like rippling water, and
flames licked my knuckles when I charred the peppers. Tierra
was all amber and ancient haze, a time traveler content to stay
put, and she was smiling at me.

I realized again how much Tierra's reactions mattered to me.
I looked to her eyes first to offer an opinion when a new song
played or when Sari asked us to make a sacrifice. I knew without
a word when she was happy, and feeling her joy as we worked
together at the fire made me happy, too.

When we were done cooking food, we hauled vines and broken trellises to the fire to clean up the area. Tierra stomped on
segments of a downed limb and parts of a rotten pallet, and the
fire grew so big and all-consuming we couldn't help but laugh.
The smoke and heat created ecstatic swirls, egging on our gasps
and shrieks.

Later, Sari found me chugging tea in the kitchen while Tierra
was standing in the refrigerator, desperately trying to lower her
temperature. She took pity on us and led us to her dome.

It was by no means cool in Sari's house, but it was at least
cooler than the kitchen. Dark and shaded by the larger dome, it
caught less southern sun, and when she flipped on her fans and
the air conditioner in the office area, it cut some of the damp
heat.

"Here, sit, sit, my lovelies. You have been working so hard."

She threw a clean batik sheet over her old couch and then
positioned two oscillating fans right at us. Then she grabbed a

squirt gun and sprayed us with shots of a heavy mist. The water evaporated quickly under the fans.

"Mmm, mint?" Tierra asked.

"Yes, I made a jug of mint and lavender water. Fill up a spray bottle and take some when you leave. Spray it on your head when you are trying to fall asleep. Am I a genius or what?"

"You are," I said.

"How did your mama cool you off on hot days, Jamie?" Sari asked me.

I tried to think back, but my brain felt soft and the details of my past seemed to be mere snapshots fading in and out of focus. "Well, my mom wasn't around much. So, just by swimming, I guess. My brother and I used to have squirt-gun fights. And you know those ice pops you buy in plastic tubes and freeze yourself? Where you cut the top off and squeeze it out? We would get those."

"Oh, I remember those! Blue and orange and red," Tierra said.

"Yuck. We should make some good Popsicles again," Sari said. "Lemon basil. Remember, Tierra?"

"Yes! Lime and blood orange paletas. Cantaloupe. I will make some soon, don't worry." Tierra patted my hand and I felt oddly reassured, though Sari had been the one requesting the treat.

"Bang, bang." Sari flirted as she shot us again, and we kept on like that, half napping under a cool mint rain until it was time to gather for dinner.

I walked home with a tote bag of apples and peanut butter, a spray bottle of Sari's holy water, and an envelope of writing she asked me to edit for the website. Bee was still not home in the enclosure.

I opened the door to my little house and saw the puddle of white dresses on my floor, and I suddenly remembered the gift bag I had stolen and cringed. Why was I so petty and weird sometimes? They probably were going to give me one, or would have if I had bothered to ask.

Regret wouldn't change anything, and since I hoped it contained a tub of salve, I fished the bag out from under my bed and upended the contents to find a baggie of Tierra's granola, a beeswax candle, a jar of Dagmar's salve, an Atlas key chain, a very large glassine envelope holding crystalline powder, a pill bottle containing oval tablets and a fistful of large, unmarked pills in a baggie tied with a jute ribbon.

42

Setting up a bequest to benefit Atlas is the most providential service you can offer the macaques, and it's easier than you might think.

While all donations of any size are welcome and vital, nothing ensures our financial stability more than estate gifts. Without you generous patrons, we will not be able to grow or realize our full mission.

If you think about it, passing one's estate to traditional heirs is a stagnant process that lacks vitality, agency, and in many cases, proper stewardship. Land gets sold and divided between squabbling children and cousins. Family members who neglected you in life suddenly get in line to benefit from your conservation. Passive transfer of assets is a major societal problem and an irresponsible way to manage one's death.

Selecting a private entity that shares your values is the only way to go!

In most states, it's not complicated at all to name Atlas as your insurance beneficiary or asset recipient. Our attorney can assist you today! One simple sentence in your will is all it takes, and then blessings will follow.

COMMENT FROM SARI

I'm very excited about this! –xoxoS.

TRACK CHANGES FROM TIERRA

Dear Sari & Dagmar. Do we really think that strangers will do this? I'm not sure if details about wills should be on the website. Maybe this topic is more of a conversation we have with members? The legal aspect of it makes me feel very uncomfortable. But if you want it written out here, maybe somewhere it should say "The macaques are infinitely grateful."

With love and respect, Tierra.

43

I didn't recognize all of the drugs in the gift bag from the party, but the pills were clearly of two kinds. I recognized the shape and the distinctive markings of the oval tablets. Generic Xanax.

The other pills had no markings at all. They were a dirty shade of white and shaped like eggs. Some of them were rough at the edge, so between that and the lack of an imprint, they were assuredly off-market.

The powder could have been anything. I've seen plenty of coke and meth in restaurant kitchens, and I had tried both, but I was no expert, and had never bought any myself. I mostly stayed away from drug use. Jason had left me a little freaked about it. His arrest from trafficking in substances took him away from me, and so I thought of drugs as a family curse that could only lead to more ruination.

People were wrong when they thought I was high as a kite the night I stole the Tiki Hut money. I was high on impulsivity, maybe, or anger, or denial—all of which are just as powerful and probably worse than amphetamines. Then there was the tequila, which I had sweated out on my walk across the bridge. I tested very clean for drugs, much to the surprise of the officer who brought me in.

The last thing I wanted to do was try the Atlas stuff just to find out what they were. I didn't want to be amped up or zonked out alone in a cabin in the Florida brush in a July heat wave. Or maybe it was August already; I wasn't sure.

Regardless, imagining the nightmare scenario of encountering snakes, bugs or an armadillo while tripping on hallucinogens set my teeth on edge, not to mention a heat stroke from whatever amphetamines would do.

I didn't even want to handle the drugs. I was torn between the urge to save them as some sort of artifact, giving them back to Sari, or simply throwing them away. I was almost positive they were nothing to worry about. Probably just antianxiety and pain medicine Atlas was given by a big pharmaceutical company to administer to forty-two stressed monkeys, and since they treated the macaques more holistically than that, they shared them with volunteers and donors. Times are tough. Everyone knew someone who needed help affording medical care.

I would have liked to be able to talk through things like this with a friend, but I simply didn't have any left, other than the women at Atlas. Midway through my legal dramas I had decided to let attrition take its course with my connections because I couldn't stand the awkwardness—if someone asked me how I was, I inevitably started to cry. Plus I was busy all the time, driving two hours every day just to work as a hotel maid. I regretted it now, but at the time it seemed wise to let everyone off the hook, myself included, from the agony of trying to repair old friendships. I was a banged-up bucket, not good for carrying water to help myself, so how could I ask for anything from others? That's why I missed my brother in my life. Family has to put up with each other. Family deserves each other.

But I learned my lesson and was changing that tide now. I

was digging into my friendships with Tierra, Dagmar, and Sari. They offered that level of acceptance and support to each other, and now to me. I might not have done well with keeping old friends, but I would keep these women close here at Atlas if they'd let me.

My original hope had been to start over. People moved to Florida every day to toss out their old lives and start anew. They'll say they relocate to escape the snow, but then more of the story comes out. They wanted to leave someone or something behind, or leave the absence of someone or something behind. People flood to Florida because it is the end of the country, the end of the line, last stop, last call, last chance to start again, and so I had planned to start again, too.

But then I got to know the women and the monkeys. The Atlas women knew something about how to live and take care of each other, and I hoped they let me stay. But the insecure part of me second-guessed even the simplest gesture, and I made every situation more complicated than it needed to be. Why did I keep getting in my own way? I wished I hadn't taken a gift bag in the first place. I pushed it all, save the salve, back under the bed.

The morning clouds were speared by the treetops, holding the heat close. I begged them to rain, even though I knew the drops would turn to steam before they touched the sandy earth.

I took a few minutes in my cabin to write a letter to Kayla, asking her to update me about how my house arrest requirements would draw to a close, because it seemed as though I should start doing something to actively manage my case. I shoved it in my pocket, hoping for a good opportunity to talk to Sari later.

On my way to the dome I saw that Bee was back in the enclosure, looking healthy and active, and I squeaked at her in relief.

I shouldn't have bemoaned the heat because our canning project went quickly. We boiled the jars while having breakfast, and the rest took no time. Sari stayed and watched while eating cold

grapes, topless and in a bikini bottom again, wearing a red bandanna in a triangle over her hair.

As I washed the last of the dishes, Tierra popped watermelon
balls in my mouth.

"This is the best job you've ever given me," I said. "I will
definitely work for watermelon today."

"Good to know," Tierra said. "I wonder what else you would
do for watermelon?"

"Absolutely no telling," I said. She rested a piece on my lower
lip and then slowly pushed it in.

"Oh, I have ways of finding out," she said.

Sari growled at us and slammed her bowl of grapes upside
down on the table.

That afternoon I cleaned the monkey toys and straps for Dagmar. Rubber balls had been tethered to the play apparatus for a
few days, and Dagmar swapped them out for a series of rings.
The macaques disliked the fact that I had their belongings outside the enclosure. Ghost shook the cage, and Mercedes periodically banged her head against the fence.

"Sorry, sorry. Go give the rings a try? Maybe they're more
fun than they look," I consoled them.

I was too distracted to redirect them to another activity. I
wasn't sure, but my best guess was that Cole should be arriving
soon to check in. I realized I should have asked Sari while I was
at her desk working on the website, but I was so engrossed with
our project that it slipped my mind to notice the exact date. She
talked about me staying at Atlas in broad terms, but I needed
to be more direct about her expectations. I couldn't have more
than two weeks to go.

"Tell me what to do, little Bee. You would just come out and
ask her, wouldn't you? I admire that in you. What should I do,
Bubbles? Tell me, Colette." I loved the leaders of the clique of
mamas.

Papayas.

Clear as day, the image came to me: piles of vibrant fruit, the monkeys holding chunks in each fist, the spoiled-smelling juice covering their chins. I was overcome with the idea of bringing the monkeys papayas, and it felt as though they themselves were requesting it.

I went to Monkey Island and knocked on the door. Dagmar came outside the building and greeted me pleasantly, her wet hair spiked out from her head like feathers on a newborn baby bird.

"Okay, maybe I'm really losing it, but I feel like the monkeys are asking me to bring them papaya. Is that something I can do for them today?" I laughed, sort of happy to have something to laugh about, and she joined in.

"Aha, they have sent you to do their begging. Wonderful! Yes, sure thing, we have lots. If you have time to prep them, you can do that today. I would help you, but I am on a tight schedule. But how are you? Do you need anything?"

"No, I'm good. I just thought the papayas would be fun."

"You can make decisions like that yourself now. You have earned that privilege, Jamie, because we trust you," Dagmar said. "We don't trust everyone. But you have earned it."

I bobbed my head a little too rapidly.

"This permission is only for you. Not for volunteers."

Back at the enclosure, I fed the macaques through the pass-through drawer and stayed in the lockout to watch them peel and smack on the fruit for over an hour. They were perfectly focused and so was I. I felt like a true custodian of the wild. Mr. Nilsson waddled over and passed me a handful of fruit through the bars of the cage. It was lush and fragrant, tasting like a rum cocktail in front of a blue pool full of cold water. I thanked him. Life could be easy if I let it be so.

44

Sari's office was hot, her air conditioner having succumbed to the relentless summer temperatures and now only serving as a lackluster fan. I could see Sari was distracted, aggressively opening and sorting mail into stacks.

Her task reminded me to give her my envelope, crumpled and damp as it was from being forgotten in my pocket. "I wrote to my lawyer asking for some clarification about a few things. Can I leave this with you to mail?"

"Okay, fine." She threw it in into a pile. "Bills and bills and complaints. I need to do a money ritual, I really do." And then louder, not so much to me as the space around me, she said, "My intention is that the universe heals my relationship with money so that cash begins flowing like an unending river of hot lava."

I didn't know if I was supposed to say "blessed be" or not, so I just stayed quiet.

"Jamie, I need to detox my root chakra. It's full of sludge. I can feel it there. Thick, nasty sludge. Accumulation of problems that other people have laid upon me. I have so much material wealth, all of this land, Flora's house, all of it. So how can I possibly have money problems? Because it's stuck, it doesn't flow! I can't borrow against it because I don't have a job. I don't want to liquidate any of it. Oh, but they want from me. Taxes, attorneys, permits, suppliers, insurance."

"We're going to increase donors with the webcam, I just know it," I said. "We're so close!"

"That will help, for sure," she said. "But not if I don't clean out this root chakra garbage so that it flows. And do you know what, Jamie? I need to confess something."

I turned away from the monitor, giving her my full attention.

"I did something that haunts me, and I don't know how to get rid of it, and until I do, I'm afraid the money won't flow. Jamie, you know how we spread Flora's ashes?"

"Sure," I said softly, remembering the ash on her dress, the melting cake, the fetid smell of the lake at the Atlas cemetery.

"Flora didn't want a cremation. Cremation is for air beings. We're Earth beings. It's a wasteful practice. Burials are a beautiful return to the land, and that's what Flora wanted. That's what I wanted for her." Tears rimmed Sari's eyes and she pulled her knees up to her chest. "This is what's stuck inside me. I feel so guilty. I had no choice because we couldn't risk an autopsy, but the guilt is like smoke and ash literally blocking my flow now, I can feel it and I don't know how to dissolve it."

"I'm sure you did the best you could do at the time," I said.

"I did! Anna Beth pushed everything into a rush!"

"Anna Beth wanted your mother autopsied?" I said, not quite understanding.

"Yes, of course she would have." She sighed and closed her eyes. I could see that she was very tired and didn't need any further questions from me, or from anyone else, but she went on. "I needed Flora's death certificate in my hand before Anna Beth could know Flora was dead. To protect this land for Atlas. To save it, essentially. We needed a fast cremation or else my sister would have questioned the will, cause of death, everything. My sister hates Atlas, she hates me, and she won't admit it, but she even hated Mama. She hated our mother for giving everything to Atlas, because before that, everything went to me and her equally. Anna Beth is greedy and full of hate and dump-trucking it on me. That's blocking my chi, too."

She opened her eyes and took my palms in hers and looked at them as though they held a fortune she could borrow. "Anna Beth was never going to let Mama rest in peace in the ground, one way or the other. I had no choice."

"So you did what you thought was right, Sari. Trust that. Let yourself off the hook." I didn't know what else to say. I wished Tierra were in the room, because she would know what to do to calm Sari.

"Thank you. Truly, thank you, Jamie. I'm doing better already, now that I said it out loud." She took my hand and put it on her cheek. "I'm doing my best. We're doing our best."

Sari skipped dinner again. The intense heat made hot food unappealing, so instead of cooking, Tierra and I ate almonds and fruit and Dagmar had leftover boiled potatoes.

Afterward I lingered on a Bonding Bench as the sun melted like a bowl of raspberry and orange sherbet. I gave Bee two strands of hair, feeling guilty for being afraid of her when she visited me in the shower house.

"It's not you, little one, it's the disease you could give me. I'm sorry to push you away when all I really want to do is pick you up," I said.

Tierra joined me on my bench, something she rarely did. She woke early and worked doggedly, and so of course she was always ready to roost up, as she called it, after dinner. That night, though, she paused.

"Tucking them in for the night?" Tierra asked.

"I can't help myself, I know Dagmar hates chatter, but they love it," I said.

"I don't think it's bad, and truthfully, she doesn't hate it either," she said. "She always gives new volunteers a hard time, it's like the Dagmar test. Don't worry, you've passed—oh, wow, don't move." Her eyes opened wide.

"What, what?" I was scared she saw a spider on me. She reached for my sleeve and carefully, slowly pulled it down off my shoulder so that I could see the large tiger swallowtail peacefully perched on my shirt. It gave us a few flaps of black-striped, yellow beauty, and then it left.

Tierra said, "I always see them on the hottest days. That was a gorgeous one." Two monkeys started screeching, but I didn't turn to see if they were annoyed with each other or with us. "Anyway, I stopped by to say that I have some sake, just a little bottle that someone gave to me at Flora's house. I was wondering if you wanted to see my house and try it."

"Now?"

"Sure, it's too hot to actually sleep, right? And if you are thinking about your anklet boundaries, my house is within your zone. It's not a problem."

"I guess, yeah, that sounds amazing," I said, lifting my jar of tea in her direction. She lifted hers to meet it with a clink, and then her bracelets chimed against each other as an echo. "Atlas happy hour."

It turned out I was completely wrong about where Tierra's house was located. She lived far from the dome and the monkeys, on a path that extended beyond the other side of the shower house. I didn't know this area of Atlas existed, and it felt as though it was springing up inches ahead of us like fast-growing ferns. We passed an empty school bus—a tiny home in development, she said—and then a few more bends led us to her cottage.

Tierra's home was nicer than my A-frame, with more cleared

ground surrounding it. It was drier and free of creeping vines. It was also much larger and more finished, with a sprawling screened porch, jalousie windows and dark red pine flooring.

She put water on a stovetop to boil while I sat on a love seat in the main living area. I studied all of Tierra's belongings: her cozy space full of quilts and rocking chairs, art supplies, plants, and bookshelves. I felt at home, thrilled at the chance to know more about her through every detail.

"This place is as old as the little dome," she said. "The original residents left because palmetto bugs kept eating their watercolor paints, depositing rainbow leavings everywhere. And then four or five of us at a time lived here when Vessel was at its peak."

She turned off the pot and placed the sake bottle in the water. "You know, I don't like to talk about it, but I had nothing back then. Less than nothing. I never finished high school, so there were too many barriers to get into a real college program." She stretched and touched her fingertips to the doorframe between the kitchen and the living room, her strong shoulders flexing. I loved the fluid way she took up space. "But I was obsessed with childbirth. I read about it nonstop. I dreamed about it. I didn't know if I wanted to have a baby of my own, but I knew I wanted to help women who lacked services, whose birth experiences were destroyed by the oppressive medical model."

She tilted her head and earnestly held my gaze until I nodded slowly, checking to be sure I understood her words. I could imagine her as the perfect midwife: attentive, courageous, knowing.

"When I heard through friends that Sari was going to fund a school, I was all in. Sari didn't care that I was a dropout. She even paid for my bus ticket here. Eventually Vessel fell apart, though. It wasn't really a good fit. Some of the women didn't want men on the land. It became this whole thing with people already living here, and the red tape for the school bogged us down and was legally prohibitive. All kinds of bad drama."

Tierra shrugged, her gaze slipping somewhere far away. Her face grew tired and dark. I wanted her to forget about the water and come sit next to me.

"Things unraveled. This discord was very painful, but eventually we began to heal. By then I realized I didn't have to be a midwife. I just needed to be a part of a community. I needed to be useful."

"You are the most useful person I've ever met. Atlas would be lost without you."

"You are sweet, but sometimes I don't know," Tierra said. "Sari is the brilliant one, and generous beyond measure. And Dagmar is a genius, too. We'd be broke without her. She arrived after me, when the midwives were mostly gone, and we weren't sure what to do to make money. Dagmar worked in the region as a vet for exotics, so she brought the idea of the refuge for macaques to us. Once we really began to understand the spiritual guidance they offered, our decision was made for us."

Tierra carried the pot to the table on the porch. I followed closely behind her and noticed a small cut where a razor had nicked her scalp. I imagined running a steady hand carefully along those curves and dips, wondering if anyone helped her shave her head or if she did it on her own.

She warmed two small cups, discarded the water and then filled them with alcohol.

"Do you like sake? I love to let it melt in my mouth. It's surprisingly refreshing on the hottest of days," Tierra said.

I held the cup in my hands. The amber drink smelled like tart apples and almonds.

She slowly took off her rings and bracelets, stacking them one by one on the table. I wanted her to tell me where her midwifery dreams went. I wanted to know what she wanted now, but she kept circling back to simple answers, cushioned in long pauses. She was content, she said. She wanted global healing. She wanted wisdom. Her voice was slow and slick as satin.

"Thank you for this." I extended my hand flat on the table. She covered it with her own.

"You know what?" she asked. "It's weird because you've been helping me a lot, but still, it's as though I've missed you this week, with all of your website work. Sari said she has been in a weird state of mind and may have laid some odd problems on your lap, and I wanted to check in. Is there anything on your mind?"

Tierra was leaning in, almost knee to knee, rapt on my every expression. I wanted to spill each thought and concern that was plaguing me right then, but I almost couldn't bear how expectantly she watched me. I didn't want to say anything that would ruin this. I looked away, studying a basket constructed from a tangle of kudzu vines that was full of yarn.

"Sari was fine. She'll be okay," I said.

Tierra smiled and sipped her sake. I took one sip of mine, letting the drops evaporate against the roof of my mouth.

"One way or the other, I hope that if you have any questions, that you share them with me. We want everything to work out."

I took another tiny sip of my drink, just enough to wet my lips, and pushed the rest away. At the onset of the evening I thought Tierra might have been flirting with me, but I was starting to wonder if I had misread the signals. She was just checking in on behalf of all of them, which of course was okay, but was also disappointing.

I cleared my throat. "I'm so glad you can envision me staying here, Tierra. Believe me, I know how lucky I am."

"This is nice, having you over," she said, leaning back. "Truthfully, I don't know why we got in the habit of not allowing little visits at night. It started a while ago because we had some community members staying here that Dagmar didn't care for, and then it kind of stuck. But the monkeys really aren't bothered by it. We should reconsider that rule."

I thought about the monkeys howling, how they did indeed

seem bothered. I wanted to confess that I had witnessed one of their nighttime rituals. I wanted to ask her how long it would be before I was invited to the Bonding Benches, but I hushed myself. I was a puppy wagging her tail at a wolf pack. I needed to be patient and wait my turn.

"Well," I said, "since it is still a rule, I guess I should head back before it gets darker."

"Here, let me walk you down the path before you turn into a pumpkin. That way I don't have to worry about you getting lost."

Tierra reached across the table, and I thought she was going to take my hand. But instead, she took my sake cup, gave me a wink, and then downed what was left in one long, quick swallow.

Outside, I followed her silently through the dark, winding pathway to the shower house. Before I could tell her I knew the rest of the way home myself, she led me inside and then turned to kiss me tenderly against the rough screen door, her long, bare fingers cupping my face, my hands slowly finding the exquisite dip at the nape of her neck, her teeth just once tugging at my right earlobe where she whispered only a few words. It wasn't until Tierra stole away and I was almost in my own room that I could regain my breath and replay her voice in my head to understand what she said.

"Try the white ones. Just a half. Dagmar makes them," she whispered.

45

How can we help you understand our deep commitment to you, whether you are here on the Atlas campus or whether you are part of our community from your own homes?

Sit for a moment in front of the livestream of our macaques. Can you see their happiness? Their safety? Their joy at being exactly where they should be, with their tribe around them?

That is you.

You are that loved, that safe, that happy.

That wanted, that healthy, that precious, that adored.

You are one of us. You have found your tribe.

COMMENT FROM SARI

I used to think I knew how to do everything, but now I'm doubting myself. It's like when you're a kid and you make a kite and it's so beautiful, you can see it in your mind—it's going to fly to the sun. But then you go outside and you run with it. You run and let go, and it plops to the ground. The wind isn't right. The kite drags behind you and never takes flight. That's Atlas. We have each other, but the local people here have no more money for us, and they stop helping whenever the drugs run short, and Zelda and Kayla stop when the money stops, and we'll never be done with the Tampa people or Anna Beth. I don't know what to do. I try and try, but this community never soars. Unless you have other solutions, it comes down to this: we've given so much already, but it hasn't been enough. We need to sacrifice something more. It's time.

46

At breakfast, Sari said suddenly and brusquely, "Let's take our coffee and go work in my dome today, Jamie. That livestream is getting turned on today, ready or not."

"We are ready," I said, trying not to sound defensive. Her annoyance made me wonder if Sari noticed Tierra being especially attentive to me this morning, or the way I had steadied Tierra's hand with my own when pouring coffee into her mug, our touch charged and full of possibility. There was a fine line between secret and private that I rarely knew how to navigate. My instinct was total protection over even the smallest personal or precious thing, especially the tender start of something new—but then again, I had never lived with a group of people like this.

I was also flooded with energy. I woke up feeling a heady rush of joy and swagger. Tierra and I did have a special connection. Now that she had broken through the barrier, everything was possible. A year ago, I would have sworn I wanted nothing to do with romance. Tierra was different, though. I was drawn to her, and this new experience of reciprocity was thrilling.

Dagmar came into the dome singing "Tu? Tu? Piccolo Iddio!" She was terribly atonal, but I didn't laugh this time, because I couldn't stop thinking about her gift bags. I wanted to know everything about Monkey Island and nothing at all.

Then Tierra, who was standing at the sink, pointed to the door, her long arm locked and trembling. Dagmar gasped, and then we all turned.

A macaque had trailed into the dome, shadowing right behind Dagmar.

"Okay, I've got this. Nobody scare Bee," Dagmar said.

Sari and I were sitting at a table with the leftover yogurt, granola and fruit bowls from breakfast. To us, Tierra said, "You two need to back away slowly from the table, because she's going to go for the food."

"When she does, I'll go get a dart," Dagmar said.

Bee ambled farther into the dome as though she had been invited to a party, her ears fanned out wide, her black eyes shining and searching the room.

"We don't need a dart. We can use the powder we have here," Tierra said.

"I need straight K, not the mix."

"We have both. The K is in the blue tin."

Dagmar nodded and went to the pantry shelf to retrieve an old cookie tin as Sari and I slowly walked away from the breakfast table.

"So far it's always only been Bee. It's inexplicable," Dagmar said.

"Outrageous," said Sari. "You better go check that the others are safe."

"Yes, of course, we will," Dagmar said.

"Give me a banana but don't let her see," Tierra said. "And get a tablecloth."

"Let's use the dart this time, the powder is so inexact," Dagmar cautioned, running out of the dome.

"I know how to dose," Tierra said. She slowly collected the items from the pantry area herself. Just as predicted, Bee moved in the direction of the breakfast table, crawling slowly on all fours like a friendly dog.

With her back half turned to the monkey, Tierra unpeeled the banana and sprinkled it with white powder from the tin. She grabbed a frying pan from the dish drain and placed the banana in the pan. Then she put that on the counter and pushed it as far away from her as she could.

"Bee, do you see the banana? Banana for Bee," Tierra crooned.

"Are you sure it's Bee?" Sari asked. "And Bee is positive, right?"

"Yes, it's Bee, and yes, she's a virus carrier," Tierra said.

"Wait for Dagmar!" Sari said.

Bee jumped on the breakfast table. Several dishes clamored to the floor. She investigated a yogurt bowl, burying her face in it and loudly slurping.

Instead of waiting, Tierra grabbed a spatula and pushed the pan a few more inches toward her. Bee screeched and slammed the yogurt bowl down. Everything inside me told me to run, and I looked at Sari. She was standing firm, on guard and eyeing Bee cautiously.

I had considered their midnight rituals inside the monkey enclosure many times, and still couldn't reconcile them with their obvious concern for contracting the lethal virus. But I had promised to learn and to observe, and to let their inconsistencies roll off my back, sure at some point I would understand them. They must know tricks for minimizing the risks, like shamans who organize firewalks where they rush people across coals that only appear to be searing hot. Dagmar and Sari must know how to keep people safe, I reasoned.

But then again, I sensed their very real fear of Bee here in the dome.

"Bananas for Bee, only for Bee, no other monkeys do I see," said Tierra, as though she were a librarian at a story time circle, competent and measured.

In fact, her voice tone was so perfectly calculated to calm and trap Bee that I couldn't help but think of the way she told me to take Dagmar's pills, right after kissing me. Her touch had been intoxicating and disarming—I was still spinning at the memory of it. But Tierra had been in charge: I was the one left swooning.

No. I pushed the thought from my mind as yet another self-defeating scrap of paranoia, and made myself focus on the problem at hand.

Dagmar slowly walked back in the dome with her tablecloth, red and drenched in sweat.

"Bananas for Bee, only for Bee, no other monkeys do I see," Tierra sang.

It worked. Bee bridged over to the counter with an effortless leap, plucked up the banana, kissed it, and then cradled it in her arms like a baby.

"Oh, come on," Sari said.

Dagmar brought her finger to her lips and hissed, "Be patient, Sari. We need to wait for her to eat or she'll just fight."

Tierra held her position with the tablecloth. Finally, Bee started to eat the banana. By the time she was five bites in, her spring-tight limbs collapsed, and she sprawled limp on the counter for a nap. Tierra swept in, threw the cloth as a cast net and scooped up Bee like a load of fish.

Sari loudly exhaled.

"It's time to admit we have a problem, Dagmar," Tierra hissed. Moments ago, she had been singing, but now her voice was full of disdain, as though she had discovered weevils in the flour.

"The entire troop is locked in as usual." Dagmar shook her head. "She must know where there is a break in the cage, but I can't find it."

"She's been out of the cage too much. Next time, she's going to get away or hurt someone," Tierra said.

"I feel like she's trying to tell us something very, very important," Sari said. "Bee is telling us a storm is barreling toward us. She is trying to reach us. She wants a sacrifice, something we haven't offered her yet. Maybe she wants—"

"Sari, I really wish you would contemplate more and talk less," Dagmar said. "Please."

"Well, Dagmar, I really wish you would not let our monkeys roam at will," Sari snapped. "I really wish a lot of things."

Ignoring her, Dagmar trotted to the walk-in refrigerator and returned with a produce box to carry Bee, and then she and Tierra silently left to take her down to Monkey Island.

I gave Sari a hug. "It's going to be okay."

"Yeah, it probably is. Let's clean and sanitize this area. Let's not leave that for Tierra. And then when they give us the all-clear, we can get to work in my office."

We put on gloves and made a bleach solution, carefully throwing away the doped banana as well as the dishes Bee had touched, just to be safe.

"Sari, why would Tierra have this sizable quantity of ketamine in the kitchen?" I tried to sound blasé, but my voice was certainly stilted. I plunged my hands into the hot water and wrung out a rag, my blood still jumping with fight-or-flight chemicals that were stronger than the bleach.

Sari simply shrugged. "For times just like this. It's a common veterinary tool. And thank goodness she did. Ugh, this hurts to waste these lovely dishes, especially this beautiful mug," she lamented. "But there's a lot we don't know about the virus, so I think we just have to sacrifice these. Protocol."

Tierra returned. "Bee is sleeping it off under Dagmar's supervision. We're certain no other macaques were out. We counted ten times. Sari, we think Anna Beth is sneaking on the land and letting her out."

"That's not possible. Not Anna Beth's style—she's terrified of the virus and the monkeys. And to only let out Bee, more than once? No way. Did Dagmar change the locks just to be safe?"

"Yes, and she now has the only key. It all has me shook. I thought it was happening because maybe a disgruntled volunteer somehow had access, but that doesn't make sense. Maybe sabotage from Anna Beth is something we need to consider."

Sari though about it for a second. "Even if she could do this, which she can't, she has nothing to gain. She's got her big lawyers working on her behalf. There's no reason for her to come here to stir up trouble any longer. And she is going to lose her claim. The new will was filed while Flora was alive. There's no body for Anna Beth to exhume, and her accusations… I'm not worried, except about how much she'll cost us in legal fees."

"Maybe just out of anger? Revenge? Trying to scare you off?" Tierra said.

"Should we install more cameras?" I asked. "Maybe add one that will give us a view of the doors or the entire enclosure?"

"Hmm. Someone's trying to send us a message, but it's not Anna Beth. It's Bee." Sari looked at me. "But honestly, I'm not going to let this drama hijack my day. We need to get our livestream and the website working ASAP. Let's just turn the camera on, Jamie."

"I'm on it," I said. This I could do.

Tierra gave Sari a long, rocking embrace. I tried to look away, feeling foolish, but also hyperaware that looking away could make me seem petty. I wished Tierra had never kissed me in the first place. But then Sari and Tierra opened up their arms to let me join in, their embrace clumsy, so many heads and shoulders, all of us sweaty and still full of panic, but it felt right, and we ended up laughing.

"I still think Bee wants a sacrifice," Sari said. "A big sacrifice."

"It wasn't us," Tierra said. "At least not today."

★ ★ ★

"I can't even believe this morning. Dealing with Bee is not what we envisioned for our day, is it?" Sari was sprawled face-down on her bed, her voice muffled by piles of quilts. I moved two shoeboxes to sit on a pouf nearby, which sank considerably more than I anticipated, absorbing me into the cushion.

"We don't have to meet today if you need a break," I said. "But we've done all the preliminary work and I'm ready to go when you are."

"Let me ask you a question, Jamie. Do you not like me? Are you trying to get away from me?"

"What, no! I want to work with you. I meant if you aren't feeling up to it, I would let you rest."

"I'm asking you if you are pretending to like me because I'm basically your boss and can essentially make you homeless or worse, with one email." She rolled over and sat up, eyes flashing. "Let's be honest. Because you must know I could, right? That's what I'm asking. I don't like having this power over you. I want us to be equals. With infinite trust."

"I'm grateful and everything. I want to earn my keep, and I certainly don't want to be a burden. But on top of that, obviously I like you. You're amazing."

"It's not obvious." Her voice was barbed, and it stung.

"I'm sorry. I can be super weird and reserved sometimes. I know you are busy with bigger things and mostly I don't want to bother you. That's all," I said.

"It's okay. You'll get better at it. Sometimes it just feels like I give and give and give, and sometimes I'm just surprised at how patient I have to be. I thought we'd be instantly connected." She stretched like a cat, arching her back and twisting her shoulders. "But no worries, we'll get there. Okay, let's get logged in. What do we need to do to get the feed rolling?"

I felt off-kilter at her words, my cheeks flushed from being called out, but I forced myself to concentrate by visualizing the setup: the camera in the enclosure, the transmitter, the invisible data coursing through the internet, the video playing for viewers at home.

I could feel Sari's wolf pelt staring at me as we stepped across it and into the office.

"I think the feed is ready. We just need to test it again, and then I'll encode it to run on YouTube, which will also feed into the player page I set up on the Atlas site. It's all going to be entirely automatic, running live 24/7. People at home will see exactly what is happening in the enclosure as soon as we turn it on."

"We have got to do this today. I want it now. I have emails ready to send out to our donor list."

Her new screensaver caught my eye, because at a distance it looked familiar, sort of like the photo of me and my mom at the beach on my dresser, but I soon saw it was just another photo of Sari. She, too, was at the beach, walking toward the water and captured midtwirl as she laughed back at the camera.

"I am more than ready." I nodded and then dug right in, writing descriptions, hashtagging the content, and tweaking the Atlas site.

"You are so brave the way you move sections and photos around. It's a little like magic, isn't it?" Sari said. "I've got hours and hours of documentary footage, and so many plans for how to reach more people with our messages. For years I've wanted to learn this, even before the macaques, but now especially with them. Don't you think they'll be stars? In a much deeper way than ARC uses their monkeys, or any other refuge, for that matter. Much deeper."

"I think so! And people are going to want to read your writings, Sari. Your thoughts are very complex and interesting."

"Atlas is going to change millions of lives. I can feel it starting already." Sari lit a green candle, and I caught the sharp scent of eucalyptus. "Make sure the livestream page links to the donation page, by the way."

"It all links to the donation page, and unless you want to, you won't have to do anything except check your email." I said a few silent prayers that the camera feed would turn on properly, because that was the only thing left standing in my way of success. But I didn't want to tell Sari I was worried it might not work.

"That's what my mother wanted, prosperity for Atlas."

I turned from the screen to give Sari a gentle look of empathy, but I noticed she was logging onto a Tor browser on her laptop. She turned it away as soon as she felt me looking over her shoulder.

In that moment, standing at Sari's desk, I wondered if I could get away with checking my own email or running some searches through Google. I would probably start by researching veterinary drugs, the cost of tiger pelts, contracting herpes B, Flora's obituary, old coworkers, and my brother. I used to key in his name every month or so to see if he had surfaced.

But first I would research Tierra. I was hungry for information about her life before Atlas, before Vessel. I wanted to see if she had a Facebook page that would link to exes or relatives, or maybe an old, forgotten Tumblr full of her heart's secret longings. I didn't realize how much googling had become my way of coping with the world, and maybe even understanding it, until it was taken away from me. It wasn't tempted for long. Nothing was worth losing Sari's trust or messing up the livestream.

Since she had the only new keys to the enclosure, I needed Dagmar to give me access to the camera box and to Monkey Island. Dagmar was grumpy about being bothered, but she didn't simply hand me the keys, either.

The camera in the cage was controlled from a mounted box in the small lockout area between the two cage gates. She led me inside. We opened the weatherproof box, checked all the cords, and then turned the device on.

"Everything is the same as when it was installed?" she asked. "The camera only shows the tire swing area, not any part of my work areas, correct? And there is no audio, only visuals?"

"Nothing has changed, except now it is on and filming," I confirmed.

Dagmar still didn't seem stoked, but I was. When I returned to Sari, she was already watching the footage stream. We checked our site and our YouTube page and there they were, the macaques of Atlas, live and streaming. Odin and Henri were the opening act, crawling into the camera frame and jostling each other on the tire swing. Sari and I cheered like proud stage parents.

"This is an awesome first shot," I said, exploding with too many thoughts I couldn't express, no matter how quickly I talked. "Remember, this camera angle doesn't show the enclosure gates. We need more cameras installed if you want complete oversight to figure out how Bee is getting out. But it's perfect for the livestream. Don't you love this framing on the swing? Look at Cornelius, entering stage left!"

"Dagmar says she will figure out the Bee problem," Sari said. "I'm not so worried about installing more cameras, and we have several ready in the new enclosure for later. Getting the livestream and donation account up for our community is what I wanted, and you did it. Jamie, this is stellar! It's so peaceful and meditative. I am obsessed with it!"

The feed showed the troop happily playing on their tire swing, and below it, we watched the viewer count go up to two.

"Someone has already found it on YouTube!"

"I love it! Love it so much! Atlas TV! This is going to change everything!"

47

After such a triumph, I hoped we would celebrate the launch of our channel that evening, but dinner was chaotic. Dark gray storm clouds pushed past us overhead, threatening to dump torrents if they were delayed one second too long, and the weather suited everyone's sour moods.

It might have been the workmen who left in crisis that afternoon when one was bitten by a water moccasin, and another was swarmed by enough fire ants to suffer a serious anaphylactic reaction. Even before the accidents the crew was disruptive, loud and attention-seeking, not at all like the typically quiet and respectful volunteers.

Their drama was bad enough that the volunteer who had waved to me at Flora's funeral arrived to deal with the men. Tierra rushed me from the garden to the dome, but I could see him in the distance, Sari at his side, standing up to the crew with his commanding presence.

"Who is that guy, Tierra?"

"Oh, Jamie," Tierra said. "Let's please ignore them out there.

It's ridiculous that those workers can't listen to Sari or Dagmar without a man getting involved."

"Is he a friend of Sari's, or a volunteer? What's his name?"

"Wolfie," she huffed. "Now, can't we just finish cooking dinner, please? Everyone is going to be hungry."

Tierra, Sari, and Dagmar needed a break from all of the building stress. I knew a day off would help, and I wished we could pile in the Atlas van and take an easy ride to the east, back to the Anastasia Island beaches where Jason and I grew up. My body needed it too, a long soak in the healing waves of the ocean, sandy pumice scrubbing my hands and feet, salt biting away infection and pain. A volunteer could stay with the monkeys while we took a day off, windows down on the ride over, radio blaring, a full cooler in the back, and the four of us ready to let the wind and water carry every worry away.

Things didn't calm down when the men left. At dinner, Tierra mentioned that something stressful happened with Anna Beth, but Sari didn't share the details. Dagmar left the supper table and slammed the door to Monkey Island, all the more shocking because I knew that Bee was inside the building, sleeping off the kitchen ketamine. Tierra quietly finished eating, and then she and Sari left to check on Dagmar.

Then Cole dropped by. I was washing dishes and saw him casually walking outside the dome, talking with Sari and Tierra. Eels in my stomach churned in that way they do when a cop pulls behind me on the road even though I know I'm not speeding, but I reminded myself his visit was a good thing. I would get to show him what I had done on the livestream. I would tell him how therapeutic the monkeys had been. I would tell him it felt good to be a productive contributor to the growing success of Atlas. I would not mention Flora, or tiger taxidermy, or rituals, or anything at all about drugs—not darts, not pills, not powder. It would be fine, and my house arrest stint would be closing on a positive note.

Then he left. I watched him through one of the hexagon-shaped windows as he walked the opposite way past the dome toward the parking lot, still talking with Sari.

Tierra came in alone. I looked at her, waiting to be given a summary of their meeting, but she offered nothing, not even typical kitchen banter. I tried to return to cubing the potatoes for roasting, but I was bristling with frustration, so I put the knife down.

"I figured Cole was here to see me," I said. "Did he leave already?"

"I'm not sure," she said flatly.

"Is there a problem that I should be worried about? What's going on?"

"Nothing is going on," she said, without looking at me.

"Did Sari show you the livestream on her computer? It's so weird she didn't mention it at dinner, because it's a pretty big deal. We're excited."

"No, not yet."

My chest started to constrict. It wasn't normal for Tierra to be this stiff with me, and for her mood to be so icy right after talking with Cole was too much. I was drowning from both an overload of information and a lack of it, and a headache was brewing behind my eyes.

Tierra finally spoke. "Everyone is so tired, I don't know if we'll want hot food for supper. We better stay hydrated," she said, pouring two jars of tea and placidly handing me a glass.

I knew not to expect one kiss to change the world. But I wanted her affection for me to be real, to be the type of connection that was constant, that protects people from harm. I wanted more time in her arms, in her kitchen, and in her garden. I wanted to help her solve problems here and to let her help me with mine. But something had run cold, and I needed to spend some time alone to get myself steady.

"You know what? You're right. The heat is taking me down. I'm going to skip dinner and try to sleep off this headache. These are ready to roast, though, if anyone wants them." I smiled weakly.

Tierra plucked an apple from the bowl on the counter and extended it to me, and she screwed a lid on my mason jar. "A nap should help your headache. If you need anything…" Her tone was cordial, like she was thanking a volunteer for a good day's work. I looked down and shook my head.

On the way home I tried to not think about wanting Tierra's attention. I had hoped she would ask me to stay. Assure me I had a place at Atlas and a connection with her. I wanted her to push through the space between us again, maybe at my cabin, maybe in a stolen moment near the peapod vines, to tell me with one more embrace that my doubts were unfounded and that real and beautiful things were blooming between us.

I tried to avoid thinking about Sari or the ways I had hoped my time with her would turn into something more, too. Cole's meeting with Tierra and Sari almost certainly meant my time was up and Atlas was done with me, and I would eventually have to make my peace with that. I vowed to wake up the next morning, calculate my days and then ask to call Kayla so that I at least felt in charge about one part of my life.

I stopped for only a minute at the monkey enclosures. I couldn't help but look for Bee, but she was nowhere to be found. John Doe and Colette were grooming in the swing area, and that at least made me smile.

"You are television stars, babies. Work it!" I told them. "We can still celebrate, even if no one else will." I was glad we weren't transmitting sound so viewers wouldn't hear all of the things I said to my monkey friends. And then I realized, my heart sinking, that I would soon be one of those viewers, only ever able to watch the macaques via YouTube.

Even before I was home, the smell of Tierra's apple soured my stomach. I tossed it deep into the palmetto undergrowth for an armadillo to find, opened my door, and saw Cole sitting at my table in his Sunshine Monitoring shirt, all of the gift bag drugs splayed in front of him.

We can build something, something, something.

Jfkalsdfuyxcznslu it's all falling apart I can't do this anymore

COMMENT FROM SARI

I thought I would feel better about this project now that Flora is gone, but I still feel stuck. Dagmar and Tierra, do you have any ideas on what else we should say? I feel like I'm repeating myself at this point, and I don't think I say enough about the macaques. The macaques are the hook, clearly, because the livestream is up and we already have hundreds of viewers and even some small donations, hurrah! We emailed our community, and some of these are new subscribers, I know it. We've had to make some compromises to our messages upfront because we need to make sure people feel the sad plight of abandoned animals, because that will make them want to donate. Me being my typical Aquarian self, I've written too much about community and philosophy, go figure. I think I did a lot of writing to answer the question "what does Jamie need to hear" because I thought she was a great example of how to introduce someone new to our ideas, but that didn't work out like I thought it would. Wolfie says to keep it simple, that it takes time for people to trust us before we can help them understand the necessity of reducing waste, including the prolonged existence of humans, and the value of the ritual. So just let the monkeys draw people in at first and then we take our time.

He says that he plans to talk to Jamie soon. Truthfully, between us, sometimes I just want to throw her in with the monkeys and be done.

Anyone else, feel free to pipe in, today was horrendous and I'm tapped. Please don't make me do this alone.

TRACK CHANGES FROM DAGMAR

Hello, this is Dagmar. The macaques are the hook, of course they are. Why would they not be? People are lucky to watch them. They will know this, and they will donate. But don't forget that is only an entry-level goal. The real growth—and of course, the funding—will happen when we have top tier Atlas members who want to watch and participate in rituals. The second enclosure is almost ready. We are very close.

But we can only do as much work as our current numbers allow. Sari, I have two more batches to make and three more to cut, and that will only get us caught up. Chaanda's bones are almost dry enough, but the pelt needs work. I simply don't have time for more. Just finish it, Sari. Put what you have already written on the website and we can add to it later.

COMMENT FROM SARI

It's not all about the donations. It's about recruiting. And I don't want to be disorganized because we don't want to look like we are making it up as we go along.

TRACK CHANGES FROM DAGMAR

Aren't we?

COMMENT FROM SARI

You need to understand how tricky this is. We can't talk about sacrifices, real sacrifices, at length on the website. Maybe I'll just ask Jamie what she thinks.

TRACK CHANGES FROM DAGMAR

Do what Wolfie says. I must again emphasize that we need to wait before involving Jamie any further.

COMMENT FROM SARI

We are ever mindful that you are not happy she is here, and you were right, she's a major complication. If we can't resolve it all, we know what we have to do. We all agree.

TRACK CHANGES FROM DAGMAR

Even Wolfie?

COMMENT FROM SARI

Especially Wolfie. But sometimes I think we've done all of this for nothing, because what if these problems mean that we are close to the time for the big sacrifice? If we don't make money soon, the universe might be telling us we ourselves are becoming wasteful.

Maybe Bee has been trying to warn us all along. I'm trying to solve all of the problems, and we need to keep working, hold a community ritual, see what happens. But if things don't turn around soon, get ready, beloveds. The more I think about it, the more I'm sure of it. It's time.

TRACK CHANGES FROM TIERRA

I've been ready.

49

Cole Calhoun looked completely at home at my table, a big, bad wolf who wasted no energy huffing or puffing.

"Hello, Jamie. Take a seat. We need to have a brief meeting. Looks like you have been up to some real monkey business out here in these woods."

The bottom dropped out of my stomach, but I tried to speak as calmly as possible. "Cole, please believe me, I can explain absolutely everything. Listen, those are not my pills. And I've never taken drugs during my house arrest. I promise, please, let me take a urine test. Let me take a blood test. I will voluntarily submit to examination, because I am clean. Those aren't mine. I don't even know what kind of drugs they are!"

Cole smacked his lips and put up both of his hands to stop me. "Anyone with eyes would know that you've been drugging."

"I swear I haven't!"

"I can see how much weight you've lost. You've got the wild-eyed look, Jamie Hawthorne."

"I've been working in the heat, Cole. I've been killing it here. Working at Atlas would make anyone look wild."

"I think that's the first true thing you've said." He picked up the glassine envelope and flicked at the powder with his fingers. "The thing is, whether or not you are using drugs is not what I want to talk about."

Cole surveyed the A-frame, my unmade bed, filthy clothes on the rough floor like barren nests, apple cores moldering on the dresser. I wished I were strong enough to run from him, through the back side of the property, maybe to Tierra's house, maybe to Flora's, maybe to the nearest street to hitchhike south. I was acutely aware of how much everything hurt: my muscles, my ankle, my head, and then something deeper. Exhaustion. Fleeing was a pointless impulse, anyway. I was as captive as any bear in a steel-jaw trap, and trying to run would only make the carnage worse.

"Jamie, the last thing I personally want is to send you back on a violation. In my mind, that's a failure scenario for both of us. I'll do it, don't get me wrong, but I won't enjoy it. What I want is my last payment. That's how it works."

"I don't owe anything, I swear. I sold my truck so I could pay everything upfront. Some sort of accounting error has happened if there's still money outstanding. I'll find my receipts."

"Not true. You are paid up with the official fees, yes. Those go to the court and to Sunshine Monitoring. I'm talking about my personal fees. Kayla didn't give me the last payment, and instead, she sent me to Sari. I've been here twice to collect, but each time they gave me the run-around."

"I don't know anything about this," I said. "I swear, no one has said anything."

Cole walked through the room and did a push-up against the slanted wall of the A-frame. "Well, I'm telling you now, you need to pressure them to pay. Beg, or promise to work it off. Do what you need to do. Just pay up and we will in fact be done. And then I suggest you disappear. Poof. Like magic."

"Kayla knows about this?"

He laughed and sat down backward in the chair. "Kayla and I have done a few mutually advantageous deals like this in the past. You can't get the kind of home detention sentence Kayla got for you unless a private e-carceration company accepts the contract. Do you really think they would agree to monitor you here without extra incentives? She pays me directly for her clients who need special handling or have unique circumstances, on top of their regular fees. Though none have been as unique as this one."

"I had no idea." I felt like I might throw up. I had no more money to pay off Cole. And if everything about the monitoring program had been a lie, I didn't know where that would leave me, except jail.

"If she had just paid like always, we'd be fine. Looking the other way is the point of the service. But she said your benefactor was late and that Sari would pay directly."

"My benefactor? I don't have a benefactor!"

"Yeah, ya do. If you think Kayla sorted out your crap because she loves pelicans, you don't know Kayla." He stood up briskly. "Listen, this conversation has gone on much too long. Talk Sari into coughing up some cash. It's not even a lot of money. Ten large, next week, and we're done. Happily, because y'all kind of creep my wife out, and I can't say that I disagree with her on this one. Otherwise I will violate you for drugs and you'll go to jail."

"Okay, got it. I'll make sure you are paid. I will." I looked deep into his eyes. "Cole. Thank you for letting me fix this."

He straightened his twisted pant leg, and I realized he was holstering a gun against his ankle. "I couldn't care less what you do after that point, but if you were smart, you might not want to stick around people who don't think you're worth ten K. They spend more than that on bananas, is all I'm saying, and they're sitting on a pot of gold worth killing for."

★ ★ ★

I sat in my room as the dark sky crawled in through the vine-wrapped screens surrounding me, the nighttime heat choking me like a gag. I was unable to rest, hot and savage with anger. I packed my tote boxes, horrified that I would have to stay until I could convince Sari or Kayla to pay my ransom, livid with myself for having no one to call and nowhere to go.

I needed to reconstruct my weeks at Atlas. I needed to map it out, so I tried to think of sequences of activities or meals that might anchor me. Oysters. Baking bread. Sari's website project. Flora rooting through the compost. Jodie picking up O-Ren. My missing plate of rocks. Anna Beth screaming in the parking lot. It was all as slippery as snakes across my bed, and each of the concerns I had talked myself into ignoring writhed and constricted around me. Baggies of drugs. Flora's funeral. Zelda's tiger. The midnight ritual.

It ultimately didn't matter because out of everyone, I believed Cole, and I knew I needed to figure out how to pay him.

I was furious with all of them for letting me work so hard, for never telling me about this side deal, but I was going to have to hide my emotions if I had any chance of receiving help from Sari. I knew Sari, and confronting her with anger would be disastrous. What could they say about a betrayal this massive, anyway? I knew Kayla was too good to be true. Atlas had been doomed from the beginning.

But I needed Atlas on every level. It was my only home, I had no other friends, and now I had to get them to help me pay Cole or I would be sent to jail. The only other options would be to run (but I had no funds) or to throw myself in the arms of the sheriff (and I knew better than to trust that). Based on what Cole revealed, between the corruption and incompetence of the authorities, the likelihood of finding help that didn't punish me further was nil. If I couldn't put together Cole's 10K payment and some money to live on while I started over, I was facing years of incarceration or else years of being penniless and alone in Georgia or Louisiana—and I didn't know which would be worse.

Just as I was about to lie down and force myself to rest, a sound hurtled though the dark like a knife.

The monkeys began screaming, louder than I had ever heard them. Atlas was either holding a more terrifying ritual than ever before, or more monkeys were loose, or Anna Beth was on the grounds. I realized I had been holding my breath since Flora's funeral, waiting for Anna Beth's return.

The moon was almost full, so I knew it would be fairly light at the enclosure. They would easily see me. I told myself to stay in my house. Their rituals were none of my business any longer, and yet I hated the fact that I was drawn to them still, even knowing everything I knew. All the more reason I should stay away.

It didn't serve me to make Anna Beth my business, either. What Sari did or didn't do to hasten Flora's death or to rush her cremation—it wasn't my problem to solve. Sari didn't need my protection. She had Tierra and Dagmar, who wouldn't hesitate to send a poisoned dart right to Anna Beth's neck if she were to mess with the macaques.

I knew I should lay low.

And yet the howling was a magnet. The monkeys were riled up, and I did feel responsible for them, for Bee and Cornelius, and for Ghost and Meaty Joe. They were calling for help. I had come to love all of them, and they were entirely dependent on human intervention.

If they were roaming, I did need to save them. Monkeys like Stella, Charlie, and Henri wouldn't survive in the wild. I could see Nora-Nora-Nora ending up in a fight with a snake or trying to ride an alligator's back. Townspeople or wildlife officers would shoot them, thinking they were another animal or for fear of the virus. Atlas could fail itself and each other again and again, and that was one thing. But for me to stand by while they failed their animals wasn't something I could live with.

I looked around my room for a weapon, and grabbed a flashlight and a beach towel in case I needed to try and capture one of my little friends.

I kept the flashlight off to avoid attention, navigating the path by following the moon through the canopy cap. I moved slowly and quietly, trying not to let the monkey howls escalate my already seething anger. I marveled at how I had learned this path over the summer's weeks. I knew which root wads to ignore. I knew the bends and twists it would take.

Even before reaching the enclosure, I could see the Bonding Benches were empty. The troop was unhinged, running and screeching. Though there was no way to count them at night while they were agitated, their doors were closed, and the enclosure seemed to be full. If some monkeys were loose, at least it was not all of them, and that was a tremendous relief.

"What's going on, little mamas? What is going on?" I whispered.

I stopped at my favorite bench to reassess, and heard a loud conversation coming from inside one of the domes, or more likely, the open area between Monkey Island and the dome. I paused. It was Sari and a man.

"I'm taking it with me," he shouted, a deep rumble full of oil and threat.

"You need to leave!" Sari yelled. "Tomorrow, we'll have it organized! But you need to leave!"

I crept closer, taking cover at the side of the Monkey Island building. What I could see looked like a standoff. Sari and Tierra were on the dome porch, silhouetted from the light of the one porch bulb. The stranger had his back to me. At first I thought it was Wolfie, but this guy was different, a short cannon of a man I had never seen before. I wondered if he was a volunteer, but it didn't seem likely. This man wasn't the type to meditate with macaques.

He pushed toward the dome, his voice louder and angrier

with each step. "Where is it? I drove all day and I ain't turning around without it. Where is it?"

Sari said, more evenly now, "I know we are late, but don't worry. We will bring it all to you, as soon as possible. It's hidden in various places because we have inspectors coming. But we'll get it."

"I paid early as a gesture, and you're late. It's not good. Get it. Now!"

The "now" was shouted so adamantly that it resounded against the chain link of the enclosure. I flinched and pressed my back harder against the building.

I couldn't see Sari's face, but I could hear her pleading. "Okay, okay. Listen. Can we talk? My mom died. We had unexpected delays. The tiger bones are not dry enough yet. Things take time. Come back tomorrow, and you'll have it all, or we'll bring it to you personally, even if it means taking on the risk of transport again."

"I will dry it myself. Make sure it's all there. Every tooth, every organ!" the man bellowed.

"Or I'll refund your money and you can pay me after delivery. But why not just come back tomorrow?" Sari said.

"Where is it?"

"Please, let's be smart," Tierra said.

I heard a hissing behind my head and froze. My limbic system lit up with flight commands.

"Get in here!"

It was Dagmar, coaxing me through the cracked door of Monkey Island. I quietly obeyed, sliding over to the door and easing my way in.

The lights were off, with Dagmar squatting on the floor by the door, illuminated by the glow of a laptop. I sat down next to her.

"What the hell?" I whispered.

"It's super bad. It's a complicated deal. The point is, I need to return his twenty thousand dollars, but I can't concentrate on this stupid cyberbanking portal. I think I refunded it, but I'm not sure. I need to go out there to protect them." She pointed to a handgun gleaming on the floor.

"Dagmar, are you serious?"

"You better be happy I have a gun. Because if that man finds out I sold the tiger parts to someone else while we borrowed his payment, it won't be good."

"Borrowed?" I whispered. The tussle outside was escalating.

"Check this, see if I did the refund right," she said. She pushed the laptop and a notebook at me, grabbed her gun and left the building, slamming the door. I instinctively reached up and locked the door, then ran past a steel table looking for a place to hide.

The monkeys started screeching louder.

Tierra shouted, "I'm calling the sheriff."

"How about I pop off monkeys one by one until you find my tiger bones," he yelled.

"Leave," Dagmar yelled.

"Leave or I'm calling the sheriff," Tierra shouted.

"Hey now, okay, she's not calling anyone. Put down the phone, Tierra," Sari said.

"Put down the phone!" the man yelled, and then he yelled it again. I started to wonder what everyone would say when the sheriff arrived to arrest the intruder—and then two shots thundered. When the air cleared, Sari was screaming and monkeys were howling, and that's all I could hear.

I was overwhelmed with fear, my pulse pounding in my ears. My hands were shaking, and it took all of my will to stay focused.

Then after a beat, one more shot rang out.

Sari shrieked again, and then there was more clamoring. I heard Dagmar's voice but not Tierra's, and through it all, monkeys screeched at each other in a vicious echo.

I took a deep breath, tried to settle myself. I needed presence of mind in order to survive.

After a few minutes, hearing no more commotion, I cautiously left the building, terrified of what I might find. I peered around the corner. The three women of Atlas were all clustered around the body. Despite everything, I was relieved to see them alive—only the man was down, splayed on the dirt. Tierra stood still, somehow the one holding a handgun. Dagmar knelt uselessly at the man's side, as did Sari, her arms raised in beseeching prayer, or perhaps in triumph.

A horrific flood of blood covered him and was still seeping out from his shirt. I handed Dagmar the bandanna from my head, but I knew it was too late for the applied pressure to help. There was no way he wasn't already dead.

"Have you called the sheriff? Are they on the way?" I asked.

"No." Sari sobbed, sitting down on the ground.

"What did you do, Dagmar? What have we done?" Tierra lamented.

"What I did is save your life. What I'm going to do is put this monster into the lake, that's what I'm going to do."

I crouched down and touched Sari. The carnage was vivid and inescapable. Bile rose in my throat. I helped her stand up.

The women began to talk rapidly, their staccato pressure sailing over my head like more bullets.

"I'm putting him in the lake. I'm giving him to the gators."

"No, you are not."

"Tierra, put down his gun."

"I'm calling Zelda."

"Will she take him?"

"She better."

"What else can we do?"

"We need Wolfie."

"We need to tell Jamie everything."

"The lake."

"Should I call him?"

"Not yet."

"Tell Zelda to come here and we'll talk. Don't give her details over the phone," Dagmar said.

"Of course," Sari said. "I'll 911 her."

"We need to call the real 911," I said. "You have to call the sheriff or I will." I knew involving law enforcement would land us all in trouble, myself included, but standing there, in front of all of the blood, my problems with Cole receded. I saw no other safe choice.

"No, Jamie, we can't," Sari said.

"But aren't we in danger—somebody is going to come looking for him. And right now if you call the sheriff, they'll be able to see it was a necessary act of self-defense."

"I was protecting us! He pulled a gun on Tierra!" Dagmar cried. The monkeys moaned with her.

Sari started walking off, and in the dead of the dark night, she placed a call.

"You need to put the guns away," I said, raising my voice to get their attention.

"You need to shut up, Jamie. You don't know what you are talking about," Tierra said. I closed my eyes against the sting of her voice. I needed to fully hear and remember it.

"Okay, okay, listen," Dagmar said. "Everybody, calm down."

"How can I calm down?" I yelled. All at once, I felt the full freight of their betrayals and crimes and of my own desperate situation bearing down on me. "None of you know what you are doing!"

Sari walked back toward us, and it struck me that she looked exactly the same as when I arrived, blond hair flowing, tan legs making long strides. I felt a righteous fever coursing through me, an indignation fueled with panic and urgency.

Dagmar winced and cocked her head at Sari. "Do you see

what I mean? Tell me you understand." The three of them locked
eyes and nodded.

"I get it." Tierra sighed.

"Zelda's on her way," Sari said. She sat on the ground.

"Give me the phone!" I yelled, ready to lunge toward them,
but before I could spring forward Dagmar pointed her gun at me.

"Stop right there!" she said.

I caught myself and stumbled backward.

"Listen!" Sari stood up and pointed at me. "You are going to
follow Dagmar into the dome right now, and you are going to
sit down. Don't say a damned thing. You don't know what you
are talking about, so listen. We're right behind you."

I did as I was told, regretting that I didn't think to message
anyone when I had the laptop in my hands mere minutes ago in
Monkey Island. But who would I have reached out to, anyway?
There was no use waiting for someone to save me or to tell me
what to do. I was utterly, gravely alone.

50

Dagmar duct-taped my wrists to each other, and then she used scissors to notch the band of my monitor before wiggling it off my ankle and onto her own upper arm. She had threatened to tape my mouth closed if needed. I shook my head vehemently and kept quiet, and she relented.

Tierra put the guns on the counter, but she kept guard next to them.

"You were a mistake." She sniffed dismissively. "I can't believe you turned on us. This betrayal really hurts."

"Calling the sheriff? I didn't mean it. Please. You know I didn't mean it."

Dagmar shouted, "If you are going to talk, I will tape you shut."

I thought back to when Tierra caught Bee in the dome. First, she sang sweet songs to her, then trapped her with a banana, then brutally dismissed her. How had Tierra put it? Bee was a problem who had been out of her cage too many times.

Right after our kiss, she had suggested that I try Dagmar's pills. And now, right there on the counter, sat a gun.

Calling me a mistake cut deep. I had allowed myself to fall for Tierra because I thought we had a singular connection. She patiently taught me so much about the practicalities of Atlas life. She had modeled serving others. But I had been foolish to tumble headfirst into a sinkhole of feelings for her, when she had been offering me what she offered everyone at Atlas. I was a volunteer to be fed, a new worker to be trained, or at best, a long-term resident to befriend—so she invested time in me. It was my own fault for thinking it could be more.

After Flora's funeral I knew I needed to back away and get my feelings in check, and then her kiss felt real, tangible, like possibility compressed into passion. But now that I was duct-taped right where I had enjoyed so many carefully prepared meals, it all made an uglier sense. She had been managing me. She knew I nursed a crush; she knew I needed reassurance. Nothing really mattered to her except Atlas. And just like a bug-infested plant or a burnt pot of beans, she saw me as a mistake that needs to be scrubbed away and forgotten.

Sari brought Tierra a mug of coffee.

"Let's quietly drink our coffee and wait for Zelda. She'll be here in about an hour."

"I don't see why we need to bother with Zelda," Dagmar said. "Just put him in the lake."

"Because Jamie's right. We need to solve this problem in total or it will steamroll," Sari said. "Somebody is going to come looking here for him."

"Maybe not," Dagmar said. "I refunded his twenty thousand in full."

Sari sat down and stared into space. Dagmar ran in and out of the dome. Tierra cried silently, her face a mess of sweat and tears, and sat down and rocked herself.

I ran through every scenario in my head. I needed to gain back their trust, get free, and then run.

Eventually we heard a horn. Dagmar sprinted out. Sari ran water on her hands and patted her face. She brought me a glass of water. A few moments later we heard Zelda cursing, and then she and Dagmar came in the dome. Sari immediately hugged her.

Zelda's hair stood on end, making her look like an angry cassowary on the attack. "What happened? Gunfire? Sari, this is beyond."

"It doesn't matter what happened. We're fine, but we need your help with his disposal. You know that's William Landry, right?"

Zelda pointed at me. "Did she do this?"

"No, but I don't know what to do about her, honestly," Sari said.

"I told you she was a problem."

"You and Dagmar were right, okay? Everyone is clear on that point."

"Where's Wolfie?" Zelda asked.

"He was on his way to Miami, but he's heading back," Sari said.

"Well, why did you have to shoot William? Did he find out you sold Chaanda to someone else?"

"No, he was here to pick up the tiger because he thought it was his…because we hadn't refunded his money yet."

Zelda's eyes bugged. "You still had his payment?"

"Just temporarily," Dagmar said. "We are juggling money right now and we were going to tell him and return it soon, but he pulled a gun on Tierra."

Zelda stared at Tierra for a few seconds, then Dagmar. Finally, she nodded, paying her respects. "So what's the plan?"

Sari spoke in measured, gentle tones. "The gunshots could be linked to us. Can you please cremate him?"

Zelda thought for a minute and sighed. "I can't do another

cremation for you right now because the equipment tracks how many times I fire up the chamber, and I don't currently have a big animal cadaver that I can switch out in his place to throw off suspicion. Remember all the forms I had to falsify last time?"

Dagmar asked, "Do we need to arrange for a fake death certificate?"

"That won't help. And my doc won't do another dealio so quickly after the last one. But you don't need to cover up the cause of death. It's not like you are related to the guy. It's better if he remains a missing person. You just need to bury him and hope he's never found." She swept her arms wide, as if reminding Sari of the deep woods surrounding us.

"Please take him," said Sari. "I'll pay whatever you want to handle the cremation. I don't want his body in my lake, or I'd do it myself."

"I don't like it," Zelda said. "There are way too many moving parts. Why don't we pay for the big cat refuge to have their hyenas take care of it? Hyenas are better than alligators. They're more thorough. Plus it'll happen away from Atlas. They'll be thrilled to do it."

I was close to passing out, hearing about all of these options, but I willed myself to stay quiet, hoping they would forget about me when they left to move the body. Then I would be able to break free.

"Hyena solution," Sari said.

"I'll extract the bullets first," Dagmar said.

Just when it felt resolved, Zelda continued, gesturing at me. "And then what about her? You going to call me about her next? Don't even think about it. Nope, this is it. I'm maxed out. Sari, you need to get hyenas of your own."

"We know. We're working on it. It's okay," Dagmar said, though her tone said nothing was close to okay.

They took off—presumably to wrangle the body—leaving Tierra to watch over me.

I tried to remember dates and exchanges to match what I had learned. Poor Flora. This must be how Sari obtained such a fast cremation, and maybe that's how Dagmar ended up with the taxidermy project. Zelda cremated Flora instead of the tiger and paid a doctor for a death certificate. I couldn't get all of the facts to line up, but the chill down my spine told me I was close to the truth.

Tierra sighed. "Between you and me, I'm tired about hearing about the big cats and the hyenas that the other exotic places have. They get all the big donations. Yeah, sure, jaguars and cheetahs are more glamorous." She went to the freezer and pulled out an ice pack for her knees. "So what if our monkeys don't eat bones like savages? They are infinitely wiser. We have an abiding spirituality here at Atlas because of the macaques. They are the future. We have to protect that," Tierra said. "Hyenas are demonic."

I had no idea who this woman was.

51

Sari stumbled back into the dome. I had my head down on the table per Tierra's instruction. I desperately wanted them to let me drink the glass of water.

"Tierra, Dagmar needs you, so I'll take over and guard her. The sun is up, and the monkeys need food. She's over there now," Sari said.

Peeking, just as I had done during elementary school rounds of Seven Up, I could see Tierra comforting Sari. What a nest of manipulative snakes they were. The guns were untended on the counter a few paces behind them. I didn't know how to get to them fast enough, even if I convinced Sari to release me from duct tape. If I had something heavy enough on the table to throw in the other direction, I could distract them; they were surely jumpy. But I didn't, and I couldn't guarantee success. Their jumpiness could also cost me my life.

"Sari," I said, working hard to keep my tone fluid and light. "Can we maybe talk about an idea I have to be of help? Can we maybe have a cup of tea and talk?"

Sari didn't respond, but she put a gun in her waistband, checking the safety first. She then clicked on the pilot light to heat water.

"I don't think I really want your ideas, Jamie."

"That guy came in a truck or a van, right? We have to get rid of whatever he was driving. I can take it out of state. You already cut off my monitor, so just tell Cole I ran off on foot, and I'll already be long gone."

Sari said nothing, but she brought the teapot and two cups to the table.

"And instead, you'll drive straight to the cops. I heard you. You want to tell the sheriff everything. Everything."

"I am not going to do that. I was just panicking. Now that everything is calm, why would I do that? I don't want to go to jail. I don't want to hurt you either."

I couldn't drink the tea with my hands tied so it sat there next to the water. I tried to look deep into Sari's eyes and to speak as gently as possible, just as I had seen Sari speak to so many volunteers. "I care about you. I care about Atlas. Atlas is beautiful, and you can fix all of your problems here. I care about Dagmar and Tierra and the monkeys. I don't want all of Atlas to crash down. Believe me, I would not wish the legal system on anyone, friend or enemy. Your grief is enough for you to grapple with. I wish you only peace."

Sari's eyes welled up.

"I could leave his vehicle on this abandoned road in the Okefenokee swamp area. It's perfect. And then from there I'll just disappear. I am mentally prepared to disappear, seriously, I was thinking about running before I got the house arrest arrangement, because jail is awful. You can trust that."

She said nothing.

"I promise you I will never, ever contact you again. Let me help you, and then you'll never hear from me again."

"Oh, I wish that were possible. It's much more complicated

than that." Sari drained her tea and held the cup to her cheek. "You know, it's time that we chat about your brother. How long has it been since you've seen spoken with Jason?"

My pulse raced.

"Not since he left town almost a decade ago. Not once."

She stared blankly, so I continued.

"I was in foster care by the time he was arrested when he was about twenty, and then he skipped town instead of facing the charges. He never contacted me, and I have searched for him, but I haven't found him yet. Honestly, I don't even know if he's alive."

"Oh, he's alive. And he saw your pelican video, Jamie. Everyone saw the Florida Woman burn down the bar, didn't they?"

I didn't like the ways her lips curled when she said that. Sari loathed me. Like her sister, she thought I was trash.

She slowly shook her head. "He saw it a million times. How do you think you ended up with such a good lawyer calling you out of the blue? Who do you think paid her? And this placement here? Jason cooked up this whole plan to help you."

She let that land like a block of ice on my heart.

"Jamie, I've known Jason since you were a child. Didn't he ever talk about having a posse of friends he ran wild with out in the county? His friends from when he got busted? Jason took the fall for us, way back in the day, when you were still in foster care." She was very deliberate, slowly delivering each detail. "He used to visit you until he decided to jump bail and had to lay low."

It was like a hard oyster shell I had been pounding and pounding finally cracked open. I thought about what Cole told me, that a benefactor was late in paying my fees. Jason must have paid my bail and secured Kayla's services. I thought I was empty and would never cry again, but fresh tears flooded my face when it all sunk in. Jason was alive, and Sari was in contact with him even now.

"We started building an amazing community back then. Jason actually led the construction of these domes—he called them his ships, and that's why we named the community The Argo. But every community needs money. We started dealing. When he was busted on the road, he took the entire rap for all of us. If he had turned me in, I would have lost everything, this land and more. And now it will all be lost anyway." She threw her arms into the air.

I knew, watching her now, that Sari was more like me than she wanted to admit. It didn't matter how hard she worked or how many times she reinvented herself, she always hit a wall, and now she was stone cold spinning out of control.

But Jason. Jason was alive and well, and he had been helping me. I needed to talk to him.

"Sari, if you had only told me about Jason earlier. Where did he go when he skipped town? How can I contact him? Why didn't you tell me he was helping me?"

"We wanted to wait until you finished your house arrest sentence first. Our community, our rituals, Jason wanted to temporarily keep it all from you. That way, when you appeared in front of the judge for the last time, you wouldn't have to lie if they asked you about him, or about what we did here. We thought you could just hang out, get through your sentence, and then he'd tell you everything about Atlas."

"But I don't understand." I was certain she said *he would tell me*, but that didn't make sense. If Jason knew everything about Atlas, why would he send me to live here?

"It wasn't supposed to be like this. We don't know what to do."

At that very moment, Dagmar came into the dome and marched straight to the table, grabbed my arm and speared it with a dart. I was out before she could pour herself a cup of tea.

52

Not quite inside myself, I woke aware of only heat and pain, as though the agony shredding my head and blazing through my body was the real me, the real Jamie, and the old me was just a small memory observing this forsaken husk from the bottom of a deep, dank swamp.

Details tumbled into place like clods of dirt from a shovel. It was so dark. My bladder stung, my hips, neck, and back ached. The details of my pain helped me in their own awful way to feel human again, feel whole again, and then I remembered the previous day. I remembered the people, the monkeys, the violence. My first solid thought: I've been sent to prison for that man's murder. And then the sour awareness of the man's blood, of Dagmar pushing the laptop at me and bolting with the gun, of Tierra's betrayal, of Zelda and Sari with their complicated schemes. I could only hope they end up in a prison that is far from mine.

I was lucky they hadn't killed me. Yet.

Jason.

Bit by bit I woke up. Flora, dead. A man, dead, just like that. I would never be okay now, knowing what a bullet-riddled body can look like, knowing the violence women I knew and trusted—people who, on the surface, appeared to be so caring and thoughtful—were capable of rationalizing.

But Jason was miraculously alive. He had seen me, recognized his little sister, and had risked his freedom to try to save me, first through Kayla, and then through Atlas. Though why bring me here, into this mess? If Sari was telling the truth, he hadn't saved my life, he had doubly ruined it. If he had left me in jail, I would have served my time by now instead of becoming treacherously embroiled in Atlas's criminal abyss.

I felt mosquitos swarming my face and nipping at my sweaty skin. I became fully aware that I was outside, and then I felt a wooden pallet beneath me. I tried to quiet my movements, but I felt motion around me in response.

Monkeys. I could smell their acrid musk nearby. I could feel them moving against their enclosure and hear them quietly chittering—not alarmed, but aware. Aware of me.

I pushed myself up. It was a humid night with thick wet clouds holding the moon back, but when my eyes adjusted, I saw diffused moonlight toying against the familiar pattern of chain link. I wasn't in the garden shed or in the shower house. Anger hot as the summer sun rose inside me.

I walked toward the fencing, slowly to avoid tripping, and turned around to take in the full horror of my situation.

I ran to the gate to confirm what I already suspected: I was locked in the brand-new monkey enclosure.

I wanted to scream, but I knew better. I forced myself up over the waves of fury and pain in silence. I didn't want to upset the macaques or summon the women—and I wasn't certain I was alone in the cage. I fought the primal desire to howl because every choice, every minute mattered. I sat on the ground by the gate, digging deep inside for the strength to stay quiet until daylight.

The new enclosure ran parallel to the old one, with a clearing between them. There was room for three rows of Bonding Benches, plus plenty of space for visitors to walk. Dagmar thought this would keep the monkeys close enough to each other to feel connected, but not enough to unsettle them.

When the faintest early-morning light broke in enough for me to see more than shadows, I found two sleeping bags and a gallon of water in the lean-to. The cage was free of other animals. I almost drowned myself gulping water, forcing it down my swollen throat.

I tried to tell myself to count my blessings. It was oppressively hot, but I could still hydrate. I was hurt, somewhat bruised, but not horribly. I could walk and move, so they probably banged me up when they transitioned me into the enclosure, but likely had not beaten me.

I told myself to rest and look for an opportunity to fight back or negotiate, or I was destined to die in the brand-new Atlas cage.

53

First, the macaques stirred, cheerfully squawking and clanging to greet the day. I willed myself to feel their optimism. Signs of life. Beacons of survival.

The full morning sun hit the open side of the lean-to, so I took cover outside it. I watched two green anoles travel up and down the wall, either flirting or in a territorial fight for shelter. I was rooting for their love. I knew I was going to lose my own fight and would likely die trying to survive Sari, but I hoped both lizards fared better.

I stopped myself. Emotional detours wouldn't help. I needed to focus. I walked the enclosure, eyes trained on the ground. Any small scrap of construction debris was a potential tool I could use for survival.

I walked the fencerow of my cage. I knew for certain no part of my enclosure could be seen in the livestream camera. Dagmar had made sure only a tight shot of the tire swing transmitted, because she didn't want random Atlas activity to become content fodder. But what if the camera had been jostled? I walked up and down the line on the very small chance that I could be seen. Any effort was worth the chance at survival.

The monkeys eyed me warily from their own cage. They probably thought I should be making their breakfast.

"I would if I could," I said. "If only, little ones, if only."

After a while, Dagmar arrived. I heard the door to Monkey Island swing open and moved to the fencerow to watch. The monkeys were watching too, eagerly anticipating their breakfast. They burst into boisterous glee when Dagmar emerged wheeling containers and bowls their way.

I knew she would take care of the monkeys, and I hoped she would at least offer me the same basics of food and more water, so I decided it was best not to call out to her. I'd trust that she would see to my needs, and talk with her then. There was no way to sound calm while yelling across a distance like that. I definitely wanted to sound calm. Not angry, scared or desperate. Agreeable, understanding, and compliant were my only paths.

Beneath it, though, I was wholly angry, scared, and desperate.

But I needed to be strategic. I needed information. If they doubted my loyalty, I would remind them that I would never do anything that would get Jason in trouble.

Seeing Dagmar feeding the macaques as she has done hundreds of times before was infuriating. She had once intimidated me, the good doctor who cared for all beings with grace and conviction. I wanted to scream, but I knew it would mean nothing to Dagmar. She had created her own inscrutable ethics and would do as she pleased.

I calmed myself by sipping the last of my water, banking on a refill from Dagmar. If they kept me in the enclosure without it, I would die within the day, but I didn't see them doing that. Dagmar would rather dart me with ketamine than let me writhe in dehydrated agony, because my screams would scare the nearby macaques. I walked my cage border while the monkeys feasted. Watermelon in their bowls. I used to love watching them delightfully slurp their way through watermelon. Now I was simply envious.

"Don't worry, you're next," Dagmar shouted.

I felt my chest thud at being addressed directly by her as though I were a gorilla in the neighboring zoo cage. I reminded myself of my choices. I said nothing. Game on.

I watched the macaques for a few minutes, and then went back to combing the ground to look for a last-minute discovery of a stray nail or bit of fencing. Sometimes I was lucky like that: the very thing I needed—a forgotten sixty-dollar refund arriving just in time to keep the lights on for the month, meeting someone who needed a roommate right before losing my lease—landed from the sky a hair before the deadline.

A piece of wire, an errant bolt, anything would have been promising.

Did it matter, though? They were either holding me until Zelda could arrange my demise, or they were going to take care of it themselves. I could practically hear Sari's "blessed be." Atlas loved nothing more than a sacrifice.

Or, if I were lucky, a burial and cryptic headstone near the cemetery pergola. I realized Bee had predicted as much when she brought me the porcelain mermaid statue from their menacing, macabre altar.

I had to wait at least half an hour before Dagmar came to me. My enclosure was outfitted with several large food drawers that Dagmar herself had designed to safely push food into the enclosure, then later pull back to the outside to clean. She placed several items in one of the drawers for me, including a sandwich, a gallon of water, a jug of tea, half of a small watermelon, and a plastic mug I recognized as one of the toys the monkeys used in their swimming pool.

I picked up the red mug and smelled its contents. "Coffee? This is really nice, Dagmar. This is more than I expected." I looked directly at her, hoping to exude warmth and gratitude. "Thank you."

"I'm a Dane. Coffee is dignity," she quipped. "It might feel otherwise, but we aren't trying to punish you. We're not intending to torture you, but we do need to contain you. And we really don't know what to do next."

I wanted to wail. Punishing me when she is the real criminal. How dare she. How dare Sari, with her meaningless spiritual manifestos. How dare Tierra, with her superficial care and cunning touch.

But anger without agency wouldn't benefit me, so I cloaked every vengeful ember with composure.

"I really appreciate this, Dagmar. What if you tell me exactly what you are trying to do. I want to help. You've cut off my ankle monitor. Does that mean Cole or the sheriff is going to come soon to get me today? I understand. Let's just get our stories straight. I'll go and I won't implicate anyone here in anything, I swear. What do you want me to say to them?"

"The sheriff is not coming."

Dagmar sat on the ground with her back to the fencing. She must be so tired, I thought. It was not like her to sit when she could stand, especially near a cage. Even though she was a heartbeat away, I had no way to fight her with the fence between us. Instead, I sat down on my side of the fence to join her.

"Someone will come. I'm a violator now."

"We had to remove it. Kayla told us how to do it by notching the edges without cutting wires. And now it's gone, far away. Tierra drove it, and then she ditched it in the ocean. This morning Sari told Cole you were missing. So basically, you escaped. On paper."

"Okay, makes sense, so now I can just live off the grid. I understand."

"The funny thing is the signal actually stopped in Orlando. The monitors are terrible, that's what Kayla says, but the court believes them. So anyway, Cole will write a report that says you ran away, forgetting everything else he learned, and that will probably be that. And now we owe him quite a bit."

"Dagmar! This is good news. So y'all can just let me go then. I'll go north and I will never breathe a word of any of this to anyone, for your safety and mine. We can put all of this mess behind us. And if it's okay with Sari, she can put me in touch with Jason. He'll teach me how to live on the lam."

Dagmar said nothing. Many of the macaques had gathered near the bars of their enclosure, watching our exchange.

I felt my heart sink in her silence, but I tried to sound upbeat. "Or not. I don't have to call Jason. It's enough to know he's okay. I can just travel on my own, disappear. No worries. Either way, I'm going to do my part. Atlas will be fine."

Again, Dagmar stayed silent.

Sweat pooled behind my knees. Dagmar drank water from her bottle. I wanted to go collect mine, but instead stayed put. I slowly drained the last ounce of coffee from the plastic cup, eyeing bite marks embedded in the rim.

I took a deep breath. I reminded myself to be soothing, submissive. "Dagmar, you know I would do anything for you, not only because I want these monkeys to have a good life at Atlas with you and Sari, but also because all I really want is to live. It's a little sad, really, because I've spent so much of my life depressed, in limbo, waiting for something to happen or waiting for my brother to come home, feeling stuck and alone. But now I have clarity, thanks to you. I want to live. I want you to let me live. I will do anything for you if you and Sari and Tierra let me live. And, Dagmar, I'm not going to guess what it is that you want from me. Tell me. What do you want? What does Atlas want? I swear to you I will do it."

The monkeys started squabbling over a breach of etiquette on the tire swing. Several of them started howling and tussling while others ran in wild circles until the drama calmed down. I bet livestream viewers loved it.

"What do we want? We want this land to be a safe place that provides for us and our monkeys. They are sacred, they truly are. We're not worthy of them. So I suppose that's what I want, to be worthy of them. To do my work and learn from them. Sari, Wolfie, and Tierra want the same thing: our spiritual community to grow and reach a world that needs what we have here at Atlas." She sighed. "And we want all of these problems to go away."

"Yes! That makes complete sense. It really does. Dagmar, I will go away."

"You are not our only problem," Dagmar said, standing up. "We don't know what to do about you because you are a fingernail's worth of our problems. This situation is absolutely overwhelming. Truthfully, Sari is not holding herself together. She is desperate." Dagmar stretched her back. I stayed on the ground. "The only thing we could agree upon is to attack our problems in an orderly fashion, one at a time, and to narrow our risks. You aren't at the top of the list yet, Jamie. Getting the orders delivered is at the top of our list. Making sure the estate transfer goes through without Anna Beth ruining it is top of the list. Paying our other bills is top of the list, so therefore continuing to earn money is at the top of the list. All of these disasters have been impossibly expensive. So yes, we've continued selling veterinary drugs and animal products. It's hard work, but we do what we must to survive. We will sacrifice and we will triumph."

I knew I only had one last shot at negotiating my release. "Truly, all you need is money and everything else will be okay. I know how to get your cyber coin back from the transfer you made. Twenty thousand dollars. I can get that money back to you without a trace. Use me, Dagmar. Don't kill me. That would be a waste. You need help! Why not just let me get donations rolling? I can raise money from anywhere. I can..."

Dagmar sighed. "We just aren't ready to deal with you. Not yet."

"I'll do anything, Dagmar. Anything."

She laughed. "You won't volunteer to do what I really need."

"Try me!"

She snapped at me with a cold, rapid-fire round of questions. "Will you willingly let the monkeys infect you with herpes B so that I can study the disease progression? No. You are too selfish. You just said as much yourself. Will you willingly offer yourself in a ritual sacrifice for the good of Atlas? No. You want to survive."

"I don't want to be infected. None of you do either, do you? You are very careful. I know you have a ritual where people go in the cages, but that's controlled, somehow, isn't it? Like a firewalk with no real risk."

"The risk is very real."

I felt the truth blooming around Dagmar's words like red algae on a pond, and clarity finally emerged, the bud of something I knew subconsciously pushing through the skim and flowering on the surface. "Dagmar, Flora didn't die of a natural disease, did she? You let the monkeys infect her."

"She volunteered to let the monkeys infect her. She wanted to die. It's okay to want to die. It's a good sacrifice to make," Dagmar said evenly. "She had her reasons. Sari had her reasons. You think of death as a waste, but it's the opposite. Death is conservation. Facing death motivates you to reduce waste, live more ethically, protect the planet, and volunteer when the time is right. Death makes you love life—you said as much yourself! And, Jamie, you know the rituals are very powerful. You knew all of this was happening."

"I knew she was forgoing medical treatment, but I assumed she had cancer. Are you saying you let the monkeys bite her to transmit a lethal disease to an otherwise healthy person?"

"The monkeys decided to bite her, and Flora was happy to

comply. She knew it was time to relinquish control of her land and in doing so, to let Atlas grow. And by studying the disease progression, we will be able to share this virus on a large scale. I have preserved saliva from a carrier macaque, and I can administer it via an eyedropper," she boasted. "I'm learning so much from the macaques. Sari wants more rituals here, as do I, but I am thinking bigger, as well. Unless it is all ruined."

A grotesque future seemed certain for Atlas. My pulse roared in my ears, but I instantly contained my revulsion. Above all, I needed to assuage Dagmar, allowing her to save face.

"You're right," I demurred. "I knew some things, and I was intrigued, but I understand if you want me to move away. I will always admire your vision and your dedication, Dagmar, always. Nothing is ruined. I promise I will tell no one about Atlas."

She sighed, exhausted. "As far as you are concerned, the outcome is the same today. We'll deal with you when Wolfie gets here." Dagmar smiled tightly and started to walk away.

As she left, I began to panic. So Wolfie was the bearded man who chased me at the funeral and walked with Sari at the ritual, the man who helped Sari when the work crews were aggressive. "Why are you waiting for Wolfie?" I called out.

Dagmar shook her head. "Because Sari wants him to deal with you."

"Dagmar, tell Sari I will do anything to help. Tell her I know how to get her the twenty grand back if she lets me go."

She spun around. "The quickest thing would be a ritual streamed onto the dark web that shows the monkeys deciding your fate," she snapped. "If they bite you, that will be a game changer."

Dagmar continued to walk away, the macaques jumping and babbling to her as she passed. I saw Bee, sweet pink-cheeked Bee, and I remembered how she stared at me when I opened the shower house door, and how she threw the yogurt bowl to the floor in the dome. Sari was right. Anna Beth would never be able to let the same monkey out of the enclosure twice.

But Dagmar could.

Dagmar had been the one to let Bee roam around the campus, hoping Bee would sink her teeth into me to make me sick.

I retreated to the corner of my shelter, eyes on the gate. How easy it would be to add a monkey to this new enclosure. How easy it would be to add two, or three, or even a whole colony distressed from transport, anxious to establish the safety of a pecking order, agitated and gnashing their jagged sawblade teeth.

54

I drank from the water jug but otherwise refused food the rest of the day. I asked only to speak with Sari. I desperately wanted a painkiller to curb the throbs in my head, but I certainly couldn't trust medicine from Dagmar, so I didn't bother requesting it.

Dagmar looked exhausted and defeated. I must have as well. Humidity drenched my hair and clothes. I'm sure I looked like a woman who had recently emerged from the depths of a swamp, and I felt like one who was still submerged.

"Jamie, if you aren't going to eat, at least drink your tea. It will make you feel better."

"What does Tierra put in the tea, Dagmar? You may as well tell me now. I know it can't be bad because you love it yourself. But there's something in there. What's in your white powder?"

"It's just a booster, Jamie," she said, pushing a new batch of bowls and jars in toward me. "A little painkiller, a little MDMA, a little of this and a little of that to open up your planetary awareness. It allows you to eat less, work optimally, and waste less. It's not dangerous. Don't stop drinking it now. It will help with your pain."

I poured the jar out at my feet. "Tell Sari I sacrificed my lunch so that she will come talk to me."

Dagmar shook her head. "Stubborn monkey."

That is how I got through the day: stubbornly looking for bits of wire or weak points in the fence, resting, planning, and talking with the monkeys.

The only true thing in those long hours was my time with the macaques. It felt natural to lose myself in their company, even though I was a cage away. When my mind spiraled into darkness, they could almost always calm me down. I watched Odin and Bee, Charlie and Curious Georgia O'Keeffe—all of them, and I wrapped myself in their comforting chirps and squeals. One way or another, I knew I would be leaving them soon.

At dinner I confirmed what I had noticed at lunchtime. There was supposed to be two locked gates with a transition space between them. Protocol was that a keeper always entered the cage through the small lockout area, and then fastened the first door behind her. Then, if an animal got past her when she opened the main gate, the transition space served as an air lock—an antechamber that prevented the animal from running free.

But Dagmar didn't plan on coming into my cage, so she had been leaving the exterior door of the transition space unlocked. I wasn't double-locked in here. It gave me hope.

When she pushed a sandwich and an apple into my cage, I decided to keep it for energy, just in case. "I'm going to die if you don't let me out today," I said. "I'm not doing well. When will Wolfie get here?"

"Oh, he's here."

"Then what are we waiting for, Dagmar? I thought you said he was going to deal with me." I searched her eyes but found nothing. "Or please, just let me call Jason instead. I just know he can fix everything."

"Eat. Your brain clearly needs glucose, because you don't understand. Jason *is* Wolfie. He changed his name years ago, back when he married Sari."

My heart dissolved and pain rose from my chest to my throat. "Jason is here?" I whispered.

"Go to sleep, Jamie," she said, and then she walked away.

No one arrived to talk with me, and I didn't hear anyone on campus anywhere, either. I was utterly alone, no one was coming to rescue me, and there was no end to the danger I was in. I didn't know if Dagmar was telling me the entire story about Jason, but enough of it rang true for me to understand that I was on my own. I always had been.

I paced in my enclosure on and off again, inspecting every joint, scouring for any forgotten connection point or bit of rubbish that might help.

I listened intently for the crunch of tires on gravel or other signs of assistance. Anyone would be welcome. An errant volunteer. A workman. A sheriff's deputy. The oyster guys. But I knew no one was coming.

I'm going to get out. I'm going to get out.

By the time dusk fell, I began rocking and repeating that one phrase like a prayer. Like an incantation.

It was harder to hold on during the night. I promised the monkeys I was going to get out, if only to hear myself say it out loud. "No one is coming back to save me, but I'm going to get out."

Now my only hope was to fight for myself, actively fight, if given a wisp of a chance, and then to run. My hands and feet were already swollen from the heat and my head ached. Something needed to give by tomorrow, or I would die in this cage.

They were either going to put me through a ritual or kill me outright, and I could not count on Jason or Tierra to save me. I needed to find an opportunity and not falter when it was time to push through and survive. I deserved to survive, but I was the only one who could make it happen.

I settled in to try to rest. To attempt to braid all of my frayed emotions—fear, fury, worry—into a coil of rebirth.

I allowed myself a generous sip of water and listened to my breath. I asked any nearby snakes to please stand down and save their venom for my enemies. A ribbon of cool night air ran through my cage as if in assenting response.

55

Dear Ones,

Join us at the most important ritual we have conducted so far. Prepare now to hold Atlas firmly in your arms as we make ever more meaningful sacrifices. When opportunities arrive, we revel in them! We do not waste them! The community is wise and strong where individuals are weak, and we will always fix our mistakes. We are ready to let the monkeys decide tomorrow at midnight.

COMMENT FROM SARI
Email has been sent. This is going to be magnificent. –xoxoS.

COMMENT FROM TIERRA
Dear Sari & Dagmar, I'm okay if Wolfie is. With love and respect, Tierra

COMMENT FROM WOLFIE
More than okay. Our success is 99 percent mental. Come on now, we can't let our mental game lag when we need it most.

Get your head up. The tide is telling us to go ahead and broadcast sooner than we planned, that's all! We're going to shred it with the livestream and everything will be awesome again.

TRACK CHANGES FROM DAGMAR

Hello, this is Dagmar. I have a few strategies to put into place that will ensure success, so tomorrow will be busy, but we're finally on the upswing and the optimism is exciting. Rest well, all!

56

When I woke, I knew that one way or another, it would be my last day at Atlas. I could feel it. My body was breaking down and my vision was blurry. I drank what remained of my water and told myself it was enough.

Suddenly, a metallic creak electrified the hair on the nape of my neck. Then a clang. I shivered.

This is it; this is it. I will not let them kill me.

I squinted into the harsh early sun. And then another clang, closer, at my own fence. I rose, shot through with fire. Were they coming to sentence me to a ritual?

Something firm (a paw, a stick?) rubbed slowly against the enclosure. A shadow crept outside, but I resisted the impulse to call out. I wouldn't give them the pleasure, whoever it was. I needed an advantage. I wouldn't reveal the fear in my throat. I couldn't afford to.

The body behind the shadow was small, though. I finally saw it, then, the familiar hunch and bounce of a macaque, pacing back and forth outside my cage just as they loped along the fencerow inside their own enclosure.

A monkey was out.

Or maybe all of the monkeys were out. I tried to center myself. It could be one monkey like the other times. I had no need to panic. I was safely in my cage.

Nonetheless, paranoid thoughts hit like hail. It could be one monkey who is trained or controlled by Dagmar. One monkey let out intentionally to frighten me. A monkey on a remote-controlled leash of some sort who would trap and kill me.

It could be a macaque that would soon be inside my enclosure, ready to turn me into Science Exhibit B.

I moved closer.

"Good morning, friend. Thanks for visiting me. Look at us. Tables are turned, and you're here to study me. Which little monk are you? Is it you, Bee?"

She cooed. It was definitely Bee, with her distinctive smoky cheeks and lush, brown fur. There she was, out of her enclosure again.

"Oh, Bee, why are you wandering? Have you come to comfort me or to hurt me? Did Dagmar let you out?"

Bee chattered in response, either mimicking or reassuring me.

"What are you doing over here, Bee? And how the hell are you getting out, anyway?"

Bee walked the boundaries of the enclosure, sometimes scaling up the chain link, and then squirreling back down to pad forward with me. She was leading me like a herd dog, checking over her shoulder if I lagged, hustling me to catch up. I scanned for Dagmar but didn't see any sign of her.

Finally, we got to the back of the enclosure, and I couldn't follow along any farther because the lockout room put an additional row of fencing between us.

Bee climbed the unlocked exterior door, swinging on it like a carnival ride. She messed around with the door a bit, climbing up and down, then returning to the ground and batting it back and forth.

"Don't get stuck in that little cage, Bee."

Bee was intrepid, eventually working her way inside the lock-out room, where she quickly found a container of mixed nuts in the food box that I had rejected. Bee laughed and hopped in celebration at her treasure. She expertly tore the lid off the container and plucked up bits of the snack, smacking her lips in triumph and pleasure.

I panicked. Those nuts were meant for me. What if they were laced with ketamine, or worse, and Bee got sick? Her celebration rousted some of the monkeys. What would they do if they heard Bee bragging?

Bee calmed down and returned to investigating the area. I calmed down, too, when it was clear that the nuts had not been laced with their fast-acting tranquilizer—although that might have meant I had been starving without good cause.

"That's okay, Bee. Eat all of my nuts. Why not? How about you bring me over an oyster next time you get some. Bring your neighbor an oyster, Bee. Or are you going to stay over here tonight. Is this a slumber party, my sweet little friend?"

She liked my chatter and babbled back.

"Clever, clever Bee. Teach me your ways, little love. Do you have your own key to the locks in your cage?"

Bee climbed all around the gate of the second enclosure, and then settled in on the lock, pulling and tugging at it. Did she know the word *lock*?

"That lock is my enemy. Exactly how much do you know about locks? How in the world have you been defeating yours?"

Bee reached into the fur that swaddled her paunchy belly and pulled out a thin glint of metal. It was a coin, no, a paper clip or some other piece of metal—a glorious scrap of glistening contraband.

"Show me, Bee. Come closer? Is that a key?"

Bee reached her paw through my cage to show me a gold charm in the shape of a soaring bird—the prize piece from the necklace that Cornelius snatched from Willow's neck.

I reached out to take it from her fingers, but she closed her fist and yanked back her arm. Bee walked to the closed gate and balanced as best she could, sometimes swaying and repositioning herself against the chain link, and she began attentively picking my lock with the wings of the golden hawk.

57

It didn't take Bee long. She poked and wiggled the wire until she felt the chambers release in the heavenly order that led to a satisfying series of pops. She removed the lock from the gate, threw it to the ground, and did a celebratory dance.

"Bee! You amazing beast. I can't believe you!" I whispered.

I wanted to bolt out of the cage, but I could barely move. I needed to go slowly anyway, to avoid alerting Dagmar, and maybe just as importantly, to avoid frightening Bee. The lock was down but walking into the small transition room with Bee might be seen as an aggressive move. Would Bee jump onto me if I then bolted out the door? Would she scratch or bite me? I needed to risk it, but I took one second to let her settle.

I listened. Some of the monkeys were chattering with each other, but I didn't think any of them were out of their enclosure or circling the grounds like a toxic army.

But also, the longer I waited, the more likely Dagmar or Sari would arrive to slam my lock back on, or to push Bee all the way into my cage. Or worse. Maybe that had been Dagmar's cruel plan all along.

I needed to act.

Could I trust Bee? She hadn't bitten me so far, and I would be facing much worse otherwise.

"Thank you, Bee, sweetheart, beauty." I did my best to sing in a gentle way. Bee was there, my only helper, with her nimble fingers and razor-sharp teeth.

A screen door slammed in the distance. Someone was in the dome having coffee. Again, another slam. I needed to move.

I kept my eyes on Bee, trying to tell her on the deepest level that all would be well if she let me leave without contact.

"Bee, Bee, Bee. Help me with my plan. Lead me out of here."

An idea hit me in a flash.

Floss.

I imagined a snapshot of Bee, happily tending to her teeth with a long strand of hair, almost as though Bee herself were sending a postcard directly to my mind.

"I want to give you a present, Bee, a little thank you gift." I plucked several long hairs from the back of my head. "For your teeth, Bee. Do you want to floss your teeth?"

She jumped to the ground. I slowly opened the enclosure gate while dangling the hair strands as far from the rest of my body as possible.

Bee eyed me up and down, and then she bounced upward with a grimace that made me suck in my breath, certain she was pouncing to claim all of the hair on my head with her own two hands. But—*oh, Bee the champion*—she was merely celebrating, springing up and down with joy.

Bee daintily accepted the hair and let me slowly pass her. I took off out of the cage without looking back.

Almost immediately, the rest of the monkeys of Atlas began screaming.

★ ★ ★

I knew I had very little time. I could not waiver; I could not afford to second-guess myself. I had to follow through, adapt quickly to missteps, and make the most of my only shot at freedom.

If I ran straight for the exit, I was very likely to encounter Sari, Tierra, or Zelda. Someone would be posted as guard. I did not know any way out of the compound that the women of Atlas wouldn't know better, and they had the guns.

I didn't want to die in a cage, but I also didn't want to die alone in the Florida wilderness, dehydrated, skin shredded by saw palmettos, body bloated with snake venom, a snack for a gator or a wild boar.

All night, I had thought about how the fantasy of being rescued is really an indulgence in mattering. At the moment I didn't matter to anyone, not even the court. I had disappeared and no one missed me. I was caged and not a single person had freed me—including my own brother. If I couldn't make it to safety on my own, I needed to matter in some other way.

I saw only one opportunity.

I ran straight to the old monkey enclosure, aware my breathing and stomping was conspicuously loud, hoping the squalling monkeys drowned out my panting.

I was dead unless Bee had left her enclosure doors—both of them—unlocked.

The first gate, the door to that enclosure's transition space, was wide open. The macaques immediately ran to the food bin on their side of the tray, hoping I was there to serve them breakfast.

I didn't like disappointing them, and I really didn't want them angry with me. Oysters would have been a perfect distraction right then, but I didn't have time to risk getting food from Monkey Island.

Focus.

I checked the second gate, the door between me and the ma-

caques, to see if I stood a chance. Just as with my own enclosure, Bee had opened the lock and thrown it to the ground. I
swooped down to grab it—and then remembered to double back
and grab the lock from the exterior door. I didn't want Dagmar
to use them to trap me in again. The risk of being discovered
and locked in the enclosure was massive, but I wasn't going to
make it easy for them. I tucked one lock into my waistband and
the other in the front of my bra.

Next step: I needed to try to turn on the microphone. The
camera was my shining lighthouse. My possible redemption.

Best case scenario, it could lead to a rescue. If I failed, it would
at least leave a record of what happened when I died trying to
flee. It terrified me to want something that much.

The weatherproof box protecting the camera transmitter was
secured with a small lock. I needed Bee to pick it but couldn't
wait, so I deployed the macaques' other go-to strategy. I grabbed
the lock from my waistband and used it as a blunt wedge against
the small lock, just like the macaques used stones to crack open
oysters.

The first hit sent a fiery reverberation from my wrist up to
my jaw, but it didn't budge the lock. Each slam resounded louder
than the last. This surely would be my undoing. The women
would come running soon, and if so, I committed to using the
lock against my challenger's head—whatever it took to get away.

The macaques gathered behind me, fussing and quarreling.
They probably thought I was working on a food puzzle to share
with them. The tension felt like a bonfire shooting sparks against
my neck. The more riled up the monkeys became, the greater
the risk, the more my blood throbbed in my temples. Then, at
last, with what I told myself would be my last shot either way,
the lock popped off.

Shaking, hands slick with sweat, I opened the box. The transmitter was on. I easily found the button for the microphone and

toggled it on, too. There was no guarantee it would work—I had never tested it—but I was as ready as I could be.

Now I needed to get within eyeshot of the remote lens.

When we set it up, the fact that the livestream camera was focused on the tire swing seemed like a good strategy for ensuring engaging content for viewers—but that placement only made my mission riskier.

Now I understood that eventually Atlas planned to use the close-up shots to show ritual participants being attacked by monkeys, and I worried I was stepping into a certain trap. Even that risk aside, scaling the apparatus to get into the camera's lens was daunting. I had mapped the angles in my head countless times already trying to find an alternative that would be safer, but there was no way around it. I needed to go inside and crouch on the tire swing.

Hands on the clasp to their enclosure, I took a moment to appeal to the macaques.

"Little friends, sweet neighbors, you know I love you. Just please let me do my thing, okay? I'm not going to hurt you, I'm just going to slowly open this, and come in there with you, and then we're going to make a little movie for the good people out in the big world. For your fans! Okay, little loves? You with me?"

For a split second I considered leaving the gate open to let the monkeys roam outside. It would be safer for me. Every macaque wandering Atlas would be one less that could bite me in the enclosure.

But I couldn't do that. Not to the macaques—they wouldn't make it in the wild. Atlas was responsible for them now. And many of them carried herpes B. A positive monkey could bite someone pumping gas in town. A kid out on his own swing set, weeks from now. Or other wildlife, causing an epidemic. No, not an option.

I needed to keep them contained and join their containment. I needed to act calmly and carefully, and if I became infected in the process, I would deal with that if I was lucky enough to make it to a doctor.

"I am your friend, remember that? Your good ole pal. I need you guys to help me. Who's ready for their close-up? Who wants to be a star?"

I opened the gate and slipped in without letting one monkey out. The troop immediately rushed toward me, circling my legs, plucking at my clothes, chattering with each other as though I were a fresh bucket of oysters or a new puzzle box to tear apart.

58

For no reason other than pure instinct, I began singing to the monkeys to calm them. Maybe I also sang to calm myself. The lullaby came from somewhere old and deep, a tune I vaguely associated with my mother, with my mother's voice, but I didn't have a specific memory of the song or of ever hearing it. I sang because it was all that I had to offer myself and the monkeys at the moment.

If you want to be free, be free.

I sang softly, breathily, willing the macaques to stay calm, walking slowly with my hands tucked under my arms, each step a small victory. I needed them to let me in and to help me as though I were Snow White, as though I had lived with them in their forest forever.

About half of the monkeys were clustered right around me as I walked toward the tire swing. They seemed so much bigger than they did from outside the cage. From a Bonding Bench they look like sweet children, but among them I felt the full bulk of their bodies, their chaotic energy.

The boldest, including Bubbles and Charlie, tugged on my legs like demanding toddlers who wanted to be carried.

The others held a bit more distance, some up on perches and others pacing or clustered on the ground. Stella and Curious Georgia O'Keeffe clutched each other on a beam as though they were weathering a monsoon.

They let me move through the enclosure. So far so good.

I paused at the tire swing and took a deep breath. It was possible that I could be seen on the camera's livestream already, but viewers most likely wouldn't be worried yet. It was possible I could be heard if I simply started yelling, but since I hadn't tested the sound, it didn't seem smart to rely on it. Yelling would certainly bring Dagmar out, too.

The macaques were likely to see my next move as a challenge. I would be taking possession of a coveted perch, physically elevating my stature. It was also possible they would take my climbing as an invitation to play. It didn't matter; I was committed. It was the only way I could ensure that I would be seen by the camera.

I started climbing the ladder. It was narrower than I anticipated, and slimy and grungy, which felt dangerous in and of itself. I pushed on, singing, buoyed by adrenaline, heart pounding in my ears, face on fire. Halfway up I scanned the beam that held the camera. I was the primary subject in the camera's frame, I was sure of it, so I was already on air. I could feel eyes on me from miles away, from hundreds of miles away.

I hoped.

It was also possible that no one was watching. A post or a video is a lonesome valentine simultaneously sent out to everyone and to no one. A few minutes of a livestream was more likely to echo and bounce into endless vacant digital caves than actually snag someone's attention. It was around eight in the morning, Eastern time. The odds were against me.

And then on top of being seen, my plight needed to be understood clearly enough to compel someone to action. Receiving the message wasn't enough. Viewers conditioned to see everything as entertainment needed to recognize my true emergency. I needed someone to be my proxy and run for help.

Monkeys were below me, their skinny fingers on my feet and ankles. They were above me, blocking my way. And now that they could tell where I was headed, they were already on the swing, claiming that prime territory before I could get there. Odin was mugging for the camera, my warm-up act.

The video of this scene alone, a woman with macaques on a ladder near a swing, could maybe seize some attention. But was it enough to inspire rescue? I could be a zookeeper, a vet. I might be someone to laugh at.

I needed to tell a different story. I needed to rip dollars from the wall.

I steadied myself against the tire and began to climb inside it. It occurred to me that the swing might not support my weight, but I had seen many monkeys on it all at once, so I trusted the creaking metal chains. Meaty Joe and the other macaques on the swing let me squeeze in without a fuss. River tilted his head at me quizzically. Nora-Nora-Nora was laughing her red head off at this new, dumb monkey. Their accommodation of my mission felt tender and helpful, a kindness of sorts.

"Thank you, Joe. I've always liked you, sir. Thank you, babies. We are doing this together."

I stared at the camera lens. I steadied myself as best as I could, perched there on the edge of the tire. I knew exactly what I needed to do.

I let the full measure of my fear and desperation settle into my face. If my song had chased those feelings away long enough for me to get into the cage and onto the swing, I now needed the darkness back. I needed the urgency to transmit, to be felt honestly and not misinterpreted as comedy or camp. It didn't take but a second: as soon as I gave myself permission to fully feel my emotions, decades of tears flooded my face.

"Please call for help. This is not a joke, please." I spoke as slowly and clearly as I could, hoping that even if the sound wasn't transmitting, my words could be discerned. "I am being held prisoner. I am in danger. I need law enforcement and medical help immediately."

Bubbles bounded up the ladder and onto the swing and began grooming my hair. Behind me, Ghost made a noise that sounded like sobs, and others cooed and rocked themselves or clutched each other.

"Emergency. *Please help me.*"

My voice was shallow, overcome with fear that no one would see me or take my request seriously. I dug deep, wanting to record specific information in case it might help some forensic investigator in the future solve the mystery and find my body in the deep Florida forest, if nothing else.

"Please help. I am being held against my will at the Atlas Wildlife Refuge near Crescent Springs, Florida, near Triangle Lake, on the Sutherland property, where the owners are distributing drugs, trafficking animals, and have committed murder. I am in mortal danger. Please help me immediately. Call 911. My name is Jamie Hawthorne. Google me. I am a real person. I was in viral video last year for saving a pelican from a fire at a Florida Tiki Bar. Now I'm imprisoned at Atlas Wildlife Refuge. Please find me."

That was the best I could do. I knew I had a very tiny shot. If anyone did see my few minutes on-screen, I had to hope they would understand my danger and figure out who to call and how to follow-through, or at least forward the video to someone who would.

Maybe it was too much to expect. Maybe I shouldn't have bothered. Maybe I should have run.

I started to climb down. I asked the monkeys to summon their fans into action, just in case. I tried to picture people in the cage with me, my ideal helpers: maybe one woman who watched the Atlas livecam with her morning coffee before driving to some office job. Or one man who dialed in to chill out after his commute home from the graveyard shift sorting packages for delivery trucks. Or one teenage girl who couldn't face the school day until she saw something good, something cheerful, something promising, so she surfed from zoo cam to zoo cam, watching tigers and monkeys and penguins wake up.

Maybe I was spitting into the ocean. I was shouting from too deep in the forest, counting on these random, unknown and invisible people. But I only needed one.

The monkeys hovered closer, plucking at my hair, reaching for my hand. Not one bared her teeth or tried to scratch me, not one. They huddled and swayed. They chattered and stayed quiet, my troop of wild friends. I slipped out of the cage, closed their gate, and locked them in.

I headed to the western woods, intending to lay low in the surrounding foliage until I could center myself and decide if it was worth waiting for a rescuer to arrive.

Then, Tierra shouted, "Jamie! Jamie! Stop!"

I stopped and turned, my breath seizing.

"Did Dagmar let you out? You can't leave, Jamie." She looked terrified, as though she were the one trapped in a monkey's cage and I were the torturer. Despite every horror, I felt a twinge in my heart. Not long ago this woman held my face in her hands and kissed me with such a startling tenderness that I felt sure I was loved—not only by her, but by something beyond us. I still wanted to believe in the goodness of that.

Yet I knew people performed unthinkable violence to each other every day, even to people they love. I couldn't be sure I knew the real Tierra, and I certainly didn't know what she might do to survive. Three things I did know: she drugged me, she allowed me to be locked in a cage, and she potentially had a gun.

I maintained eye contact and backed away from her, small steps at a time.

"Where's Dagmar? How did you get out?"

"You won't believe it when you hear it," I said. Part of me wanted to tell her the story so that we could celebrate Bee's brilliance together. The Tierra I knew would marvel at Bee's ingenuity and would appreciate her industry. She would hang on every detail. But I bit back my words.

Dagmar appeared, pushing a blue wheelbarrow full of food and ready for breakfast like any other day. Then she saw us. She rushed to Tierra's side and protectively pulled her back, as though I were the dangerous one.

"Tierra," I said, "just let me go. I promise I won't tell a soul."

Dagmar said, "Stubborn Jamie. Why did you go to all the trouble of escaping? You never have faith. We were coming to get you out. We weren't ready yesterday, but now we are. Tierra, go tell them I'm bringing Jamie to Flora's house."

I watched Tierra leave until there was nothing left of her to see. She didn't turn around to look at me, not even once.

"I want you to come and stay with me at Flora's house," Dagmar said. "You're dehydrated. You can eat and build up your strength in the air-conditioning, and then Wolfie will help you start over in a new town in a few days. If that's what you want. We trust you, Jamie."

I let this soak in. Dagmar exuded icy competence. She certainly hadn't seen my video, that much was clear.

Luring me to Flora's house, luring me with Jason—it all sounded like a trap. They didn't trust me, and I definitely didn't trust them.

I nodded, but I didn't move.

"Dagmar, I don't know if you know this or not, but Bee is loose, and she might be in the other enclosure without water. She'll need breakfast." I twined my last bits of energy. "And I need to tell you this. Bee can pick locks. She picked my lock and let me out."

Dagmar stopped in her tracks, considering. She looked around, taking a few steps back toward Monkey Island to survey the enclosures, and when she did, I bolted toward the gate to the road.

59

I didn't know if anyone saw my livestream or if help was on the way, but I knew if Dagmar wanted me to go to Flora's house, I needed to go in the opposite direction.

I took off and plowed a few feet into the palmettos brush leading to the parking lot. The razor-sharp fronds and thorns of the underbrush tore into my legs. I moved clumsily, pressing farther toward the entranceway to the property. I had to believe it was possible to escape.

Dagmar called out, "Jamie, don't be silly. You are dehydrated. Jamie, let me help you."

Then I heard gravel, the blessed sound of help arriving. I ran into the parking lot. Dagmar would never shoot me in front of a rescuer. The vehicle drove in and Sari exited from its passenger side to close the gate behind them, and my soul sank. It was a beat-up white van with clay caking the tires and spitting up the sides as though it had been ridden into a mud bogging pit.

I backed away. I needed to run but I doubted my strength. I had nothing left after the tire swing. I was thirsty, and the day was getting hotter each minute. I was filthy and contaminated from the monkeys. I needed to go, but I couldn't outrun a van, much less a bullet or tranquilizer from Dagmar. They had me.

I didn't have to make it easy for them, though. I would put up a fight. I would leave a trace.

I continued to inch toward the front fence, away from the white van.

And then the bearded man climbed out of the driver's seat.

"She's all yours, Wolfie," Sari said.

"Jamie," he said. "James, James, wild child. It's been torture not to hug you. I'm so sorry. Jamie, come over here!"

I froze.

Jason. That voice was home—it sent me free-falling. It flooded me with a blinding, unfiltered light, with the taste of gas station cherry pies and blow-up pool toys. That voice filled the space between us, but how could it come from this man? Jason was a scrawny beach-baked teenager in my memories. This thirty-year-old man had turned a corner and come into his own. He was twice as big, brawny with a Viking's beard, and looked entirely different.

He opened his arms wide and shook both of his hands in shaka signs as though we were still children, as though he hadn't just left me in a cage to rot. It was my brother, all right, my heart, my missing piece: I could finally see it then, the slope of his shoulders, the way his left foot tucked a few degrees inward, the exact tilt of his head. He was older, his silhouette infinitely beefier and burlier, his face almost hidden in that big grip of a beard. But I could see it. Inside was still the boy who ran on the shore with me, the kid who made sure I could sleep at night, my brother.

"Why did you do this to me, Jason? How could you?"

"Of course we didn't mean any of this to happen. I wanted to help. I'll explain it all at Flora's house, Jamie. Let's go sit down."

"We can drive over," Sari said, much too breezily, opening the back door of the van. "Help her, Wolfie. She looks tired."

I stepped away from Jason's reach.

"It's okay, it really is," he said. "Listen, there's too much to explain right here. But I'll catch you up about everything."

I looked into his eyes. All my adult life, I had worried about him living on the lam, lost and somewhere far from home, but he had been fifty miles away, living with Sari. I waited for his return, but he had been here all along, surfacing in my life only to bring me down with him.

And worse, he had been here this whole summer, and he stood back while I had been drugged and held captive.

I said, "So it was you. You were the man at the ritual when Mischa went in the cage. I saw you. And at Flora's house. You've been hiding from me."

"Yes. You weren't supposed to see that. We wanted to wait until you were done with your own court battles. After you were cleared, I was going to tell you everything—and I was kinda hoping you'd want to stay and help us expand the community. We didn't count on you freaking out, but I know we had some unforeseen problems. Bad timing. We haven't managed this very well, and I am very sorry, James. That's on me. Just give me a chance to explain, and you'll understand." He motioned to the van.

"All this time, you let me be alone. You let them drug me. Knock me out. And you let them cage me? Threaten to make a sacrifice of me, to your messed up cult on the skids?" Fury ripped through my broken body, overtaking the pain.

"We didn't know if you'd be loyal to Atlas," Sari said. "We—"

Jason cut her off. "I said I'll explain. In the van, Jamie." His voice was now sharp and commanding.

I didn't move. I reminded myself not to get distracted. To trust only myself.

I looked at Dagmar to make sure she didn't have her gun out, and I saw Tierra leaning against her, head down, silently crying. She looked up to meet my gaze, brought her right hand to the top of her chest, and mouthed what I knew were parting words—I was almost certain she said *I'm sorry*, though maybe she said *goodbye*—or maybe just a secret, whispered only to herself.

"We just got in over our heads. And we're gonna get out," Jason said. "I can fix this. Let's go talk. Just you and me."

My pulse was racing, but I couldn't make myself move. I loved him. My memories of him felt safe and true to me: complex, traumatic, yes, but also good. Something in me wanted to trust my brother.

But Tierra's tears were telling me otherwise.

Everything about Sari and Dagmar was telling me otherwise.

The hours they left me in a cage, the dart in my arm, and the dead man that was fed to hyenas were telling me otherwise.

Flora, the spirit of Flora herself on her own land, was telling me otherwise. I might never know if they convinced her to die or if she convinced herself, but either way, her death was a tragic waste, and they were responsible.

Jason was responsible.

I couldn't hold on to an old idea of him any longer. I wasn't fifteen anymore. He wasn't going to save me. He hadn't saved me for years. The one real thing he did for me was bring me to Atlas, and it risked my life. I could no longer count on him for anything.

I took off running for the gate.

My limbs felt awkward and clumsy, and there was not enough oxygen in the world for my lungs to transport me. I begged for superhuman chemicals to kick in. I begged my body to fire and fly, to save me, to follow through and win for once.

The van doors slammed, and Sari sped forward, churning up gravel. She would close in on me in an instant if I didn't clear the gate.

I veered toward the fence to scale it, like the monkeys would do. I thought I could make it there, but climbing it was another

matter—and if I didn't scale high enough in time, I would be
pinned.

The shrieks of the monkeys pierced my temples; my pulse
was loud in my ears and jaw. My hands shook, slick with sweat.
One foot in the slat, trying to find leverage, I tugged myself
up, feeling ill-equipped but hell-bent, a cat running from ravenous wolves.

I tried not to look. I prayed Sari would hit the brakes, that
some goodness, fear, or squeamishness would kick in or that
Jason would stop her—I hoped that I held enough space in Jason's heart for him to at least not crush me—

Sari stopped the van. "Do it, Dagmar," she yelled.

I kept climbing. If I could make it two or three steps down,
I figured I could jump without breaking my ankle—and then
a gunshot rang out, ricocheting from the fence near me.

"Get back over here and get in the van," Dagmar shouted.

I froze—I shouldn't have, it made me a steady target, but I
couldn't help it, because just then I heard the most promising
sound in the world: gravel grinding as a car turned from the
dirt road down onto our driveway.

Sari howled. She knew approaching tires did not benefit everyone, not now. It might be good for me or it might be good
for them, but it wouldn't be good for both of us.

I would accept almost anyone as salvation. Cops or a stranger.
An Atlas volunteer. Anna Beth, because even Sari's enemies
would be better than someone like Zelda.

I stayed frozen on the top of the fence, ready to either drop
and run toward or away from the arriving car. Then we saw
it, slowly emerging in the driveway: another white utility van.

Jason ran toward the lake.

Tierra shrieked, and I knew I was about to catch a bullet. I
pivoted to jump down on the free side of Atlas—and then I saw
Bee's pink face, her weight on her genius hands as she ran across
the parking lot on all fours to Dagmar.

Dagmar immediately trained the gun on her.

"Don't you dare shoot Bee," I yelled.

"Dagmar!" Tierra screamed.

"Go home, Bee!" I yelled.

"Bee wants a sacrifice!" Sari said.

Tierra opened her arms high and wide and Bee leapt into them, wrapping her limbs around Tierra's neck.

Dagmar holstered her gun. She and Tierra slowly walked back into the heart of Atlas, back toward the monkeys, Bee in tow.

The white van pulled all the way up to the closed gate and stopped. Both front car doors opened. Two people in polos and khakis stepped out.

I flew down the fence in two pounces and scrambled through thigh-high rows of azaleas, sending white petals flying, and moved to take cover behind their van.

Confused, one of them said, "We're here from Fish and Wildlife for a compliance inspection, ma'am. Can you open the gates, please?"

60

The ER was terrifying because I was sure they were going to haul me away. I was heat sick and exhausted. I was hurt more than I had known, with countless gashes, scratches, and sores—though my injuries are probably what saved me in the end, since my appearance terrified the wildlife inspectors enough to scoop me into their van without hesitation.

At the hospital, the inspectors made sure the doctors understood the severity of my exposure to the macaques. Adrenaline may have protected me from feeling scratches or bites from monkeys, plus cuts from the cages could have spread contagion. They needed to assume I was infected until tests could verify otherwise.

I didn't know the reach of local law enforcement, or whether they might be in Sari's pocket, so I was petrified someone was moments away from locking me up. I told the doctors I was a crime victim and that everything needed to be documented with strict evidentiary protocols. I did my best to be my own bodyguard and to kick CSI ass, to be an advocate for myself until at least six hours later when the FBI showed up and took over.

Then they transferred me to a bigger teaching hospital. *Herpesvirus simiae* was rare, but with the growing wild monkey problem in Florida and ever-increasing concerns about viruses, the researchers and physicians, much like Dagmar, were enthused to learn as much as they could about my exposure and possible virus or antibody progression.

For three days I asked for blankets every time I woke up. The hospital air-conditioning was icy, and that's the only concrete thing I could muster when they asked how I felt. By the end of every day, I was covered in layer upon layer, like an inverse of the princess who couldn't tolerate even a pea-sized discomfort. Imagine being bruised by a pea. Poor, miserable princess. I wouldn't change places with her for the world. I'm glad I know what I can withstand.

By the end of the week, I was assigned both a victim advocate and a new lawyer: a short woman with elaborate, bejeweled nails named Brianna. She told me investigating Atlas would take a long time, but she wasn't worried. I asked her if she had any plants and she said one, an air plant in a conch shell that did fine on its own.

She also told me that Jason hadn't been found. We decided he left me with no choice but to answer investigation questions about him fully and truthfully. I had to fight back a powerful instinct to protect him, but he's long been the expert at taking care of himself, and I need to learn how to be the expert at taking care of me.

No one at Atlas had seen the livestream of me climbing up the ladder with the monkeys, but it turns out that plenty of other people did. Only a few dozen at first, but they made the necessary phone calls, and two even drove up from the Keys and arrived at Atlas later that day, ready to find me, as did a few local volunteers including Jodie and her husband, and sheriff deputies after that. Even Anna Beth came, but by that point, I was already safely gone. I'm not sorry I missed all of that chaos, but I am grateful for it.

According to Brianna and my nurses, the video I made in the macaque cage eventually succeeded in taking on a life of its own. It had been seen, and seen again, and then memed and memed again into the viral stratosphere.

A few of the original viewers of my tire swing video shared the links and clips on Twitter and Facebook, TikTok users made reaction videos, an Instagram animal rights influencer covered it, and news outlets followed. People saw me climb up to the swing, they saw the monkeys contorting around me with delight, and then they saw my plea for help, and the sudden cut to black when Tierra screamed.

The comments were all over the place.

She's a victim of trafficking!

She's abusing the animals!

Check time stamp 2:04 and you'll see strings. Those monkeys are clearly puppets.

I think this is from an old 1970s filmstrip, I saw it in elementary school.

She must be a PETA terrorist!

Obviously a deep fake.

Wait a minute, is that the same Florida Woman who burnt down a bar and stole a pelican?!?

The video gained traction the following day. By then the story had been corroborated, linked to the developing Atlas news story, and also linked to my old Tiki video. The weird news cycle brought it to social media platforms where it blazed like a river on fire.

FLORIDA WOMAN STRIKES AGAIN, THIS TIME WITH MONKEYS!

I didn't mind the viral infamy as much the second time around. I was still ashamed to be known for the Tiki Hut theft, but this time I was simply happy to have survived the summer. Marion, my favorite nurse, showed me a T-shirt she planned to buy for herself. It was a collage of two images: a photo of me and the pelican on the right, and one of me on the tire swing surrounded by monkeys on the left. The caption read *Florida Woman, Before and After.*

"I don't understand," I said. "Before and after what?"

"That's right, before and after what?" She chuckled. "Life, I guess. Now, I left a comb in the washroom so you can spruce yourself up before the students swing through here on their rounds."

"I don't need doctors. You tell them I'm healing just fine. I know you're the real expert around here, Marion."

"We can tell them, but they won't believe us. We're just a bunch of Florida Women to them, you know that." Marion started pulling the sheets off my bed, leaving me no choice except to rise.

"Are we *before* or are we *after*?" I asked.

Marion laughed and then gave it a little thought. "Both, Miss Jamie. I'd say most of us are a little bit of both."

61

Brianna picked me up first thing from my hotel. We had a bit of a drive to make, and visiting hours closed at two o'clock. It was finally chilly enough for a hoodie, but I knew I would be peeling it off within an hour. Autumn in north Florida is gorgeous, with an amber sun and an abundance of flowers blooming in earnest after surviving the last of the late summer storms.

My Tiki Hut case was resolved. I will have depositions and maybe even trials ahead for the Atlas cases, but as long as I continue to cooperate, I'm on track to avoid any charges. The civil cases for my damages from Kayla, from Sunshine Monitoring and with Sari and Flora's property liability insurance companies will likely be settled out of court, but even that will take years.

"Nobody's admitting much of anything, but Sari and Tierra continue to talk in ways that justify their behavior, with no idea they're implicating themselves. Sari printed tons of written documents full of her philosophies and plans, and she has years of video footage. Gotta love that. Zelda is begging prosecutors for a deal and has offered to flip. Dagmar's petitioning to be released to Denmark. Jason is gone. Expect it all to take a long, long time," she said.

"I'm going to focus on working and building myself back up," I assured her.

"That's what I like to hear. Sari will probably end up running a hippie gang in prison or something. We're not going to worry about her."

"They might like it. They do so well living in communities," I said.

I knew that wasn't true. I was trying to keep it light with Brianna, but I felt sad for everyone. Even saying Tierra's name out loud made my chest constrict, and I knew that when I could afford a home of my own, I would think about her every time I made bread or rinsed sprouts. She would suffer massively without daily graces like those in her life. Sari wouldn't last long away from the pine trees and cypress knees of Atlas's wild land, either. Part of me wished they could stay there and pay their debts to society some other way. House arrest, maybe.

Brianna kept her eyes on the road. "By the way, the only other thing I needed to mention is the Feds never figured out where that twenty-thousand-dollar cybercurrency transfer went. Funniest thing, it went stone cold missing. They verified that Atlas received the money from the trafficker, and then Dagmar said she refunded it to him. The currency seemed to have moved that day into an anonymous chain, but the trail ends there. It just vanished, and forensics can't trace where it ended up."

"Isn't that why people like cybercurrencies?" I asked. "Untraceable."

"It sure is. Dagmar probably stole it for herself and plans to extract it in Europe, is what they figure."

I kept my eyes ahead on US I-95 too, but I could feel Brianna glancing over at me.

"Or maybe Sari has it," she said.

"Or maybe Jason," I said.

I stared straight ahead at an RV plastered with at least half a dozen Disney stickers.

"Hypothetically, if whoever ended up with that coin transfer was my client, I would tell them not to make any purchases for a long while. Not to draw attention with any spending whatsoever that couldn't otherwise be explained via income." She clicked her painted nails on the steering wheel, sending tiny palm trees and flamingos dancing. "For a long time. Because that would be the only way they would get caught. Hypothetically."

Point taken.

I couldn't ask Brianna how she knew I took the missing money, but I liked how clever she was.

She was right. I transferred the money to my own cyberwallet when we were at Atlas. Dagmar hadn't accomplished sending the currency anywhere. When she shoved the laptop at me, I was desperately afraid that I still needed to pay Cole, and that I might need to run for my life from whoever survived the shootout. Thanks to Duke, I had several anonymous accounts and knew how dark web money exchanges worked.

An act of pure self-preservation.

When I was safe, I sent it where it belonged. I transferred a series of small anonymous donations to wildlife refuges, including the Atlantic Rescue Center, the well-run facility where most of my macaque friends have been re-homed in the aftermath of Atlas's fall. After all, it truly was the monkeys' money, not mine. I'm waiting tables again. I'll survive.

"You up for this, Jamie? Now, if seeing all of the bars are triggering, you tell me and we'll leave," she said with a gentle smile.

"I'm more than up for it. I am really excited to see her. I need to see her."

We were making good time headed down the highway to visit Bee during feeding time at the center. Soon enough I would travel elsewhere to see the other monkeys, too—Curious Georgia O'Keeffe, Bubbles, Isak. All of them, when I could.

But Bee was first and would always hold my heart in her skillful, lock-picking hands. She saved me, and I would never forget her.

In fact, some nights I wondered if I should accept the offers to share my stories before they dry up and use the money to start a wildlife refuge of my own. I bet I could manage it better than Sari and Dagmar had. I mean, who couldn't? Other like-minded people would be welcome to help. We could build a whole community, living with the upmost respect for our environment, each other and the animals in our care.

We would need a beautiful piece of Florida land, with dripping live oak trees to provide shade and space for blueberry bushes, rows of kale, and a papaya grove. We would start small, with Bee and a few friends, but then we could grow. So many creatures need our affection and dedication.

Or. No.

Or, I could just visit Bee. Enjoy a gorgeous ride with Brianna, who will roll down the windows as soon as we're off the highway and blare some Tom Petty like a good Florida girl. Maybe stop at a Waffle House on the way home.

I don't know how much I learned by watching the monkeys at Atlas, but I do know I've decided to live, even if I don't quite know how. Soon enough, I'll find a way to shape a solid life near the beach. Make a few friends and come to know them deeply. Learn to take better care of myself. Maybe adopt a dog or cat. Decide what I want to do next.

Right now, the monkeys I already know and dearly miss need buckets of oysters and safe places to call home, so I'm going to start there. I'll begin by filling their hands with briny shells, with slabs of melon—with everything they love and deserve.

★ ★ ★ ★ ★

Acknowledgments

First and foremost I want to acknowledge that this book was written on land that remains scarred by the histories and ongoing legacies of colonial dispossession and is the ancestral and traditional territory of the Republic of Timucua and the Seminole Tribe of Florida. I pay respect to their Elders past, present and future, and to all Indigenous people.

Publishing a debut novel is a dream come true. My undying appreciation goes to my agent, Hannah Brattesani, for her bold belief in this book. I am so grateful for her developmental genius, exquisite stewardship, and keen matchmaking and deal-making acumen. Thank you, Hannah, and thank you to the entire intrepid team at the Friedrich Agency for going above and beyond to champion this book: Molly Friedrich, Lucy Carson and Heather Carr, who offered invaluable editorial guidance.

I remain stunned by my good fortune to publish with Hanover Square Press. I am deeply grateful to my extraordinary editor, Grace Towery, who dove headfirst into the gator-filled weeds with me, who understood this wild story and characters like no one else could have, and who insightfully guided me through the editorial process with unfailing brilliance. Thank you, Grace, and thank you to the dream team you led at Hanover

Square Press on behalf of our little monkeys. The editorial and production teams consistently humbled me with their skill and devotion, and I'm ever indebted to every single person, including copy editor extraordinaire Cathy Joyce, Tamara Shifman, Lisa Basnett and Sally Glover in Proofreading, and Managing Editor Angela Hill, as well as Janet Chow, Sara Watson, and Amanda Roberts in Typesetting, and cover designer Quinn Banting, all of whom made every pica and pixel of the book beautiful inside and out. A million thank-yous to the heroes who connected my outsider story with booksellers and readers, including the entire Harlequin sales squad, the social media team, Eden Church—who led marketing alongside Randy Chan—and Laura Gianino, who spearheaded public relations.

I owe specific gratitude to Sisters in Crime and to Eckerd College Writer's Conference, both of which granted me funding so that I could workshop an early draft of this novel with Laura Lippman at Writers in Paradise; and to Sevilla Writers House, which granted me a scholarship to attend an invaluable workshop led by Anna Dorn at a crucial time in revisions. Thank you to writer Ann Imig for supportive beta reading; to Julia Nusbaum at HerStry for a lifesaving Babes Who Write workshop; and to the bloggers, BlogHer OGs, booksellers, bookstagrammers, booktokkers, librarians, reviewers and authors who so generously boosted an unknown writer. Your support has been nothing short of miraculous.

And lastly, thank you to my steadfast crew near and far; and to my mother, Diane, who as an artist herself taught me to prize the transformative thrill of creative work and who has always been in my court; and to Sean, the most magnificent animal whisperer, who teaches me how to dig deep and never give up; and to Adam, whose fascination with snakes, lizards and waterways taught me how to fall in love with Florida in the first place, and who knows how to hold everything exactly right. All that I do is because of and for you, always.